DAR & EARTH
EVOLUTION

Athena M. Kaiman

Athena Productions Inc.

Copyright © 2025 by Athena Millas Kaiman. All rights reserved. Printed in the United States of America.
For more information, please visit www.athenamkaiman.com.

Cover illustration, cover design, and book designed by Kent Hernández.

Author photo by Sara Bill.

The Library of Congress Cataloging-in-Publication Data is available upon request.

ISBN 978-1-7339828-6-3

For my daughter Cady
An angel who walks among us.

Thank you for being the light in my life that
guides me to exactly where I'm supposed to be.

ALSO BY

Athena M. Kaiman

DAR & Earth: Oraculi

DAR & Earth: Revelations

DAR & Earth: Yasteron

DAR & EARTH

EVOLUTION

CONTENTS

1

ABUELA

T HAGAR KISSED KALEIGH'S forehead as he cast the Deep Slumber spell on her. He headed toward the hospital wing where Abuela lay dying from the carbon monoxide poisoning that both she and Kaleigh had been exposed to yesterday in the Torres house.

He spent the entire night with Kaleigh in the pediatric unit of Wainbridge Medical Center. She'd been given pressurized oxygen as a precaution, but the doctors still couldn't understand how she'd never even lost consciousness. The fact that it was now Thursday and Thagar still hadn't heard from Aelish, in addition to all the interest over Kaleigh's medical condition, had frayed his nerves completely. He couldn't wait for Kaleigh to be released from the hospital this afternoon so all the fascination over her would end.

Kaleigh was furious that her mother had not returned from the magical world to see her, but Thagar was grateful she was alive to *be* furious with her mother. Throughout the night he thought many times about the parents of the girl whose donated cornea was in his own eye. He could not imagine what they had suffered the night she was killed. If he had lost his beloved Kaleigh, he did not know how he could go on.

Thagar gently knocked on the door of Abuela's hospital room and quietly entered. The scene was grim and the sorrow palpable. Jorge greeted him at the door and told him Abuela was not expected to survive another hour. She was not in any pain, but her imminent death was causing immeasurable pain to her immediate family gathered around her bedside. Marisol had kept Thagar apprised by text of everything that had transpired during the night. Javier had flown in from California on the red-eye flight, and Isabela had been permitted to leave the psychiatric facility so she could say goodbye to Abuela.

Isabela got up from her chair and embraced Thagar with tears flowing down her face. She had dark circles under her tear-laden eyes and had lost weight since the last time he'd seen her. She seemed older than her nineteen years and Thagar's heart broke for her.

"Why did this have to happen, Thagar?" Thagar shook his head and held Isabela tightly. "Where is Aelish?" she asked. Thagar glanced over at Marisol, who was holding Abuela's lifeless hand in hers. She quickly shook her head, no, indicating he should not tell Isabela that Aelish had gone to Yasteron after Sartaine and Naz' Commitments Ceremony to sign the Peace Accord.

Following Marisol's lead, Thagar lied and said, "She was here during the night before you and Javier arrived."

"Oh, okay," Isabela replied.

Javier came over to shake Thagar's hand and asked, "How

is Kaleigh doing?" Thagar noticed how much he'd matured. His physique reflected his professional athlete status, and his demeanor was gracious and sincere.

"Kaleigh is resting comfortably and has not experienced any additional symptoms. Whilst I have not explicitly told her that Abuela will not survive, she is devastated. I'm so sorry this has happened to one of the kindest people I have ever known. It is cruel and unfair." Thagar embraced Javier who began crying. As he pulled out of the embrace, Thagar asked Jorge, "Have the authorities determined the definitive cause of this tragedy?"

"Their investigation will be finished this afternoon," replied Jorge. "But it does appear the standby generator did, indeed, malfunction, and the carbon monoxide detector battery was leaking and ineffective. Once the power blew, the detector simply stopped working as the battery did not provide the proper backup. I just can't believe our family could be this unlucky." Jorge shook his head and began crying again. Javier guided his father over to a chair so he could compose himself.

Isabela took Thagar's arm and said, "Come, say goodbye to her. Abuela may still be able to hear you." She guided him over to Abuela's bedside.

Thagar stared down at Abuela and knew she was yet another victim of the climate crisis, just like the refugees at the Climate Refugee Intake Centers. Imperfect backup power systems were now a necessity not only because of the endless outages up and down the Eastern Seaboard caused by the Perfect Storm but also because of the relentless storms now occurring out of their normal season. Her death was caused by the escalating climate crisis, and he knew it was only going to get worse here on Earth. Why Kaleigh had not succumbed to the carbon monoxide poisoning was still a mystery, but he was determined to find out the reason.

He looked down at Abuela's face and remembered their first

encounter. She'd asked him, "What kind of name is Thagar?" And then, she pronounced it in a way he'd never heard before.

He laughed at her directness and replied, "And what should I call you?"

"Abuela," she responded flatly. And just like that, he had a grandmother. He sat down in the chair where Isabela had been sitting and gently stroked Abuela's forehead. He grabbed hold of Abuela's hand, which was cool to the touch. She was intubated and a ventilator forced air into her lungs, artificially moving her chest up and down. Yes, Abuela had been slowing down, but the balance of her life had been stolen from her. And if he discovered this tragedy was orchestrated by any being in Yasteron, he silently vowed to Abuela that he would break his Oath of Peace and end their life.

"You've always been so kind to my family," Thagar said softly. "Thank you for caring for my daughter as if she were your own. She loves you so very much, and I don't want you to worry—Kaleigh is going to be fine."

"Thank God," he heard Marisol whisper.

Thagar continued. "However, before you leave us, there's something I have to confess." Everyone lifted up their heads and stared at Thagar. "I mostly let you win at our poker games, just so I could watch you do shots of tequila." The Torres family surprised themselves when they all burst out laughing. "I'm glad I got a chance to tell you that because you're going to need to work on your game if you're planning on playing in heaven."

Thagar stood up and gently touched her forehead. He kissed it before walking away from Abuela's bedside. She'd given his child so much love and care, and until this moment, he never realized just how much he and Aelish relied on her to always be there for Kaleigh. He could not imagine how the Torres family was going to cope with this loss; Abuela truly was a force of nature. He wiped his eyes and hugged each one of the family members before Marisol walked him out of the hospital room.

"Thank you for lying about Aelish," said Marisol. "Forgive me for asking you to do so but, in my heart, I know Izzy is going to feel like her last cruel words to Aelish propelled her to venture to Yasteron. I'm praying Aelish returns safely not only for her sake but also for Izzy's. I don't think Izzy could cope with worrying about Aelish, on top of losing Abuela.

"Agreed," said Thagar.

Marisol continued. "We are in the process of making all the funeral arrangements. We need to fly Abuela's remains to California so she can be buried in the plot next to my dad. We are also contacting our extended family, so they can attend the service and the repast luncheon. We want everyone to be there so we can give her the best possible send-off. The funeral will most likely be next Wednesday."

Thagar nodded and said, "If Aelish has not returned by the time of the funeral, we can simply tell Isabela that she is caring for Kaleigh. I don't think Kaleigh should attend Abuela's funeral. What do you think?"

"I absolutely agree with that decision," said Marisol. "Kaleigh should resume a normal schedule as soon as possible. Also, since the funeral will be in California, I think we can continue playing cat and mouse about Aelish's absence with Izzy. There will be so many friends and family members present, Izzy will be suitably distracted and not focused on Aelish. But once we return from the funeral, if God forbid Aelish is still not back, we'll have to tell Izzy that she went to Yasteron to sign the Peace Accord."

Thagar nodded. "I can't wait until Kaleigh is released from the hospital this afternoon, despite the fact that Aelish has not yet returned. The scrutiny of my child by so many inquisitive Humans has become unbearable."

"I understand," said Marisol. "Oh, and one other thing."

Thagar looked at Marisol.

"I think you should try and contact Aelish in Yasteron tomorrow. I know tomorrow's only Friday and you both agreed to wait until Saturday, but Aelish may get very angry at you for not telling her anything about Abuela, let alone Kaleigh."

"Thank you, Marisol. That's excellent advice. I will get word to her tomorrow. Enough is enough."

"Please give Kaleigh a kiss for me, and tell her how much I love her, okay?"

"Of course." Thagar embraced Marisol and they both began crying. "I'm so sorry you are going through all of this, Marisol."

"Thank you, Thagar. I will keep Aelish and Kaleigh in my prayers." Thagar nodded and walked away. A short while later, Marisol texted him that Abuela had died.

‡‡‡‡

After Cardissius left the bedchamber and Aelish was no longer immobilized from his spell, she just laid there thinking. She could not believe how easily he had captured her, and she wondered if the delegation had all been killed once they realized what he'd done. She thought about her beautiful parents, murdered by Cardissius and his father, Nevuna, before him. Centuries ago, Yasteron had aligned themselves with King Gidius of Komprathia, who used Komprathian drone rats to spread the plague on Earth with abandon. She wiped away tears for her mother, Saoirse, and her father, Cian, and began to feel something she hadn't felt in years: a fresh grief brought on by a renewed panic about acquiring Magical Interruption Syndrome, or MIS.

Her magical powers had once again been taken from her, just like they'd been taken during her imprisonment in the N.W.

Quadrant Detention Center in DAR. By holding her captive with no magical powers, Cardissius had made her susceptible, yet again, to this rare magical disorder. And Thagar was not here to wrap his muscular frame around her, his strength quelling her panic.

She tried to calm herself with breathing techniques she'd learned long ago and began to think about all the females in both the magical and Human world who continued to be sexually assaulted as a weapon of war, including those as young as Kaleigh. What defect lived inside of the male species, both magical and Human, which allowed them to do such a thing to innocents? The thought of it nauseated her, especially in light of the fact that tomorrow Cardissius planned on perpetrating this same heinous act upon her own body. She could feel herself descending into madness and needed to find some way to maintain her sanity.

Curled up on her left side with her eyes closed, her back was facing the entrance to the bedchamber. She heard someone enter.

"Good evening, Lady Aelish," said a soft female voice. "I am your lower-order-in-waiting. I'm going to prepare a bath for you."

Aelish didn't even open her eyes and quietly said, "Leave me, please." She listened as soft footsteps walked away.

Later on, a male voice startled her. "I have prepared your dinner, Lady Aelish." She silently thanked God the male voice was not Cardissius. While his voice was stronger than her lower-order-in-waiting, she knew he remained respectfully at the threshold of the bedchamber. Still curled up on the bed with her eyes closed, she quietly said, "Please, take it away." She listened and heard footsteps retreat along with the clatter of covered plates being wheeled away.

Hours passed and she remained awake in the same black and white gown she wore for the signing of the Peace Accord. She'd specifically chosen it to match the black and white striped velvet seat cushions for the Yasteron ministers in Legislative Hall, located in the Royal Governmental Affairs building. It felt like a year had passed since she'd put on the gown.

There were no windows in any part of the bedchamber and there was no noise, whatsoever. Silence emanated from the bedchamber and the entire suite of rooms beyond it. There were no sounds from the outside world either, like birdsong. This kind of sensory deprivation could potentially cause her to lose her sanity much faster than worrying about MIS. There were also no clocks in any of the rooms, so the only way she could gauge the time was by the servants who came to wait on her.

Suddenly, she heard the distant sound of a door opening. But the sound seemed to come from the opposite direction of where she'd first entered the suite of rooms, subsequent to being tricked inside with an urgent message from Earth by Chief Minister Stannon. She only just realized the servants were using a door from the *back* of the suite of rooms. So, there were two ways in and out of this horrible place.

A platinum blond female, no older than fourteen years of age, entered her bedchamber. "Good morning, Lady Aelish. I am your lower-order-in-waiting. I am here to bathe and dress you for the day."

Aelish thought she'd go mad hearing her Earthly title over and over after all these centuries. She stared at the young female before her who appeared quite malnourished. She had the same pallor as those who suffered from famine. "You do not have to address me as Lady Aelish. Please, just call me Aelish."

"Forgive me, Your Ladyship, but I am not allowed to do that. I must call you by your full and proper title."

"What is your name?" asked Aelish, sitting up higher on the bed. The female hesitated and dropped her eyes. "You do have a name, don't you?"

"Yes, Lady Aelish. But I am not supposed to relay that

information to you. I am only referred to as lower-order or lower-order-in-waiting."

"That's preposterous!" exclaimed Aelish. "You're supposed to do as I say, correct?" The lower-order nodded. "Well, then, this is something I am directing you to do. Now, let's start over. What is your name?"

"My name is Katrina, Lady Aelish."

Aelish felt her stomach flip. She couldn't believe the malnourished young female standing before her had the same name as her beloved servant, Catríona, in Ireland. "Catríona? How do you spell your name?"

Aelish observed the female mentally struggling and immediately realized she was illiterate. "My mother says it begins with the letter -K- in English."

"Well, the first thing we are going to do is teach you how to spell your name." Aelish saw terror cross her face. "Why are you so afraid?"

"Forgive me, Lady Aelish. But other than my family, no one has ever cared what my name is. And I fear I will get into trouble if I learn how to spell my name."

"Please, look inside that desk," instructed Aelish, gesturing toward a small writing desk inside the bedchamber. "See if there is some paper and something to write with."

"Yes, Your Ladyship." The female walked over to the desk and found some paper and a pen. She handed them to Aelish.

"If your name is spelled the English way, it is most likely spelled like this." Aelish began slowly writing the letters of the name K-A-T-R-I-N-A. "Watch my hands and see how each letter is formed. We will practice every day until you can legibly write your own name correctly." Aelish observed Katrina becoming severely uncomfortable. "Again, you are to do as I say, correct?" Katrina nodded. "Then, this is something I am directing you to do. And we will keep it a secret from everyone else, understood?" Katrina nodded again.

"Now, tell me a little bit about your family and why you don't speak Yasteron."

"I have a mother, a father, three brothers, and three sisters. I am in the middle. The lower-orders speak English, as it was deemed the easier language for us to use."

"Do you go to school?"

"What is school, m'Lady?" asked Katrina. She paused for a moment. "Oh, you mean an educational institution. That is what they are called here. And, no, I do not."

Aelish sighed. "Well, you are very blessed to have such a large family."

"It is not really much of a blessing, Lady Aelish."

"Why not?"

"Because we do not have enough food. I only eat on designated days so there is enough for everyone."

Aelish was horrified. "So, for example, you eat on Mondays, Wednesdays, and Fridays, and you have no other food except on those specific days?"

"Yes, Your Ladyship. I eat on Monday, Thursday, and Saturday."

"Yesterday was Wednesday, so you must still be very hungry."

"I'm fine, thank you, Lady Aelish."

"This is what I propose we do. When the cook brings my meals, I will only eat half of it and I will hide the rest. You will then take it home so you and your family members have more to eat."

"Oh no, Lady Aelish! I could be killed for doing such a thing!"

"Killed? Why would you be killed?"

"They would hang me in the town square in the capital city of Shamalaya. They do weekly hangings there of lower-orders who have committed crimes. And stealing food from a noble is most definitely a crime."

"But you would not be stealing it. I would be giving it to you." Aelish watched Katrina weigh the difference between what she was proposing and the actual crime of stealing. "No one will ever find out. We can try it out today. But if you do not wish to share my food with me, I will not force you to do so. However, it would make me happy to do this for you. I am very sad about where I am, Katrina. I cannot leave this suite of rooms, and I have no use of my magical abilities."

"We all feel very badly for you, Lady Aelish."

"When you say, we, whom do you mean?"

"All the lower-orders know King Cardissius is holding you captive to bear him a male heir. I am so sorry for you, m'Lady."

"Katrina, how many lower-orders live in Yasteron?"

"There are over two million lower-orders."

For the first time since being captured, Aelish felt a glimmer of hope. The lower-orders were definitely where unrest was brewing in Yasteron. How could they possibly already know what happened to her? Aelish knew this frail, terrified young female had never been told directly about her situation. The information had permeated throughout the lower-order community, and she wondered which noble was relaying such incredible intel to them.

Aelish smiled at Katrina. "Did you know I was born on Earth of Human parents?" Katrina shook her head. "That is why my skin color is lavender. Whilst my provenance is of DAR, I was born into a noble family on Earth. My father was an Earl and my proper title was Lady Aelish. I also had a servant named Catríona. It was spelled very differently from yours, but it was pronounced the same."

"Forgive me, Lady Aelish, but what is a servant?" asked Katrina.

"You've never heard of this term before?" Katrina shook her head. "It comes from the larger term, servitude. It means being a slave or completely subject to others who are more powerful, like a royal or a noble. It is not something chosen of your own free will. It's simply an accident of birth."

"Ah, I understand, Lady Aelish. That is what the lower-orders are, but we are not called servants. We are not educated, and we are, indeed, forced to serve the royals and the nobles."

Aelish ascertained that in Yasteron, it was more like the 1500s on Earth rather than the year 2026. And she found it ironic that the lower-orders spoke the language of England, historically, one of the most renowned countries on Earth for servitude. But Katrina lived in the magical world of Yasteron. It was as if Yasteron only picked the worst traits of Earth to subjugate those not born of royal or noble birth.

"Thank you, Katrina, for reminding me of the wonderful relationship I shared with my former servant, Catríona." Katrina slightly curtsied and Aelish felt bile rise in her throat. How she detested a monarchical society with its royals, nobles, servants, and curtsies.

"I should begin your bath, m'Lady, or I will get into trouble with the kitchen staff. They are awaiting my return with a list of your favorite foods for breakfast," said Katrina, smiling.

"Well, then, let's do what you came to do so you're not running late. Do you know who will be preparing my food?"

"Yes, his name is Aaron. And he is an excellent cook. He has cooked for many different noble families. He is also very kind."

"Excellent. And is Aaron also a lower-order?"

"Yes, Lady Aelish. But like me, he has been given one of the most coveted positions within the entire kingdom."

"I understand how important a position this is for you, Katrina, and I will not endanger your life or the lives of your family members. Of that, you can be certain. Do you have clothes here for me to change into after my bath?"

"Yes, Lady Aelish. There are many gowns in the dressing area, which is near to the bathing room. Are you ready for your bath, then?"

"Yes, Katrina, I am ready."

Aelish was already scheming how she could garner intelligence on the unrest brewing in Yasteron, despite being a captive. It was the only reason she was able to rise from the bed.

2

THIS ENTIRE DEBACLE

KALEIGH WAS EXTREMELY quiet on the ride home from the hospital. She sat in the back of the SUV in her booster seat, mostly looking out the window. Thagar decided to take her to the beautiful lake by their house, to see if he could get her to open up about her feelings. She always enjoyed feeding the ducks on the shoreline, and he hoped seeing them again would do the trick.

He pulled the SUV into a parking spot, but before he'd even turned off the engine, Kaleigh had unstrapped herself, opened the door, and began running toward the edge of the lake. "Be careful!" Thagar shouted at her. He magically produced some food in a bag and walked to where the ducks had already congregated to meet her.

"Do you have any food, Daddy?" she asked. He lifted the bag in the air and she gestured for him to give it to her. The ducks began quacking in anticipation. She reached into the bag and retrieved her first handful and threw the food at the ducks.

"Nice throw, Kaleigh."

"Thanks, Daddy."

Kaleigh's sneakers were getting wet as she ventured off the shoreline and into the water. She was smiling and laughing, and the ducks were equally happy being fed by a little girl with absolutely no fear of them. Although it was January, the water in the lake was as warm as the outside air. She wasn't cold and was completely unaware that she was now knee-deep in the lake.

"Are you planning to go swimming with the ducks?" teased Thagar.

"Oh, my gosh! Daddy, my jeans and sneakers are so wet!" She began laughing and came running over to where he was sitting on the shore. After giving him a big kiss, she plopped down next to him.

"I think these ducks have really come to know you, Kaleigh."

"They're so beautiful and I love all animals," she said. "In school, we're learning about animals that are going extinct, and it makes me so sad to think that, one day, these ducks might not be here anymore." She paused for a moment and looked at him with tears brimming in her eyes. "Is Abuela dead?"

Thagar put his arm around her shoulders and pulled her closer to him. "Yes, Kaleigh. She died a few hours ago."

"But I love her so much. How is it possible that I'm never going to see her again?"

"When we lose those we love during our lifetime, the memories we shared with them live on in our heart and in our mind. And when we think of those memories, it's as if they are alive again. We keep them with us by never forgetting them. Do you understand what I'm saying?"

"I dreamt of her before I left the hospital. In the dream I was sad. But when I saw her smiling face and she spoke Spanish to me, I felt happy again. Then, I woke up and felt very confused.

Do you think she came to say goodbye to me in my dream?"

"Many have experienced something very similar to what you are describing. I think it is possible she came to say goodbye to you. Perhaps she wanted you to know that she was going to be all right and was going to a better place."

"Like heaven?"

"I don't know for sure if there is a heaven, but I know this, Kaleigh—if there is, Abuela will definitely be there. And you can cry as much as you want when you miss her."

Kaleigh exhaled a deep breath. "I don't think Momma loves me anymore, Daddy."

"You know that's not true, Kaleigh."

"I heard the doctors and nurses talking about me. They were all saying it was a miracle I wasn't going to die like Abuela. Whatever Momma is doing in the magical world is obviously more important than being here with me, even though I could have died. So, I do think it's true."

Kaleigh's deductive reasoning was hard to argue with. He decided to finally tell her the truth and fall on his sword. He'd rather she be angry with him than angry with her mother. "Momma doesn't know what happened to Abuela or to you, Kaleigh. I haven't told her."

"What?" Kaleigh stood up and glared at her father. "Why not? Why didn't you tell her?"

"I didn't want to put her in a position where she'd have to interrupt a very important peace mission. She's been working on it for many years. And if she's successful, she could not only help the beings in the magical world but also the Humans on Earth, as well as the animals you love so much. If I had told her, she would've left the magical world in a second to be here with you."

Kaleigh began angrily pacing back and forth, her wet sneakers digging into the sand. "Why would you let me think for one minute that she didn't love me, Daddy? Why didn't you tell me this yesterday? I've been mad at Momma this whole time, and she doesn't even know what happened to me or that Abuela died? That is so *mean!*"

Kaleigh was just like Aelish. At the age of six, she had the ability to make him question his own judgement. He put himself in her wet sneakers and agreed with her; he would be quite angry.

"It was a very hard decision to make, Kaleigh. Please don't be angry with me. I knew from the moment we were in the ambulance that you were going to be fine. Please forgive me for not telling you sooner, but you were so upset about Abuela, I didn't think telling you about Momma would help in any way. Also, your mom was supposed to be home last night, so I kept hoping she'd walk into your hospital room at any minute."

"*That's* why you kept telling me she'd be here soon? She was supposed to be home yesterday? Have you spoken to her at all? Is she all right? Don't you think by now you should have told her everything? Because I can tell you right now, she is going to be so mad that you didn't." Kaleigh sat back down on the shore next to him with her knees pulled up against her chest. She looked out at the lake and then turned and looked at him. "Well? When are you going to tell her?"

Thagar loved his daughter so much; sometimes, it literally made his heart ache. And while she was still so very young, he trusted her assessment of things. Even though he'd quickly discussed with Marisol at the hospital about telling Aelish everything, once he'd told Kaleigh the truth, he knew interrupting Aelish's mission was the right thing to do.

"I will send word to her first thing tomorrow. We'd agreed not to speak until Saturday, but you're right, I should contact her sooner."

Kaleigh shook her head at him. He knew her estimation of

him had dropped, but he also knew she'd allow him to redeem himself. He deeply sighed and ran his hands through his curls.

"It's all right, Daddy. Thank you for telling me the truth. But please, don't ever do that again, okay?"

"All right, Kaleigh. Do you still love me?"

"I could never not love you, Daddy, but that was one dumb decision."

Thagar burst out laughing. Being schooled by his daughter only made him love her more. "Come on," he said, standing up. "I'll race you to our favorite rock."

Kaleigh stood up and began running. She yelled back at him, "You're going to lose as usual." He saw her laughing and promised himself to, one day, tell her that he'd always let her win the race—just like he'd let Abuela win at poker.

‡‡‡‡

Later that day, after Drummond had plied him and Kaleigh with enough sweets to put them both in a sugar coma, Thagar decided to call Drew and tell him everything that had happened, including the fact that Aelish was still in the magical world.

Ever the benevolent billionaire, Drew surprised everyone when he took it upon himself to organize and pay for all the arrangements for Abuela's burial after speaking with Marisol. He was like a breath of fresh air after the family's devastating loss. And while everyone knew he was doing it out of his love for Isabela, she was still too mentally unwell to recognize that fact. Drew planned to fly the entire family, along with Abuela's casket, on one of his private jets. His staff arranged for everything in L.A. with the church, the funeral home, the cemetery where she was to be buried, as well as the repast luncheon venue, conveniently located near most of the extended family.

Thagar was upfront with Kaleigh and told her at the lake, he did not want her to attend Abuela's funeral in California. He explained that he felt it was best for her to resume her normal schedule with school and friends. He was surprised when she didn't put up a fight and could see she also wanted life to get back to normal. He hoped after speaking with Aelish tomorrow, she'd confirm she would be home in time for the funeral next Wednesday. But if she didn't, he planned to transport to California and back to Tennessee in time to pick up Kaleigh from school.

While he anticipated being on the receiving end of Aelish's anger, he was still greatly looking forward to speaking with her. So much had transpired. And now that he'd made the decision to contact her before Saturday, he was anxious to hear the sound of her sweet voice, even if it was filled with anger and resentment. Without her, his world felt uncentered. And in making the decision to tell her, he finally allowed himself to embrace how much he missed her.

‡‡‡‡

Aelish was working on a simple spell to teach Katrina. Despite being illiterate, Katrina was still a magical being. The spell would enable Katrina to magically send the food Aelish was hiding, directly to her family. Aelish was in the living area, when she heard the back door open.

"Excuse me, Lady Aelish, but Chief Minister Stannon is here to see you," said Katrina.

Aelish was furious Stannon had ambushed her with a surprise visit, as she was only wearing a robe. She'd been trying on gowns all afternoon, but got distracted by the spell she was preparing, and forgot to put back on the gown Katrina had dressed her in this morning.

Tightening her robe, she stood up from the settee in the living area to greet him. He stood before her and bowed ever so slightly. She heard Katrina leave the room.

"I've just come to tell you that I completely disagree with the king regarding this . . . this arrangement," said Stannon. He gestured toward the suite of rooms.

"Well, on that we can agree," said Aelish.

He rudely looked at her from head to toe. "Further, you are to dress properly every day, like the future mother of the heir to the throne. Never has a King Mother of Yasteron sat around all day in a robe—it is disgraceful." Stannon turned away from her and suddenly pivoted. "I don't know what the king is thinking. Look at you—lavender skin, red hair, one can only wonder what the heir apparent will look like. He is diluting the purity of the line of succession. You may be of noble Earthly birth, but look at you!" His middle-aged porcelain skin was red with anger, his blue eyes became icy, and a section of his neatly-styled short blond hair came out of place.

"You do know only DARlings born of the Earth have lavender skin, correct?" asked Aelish. "It is not a genetic trait which can be passed on."

"Regardless, I am opposed to this entire debacle."

"Whereas, I am enthralled with having been kidnapped from my commonwealth and my family whilst on a peace mission. I'm being held in captivity with no magical powers as I await to be raped, in order to procreate a male heir for a kingdom that DAR has been in a proxy war with for centuries. King Cardissius and Queen Saia have three beautiful female heirs who could continue his reign. What he has done to me is immoral. And in all likelihood, it will start a war within the magical world."

Stannon shifted uncomfortably.

"Or maybe the war has already begun?"

Stannon glared at her.

"I wonder, Chief Minister, perhaps you fear the king's decision to procreate with me will somehow diminish your own power. I think you oppose this entire debacle, as you call it, for the changes it will mean for you personally."

"You're a cunning female, Director Aelish. And to this day, I will never understand how you turned the Kingdom of Komprathia against us. You are nothing more than Earthly scum."

"Shouldn't I be dressed more properly before you call me Earthly scum? And further, just because I'm a captive here, doesn't mean you may enter my prison on a whim. It is rude and undignified. Next time you wish to see me, make an appointment."

Stannon uttered a disgusted sound and turned on his heel to leave.

"Thank you for coming!" Aelish sarcastically yelled after him.

The momentary victory she felt over Stannon was short-lived. Katrina entered the living area with a garment bag in her hand.

"What is this?" asked Aelish.

"Chief Minister Stannon gave it to me when he first arrived. It's a peignoir set you are to be wearing by eight o'clock this evening, when King Cardissius is planning to visit." Katrina could barely get the words out.

"So, let's see what he has chosen for my first sexual assault." Aelish reached up and unzipped the garment bag. Two velvet hangers hung inside the bag. Both the gown and the robe were made of a stunning gold fabric. The robe had a border of black fur from the neckline to the hemline, and the gown had a deep neckline with thin spaghetti straps.

Katrina whispered, "Chief Minster Stannon also instructed that you be clean, wear a designated perfume he brought with him, which I left in the bathing room, and you are to wear your hair loose and untethered."

"Good God!" exclaimed Aelish, who ran out of the living room and into the bathing room. She found the bottle of perfume, sat down at the dressing table, put her head in her hands, and began sobbing. She heard Katrina hang the garment bag up in the dressing area and leave.

Aelish felt desperate. She wanted to run as far away as possible from this room. She didn't care if the King's Guard killed her on sight. But then, she remembered the threat of Cardissius, *'If you try to escape, I will kill Thagar and Kaleigh.'* She was trapped and there was no way out. She dropped to her knees and began praying.

‡‡‡‡

At precisely eight o'clock, King Cardissius entered the room. His tall muscular frame stood before her as she sat on the settee in the living area. "Stand up! Let me see how beautiful you look in gold." Aelish stood up and nervously pulled the robe tighter across her body. "You are a vision, Aelish, especially with your hair down."

"May I ask you something?" she asked.

"Of course, you may ask me anything."

"Why do you wish to procreate with me? Aren't you concerned about keeping the purity of your progeny with only Yasteron blood?" She knew it was hopeless, but she tried using Chief Minister Stannon's argument from earlier in the day.

"Earth born DARlings are the most interesting of all the females in the magical world and their magical abilities are unrivaled. Your magic is so extraordinary that you created a Human daughter. And you are the only magical female who has ever dared defy me and won! I have been in love with you for centuries, and you will be mine, Aelish. Besides, you were also born of noble blood." He reached for her hand and pulled her toward the direction of the bedchamber. His long, blond locks cascaded over his black velvet robes. His excitement matched her dread.

Once they were standing near the bed, he smiled at her and asked, "Would you like to keep your robe on during the Endeavor or just the gown?"

Aelish looked at him totally confused.

Cardissius began laughing at her. "Did you think we were going to have relations like Humans, which would require we completely disrobe? Aelish, we aren't farm animals; we are evolved magical beings! Now, come lay down beside me." He got into the bed with all of his clothes on. Aelish was frozen in place. She almost fell to the floor in gratitude, realizing he was not going to physically penetrate her.

Oh, my God! He will never be inside of me! Thank you, God!

She climbed into the bed with both her robe and her gown on and lay beside him. "How can I perform such evolved magical procreation without using my own magical abilities?"

"I will take care of everything," he said, smiling. "Your magic lives inside of you and will transfer accordingly to the child. My magic will be enough for us to procreate together. After you are impregnated, which lasts about three months, I will not bother you again until the child is at least three months old. This way we can have two children per year."

Aelish nodded her head but was busy calculating the gestation and waiting time between offspring, noting it was nearly identical to having a DARlette. She chided herself for not knowing more about how Yasterons procreated with one another. "Why do you refer to your offspring as children? Why do you use the Earthly term?"

"We've been on Earth for so long, we felt speaking English instead of Yasteron would make it easier for our covert operatives." Aelish noted his English was perfect. He had no detectable accent, whatsoever. It astonished her how casually he brought up his covert operatives on Earth, who were hell-bent on destroying it, with no apology or regret for their actions.

"And once you have provided me with a male heir, I will honor all the conditions and stipulations of the Peace Accord."

"You will?" asked Aelish.

"If you promise to rule the magical world alongside me and our heirs, I will release all the prisoners from the Proelium, all the drone rat captives from Komprathia, and Yasteron will no longer steal Earthen elements and metals to create our newest bomb. And we will destroy all stockpiles of the bomb, the LECCS bioweapon, and the DARling Draft. And our covert operatives will come home."

Aelish knew Cardissius' promise to acquiesce to all the terms of the Peace Accord was said out of pure selfishness. He would use the conditions to further his long-term vision of gaining control over not only the magical capabilities of the DARling female, thereby controlling DAR, but also over the entire magical world. It was nothing more than a means to an end for him. He was seeking magical world domination, like any other megalomaniac.

"Before we begin, I do have one question for you, Aelish," said Cardissius. "When Melanthia told us to stop bombing DAR and advised that DAR possessed Roger's spell, we did not know at the time the spell had been altered to kill *only* Yasterons. DAR, and more specifically, you, single-handedly had the tactical advantage to destroy all of Yasteron, including all of our covert operatives on Earth. Why didn't you use the spell? I simply can't wrap my head around it."

"Because I took an Oath of Peace, like all DARlings. Life is the highest form of currency in DAR; we value life above all else and I am not a murderer."

"Meaning I am, correct?" he asked, smiling at her.

Aelish tilted her head to the side and raised one eyebrow. Her sarcasm was not lost on the king, who began chuckling. "Well, our newest bomb makes Yasteron and DAR evenly matched once again; our mutually assured destruction has been restored. We no longer need Roger's spell."

"So, that's it? You force one of the most brilliant minds in evil magic to exterminate himself, and all you have to say is, eh, I don't need it anymore?"

Cardissius reached across and passionately kissed her. She was caught completely off-guard, and for a moment, felt pleasure coursing through her body. Was she already under a spell? Was it subconscious gratitude on her part for not having to endure being physically raped? Whatever the reason for her pleasurable reaction, she became nauseated; the feeling disgusted her. And while she was grateful beyond compare not to be forced to share her body with him, performing the Endeavor was a horrifying betrayal of her Commitments to Thagar.

"Well, whilst I could talk with you all night, Aelish, I suggest we begin. Now, close your eyes."

Aelish closed her eyes, but after several minutes she felt nothing. She opened them to see a frustrated expression on Cardissius' face. "Hmm . . . something is blocking my magic. Ah, it must be this amethyst amulet around your neck. The stone must have magical powers."

"No, please," begged Aelish, as he aggressively grabbed the chain, snapped it off her neck, and threw it across the room. "It's just a silly stone, Aelish. I will give you far more valuable treasures than this. All right, close your eyes again."

Aelish felt tears fall from her closed eyelids. It was as though the king had ripped Thagar from her heart. She pictured Thagar's face and began to relax. She felt pleasure, similar to the Rapture, but not as intense. When the Endeavor was over, she felt confused. As she was trying to get her bearings, she felt a hard slap across her face.

"You are never to think of him again when you are with me—do you understand?"

She realized Cardissius could telepathically see her visualizing the beautiful bronzed face of Thagar during the Endeavor. The king was furious he'd encountered the deep love she had for Thagar, especially during the first time they had magical relations. She began rubbing her face as one tear fell from her eye.

Seeing the pained look on her face, as well as the welt he inflicted, he apologized. "Forgive me, that was uncalled for and I should have expected it." He got up from the bed, stood beside it, and slightly bowed to her. "We will try again tomorrow night. Sleep well, dearest."

As soon as he left the room, Aelish began feverishly searching for the amethyst necklace Thagar had given her for their Commitments. She found it on the floor of the bedchamber next to the writing desk. She kissed it and said, "Forgive me, my love," and hid it underneath the mattress of the bed along with the crucifix given to her by Stavros. Now, they were both safe.

3

NOTIFICATION

❝ DRUMMOND, THANK YOU for preparing such a beautiful breakfast, celebrating Kaleigh's return to school today. It was wonderful seeing her so happy as she devoured all of her favorite pastries. I really appreciate it," said Thagar.

"Of course, sir," said Drummond. "I hope by the time I awaken, later today, you will have some news for me about Aelish."

"Let's hope so."

"Well, if there's nothing else, sir, I'm off to bed," said Drummond.

"Have a good sleep."

Thagar continued sitting at the kitchen counter and began opening the mail that had accumulated over the last several days. He still found the mail one of the most irritating aspects of living on Earth; there was never anything pleasant to open. But he didn't want to leave it all for Aelish, who usually tended to all the annoyances in the daily mail.

He began climbing the stairs to the home office, which Aelish predominantly used for meetings with the Head Council. He rarely used the home office, preferring his office at the Climate Refugee Intake Center. But he'd already begun composing his message to her in his head and was anxious to contact her.

Halfway up the stairs, his thoughts were interrupted by the sound of the doorbell. Groaning, he turned around on the staircase and headed for the front door. He opened the door and saw Sartaine, the current Director of the POD, who should have been on his Commitments Ceremony holiday and Lieutenant Commander Stavros of the N.W. Quadrant, who had accompanied Aelish to Yasteron with the other members of the Peace Accord delegation. But what shocked him more than seeing their faces, was seeing the death notification uniforms they were both wearing. He felt his stomach hit the floor and a current of agonizing anxiety ran through his entire body. He grasped the door handle to keep himself upright.

He looked at both of them and asked, "Is she dead?"

"Can we please come inside, Thagar?" asked Sartaine.

Thagar moved aside so they could enter. "Can we please also have some whiskey?" asked Sartaine.

He walked them into the living room and gestured to where the drinks were on the home bar. Thagar sat down on one of the couches, spread his legs, and dropped his head into his hands. He raked his fingers through his curls, covered his face with his hands, as if by doing so, he could prevent himself from hearing what they were about to tell him.

Sartaine and Stavros sat down on the couch opposite Thagar. "We do not know if Aelish is dead because she was abducted during the final meeting of the delegation," said Sartaine.

"It is entirely my fault, Thagar," said Stavros.

Thagar finally lifted his head. "Explain."

Stavros said, "Chief Minister Stannon, who is the right hand of King Cardissius, came over to where we were working and told her there was an urgent transmission for her from Earth. Stannon led her into a room, no more than ten feet away from the conference table where we were working. I followed her into the room, but she told me she'd be fine and wanted some privacy. I finally confessed that I'd promised you, to never let her out of my sight. She began laughing, realizing her privacy had been invaded, even in her bedchamber. She told me not to worry and that she needed privacy during the transmission. I could tell she was very worried something had happened to either you or your daughter, Kaleigh."

"Go on," said Thagar.

Stavros continued. "I stood at the doorway and watched Stannon lead her to a settee in front of a large screen on the wall. She sat down smiling at me and said she would be out of the room as soon as her conversation was over. She blew me a kiss and Stannon closed the door as he exited the room. I stayed right outside the door, but I could hear nothing. When she didn't emerge after twenty minutes, I knocked on the door. There was no response, so I began banging on the door calling out her name. I tried the doorknob, but it was locked. I tried to magically peer inside the room and was propelled backward, landing on the far side of the conference table.

"I located Stannon and told him to open the door to the room immediately. He tried to calm me down with useless words, so I punched him in the face. The King's Guard surrounded me. By this time, Head Council Member Cheswick and Commander Baltasar were demanding to know what had happened to Director Aelish.

"Numerous soldiers surrounded our delegation, and we were all escorted out of the room where we'd been working. The entire delegation was forced to leave the Royal Governmental Affairs building, and we were rendered magically paralyzed. Right before they transported all of us back to the N.W. Quadrant, Chief Minister Stannon whispered into my ear, "You have lost her. She now belongs to King Cardissius. Tell her mate, Director Thagar, your Head Council, and the Alliance of Magical Dominions, if they retaliate in any way, we will kill her. But trust me, the king wants her alive—so stay away and she lives."

Thagar physically lifted the coffee table between the couches and threw it over the heads of Sartaine and Stavros. The glass top shattered into a million pieces, just like his heart. He'd been right all along. All the years of negotiations, with a promise of a peace between their dominions, was a ruse to secure Aelish's commitment to come to Yasteron, just so Cardissius could steal her. Why hadn't he insisted more fervently that she not attend? Why hadn't he firmly stopped her from going? He began banging his hands against his head and then stood up and began pummeling the living room wall until there was no more wall left to pummel.

Sartaine stood up and wrapped himself around his brother-in-arms, his dearest friend, and his mentor. "Thagar, please, do not injure yourself. We will get her back."

Stavros magically repaired both the wall and the table and handed Thagar a shot of whiskey. Thagar downed it in one gulp and yelled at Stavros, "Bring me the bottle. Now!" It was the first time he'd drunk alcohol since his corneal transplant.

While Stavros brought over the bottle of whiskey, placing it on the restored glass table, Sartaine managed to get Thagar to sit back down on the couch with him. Stavros dropped down on both his knees in front of Thagar, bowed, and touched his head to the floor. The DARling Deference was an element of military tradition used to demonstrate an extreme apology, which usually involved the loss of life, caused by the being on their knees. It was performed in front of an officer of higher rank as a deep apology and to beg for forgiveness.

"Please forgive me, Thagar, because I know I will never forgive myself."

Thagar had only witnessed the DARling Deference once before in his life, and it had the desired effect on him. It brought back a bevy of memories and emotions from a lifetime of service in the Protection of DAR. How he wished he still had the power as Director of the POD to declare an all-out war on Yasteron. But he didn't. He'd been forever changed after Yasteron bombed the underwater bunker nearly four years ago. And once again, Yasteron had taken something precious from his life. Perhaps the most precious thing of all—Aelish.

"I forgive you, Stavros. Please rise," said Thagar, the whiskey quelling his rage.

Stavros slowly got up with tears streaming down his face. He walked over to the home bar and splashed water on his face, drying it with the sleeve of his uniform. Thagar could see how completely distraught he was over losing Aelish. It was comforting to share her loss with someone who was in the middle of his life, had never mated, and chose to live his entire life devoted to the Protection of DAR. He knew how deeply Stavros cared for Aelish, as they shared something which bound them together: faith in a deity Thagar still had trouble accepting.

"Can you give me a report of what's happening?" Thagar asked Sartaine. "Has the Head Council authorized the POD to take any action against Yasteron?"

Sartaine replied, "At this moment, DAR is in a bit of turmoil as the news of Aelish's abduction has begun circulating throughout the commonwealth. I have spoken to Melanthia, who is planning to meet with the Alliance of Magical Dominions within the next few days, in order to determine what action should be taken against the kingdom. "It's simply unbelievable, Thagar. They just never stop. I had hoped Aelish would secure the best Commitments Ceremony gift for me: peace with Yasteron, after Naz and I returned from our holiday. But I fear it will never be."

"I'm sorry. I didn't even ask you how she was," said Thagar.

"She now knows what it means to be a military mate. Naz told me to tell you that Aelish is a Living Legend for a reason and not to give up hope for her return."

Thagar chuckled wryly. "I suppose there's some truth in that. We can only hope Cardissius does not truly understand the talents of our most famous Living Legend. What in the world am I going to tell our daughter, Kaleigh?"

Stavros replied, "The truth. She needs to know why her mother has not returned home."

Thagar nodded. "You're right. I will tell her tonight."

‡‡‡‡

Isabela looked at herself in the mirror. She barely recognized the image reflecting back. She was dressed in funeral clothing with very little makeup on and realized that in two days, on Wednesday, January 21st, the same day as Abuela's funeral, she would turn twenty years old. Her mother had profusely apologized for the dates colliding but what was the difference? She and Abuela had always been deeply connected; she didn't mind sharing her birthday with Abuela's burial. She stared at her reflection, examining the dark circles under her eyes.

I look like I'm turning forty instead of twenty.

She turned away from the mirror and sat down on the couch in the living area of her suite at the psychiatric facility. At first, she didn't think her doctors were going to let her attend Abuela's funeral. But it was deemed a long-term detriment to her mental health to miss such an important milestone in her life. Abuela, who had raised her, was gone forever. Isabela held the necklace of St. Michael around her neck, given to her by Abuela less than two weeks ago. She couldn't help but feel that in parting with it, Abuela had lost her protection. Feeling this way was in direct contradiction to her atheist beliefs, but for some reason, she knew it was true.

They'd had so much fun celebrating Cinco de Enero, or January 5th, instead of Cinco de Mayo in May. Abuela had made all of Isabela's favorite foods and simply moved the calendar up five months, to celebrate Isabela's favorite holiday in honor of her upcoming twentieth birthday. The spontaneity of Abuela and her outlook on life was what made her so special. Despite being devout, she was also completely irreverent. Her contradictions were what defined the essence of Abuela, and there was no one who could replace her.

She would also never not believe that Yasteron had a hand in her death. The standby generator *and* the carbon monoxide detector failed? The circumstances of Abuela's death solidified her paranoia and fear of Yasteron. How many times during sessions with her doctors had she wanted to discuss the truth of her life? But she'd made the commitment to secrecy about the magical world a long time ago. She tried using metaphors to describe all that had happened to her, but it was never quite the same as the reality. At least the assassination attempt was something she could almost truthfully discuss in therapy. But that event led into her detachment from Aelish on Drew's helicopter, which was an even deeper unresolved issue in her mind. One day, maybe she'd be able to get over it all. But right now, that seemed like a long way off.

As a physician-scientist, she knew something had saved

Kaleigh from certain death from the carbon monoxide poisoning. She tucked it in the back of her mind for her to-do list at the lab, but first, she had to get well enough to return to the lab. She'd taken a one-month leave of absence. But by the time she returned from the funeral, nearly two weeks of her leave would be over. How she'd get it together in the remaining two weeks seemed highly unrealistic in the moment. And she was dreading the idea of asking for more time away from her work and her research.

She tried not to read or watch the news in her downtime. The global vaccination numbers were now featured on the crawl of every cable news channel, and the low percentage of inoculation was not helping her mental health. She heard a knock on her door, checked her phone for the time, and realized it was way too early for their departure to the airport.

Isabela opened the door to the face of her beloved brother, Javier. "Javi! What are you doing here so early? Is everything all right?"

"I figured you were just waiting around doing nothing, so I thought we could just hang out together for a little before we begin the seventy-two-hour-Latino-fest," he said. Isabela began laughing and tightly embraced her brother. And then, they both began crying.

"It's so damn awful, there are moments when I simply can't stand it," said Javier. "How did this happen? First, you're admitted to the hospital for psychiatric care and then Abuela dies. I've been back to Tennessee more in the last two weeks than in the last year. I know, I know, I should visit more."

"I didn't say anything," Isabela said defensively.

"I didn't mean you," he said. "I used to get the guilt trip every week from Abuela, and it appears Mom has now picked up the mantle. Ay, Dios mío! They can both lay it on pretty thick. And it's not like I don't see our extended family in L.A."

"They just miss you, Javi—we all do."

"Izzy, please, tell me what happened. I feel like there's been a shift since you've been hospitalized, and Mom isn't as forthcoming as she used to be. She seems to be holding back with me."

What a tempting moment this was for Isabela. With Abuela gone, Javier was the only member of her immediate family who didn't know about DAR, Yasteron, Glen—all of it. How she longed to tell him and finally have a confidante her own age. And she trusted her brother with her life. But to lay it all on him now, on the first night of Abuela's wake in L.A., didn't seem fair to Javier. And then, her resentment of Aelish reared its ugly head. Aelish had unilaterally decided to tell Drew everything. Why couldn't she have that same freedom and just tell Javier everything?

"What is it, Izzy? Are you all right? Come on, let's sit down." All she had to do was think about Aelish telling Drew about the magical world and it outwardly showed on her face. She was losing the ability to hide her emotions. Maybe her unresolved anger coming to the surface wasn't necessarily a bad thing, but she didn't mean to upset Javier.

"I'm okay, Javi, don't worry."

"Are the doctors helping you? I know it hasn't been that long, but do you feel you are making any progress? I'm sure Abuela dying so soon after your admission hasn't helped, whatsoever. Talk to me, Izzy."

They both sat down on the couch and Javier wrapped his arms around her. He'd always been there for her, and she'd long forgiven him for not recognizing Glen was horrid. She had experienced an irrational anger at Javier years ago, but she no longer felt any resentment toward him. And now, he was, literally, the only person left in her family who still didn't know who Glen really was. She promised herself on the couch that, one day soon, she was going to tell him everything. It helped relax her as did his loving embrace. Sometimes, she wondered if the Human touch truly was the most powerful medicine of all.

‡‡‡‡

Isabela's suitcase was at the door and she was waiting for the limousine to arrive. It would take all of them, including Abuela's casket, to one of Drew's private planes. Then, on to California, and finally to the funeral home, where the first night of Abuela's wake would take place. She hoped to be able to sleep on the plane, as she felt emotionally exhausted at the thought of it all.

She was glad Aelish had decided to skip the funeral. One less stressor for her to have to deal with. But she was mostly happy Kaleigh wouldn't be there. After the trauma of trying to save Abuela's life in the house using CPR, it was the right decision. Kaleigh didn't need to see the laid-out, dead body of someone she loved as much as Abuela at the age of six. Isabela hoped the funeral home in Tennessee had done a good job of making her appear lifelike because Abuela's casket was going directly from the plane to the funeral home in L.A. There was no time for a retouch. She heard her mother's signature knock on the door.

"Izzy?" Her mother slowly opened the door. "I'm here. And here come the tears again." Isabela came to the door and began hugging her mother. "Oh, Izzy, just when I think I have no tears left, more come streaming down my face."

"I'm so sorry, Mom. This is all horrible. I just can't make sense of it. Is Abuela just another victim of the climate crisis? It was bad enough with the power outages after the Perfect Storm, but now we need generators because we are getting storms completely out of season. We've lived here for eight years and have never experienced winter tornadoes before. We always felt so lucky the house had never been damaged and now this? How is Dad?"

"Despite being told by the fire investigators that none of what happened was in any way his fault, he continues to blame himself for purchasing the standby generator and for not checking the battery in the carbon monoxide detector more often. It's all nonsense, but he will probably feel this way forever. He just cannot internalize it was all an accident."

Isabela took a deep breath and looked away from her mother.

"What is it mija? What are you not saying?" Isabela just shook her head, but her mother was not dissuaded. "You don't think the magical place Glen was from, I can't remember the name at the moment, would try to hurt Kaleigh or Abuela, do you?"

"I still can't believe I can talk to you about Yasteron, Mom. To be honest, I've had the feeling many times they had a hand in it. They are just so evil."

"Oh, my God, do you really think so?"

"I can't see what their motivation would be for killing Abuela. To me, Kaleigh seems the more likely target. But I never considered them to be spiteful. They're very cunning and always have a tactical reason behind their actions. This entire fiasco seems too sloppy for them. Maybe it's easier to blame them than to actually believe it was all a sequence of events which came together, resulting in the worst luck ever."

"There was a moment," said Marisol, "when I didn't think they were going to let Kaleigh leave the hospital. Thagar was freaking out they were going to want to study her. Thank God, he lied to the police officer at the scene, telling him Kaleigh had just stopped by to check on dinner's progress and wasn't there very long. By the time the investigators came to the hospital, Thagar had instructed her to lie—"

"Oh no! Kaleigh hates lying. Yet she's amazing at keeping so many of her parents' secrets."

Marisol chuckled. "You're so right. She had a fight with Thagar about telling the truth to the authorities."

"Oh, my God. What fictitious story did he come up with?"

"Kaleigh told them she'd just learned about fire safety and CPR in school, which was actually true. So, she said when she entered the house, she smelled something burning."

"But carbon monoxide is odorless. They bought that?"

"Thagar told her to tell them the smell was coming from food burning on the stove. And since Abuela had collapsed onto the floor and the flame was still on the stovetop, burning all the food for dinner, it was the truth. Kaleigh then lied and told them she put a kitchen towel over her mouth for smoke inhalation, which prevented her from directly breathing the carbon monoxide."

"Ohh, I see," said Isabela, smiling.

"I think if she were older, like sixteen, and there weren't so many legal hurdles to go through to study her, I think they would have kept her. Imagine if they had discovered she can breathe underwater? Ay, Dios Mío!"

"I know Aelish has been busy with all of this, but I'm surprised she hasn't come to visit me yet. I've texted her a couple of times, but she never texted back. Perhaps I went too far and she hasn't forgiven me for the mean things I said to her, not that I'd blame her."

Marisol shifted uncomfortably and became jittery. Changing the subject, she said, "Oh, look at the time, Izzy." Marisol had pulled out her phone and also saw a text from Jorge. "Ay, here's a text from Dad telling us get a move on. Javi and Dad are waiting for us in the limo while we're standing here gabbing." Marisol put her phone back in her purse. "It will be so nice to see everyone again. I just wish it was to celebrate Abuela's 70th birthday, two years from now, like we'd been planning, instead of her funeral."

Marisol wiped away tears as Isabela gave her a hug.

"I can't believe Drew is allowing us to use one of his private planes," said Isabela. "I love that Abuela is flying along with us."

"Shipping her body to L.A. was quite complicated," said Marisol. "Thank God, for Drew."

"I don't know why he's been so good to me, considering how much I've avoided him over the last . . . wow, it's been almost two years," said Isabela.

"Don't you know why, Izzy?" Her mother smoothed Isabela's baby hairs and cocked her head to one side.

"Mom, Drew could have any woman in the world. Don't be ridiculous. I think it's purely because he values my work and wants me to get well as soon as possible so we can continue promoting the vaccine."

"Pobrecita." Her mother shook her head at her. "Come on, we have to go, Izzy."

✠✠✠✠

When it was all over, Javier went back home to his apartment in L.A. and Isabela and her parents went to the airport. It felt so odd that two of her immediate family members were not accompanying them back to Tennessee, despite Javier moving away four years ago. She already missed him. And she felt for her parents. She wasn't technically going home either, as she was expected back at the psychiatric facility. For the first time in decades, her parents would finally have the house to themselves.

Isabela listened to the gentle snoring of her parents in tune with the airplane engine, but she remained wide awake. The seventy-two-hour-Latino-fest, as Javier called it, was over. It had been filled with so much laughter, sadness, and happy memories of growing up in L.A. It had been wonderful to see her extended family again as well as her childhood friend, Gabby. Even Drew came to the funeral service, but she couldn't find him later at the repast luncheon. Thagar told her he'd left after the service because he didn't want to intrude on such a somber family occasion. Isabela had chuckled at Thagar and said, "He's obviously never been to a Latino repast luncheon." And it was, indeed, boisterous, just like Abuela would have liked it.

But there was a hole in Isabela's heart. She reached up and fiddled with Abuela's necklace of St. Michael, which she never took off. Abuela looked beautiful in her casket and the whole time it felt like she was still with them, even after the casket was lowered into the ground next to her Abuelo. Isabela accepted her passing and was glad Abuela was at peace in her final resting place. She would miss her forever, but Abuela remained in her heart and mind, buoyant, smiling, and full of life.

Sitting on the plane, she could feel Abuela all around her. It was as if Abuela was the pilot of her heart, navigating her toward something specific. Isabela laughed when she caught herself looking out of one of the southeast windows of the plane. She was hoping to catch a glimpse of the lights in the capital city of Bencarlta in DAR, especially because it was at night. Unfortunately, there were too many clouds, but the fact that she had tried to find the lights in the pitch-black darkness illuminated something else.

She realized DAR was a huge part of her life, and she'd been steadily trying to forget about it ever since Aelish told Drew about its existence. DAR had always been hers. It was something she shared only with Aelish; it was theirs. Isabela began quietly sobbing, not for Abuela but for Aelish. The hole in her heart could only be filled by the lavender-faced being with the long, red, fishtail braid. Isabela missed her so profoundly, she could barely breathe.

Today was her twentieth birthday as well as the day Abuela

was buried. The two events would always be intertwined. And she could feel Abuela guiding her toward the best birthday gift she'd ever given her: the realization that it was time to let go of her childish anger at the lavender-faced being who had changed her life forever. Isabela had so many memories and lifetime achievements that would never have happened if Aelish had not appeared in her bedroom eight years ago.

The betrayal she felt was a childish one and she was no longer a child. It was time to lay down her feelings and forgive Aelish. She'd been living with these feelings of betrayal ever since May 15, 2024, when she was nearly killed at the World Health Organization. But most of all, it was time to forgive herself for allowing Aelish's one decision to tell Drew about DAR, to cause her so much mental illness.

Aelish always had her best interests at heart, and the meanness she'd demonstrated toward Aelish must have been even more painful than her own feelings of betrayal. What had her behavior done to Aelish? It was the first time Isabela put herself in Aelish's shoes. What had her rage done to Aelish?

During the last three days, something had been missing. Isabela kept looking for it in the funeral home, in the church, at the cemetery, and at the repast luncheon. She kept waiting to see Aelish among all her family and friends. But she'd basically thrown Aelish out of her life after that day on Drew's helicopter, and she knew until they reconciled, she would never be able to fill the hole in her heart or be well again.

She kissed the necklace of St. Michael, wiping away tears with the back of her hands, and silently thanked Abuela for giving her one last birthday gift: the wisdom to know how to get well. Isabela felt a calm envelop her entire body as if Abuela was holding her. For the first time in nearly two years, she finally relaxed and fell sound asleep for the balance of the plane ride home.

4

GLOWING

A ELISH WOKE UP startled. She reached into the drawer of her night table for the piece of paper where she kept track of the days and dates of the week. She teared up, realizing today was Isabela's twentieth birthday. However, even if she were on Earth, she doubted they would celebrate this auspicious birthday together. Most especially, if Isabela were still in the psychiatric facility. She could not believe their relationship remained fractured. How had it all gone so terribly wrong? While she still did not regret telling Drew about DAR, she did wish the outcome of her decision had not ripped her relationship with Isabela to shreds. And she certainly never anticipated it would cause Isabela such severe mental anguish. She closed her eyes and pulled the covers over her head.

Trying desperately to sleep, in order to forget about Isabela, her birthday, and their relationship, Aelish suddenly felt very odd. At first, she attributed it to her melancholy over Isabela. But then, an unexpected happiness enveloped her. And she had absolutely no reason to be happy, whatsoever. It felt like a being had cast a spell on her to remove her sadness. Was Cardissius doing something to her from afar?

She poked her head out of the covers and laid on her back analyzing why there was a smile across her face. She had endured six consecutive nights of the Endeavor with Cardissius and was tormented by the fact that after each time, she found it more and more pleasurable. Last night's session had left her peaceful, sexually satisfied, and she was disgusted with herself. The betrayal she felt toward Thagar was debilitating. So, between that and missing Isabela's birthday, why in the world was she smiling? She felt like her emotions were completely out of control and she was slowly losing her sanity.

Aelish pulled off the covers, entirely, determined to start her day so she could resume being the miserable captive that she was and not some smiling lunatic. But something caught her eye. She lifted herself up in the bed, and then she clearly saw it. There was a magical glow over her abdomen, and she instantly knew she was carrying Cardissius' heir. Having never been pregnant with a magical being before, this euphoric feeling was entirely new to her. But then, she remembered Lady Antonia discussing it endlessly. She'd told her, *'That initial feeling gets you through some trying times as a mother.'*

Aelish began massaging her abdomen, and the glow rose about a foot in the air above her belly in shimmering iridescent colors. She'd never seen anything like it. The more she massaged her abdomen, the brighter the glow became. It rose higher into the air until the entire bedchamber took on the hue. Aelish was positively mystified by the magic emanating from the life that now lived inside of her. On the one hand, she felt like her previous life had officially ended, which was horrifying. But on the other hand, she realized Cardissius would now leave her alone. She wouldn't have to perform the Endeavor again for at least six months. She was certain Cardissius would keep his word because he would never jeopardize the life of his heir.

She deeply exhaled with relief that the forced procreation sessions were over for now, and the fact that this gift was bestowed upon Isabela's birthday made it all the more special.

Thank you, Isabela! Happy birthday, sweetheart.

Aelish continued to lay there bathed in the magic of the fetus and found her anxiety of contracting Magical Interruption Syndrome had disappeared. The fetus' glow finally allowed her to feel a semblance of magic, causing her to relax and fall into a deep sleep.

‡‡‡‡

Katrina entered her bedchamber. Her gasp woke up Aelish, who slowly opened her eyes and stared at the shocked face of her lower-order-in-waiting. Aelish asked, "I assume you know what this glow means?"

"I do, Lady Aelish. Are you feeling well? Can I get you anything?"

"I suppose we will have to send word to the king at some point during the day, but for now, could we just keep this between us until I have bathed, dressed, and eaten?"

"Of course, m'Lady," replied Katrina. "But when your food is delivered, we'll need to hide the glow of your abdomen with blankets so Aaron doesn't go back to the kitchen and tell all the lower-orders before you've told the king."

"Hmm . . . good point, Katrina. Can the glow be covered up?"

Katrina looked confused. "Didn't you experience this before, Lady Aelish, when you had your daughter?"

"It's a very long story, Katrina, but no, my daughter is Human."

"Ohh, m'Lady, I did not know this. Forgive me, if I have upset you in any way. I just assumed it was the second time you'd experienced the magical glow." Katrina paused for a moment. "You truly are exceptional. How did you manage to procreate a Human if your husband is also a magical being?"

"To this day, it remains a mystery. But the fact that I was capable of doing so was, in part, why the king wanted me to bear him an heir. He feels my magical abilities are unrivaled."

"Yet he keeps you locked away without the use of those abilities," said Katrina.

Realizing she had said too much, Katrina put her hands over her mouth. "Don't worry about it; it happens to be the truth," soothed Aelish.

"I feel congratulations are in order, but I'm not sure if you feel happy or sad, m'Lady."

Aelish found it fascinating that both times she'd become pregnant, the situation was fraught with uncertainty and circumstances beyond her control. While this pregnancy gave her a magical happiness, she'd been forced to procreate with her sworn enemy. And when she was pregnant with Kaleigh, she and Thagar were at odds over whether or not to terminate the pregnancy. Once they discovered it was Human, they were confronted with having to live on Earth, as they knew Kaleigh would be unable to breathe in DAR. Would she ever become pregnant in her lifetime and feel a normality to the event?

"I think under the circumstances," said Aelish, "you should hold off congratulating me until I have delivered this child. Sometimes, things can go wrong."

"Of course, m'Lady." Katrina walked over to the dressing area and returned with a blanket. "You can use this thick blanket to cover your belly so Aaron will not see the glow. Just try not to massage it, as it makes the glow brighter."

Aelish couldn't believe her young lower-order-in-waiting knew that and she didn't until this morning. Obviously, Katrina's mother had many siblings after Katrina's birth, but nevertheless, Aelish felt naïve. She smiled at Katrina and said, "Well, let's get this momentous day started. You do know how to get a message to the king, correct?"

"It is an arduous process and involves several beings who are nobles, but yes, I can get a message to the king. In fact, let me start the process now, as it may take hours before he receives it. Do you mind if I leave you for a bit? I will return once I have completed the steps. Do you need anything before I go?"

"No, thank you, Katrina. I will just rest a bit more."

"All right, m'Lady. I will return as soon as possible."

Aelish watched Katrina leave the room and envied her ability to come and go. How was she going to birth a healthy infant, living in captivity with no sunlight or magical abilities? She unwittingly began massaging her abdomen and instantly felt the sadness leave her as the glow grew brighter.

Well, at least that's some form of magic.

✝✝✝✝

Aelish was wearing a coral chiffon gown. Its sleeves were translucent, the neckline had a deep V-neck, the waistline was form-fitting, and the bottom ballooned out in yards of coral chiffon. She wore her hair in an elegant updo and truly looked royal sitting on the settee in the living area. The gown's voluminous bottom spread out nearly the length of the settee and on her feet were matching coral satin shoes. The thick blanket was over her abdomen, hidden under the gown's numerous pleats. She planned on using her pregnancy to try and manipulate the king into allowing her to go outside. Therefore, she decided to look the part of the King Mother.

Katrina entered the living area, took one look at her, and deeply curtsied. Aelish was pleased her ensemble had the desired effect on her lower-order-in-waiting. "You changed, Lady Aelish. You look positively radiant," said Katrina. "I think this gown suits you much better than the one you chose earlier. You should have summoned me to help you."

"I decided the coral color was more appropriate than the original black gown."

"I agree, m'Lady. The king is expected at any moment, so I will leave you. I just wanted to make sure you didn't need anything before his arrival."

"Thank you so kindly, Katrina. I'm all set."

Aelish watched her deeply curtsy once more, which boosted her confidence that Cardissius might possibly let her go outside, if only for a few moments. Ten minutes later, he entered the suite of rooms.

"I'm sorry to have kept you waiting, Aelish. I've been in our OCE all morning."

"The OCE?" she asked.

"The Operations Center for Earth."

"Oh, I see. Is everything all right?"

"Apparently, the Humans are having worldwide protests today. They've decided to rise up against the banks who'd previously promised to no longer fund new fossil fuel projects by joining the Net Zero Banking Alliance. I don't know which is more ridiculous: Humans thinking they could ever effect change through peaceful protests or believing banks would ever keep their word."

Aelish felt herself getting angry. She knew about the Net Zero Banking Alliance, but she had no idea there were worldwide protests today. She was locked in this prison and unable to perform her duties as Policy Director for Earth. And the fact that Yasteron's covert operatives held top positions in those same banks, who'd long ago broken their promise to no longer create new fossil fuel projects, made her furious. She tried to stay focused, but he'd gotten her Irish up.

She asked, "Are the targeted banks: Bank of America, JPMorgan Chase, Citibank, Wells Fargo, Morgan Stanley, and Goldman Sachs?"

"I should have brought you down to the Operations Center," chuckled Cardissius. "Yes, those are the six banks chosen by the protestors because they are primarily responsible for financing fossil fuel expansion."

Aelish knew she should let it go, but she couldn't help herself. "Once an oil, gas, or coal resource is developed, or a fossil fuel infrastructure is built, there is a very strong incentive to fully extract it to the end of its economic life. It's been five years since Fatih Birol, the head of the International Energy Agency, argued that fossil fuel projects, and I quote, 'are not the solution to our urgent energy security needs and they will lock in fossil fuel use.' His quote was basically the motivation for the International Energy Agency's 2021 recommendation to the Net Zero Banking Alliance: no new oil and gas fields and no new coal mines."

Cardissius smiled and sat down in a chair across from her. "Your knowledge of this issue is quite impressive, but I'd expect nothing less, Director Aelish. But keep in mind, even if Yasteron brought home all of our covert operatives, the banking system on Earth would continue funding new fossil fuel projects, despite their promise not to do so. The Human thirst for more and more money is truly astonishing. It comes at the expense of their entire civilization, and it will ultimately cause their extinction, but they cannot stop. Yes, we are guilty of having operatives at the highest levels of these six banks, but the average Human continues to fund their life with dirty money that is killing their world. Pensions and all forms of monetary products are linked to fossil fuels, and whilst they could switch the world economy to renewables and create a new energy system, they won't—their greed is unquenchable."

Aelish replied, "I've always said in my presentations to the Head Council that money on Earth equals the desire for more sophisticated or evil magic in the magical world: money equals magic. And this particular situation reminds me of your own unquenchable thirst for magical domination. I would go so far as to say that you are the magical form of banking."

The king chuckled and smiled at her. "Well put, Aelish. But let me ask you something. Why does DAR continue to be allied with the corrupt world of Earth? It's a world that has never cared about peace; all they care about is money. Yasteron has taught them a powerful lesson about greed, bringing them to the brink of self-annihilation. Watching them destroy their own world in the pursuit of more and more currency has been incredible. DAR has never been able to stop their relentless single-mindedness about money. The actions of Humans have been worse than anything Yasteron has promulgated against them. They are incapable of learning, the same way DAR is incapable of learning the true essence of Humanity. Wouldn't you agree, Director?"

"DAR cares for the Earth because there are DARlings born of the Earth, few as they may be," said Aelish. "DAR will never abandon the Earth for their own beings are born there."

"Like your commonwealth has abandoned you?" scoffed Cardissius. "I hold you captive, yet they don't war with me or attempt to rescue you, despite the pressure they are receiving from the Alliance of Magical Dominions. What does that say about DAR? How weak is your commonwealth? One of their greatest Living Legends has been taken, and they let you languish here, just like the prisoners from the Proelium and the Komprathian drone rats.

"Until your covert mission into Komprathia, DAR never stopped King Gidius from using his drone rats from traveling to Earth in order to spread the plague. Yasteron created the invisible tunnel spells, which I might add, DAR was never able to decode until King Gidius' brother, Obredón, betrayed us."

Aelish was beet red with anger. All she could think of were her parents dead from plague.

Cardissius continued. "Yasteron fomented climate destruction on Earth, stole Earthen metals and elements to create the most destructive magical bomb ever created, and still, DAR did nothing to stop us. And now, you find yourself abandoned by DAR. Is your life not worth the lives of DARling soldiers who'd be sent to rescue you? Why would DAR not risk everything to try and save you? So, I'm confused, Aelish, why does DAR deserve your undying loyalty?"

Hearing him list all of the despicable acts Yasteron perpetrated against DAR and Earth, Aelish felt like she was going to explode. She took a deep breath and said, "DAR is more important than any one DARling. When a dominion has a true and steadfast belief system, those who serve her know they must be willing to sacrifice their own lives not only for that belief system but also for the continuation of the dominion. If Yasteron had such tenets and principles, your citizens would also be willing to die for them. But Yasteron is ruled by a king who cares only about what serves his principles and his desires. Therefore, your citizens and soldiers are forced to defend what *you* believe in, not out of a true devotion to Yasteron but out of fear.

"DAR not starting a war over my captivity is a concept you cannot understand, because to understand it would require you to believe in an ideal. An ideal of a dominion that is greater than any one king or ruler. DAR believes foremost in peace, and we are guided by a desire to foster harmony and peace within the magical world, not war."

Cardissius mockingly smiled at her, shaking his head.

Trying to remain calm, Aelish continued, "The major difference between a DARling and an Earthling is that Humans are born with a sense of entitlement. Humans behave as if they were born with inalienable rights. DARlings, on the other hand, are born with obligations to their commonwealth, their fellow citizens, and the magical world at-large. DARlings do not possess a sense of entitlement; things are not owed to them, just because they were born. They possess an obligation to contribute something meaningful in their lifetime. They desire to improve things and leave DAR and the magical world better than how they found it. Yasteron knows nothing of these ideals, which is why you so seamlessly meld into Earthly society.

"Yasterons are exactly like Humans. You keep taking and taking and always want more, just like Humans who never give anything back to Earth. Some have awoken from the endless pillaging, but it's too late. It's nearly gone. And even if all the Humans became extinct tomorrow, the Earth would still never be as it once was; it may never be able to fully recover.

"You share so much in common with Humans. You think your kingdom is the same as when your father ruled, but it isn't. Your refusal to evolve has already doomed you to losing your kingdom. You've lost the devotion of your people, male heir or not. You have sight but no vision. You live only for yourself, not for your people. You don't live for an ideal, a belief, or anything greater than yourself. You live for whatever selfish, momentary fulfillment is needed to bring you instant gratification."

The king replied, "I could live for you, Aelish. I have been living for you, for the last three hundred and sixty years."

"The concept that you are living for me or that you love me after murdering both of my parents, the Earth where I was born, which will ultimately take the life of my daughter, as well as blowing up my mate in an underwater bunker, makes you insane. It's never enough; you want more and more. In fact, the Yasteron and Human male are never satisfied. They are never at peace. They are always disquieted and destructive. They seek more and more power or more and more money, like a wrecking ball to the females who live beside them."

"Perhaps if your own mate were more like a Yasteron or a Human male, you would have trusted him with the knowledge of your covert mission into Komprathia."

The only reason Aelish didn't slap Cardissius across the face was because she was afraid to move and dislodge the blanket under her gown, disclosing the magical glow of the fetus. And after this debate with the king, all she wanted to do was terminate the fetus. How could she give him an heir to continue on with his insanity?

"Do not speak disparagingly about my mate. You know nothing of who he is."

The king replied, "I know he is the reason you suffer with anxiety of the Magical Interruption Syndrome. He didn't save you then and he won't save you now. He allowed you to be imprisoned in the N.W. Quadrant Detention Center because you didn't trust him with your covert mission."

"I would never risk another's position, life, or freedom for a mission I chose to finish."

"But if you truly loved him, if you truly trusted him with your life, you would have told him everything. Or did you know all along he would never support you? You knew he'd never support your mission against me, my father, and Gidius. He let you do it alone."

Cardissius' words stung Aelish, as there was a ring of truth to what he was saying.

"He didn't save his commonwealth from our bombs, and he hasn't saved Earth or your Humans. What has he accomplished that so deserves your endless love and devotion? Why do you stay with such a worthless protector?"

"I don't need a protector."

"Oh, but you do. Look at where you now find yourself. If he had loved you the right way, he'd have never let you walk into my kingdom, right into this room, unprotected, and alone. You may think me a brute after all I've done, but I will say this, Aelish—if you were mine, I would never allow any harm to come to you. Your mate has been careless with you."

"DARling females do not need DARling males to protect them. We are not Yasterons."

"Well, how has that worked out for you? The only attribute I envy of your mate is his ability to breathe underwater. It is an amazing magical ability which no Yasteron possesses."

"Those may be the only truthful words you have ever spoken in your life," said Aelish.

"I have professed my love for you, Aelish. Those are also true words. You are the only being who has ever had the courage to cross me and destroy all of my plans and agendas. You may have been motivated by grief or morality, but the actions you took against me were fair. You were a fair enemy, and I fell in love with you for it."

Aelish deeply exhaled. "You've taken everything away from me and hold me prisoner. That's love? Perhaps it's some twisted form of love, but I know with certitude, I will never love you. How could I after all you've done to me? How could you even remotely expect that to be possible? You've raped me for days on end, forcing me to bear you an heir, and you actually believe I could love you after that?

"You will never possess my love or my soul because I gave that away a long time ago—my whole soul, there is no part left for you. Thagar has it all. So, now you will know what it feels like to live with loss, an endless grief, and an unfulfilled love. You will never know true love the way I have. At least I knew it when I had it."

The king's face was actually pained.

"Why don't you try something novel?" asked Aelish. "Why don't you do good works in the hopes of wooing my heart? Stop the hate, stop the conquering, and start living. Be present for today, as tomorrow does not exist. Release the prisoners, stop making bombs, stop making bioweapons, and stop destroying the Earth. What is it all for? At least Humans can say it is for money. What can you say it is for—magical world domination? Okay, so now you dominate, what's next? There's no true fulfillment in domination because when your hands are holding a being or a dominion down, a part of you has to be down there too.

"Perhaps if you demonstrated some remorse for what you've done, sought redemption or sought forgiveness, it could bring a truthfulness to your life. For without truth and kindness, what is the point of living? You have everything a magical being could want, but you want a male heir when you have three female heirs. Why? Make your eldest daughter queen. Moreover, abolish the monarchy entirely and set the beings of Yasteron free to govern themselves. But first, you might want to give them something to eat!

"You are antiquated, Your Highness. The way you rule passed centuries ago. So, you can count yourself amongst those who live in the past. Why don't you work with DAR to save the Earth? You may find in doing so, you save yourself, your soul, and open your heart to experience true love. A truthful love, a real love."

"With you?" he asked.

"Yes, with me," she lied.

The king put his long, blond hair into a ponytail with a ribbon he kept in his pocket. He rubbed his face as if to push away all the words she'd used to hurt him.

Aelish stood up and let the blanket drop underneath her gown. "Is this really the life you want for *him*?" The magical glow enveloped the room and she rubbed her abdomen to make it glow even brighter.

"Ohh," uttered the king. He slipped off the chair and knelt before her, hugging the voluminous gown which surrounded the bottom of her legs. After several moments, he stood up and embraced her. "You have made me the happiest male in the magical world, and I will consider all that you have said today. I have never known a being like you, Aelish. I hope the next time we perform the Endeavor you will be a willing participant as my wife and as my queen."

"Your *wife*? I am already mated, Your Highness, I cannot marry you."

"You must or the heir will be a bastard and cannot rule."

"But it goes against my religious beliefs. I cannot be a bigamist!"

"Your Commitments to Thagar have ended, Aelish. You will rule Yasteron alongside me as an equal partner along with our heirs. And one day, I hope you will truly love me as I do you."

Aelish collapsed onto the settee and put her face in her hands crying. "Won't you at least let me go outside and see the sunshine and feel the wind on my face? Please! I cannot bear being kept inside this prison any longer, and it is not healthy for the heir if his mother is miserable. I fear I will go insane locked in this room without my magic and without any sort of life. I've done everything you've asked. Is there no reward?"

"You don't understand, Aelish. There are those who disagree with what I've done. They are furious I have left Queen Saia and chose you, an Earth born DARling, to bear me a male heir for my succession. This room was built for your protection. Until you give birth and we are married, you must remain here so I can keep you completely safe. There are those within Yasteron who wish to do you and the heir harm, even before he is born. You must trust me on this. It is for your own protection."

Aelish had never even considered that she could be in danger by anyone other than the king. Perhaps she and her unborn child could wind up unwitting victims of the unrest brewing in the kingdom. She was also shocked by what appeared to be the king's genuine and sincere concern for her safety.

The king continued. "But I have been working on an idea that I hope will please you."

"What is it?" she asked. The king was now sitting next to her on the settee. "I have always found the companionship of an animal to be most comforting, especially when I was very young. I had horses, unicorns, dogs, and many other magical creatures. They provided me with a lot of love that was not bestowed upon me by my parents."

Now this, was valuable intelligence. The king was a lonely child? His father, King Nevuna, and his mother, whose name she still did not know, neglected him? Why?

"Will you tell me about your youth?" she asked.

"At another time. But may I ask, have you ever loved a dog?"

"I like dogs very much, but I have never had one of my own. Not on Earth, when I was growing up in Ireland, nor in DAR."

"Well," said the king, "whilst we are on the subject of keeping both you and the heir safe, I was considering obtaining even more protection through a particular breed of dog which is very valued here in Yasteron."

"I see. Tell me more about this breed."

"They are known as the Great White Mountain Hund and

have extraordinary magical powers. It's a beautiful all white, long-haired breed that weighs about one hundred and fifty pounds. They have bright blue eyes and if the dog feels threatened, or if it perceives his master or mistress is threatened, it can gaze into its enemies' eyes and blind them, whilst at the same time making them mute, so they cannot even scream for help. It can also be ridden like a horse, by children up to the age of twelve. Their strength, protective nature, and hearing acuity is unrivaled by any other magical canine. Their fealty is to their master or mistress and are willing to give their life to save yours."

"I have never heard about this breed before," remarked Aelish.

"I would like you to have one, but since the breed can be deadly, both you and the dog need to have proper training. There is a unit in our military which utilizes these dogs to serve alongside them. I will reach out to the captain and see if he can spare the time to come here and work with you and the dog. Would that make you happy? You would have companionship whilst I attend to my duties."

"I would like that very much," said Aelish. "Can I sleep in bed with the dog or is too dangerous?"

"Once it is trained, I imagine it would sleep with you every night, at the foot of the bed, guarding. All right then, I will make all the necessary arrangements. I must return to the OCE now. But I would like to join you for dinner tonight so we can properly celebrate this momentous day. You've made me so happy, Aelish, and I am still considering all that you've said to me today. Do not think I have dismissed or forgotten it." He bowed and reached for her hand to kiss it. "Until tonight, dearest."

After he left, Aelish wrote down all the intelligence she'd gathered about the protests on Earth, his childhood, and the military unit which used the Great White Mountain Hund. She was surprised DAR did not also utilize this breed. How she wished she could ask Thagar about it.

Sitting at the writing desk in her bedchamber, Aelish felt conflicted. Cardissius' opinion about Thagar not being a good protector had some truth to it. She hadn't trusted Thagar. She knew he would betray her to the Head Council had he known about her covert mission into Komprathia. She also knew he would have never given up his command of the S.E. Quadrant, to join her on her covert mission and finally stop the plague on Earth.

She did end up in the N.W. Quadrant detention center because she'd had no support from DAR or from Thagar for her actions. And she did, in fact, develop a terrific fear of Magical Interruption Syndrome from being incarcerated for six months. As she sat there, she realized it had been ten days since she'd seen Thagar. Had he even considered approaching the Head Council to take some form of action to rescue her?

She violently shook her head to stop these thoughts. All of this was in the past, and her actions had been her choice and her decision. Cardissius was polluting her mind against her mate. Here she was, carrying the heir to a kingdom that had killed her parents; their grandchild, who now lived inside of her, was half Yasteron. She was utterly confused and began massaging her belly to calm herself. The glow grew so bright, it was as if the fetus sensed her distress and was trying to cheer her up.

She looked down at her abdomen and smiled. And then, was instantly disturbed to feel even a smattering of happiness, carrying Cardissius' heir. She stood up, took a deep breath, and began pacing around the bedchamber. Her inner turmoil was torture. She began to pray and thanked God for the chance to hopefully love two new things, a dog and an infant. She could only hope they might assuage her unbearable loneliness.

5

BREAKDOWN

THAGAR PRESSED THE intercom on his office phone at the Climate Refugee Intake Center. "Elle, could you please see if Mrs. Torres is free to come to my office?"

"Right away, sir," replied Elle. A few minutes later, she buzzed his intercom. "She will be here in about fifteen minutes."

"All right. Thank you, Elle." Thagar sat back in his office chair and swiveled to look out the window. It had been nearly two weeks since Sartaine and Stavros came to tell him about Aelish, and he was anxiously awaiting a transmission from Melanthia. He was desperate to know what action DAR was prepared to take against Yasteron. He was becoming more and more restless, and the only reason he remained grounded was for Kaleigh's sake.

Kaleigh took the news about her mother being held captive better than he thought she would. She was well aware of the Peace Accord her mother had been working on and had an understanding of the situation far beyond her six and a half years. She had an innate grasp of diplomacy and understood how Yasteron had tricked her mother with the promise of peace.

He knew he probably should have held back on telling her the historic details of Yasteron's despicable behavior. But she was so intelligent, it seemed to provide her with a better understanding of why they took her mother, and it gave him the ability to vent his feelings. She was of great comfort to him and told him to never give up hope that her mother was coming home. His rage at the entire situation often got the better of him, but he hid that from Kaleigh.

He heard Elle's distinctive knock on his office door, and he said, "Come on in."

Elle opened the door, saying, "Mrs. Torres is here."

Thagar gestured for her to come in and Marisol entered his office. "Thank you, Elle. Would you like some coffee or tea, Marisol?"

"No, I just finished a big cup," said Marisol. "Thank you."

"That will be all for now, Elle." He watched her close the door. Once they were alone, he asked Marisol, "How are you holding up? The loss must be unbearable."

"It makes me catch my breath at least ten times a day. The worst is when I forget she's gone and I go to call her to tell her about something. It's an emptiness that can't be filled."

"How is Isabela coping?"

"Better than I expected, but I feel like the other shoe is about to drop because we haven't told her yet about Aelish."

"Well, that's what I wanted to speak with you about."

"Oh, what's going on?"

"Isabela has called both the house line and my cell phone in the last two days, at least two times a day, looking for Aelish. I've been able to lie, but I think time's up; we have to tell her."

"Okay, Thagar. It's probably for the best, and we don't want it to appear like Aelish is ignoring her. I've already spoken to her doctors about the fact that there is some devasting news I need to share with Izzy, and they all agreed it would be best if she was told soon and in person.

"I would like to come with you and be the one to tell Isabela everything."

"Are you sure, Thagar? Her reaction might be volatile."

"Absolutely. I don't want you to have to do this alone. How about we do it today?"

"Okay. She has therapy later this afternoon, but we could do it before then. Does that work with your schedule?"

"Whenever it's convenient for you and Isabela."

"I didn't want to ask, but I assume you've heard nothing further about Aelish?"

"I'm waiting to have a virtual meeting with the Head Council Chair of DAR any day now. I hope it happens soon because I'm trying to hold it together for Kaleigh, who has been absolutely amazing. She's so much like Aelish, it brings tears to my eyes."

"Count it as a blessing, Thagar. And definitely don't let Kaleigh see your anger. It will make her feel hopeless and helpless. Trust me on this."

"I'm trying so hard not to, but it's not easy. The rage at what they've done lives right underneath my burned skin."

"Pobrecito," said Marisol. "Okay, I will drive us to the psychiatric facility, as it's nestled in the mountains and easy to get lost. Are you sure you want to do this today?"

"I am. Isabela has to be told."

"All right, then. I will be waiting outside for you in my car at one o'clock."

"Okay, see you, then." Marisol stood up and left his office. Thagar leaned back in his chair and began mentally preparing how he was going to tell Isabela, in order to soften the blow.

Thagar and Marisol stood outside of Isabela's suite at the psychiatric facility. Marisol gently knocked on the door. Isabela had been told Thagar would be joining her mother for a visit. She knew something was wrong, as Thagar had never come to see her before. She could feel her anxiety rising, making her heart race.

Isabela opened the door. "It's so good to see you, Thagar. Hi, Mom. Come on in. Do you want anything to drink? Let's sit in the living area." Thagar and Marisol followed behind her, sharing a worried look between them. They had decided Thagar would tell Isabela everything.

"This is some suite you have here, Isabela," said Thagar. He felt his throat getting dry from apprehension. "Do you have a soda?"

"Of course, one second," said Isabela. "Mom, do you want anything?"

"I will take a soda, too," said Marisol.

Isabela returned with a variety of sodas from her small refrigerator and put them on the table in front of the couch where Thagar and Marisol were sitting. She sat down in a chair across from them saying, "Well, I imagine what you're about to tell me isn't going to be good, so let's get it over with."

"First off, Isabela," said Thagar, "I want to profusely apologize for not being truthful with you."

"This is about Aelish, right?" asked Isabela. "You've come to tell me she no longer wants to be a part of my life, correct?"

"No, not at all, Isabela," said Thagar. Isabela breathed a sigh of relief. "Your mother and I thought it was best to wait until after Abuela's funeral to tell you what has happened to Aelish."

"Oh, my God! What has happened to Aelish?" Isabela's heart felt like it was going to burst out of her chest. She moved closer to the edge of her chair.

Thagar continued. "When we were in DAR at Sartaine and

Naz' Commitments Ceremony, Aelish was told by Head Council Member Cheswick that King Cardissius of Yasteron was ready to sign the Peace Accord she's been working on for years, but he had one final condition."

"Oh, God," said Isabela. "What else did he want? Aelish told me the morning of my presentation to the WHO, which was also the day Yasteron tried to assassinate me, that Cardissius constantly sabotaged the conditions and stipulations of the Peace Accord. And you both know what happened between Aelish and I after she boarded Drew's helicopter."

Thagar nodded. "Cardissius must have known she would be in DAR for the Commitments Ceremony, so he requested, which means demanded, that she attend the signing of the Peace Accord. It was scheduled to be signed the same day Abuela and Kaleigh were exposed to carbon monoxide. She was even supposed to join us for dinner that night.

"The delegation left for Yasteron the Monday after the Commitments Ceremony, and the signing was supposed to be on Wednesday. But when I returned to Earth alone on Monday, she'd magically left me a letter stating she had a feeling the Peace Accord would most likely not be signed by Wednesday, and I should expect her by Saturday. Therefore, Saturday would be the earliest we'd speak to one another."

"Is she still in Yasteron?" Isabela asked with trepidation.

"The evening of the signing, Aelish was tricked inside a room to await an urgent transmission from Earth."

"So, Yasteron did kill Abuela," said Isabela. "Of course, they did. How else would they know there was an emergency on Earth involving her daughter?"

"I have yet to determine if they made up the story of an urgent message from Earth to trick her into this room or whether they were, in fact, responsible for what happened to Abuela and

Kaleigh. I truly do not know the answer yet, Isabela, but I promise I will find out."

"They totally killed Abuela. They are absolutely unbelievable!"

Thagar and Marisol glanced at each other over Isabela's reaction.

Marisol said, "Izzy, try to stay focused. According to the men from DAR who came to tell Thagar about what happened to Aelish, the urgent message was simply a ruse to make her enter this room, unaccompanied by any other members of the delegation. Don't focus on Abuela at this moment."

Isabela stood up from the chair and began pacing. "If Yasteron didn't intentionally poison Abuela and Kaleigh, that would be a fantastical coincidence. These two events just simply collided? Yasteron knew nothing? I will never believe it."

"Izzy, please try and relax," said Marisol. "Please sit down, mija, and let Thagar finish." Isabela sat back down and began fidgeting with her hair.

Thagar continued. "Aelish is being held captive in Yasteron, in that same room, Isabela. Once she entered this room, none of the delegation ever saw her again. They were all rendered magically paralyzed and were transported back to the N.W. Quadrant in DAR. Actually, the Peace Accord was the ruse. All these years, Cardissius used the negotiations as a way to keep Aelish occupied with Yasteron so she'd be fully invested in seeing the Peace Accord come to fruition. By adding the one last condition of her physically needing to be present for the signing, Cardissius was able to kidnap and take her prisoner. She knows nothing about what happened to Abuela or Kaleigh. That's why you haven't seen her once during all this time. She isn't here. And I don't know if we will ever see her again." Thagar began wiping tears from his eyes.

As a physician-scientist, Isabela always wondered what

a break with reality would feel like. However, through all her depressions and her hospitalization in the psychiatric facility that had never happened. Suddenly, her mother and Thagar became blurry. She felt the rage about Aelish telling Drew about the magical world morph into a rage at Yasteron for sending Glen to steal her scientific research and break her heart. But mostly, she blamed herself for Aelish going to Yasteron with the Peace Accord delegation. She knew those last cruel words she'd spoken to Aelish had propelled her to go and would most likely end in her death. Isabela blamed herself for it all and no longer felt like she could live with the anguish for one more minute.

She stood up from the chair. Her speech was incoherent and disorganized. She kept switching from one topic to another and began speaking to people who were not in the room. And then, she began screaming and throwing objects which were not nailed down. She had superhuman strength and broke her chair. She used a piece of it to break other furniture in the room. She ran into the bathroom, looked into the mirror, put her fist through it, and took one of the shards and slit her wrist with it. Before she could slit the other, Thagar magically flung the shard of mirror out of her hand.

By this time, Marisol had secured assistance from the facility. She had not witnessed Isabela slit her wrist, but when she saw the blood, Marisol began screaming. Thagar embraced Marisol as they watched three enormous men wrestle Isabela to the floor, who was kicking and screaming. They finally injected her with a sedative, which rendered her unconscious. A gurney was brought in to transport her to a part of the facility designated for attempted suicides.

After Isabela was taken away, Thagar and Marisol went back into the living area. Thagar moved aside the wreckage of Isabela's break with reality, and they resumed sitting on the couch. Marisol was so pale he was concerned she might have a heart attack. He put a calming spell on her and hugged her tightly on the couch. He simply could not process what he'd just witnessed.

A psychiatrist entered the room and told them Isabela would be in the ward for suicide patients and would most likely be sedated again after she woke up. He explained that often when suicidal patients awaken, and realize they were unsuccessful in their attempt, they immediately lose control and must be sedated again. He did not know how long Isabela's psychotic break would last, but he went so far as to suggest Isabela might be a candidate for Electric Shock Therapy. Despite the calming spell, Marisol began yelling at the doctor that EST could endanger her genius and she would not allow it. The doctor did not press the issue any further and told them to go home and check back with the facility tomorrow.

Once he left the room, Thagar explained to Marisol that he was going to magically transport both of them and her car back to her house. He called Jorge and told him to leave work immediately and quickly explained everything that had happened. Once they arrived at the Torres home, Thagar used the Deep Sleep spell on Marisol so she could rest and hopefully wake up more clear-headed. When Jorge arrived, the two males sat and talked together until it was time for Thagar to pick up Kaleigh from school. Jorge was very grateful, while at the same time, terribly distraught. And Thagar felt totally responsible for the magical world irreparably injuring this family.

‡‡‡‡

Marisol's phone began ringing. It felt unbelievably sad that Abuela would never again be on the other end. She saw the incoming call was from Drew.

"Hi, Drew. This is a pleasant surprise. But before you tell me why you are calling, I just wanted to say thank you again for all you have done for our family. Your actions made Abuela's death and funeral so much more bearable."

"How are you doing with the grief, Marisol? I remember after my mother died, I felt anxious all the time. I couldn't eat and basically felt like I would never get over it."

"That pretty much describes it. The anxiety is the worst part for me."

"It was for me, too. I know you have a lot going on in your life right now, so I hesitated to call you, but I'm very concerned about Isabela."

Marisol's stomach flipped. She hadn't told Drew anything about Isabela's psychotic break or her attempted suicide last week and suddenly felt like she was going to vomit. "Oh, I see. Can you tell me what's happened?"

"Well, I received an invoice from Isabela's psychiatric facility for furniture. I just wanted to make sure I wasn't paying for a remodel," he said, chuckling. "When I pressed the facility further, they informed me that Isabela broke most of the furniture in her suite. Marisol, why did Isabela break the furniture in her suite?"

"Oh, my God, I am so sorry you got blindsided by an invoice for that. And I apologize for not giving you a heads-up on what happened to Isabela."

"I assume you told Isabela about Aelish being held captive in Yasteron? And then, Isabela completely lost it, and proceeded to break all the furniture, correct?"

"You guessed it, Drew. She went out of her mind and began literally breaking everything that wasn't nailed down in a fit of rage and anguish and had to be sedated for three days. I am so sorry I did not communicate all of this to you, but I was fighting with her doctors over the last week not to administer Electric

Shock Therapy, as I am terrified it might alter her genius."

"Oh, my God, was it as bad as all that?"

"Yes, Drew. Isabela had a psychotic break and slit one of her wrists. Thagar prevented her from slitting the other. She was in the suicide ward until two days ago."

"Oh, my God," said Drew. Marisol heard him deeply exhale. "Listen, I spoke with Thagar at the funeral about Aelish. I don't know how he's holding it together. But he did tell me you were planning to tell Isabela about Aelish once you all came home. Marisol, I've stayed away from Isabela for nearly two years. I left right after the funeral service so she wouldn't be uncomfortable at the repast luncheon. I've never even asked to visit her in the facility, but it's time. I need to see Isabela, Marisol."

"I understand, Drew, and I also agree. Let me see what day would be best, and I will get back to you. But it will be this week, okay?"

"Thank you. And again, I am so terribly sorry for everything your family is going through."

‡‡‡‡

Marisol knocked on Isabela's door in the psychiatric facility. Isabela opened the door and looked positively wretched. Marisol had no idea when or how her daughter was ever going to get out of this place. She'd been doing so much better and even handled the death of Abuela better than Marisol had ever expected. But Aelish being taken prisoner, completely broke her.

"Hi, Mom," said Isabela, opening the door. Marisol stepped inside and suggested they sit outside on the terrace.

Once they were seated in the sunshine, Marisol said, "I want you to remain tranquila."

"Oh, my God, what happened now?" asked Isabela, who

immediately stood up and began pacing.

"Drew is downstairs and he wants to see you, Isabela."

"You brought him here, *now*? And didn't think maybe you should tell me first?"

"And if I had, would you have agreed to see him?"

"Absolutely not!"

Marisol knew she was taking a big risk that Isabela could relapse and have another psychotic break, but her instincts as her mother propelled her to continue. "It's time, Isabela."

"No! I refuse to see him! I haven't seen him in almost two years, Mom, and you suddenly decide it's okay to ambush me with a visit from Drew?"

"Yes, Isabela, you are going to see him. He received a bill for all the furniture and items you destroyed in this suite, and he's extremely concerned about you. You are going to thank him for all he has done for you and for this family. He flew Abuela and all of us on his private jet, and paid for the entire funeral, and burial. He graciously came to the funeral service, but left right afterward so you wouldn't have to see him. Do you know how much he has done for us? Abuela is buried right next to Abuelo and it cost us nothing, just like all your treatments here have cost us nothing. He is an elegant, generous person who does not deserve to be treated like this by you anymore. I won't stand for it, Izzy. I raised you better than this. Basta!"

Isabela sat down on a bench and began crying. Marisol remained quiet as she sobbed. After about twenty minutes, Isabela looked up at her mother and said, "Mom, I simply can't face him today. I still feel medicated from being sedated for three days. I'm not ready."

"While I respect your feelings and the treatments you are receiving here, you are just going to have to trust me, Izzy. You need to do this, and there will never be a day when it's going to feel comfortable for you. So, I suggest you go wash your face and put on some decent clothes. I will send him up in fifteen minutes, and I will come back afterward to check on you. Do you want me to inform the nurses that you might need attention after his visit?"

"No!" exclaimed Isabela. "No more doctors! No more nurses! I just want to go home, Mom. I want to go back to my lab and to my life. What is wrong with me? Why can't I get better?"

"You are better, mi amor. You were set to come home in two weeks, and then Abuela died, and then you found out about Aelish. Those two events set you back, but they didn't set you back to the point of no return, comprendes? You are stronger than you know, and you can do this."

"Fine," Isabela finally uttered.

"I didn't expect you to be happy about this, Izzy, but I do expect you to demonstrate gratitude toward Drew." Marisol stood up and gestured for Isabela to also stand. She embraced her daughter, who began sobbing again. "It's all right to start trusting again, okay?"

"Okay, Mom."

‡‡‡‡

Isabela put on a simple black, long-sleeved dress and some flat shoes. Her hair was dirty, but it made it easier to put it up in a high ponytail. She put on a little bit of makeup because when she looked into the new mirror in her bathroom, her reflection looked worse than ever.

She heard a knock on the door, took a deep breath, and remembered all the difficult things she'd accomplished in her life. She whispered to herself, "You can do this, you can do this."

She opened the door and Drew smiled at her. He handed

her a beautiful potted plant with vibrant colors. "I assumed you wouldn't have a vase laying around," he said, smiling.

Isabela found herself chuckling at his sarcasm. "Please, come in."

Drew took off his long trench coat, and the scent of his manliness and elegant cologne enveloped her. He asked, "Where would you be most comfortable to sit with me?"

"It's a little chilly outside, so why don't we stay in the living area?"

Drew sat down on the couch and Isabela sat down on the new couch across from the old one. Isabela assumed the facility made an executive decision to have heavier objects in the rooms, to keep their patients safer. The new couch was unable to be used as a weapon, like the old chair she'd broken in half. "I'm not going to stay long, Isabela. I just wanted to tell you a few things, and then I will go."

Isabela nodded.

"First, I want to tell you how very sorry I am for the loss of your grandmother. I am sorry I never got to meet her."

"You would have liked her. She was so kind and generous, like you, and she was so funny. She could always make me laugh, no matter what." Isabela began fiddling with the necklace of St. Michael around her neck.

"Second, I am very sorry about Aelish."

Isabela fought back tears, but they came all the same. "I'm so sorry I'm crying," she said. "But I just can't forgive myself for the way I spoke to her shortly before she left for DAR. And I know my behavior and my ugly words propelled her to go to Yasteron. I don't believe she would have gone if I hadn't spoken to her the way I did. It's all my fault, Drew."

Drew got up and sat down next to Isabela. He gently hugged her and she embraced him, sobbing. "Aelish is the kindest being I have ever met," said Isabela, "and I treated her very badly. I will never forgive myself for what I said to her, and now, she's King Cardissius' prisoner all because of me."

Drew remained quiet as she spoke and cried on his shoulder. When she was finished, he lifted her chin and stared into her eyes. "While I understand what regret feels like, I think you are being a little hard on yourself. Aelish's war with this kingdom goes back long before you or I were even born, Isabela. You may be correct in that she went to Yasteron in a small way because of you, but this king has been her nemesis for hundreds of years. Aelish was always going to go to Yasteron. She would never have missed the opportunity to sign a Peace Accord with this kingdom, no matter what you said to her before she left. You have to internalize this fact."

Isabela gently nodded and began wiping her tears with the back of her hands. Drew handed her a handkerchief. "Thank you. Aelish always says she never has one of these when she needs one. Did you know we both wipe our tears off our face the same way?"

"I did not know that." Drew smiled at her. "I think you are underestimating Aelish."

"How so?"

"She's inside that kingdom now and might actually be able to effect more change from the inside than she ever could from the outside. While it may cost her dearly, she never seemed the type of being to back away from a fight for what's right and what's just. You must have faith in her as well as in Thagar to bring her home. Thagar is awaiting word from DAR to see if they will go to war with them over her abduction. He does not believe they will. This is probably for the best, as war never seems to solve anything except the killing of innocent civilians."

"I love her so much, Drew, but I was so angry with her for

telling you about the magical world without even considering how it would impact me," said Isabela.

"She made an impulsive decision. All great leaders do, Isabela. But now, it's time for you to begin trusting her again. It may all work out horribly, but Aelish does what she thinks is right. She may die for her decision to attend the Peace Accord signing, but how you spoke to her had nothing to do with her wanting to solidify peace with a kingdom she's personally been at war with for centuries. She would have gone to Yasteron if you had never spoken harshly to her.

"Thagar begged her not to go, and she didn't even listen to him. But you're taking all the blame? Come on, Isabela, you're smarter than that. And it's time for you to rejoin the world. If Aelish manages to escape, how would she feel knowing you didn't fight as hard as she did to survive? How would she feel knowing you didn't fight for a better outcome for Earth, like saving the world from LECCS? The world needs you, Isabela. I can't get the message out about the vaccine to those who are hesitant to take it, without the physician-scientist who created it. I need your help. Do you understand? We may lose the battle, just like Aelish, but we have to try."

Isabela stared at him as if she were meeting him for the first time. His knowledge of Aelish's battle with Yasteron surprised her; he'd gained quite a grasp of the magical world and Yasteron in particular. How did Aelish know on the helicopter that Drew would handle the knowledge imparted to him about the magical world with such intelligence and compassion? Most people would have thought Aelish was insane and wouldn't have believed anything she'd told him. But he not only accepted it, he also embraced it. He wanted to help Earth fight against the ravages of the climate crisis, instigated and perpetuated by Yasteron.

"And I will leave you with this," he said. "I cannot believe the scientist before me does not want to get out of here for one reason and one reason only."

"What do you mean?"

"Don't you want to know why Kaleigh didn't die in your house with Abuela? You know if she were truly one hundred percent Human, she would be dead. Don't you want to analyze her DNA, Doctor Torres? Perhaps there's something there that Aelish will need to know about if she ever gets out of captivity."

Isabela began smiling. "Wow, you really get me."

"I do, and I have ever since I first met you in Hector's kitchen on a computer. Why do you think I went forward and supported all of your research? Do you think a boy your age could possibly understand you, Isabela? We share the same birthday, and while I may be eighteen years older than you, I still find myself endlessly trying to keep up with your intelligence. And not even my money can make up for my lack of genius."

Isabela started laughing.

"Now, that is a beautiful sound. So, what do you say we get you out of here in about two weeks? Have some closing sessions with your doctors. Then, be prepared to work with me on the messaging of the vaccine while you secretly begin analyzing Kaleigh's DNA."

Isabela felt like a five-hundred-pound-guerilla had been lifted off her chest. She was so excited to get out of here.

"Okay, Drew. I will try to be back in my lab or wherever you need me to be in two weeks. I'm done being afraid."

"You don't have to be afraid of anything anymore, Isabela. I will always be here for you, and you will never feel alone again."

6

WAR & PEACE

T HAGAR WAS UPSTAIRS in the home office awaiting a live transmission from Melanthia, when the doorbell rang. He heard Drummond's feet clomping toward the bottom of the staircase.

Drummond yelled up, "I will get the door, sir."

"Thank you," Thagar yelled back.

Drummond opened the door to the olive-green face of the Council Chair, Melanthia. "Ohh," he uttered. Then, he deeply bowed and his conical hat fell to the floor.

Melanthia began chuckling and said, "May I come in, Drummond?"

"You remembered my name," he said.

"Of course, you are very dear to DAR," she said.

Drummond began broadly smiling and stepped to the side of the door so she could enter. He was completely flustered. It wasn't every day he opened the door to see the Council Chair of the Head Council of DAR. "Can I get you somethin' to drink or eat, Council Chair?"

"Perhaps in a little bit, but could you please tell Director Thagar I am here to see him?"

"Yes, yes, of course. One moment." Drummond left Melanthia standing in the entryway and walked to the bottom of the staircase. He yelled up the stairs, "Director Thagar, I think you need to come downstairs."

Thagar stood up and wondered why Drummond was using his official title. He aspirated to the front entryway and stared at Melanthia. "What are you doing here? I thought we were going to have a live transmission. It's so good to see you in the flesh." Thagar reached across and embraced Melanthia. Turning toward Drummond, he instructed, "Please make a special breakfast for the Council Chair, Drummond."

"Right away, sir." Drummond picked up his hat from the floor, bowed once more, and raced toward the kitchen.

Melanthia said, "I needed to get out of DAR for a bit, and I thought coming to Earth might lend some perspective. Would it be possible for us to speak in that beautiful room in the back of the house? I remember speaking with Aelish in there."

"Do you mean the tree-house room?"

"Yes, that's what it's called. I couldn't remember; it's so lovely."

As Thagar walked Melanthia back to the tree-house room, he said to Drummond, who was in the kitchen, "Please serve us in the tree-house room, Drummond."

"Right away, sir."

Melanthia walked over to the windows to view the beautiful acreage behind the house. "There's something magical about this room." She took a deep breath and loudly exhaled. "That might actually be the first real breath I've taken since Aelish was abducted."

Thagar sat down on one of the couches while Melanthia took

a minute to enjoy the view. He realized he only spent time in this room with Kaleigh, as it reminded him too much of Aelish. This was her favorite room in the house. She'd been gone a month now, resulting in a permanent pit in his stomach. He was barely sleeping without the aid of spells, and his appetite had disappeared along with Aelish.

But mostly, he was angry. Aelish was gone, and he didn't know how he'd ever get over witnessing Isabela slitting her wrist. She was finally released from the psychiatric hospital just yesterday, but he wondered how long she could stay mentally healthy. When he took Kaleigh to church on Sundays, he found himself praying for Isabela and Aelish. All of it was unbearable and totally unfair.

Drummond entered the tree-house room and placed all the food he'd prepared on the table between the two couches. There was enough food to feed an army.

"This is too much, Drummond. You honor me," said Melanthia.

"Thank you, Drummond," said Thagar. "You created a veritable feast in a very short time. Now, off to bed you go."

"I'm just goin' to clean up first, sir. Then, I will be off to bed."

"Okay, thank you, Drummond," said Thagar.

Drummond bowed one final time and left the room.

"So, war has begun in the magical world," said Melanthia, still standing at the window.

Thagar's head shot up. "Are DAR and Yasteron at war with one another?"

"Not exactly." She walked away from the window and sat down on the couch opposite Thagar and began making a plate of food. "Within days of Aelish's capture, Komprathia began bombing Yasteron. The Alliance of Magical Dominions has provided tremendous support for them warring with Yasteron, and DAR finds itself in a difficult situation. I don't want to directly engage with Yasteron, as I fear mutually assured destruction. The N.W. Quadrant is finally back to the way it was, prior to the bombings, and I would like it to stay that way.

"Komprathia has led the charge, as their drone rats continue to be held captive. They are still furious about the bombs dropped on DAR, which contaminated our soil and could have spread radioactive material to their own crops, to say nothing of Komprathian citizens potentially suffering from intergenerational radiation contamination. Thanks to you, we found out in time that the bombs threatened not only DAR's food supply but also Trelveland's trees and Komprathia's crops. You are quite the hero, Thagar. If you hadn't survived the underwater bunker bombing and lived to tell Aelish about the radioactive component to the bombs, I fear we all would have starved to death by now."

"I am no hero, Melanthia."

"You know that's not true, Thagar." Melanthia shook her head at him. "Komprathia is also deeply devoted to Aelish, as she is the Living Legend who freed them from the tyranny of King Gidius. They are horrified she was captured on a peace mission and is being held prisoner."

"So, what is DAR's response to Komprathia taking the lead on warring with Yasteron?"

"We are performing the delicate balance of trying to appear neutral, whilst at the same time, assisting Komprathia with reinforcing their protective grids and barriers to repel counter attacks by Yasteron. Mercifully, Yasteron is not using their newest bomb so radioactive contamination is not a concern at this time."

Melanthia took a bite of food and wore a troubled look on her face.

"But DAR is experiencing civil unrest," she said. "The citizens are severely divided over whether or not to war with Yasteron.

And the cry to war is being led by the Earth born DARlings, as there has not been a birth of an Earth born DARling in over one hundred years. The only possible explanation we can deduce for why this is the case, is because of the climate crisis here on Earth. Our experimenters are evaluating the situation, but the Earth born are convinced the slow demise of Earth is why there are no new births."

Thagar was pleased to hear DAR was in turmoil and that the Earth born, like Aelish, were pressuring the Head Council to war with Yasteron.

"DARlings born of the Earth reach the highest level of magical attainment in DAR," said Melanthia. "And the Earth born believe that is why Yasteron wants to kill off all of Humanity—to prevent any further births of Earth born DARlings. The Earth born relegate Yasteron's magical abilities to second place, and Yasteron wants to reign supreme in the magical world."

Thagar said, "I believe after Aelish freed Komprathia, Yasteron decided to ramp up their covert activities here on Earth as revenge for her posing as one of them, which undermined the relationship between King Gidius and Yasteron. Nothing was going to stop her from ending the outbreaks of plague on Earth. She knew the alliance had to be destroyed; it was the only way to stop the drone rats from traveling to Earth, in Yasteron-built tunnels, to spread the plague."

Melanthia said, "Her mission was quite brilliant, and she was only a student at the time. And during their alliance, Yasteron learned a lot about Human traits from Komprathia since they have them as well. Yasteron uses the worst of Human traits to urge Humanity to self-annihilate."

Thagar said, "But DAR attempting to remain neutral in the current war, whilst supplying Komprathia with assistance, is the same proxy war we've been engaged in with Yasteron for the last one thousand years. They use other realms to have proxy wars with us. Their alliance with Komprathia to create massive plague outbreaks on Earth is but one example.

"After Aelish broke the alliance, Yasteron turned their full attention toward harming Earth. DAR's devotion to Earth only furthered their desire for the next proxy war. Armed with the knowledge of Human traits, like greed, Yasteron encouraged Humans to continue using fossil fuels. They knew Humans would be willing to destroy their own world, all for the sake of money and an unquenchable greed. It's simply astonishing.

"I don't think Yasteron actually has a hatred for Humans; I don't think they care about them one way or the other. They do it all to aggravate us with one exception: by propelling Humans to destroy the Earth and extinct themselves through the climate crisis, Yasteron will stop the procreation of Earth born DARlings whose magical abilities exceed their own. That is, and has always been, their target."

"I agree, Thagar," said Melanthia. "The Earth born have pushed DAR toward incredible levels of magical attainment. I sympathize and understand why the Earth born wish to war with Yasteron; they are trying to eliminate their existence."

"I would like to share something with you," said Thagar, "but you must promise me that you will tell no one, Melanthia."

"I give you my word, Thagar."

"Our daughter, Kaleigh, was recently exposed to carbon monoxide poisoning."

"But that is a deadly gas for Humans."

"Exactly. But Kaleigh was able to breathe in the toxic environment and suffered no repercussions from the exposure."

"What are you saying, Thagar? Kaleigh is magical?"

"Not necessarily. I believe Aelish and I may have created the first next-generation Human who can survive the toxic atmosphere created by carbon, methane, and other greenhouse gases. If I'm right, this could mean that DARlings can potentially procreate a next-gen Human, just like Humans are able to procreate an Earth born DARling.

"I believe we are on the precipice of this, which means next-gen Humans could, theoretically, survive the toxic environment Yasteron has secretly been encouraging for centuries. I plan on having Kaleigh's DNA analyzed by Isabela to determine if I'm right. Unfortunately, Isabela has been mentally unwell for some time, but it is my hope she will soon be able to unlock the secret as to why Kaleigh survived the carbon monoxide poisoning."

"When did all of this happen?" asked Melanthia, shocked.

"The day Aelish was supposed to sign the Peace Accord, which was the same day she was taken. You must promise me that you will tell no one, Melanthia. And I, in turn, will keep you apprised of the analysis on Kaleigh."

"Absolutely incredible," remarked Melanthia. "I will tell no one, Thagar, as that would make Kaleigh a target for Yasteron. Wait, do you think they were behind the carbon monoxide poisoning?"

Thagar began to remember how much he respected Melanthia's intelligence, despite completely disagreeing with her on whether to war with Yasteron. "I don't know. And unless I find the Yasteron responsible for killing one of the kindest Humans I have ever known, we may never know."

"Whom are you referring to?" asked Melanthia.

"Isabela's grandmother did not survive the poisoning and our world has severely and unfairly affected not only Isabela but also her entire family. Isabela is very fragile from working with DAR over these last eight years. It's something we should keep in mind when asking Humans for assistance. Why can't we finally, once and for all, deal with Yasteron, Melanthia?"

"I know we disagree on this issue, Thagar. And I know your feelings have changed with regard to many of DAR's tenets and principles. They haunt you. But you know firsthand, as the former Director of the POD, using military intervention is not the surest path to achieving a dominion's political aims. DAR learned that through the endless wars of the past. Having so much faith in the use of war can easily lead to gross miscalculations, costing DARling citizens and soldiers their lives.

"I know Aelish came to believe, after much consideration over using Roger's spell, that armed victory is not the ultimate decider when trying to alter a barbaric enemy. You may defeat them and you may win the war, but they will remain barbaric and will immediately begin plotting to once again go to war."

Thagar said, "We can agree the loss of innocents is morally wrong, Melanthia. But there comes a time, when the only thing a barbaric realm understands *is* war."

"I understand what you are saying, but DAR's tenets and philosophies are different from any other magical realm. After the females took over governing DAR, they realized our commonwealth has no interest in the spoils of war, like Yasteron does, including increased power, domination of the magical world, and taking resources found in conquered realms. These are all justifications of war by Yasteron. They enjoy the spoils of war, but DAR does not."

"But sometimes, Melanthia, war is a transformative force."

"You know that assumption, more often than not, has been proven untrue, Thagar. In the face of naked aggression, such as Yasteron releasing radioactive bombs over the N.W. Quadrant to poison our soil and starve us to death, the idea of war becomes very alluring. It is an understandable reaction. I experienced it myself when I threatened Yasteron and told them we had Roger's spell and planned on using it unless they ceased the bombings.

Was I really prepared to annihilate an entire kingdom, including their innocents? Not really. But I was not going to be the first one to blink. They had to stand down, and I used mutually assured destruction as a threat. Mutually assured destruction is a form of insanity—everyone dies."

Thagar shook his head in disagreement.

"Listen to me, Thagar. The temptation to annihilate Yasteron, and having the power to do so, tortured Aelish for months. Your bravery and your willingness to risk everything, by staying until the very end of Glen's interrogation, made Aelish decide *not* to use Roger's spell against Yasteron. You imparted unknown intelligence about the unrest brewing there. She could never abide killing the innocents who live under the thumb of Cardissius and his nobles, especially when you definitively provided us with that information. You are the reason why she decided not to use Roger's spell."

"I feel so powerless," said Thagar, smoothing his beard. "And I see all the opportunities I squandered against Cardissius and his father, Nevuna, whilst I was Director of the POD. I'm tortured by all of my inactions, throughout my entire tenure at the POD. I could have altered history, which could've resulted in a different outcome for Aelish."

"They say hindsight is twenty-twenty, but it isn't," said Melanthia. "We think if we could go back in time and alter this or that decision, it would make a difference. But that's not necessarily true. Perhaps where we find ourselves is exactly where we are supposed to be. And the only way out of questioning our previous actions is to move in a forward-thinking direction. Looking back only causes regret and makes us incapable of rational thought in the present. Stop torturing yourself, Thagar. You were an outstanding commander and director, maybe even the finest I have ever known with perhaps one exception—Bathwick."

Thagar nodded and said, "But there are those in Yasteron who enjoy all the spoils of Cardissius' policies without any of the risks or sacrifices that his soldiers and their families make. There are many who oppose his policies and desperately want change, but you know as well as I do that removing a despot from power is one of the most difficult things to do. Why can't we do it for them—remove Cardissius from power once and for all? He is the most despicable being in the entire magical world. Why can't it be DAR that decides when it is time for him to be removed? He's attacked us without provocation and he's been killing the Earth for centuries. There hasn't been a birth of an Earth born DARling in over one hundred years! When is it enough?"

Melanthia replied, "Because the lines can become blurred, Thagar, between the moral distinction of a military action and a criminal act of aggression. There's a great deal of moral illiteracy within the Alliance of Magical Dominions. Therefore, DAR must always be the harbinger of peace and rational thought.

"After the war is over, the peace talks always come. So, Aelish decided, let's talk first. That's why she worked for years on the Peace Accord. She chose not to be the cause of innocent civilians losing their lives by using Roger's spell. There is always time for war, Thagar, but there is not always time for peace."

Thagar stared at Melanthia and heard the words, but he did not let them penetrate his soul as he knew what she was going to say next.

"So, even for Aelish, we will not declare an all-out war against Yasteron to rescue her. It would literally be the exact opposite of what she would want. She was always willing to die for peace but never for war."

Thagar stood up and began pacing. He'd finally heard Melanthia's refusal with his own ears in his own house. While he might have agreed with most of her arguments, this was Aelish they were talking about, not some hypothetical class being taught in the POD on war as policy. He was furious DAR was going to do nothing to rescue her.

"This place, Earth, and her devotion to it, will cost her everything," said Thagar. "She is so beautiful, body and soul. There is no DARling like her. You know this! And DAR is seriously not going to do anything to save her?"

"There are those who are trying to force my hand, as Council Chair, to make the Head Council take a vote on whether or not to declare an all-out war against Yasteron. But in this moment, Thagar, no, we are not prepared to do so, not even for Aelish. If I lose the support of the Head Council, I may ultimately be forced to put this to a vote. But until that time comes, I will never go against Aelish's wishes and declare war. It's not what she would want."

Thagar sat back down on the couch and ran his hands over his face. "I begged her not to go with the delegation."

"I understand," said Melanthia. "I know all too well what it's like to try and stop Aelish from doing something she's already made up her mind to do. She is a very determined female, perhaps, the most determined female in all of DAR."

"I know she went for our daughter, Kaleigh. It tortures her that Kaleigh's life is so endangered in this place. And now it will cost Aelish her own life."

"Cardissius will not kill her, Thagar."

"No, he prefers to keep DARlings captive in perpetuity. But she may well want to kill herself after he's done with her. He will ruin my beautiful mate."

Melanthia put her head down. Thagar knew she was thinking about what Cardissius was capable of. He watched as Melanthia physically shuddered as she pondered Aelish being subjected to his evil.

"May I ask you something?" Thagar asked.

"Of course."

If I could put together a covert operation, would you allow me to execute it to rescue her?"

"Yes. It may be the only plausible way to bring her home. The Head Council will not stand in your way. However, I do recommend you not even tell Sartaine."

Thagar nodded his head. "I need to put together a team."

"I may have some options for you."

"How about this, Melanthia? Leave the details to me, so you have plausible deniability whilst you continue to uphold the peaceful tenets and principles of DAR with the citizenry and the other members of the Head Council."

"Understood," said Melanthia, who smiled at him. "Please bring her home, Thagar."

7

THE CODE FOR LIFE

ISABELA HAD BEEN released from the psychiatric hospital on Wednesday, February 11th. She returned to her lab the following Monday and had been working ever since, day and night, analyzing the DNA of Aelish, Thagar, and Kaleigh. Aside from mandatory appointments with her psychiatrist and psychologist, all she did was work on this one project. Her staff had functioned very well without her supervision for over a month. So, they gave her space and did not try to find out what she was working on. Even David, her Clinical Trial Administrator, kept his distance. As scientists, they all understood the healing power of the microscope. With each passing day, Isabela felt more like her old self. And it showed on her face, which lifted the spirits of everyone in the lab.

She couldn't believe how long she'd been in possession of Aelish and Kaleigh's DNA without analyzing it. Secured in another magical vault in the new LECCS lab, their DNA remained in perfect condition. Aelish had bestowed cheek swabs, urine, blood, and hair samples from both of them, when Isabela was in the early stages of creating the LECCS vaccine using Kaleigh's stool samples.

Inspired by her recent conversation with Drew at the psychiatric hospital, Isabela was determined to find out why Kaleigh had not died from the carbon monoxide poisoning that had killed Abuela. The day after she was released from the hospital, Isabela went over to Aelish's house to obtain DNA samples from Thagar. When she'd first conceived the idea to potentially use Kaleigh's stool samples as the foundation for the LECCS vaccine, Thagar was still residing in Wainbridge Rehabilitation Center. As she secured his DNA samples, she remembered how casually Aelish had signed Thagar's signature in the coffee shop, without his permission, so Isabela could obtain Kaleigh's stool and DNA samples because she was a minor. She quietly chuckled at the memory, longing for her Oraculi. Being in Aelish's home without her was a specific kind of torture. She had no idea how Thagar and Kaleigh were coping with her absence.

Why it had taken her so long to analyze Aelish and Kaleigh's DNA would always remain a mystery. She had clearly been obsessed with creating a vaccine for LECCS, but even still, how had her scientific curiosity not gotten the better of her? What she'd discovered over the last two weeks was simply astonishing. Staring back at her from the high-resolution monitors of the electron microscope's computer system was the answer to how Humans could survive the ravages of climate change. And it had been locked away for years while she focused solely on LECCS.

She imagined this was how Rosalind Franklin must have felt when she discovered the double helix structure of Human DNA. Isabela knew she would spend the rest of her scientific life working on the *triple* helix that she was now looking at. Instead of one twisted ladder with two strands, the triple helix had two sides with a shared strand in the *center*; in essence, she was looking at two twisted ladders, entwined. And it was most definitely not the rare triple or quadruple DNA sometimes found in the Human genome.

The first thing Isabela did was name the third strand to the right of the center strand. She called it MNA for Magical Nucleic Acid. Kaleigh's magical strand was actually quite sparse, demonstrating she'd only inherited a smattering of magical genes from her parents; she was not a full-fledged magical being. Aelish's MNA was the most complicated of the three, exemplifying her incredible magical capabilities.

The first ladder in the triple helix represented the DNA within all three of them. While Aelish's DNA was far more reflective of Human DNA, it was extraordinarily complex. It revealed her Earth born heritage from her Human parents, coupled with the DNA of a DARling. Thagar's DNA was entirely unique from Aelish and Kaleigh's. Since both his parents were magical beings, he did not possess any Human genes. And while his MNA was quite involved, it was far less complex than Aelish's MNA.

But Isabela immediately noted Thagar's magical gene for breathing underwater, as it was identical to one of only four magical genes in Kaleigh's MNA. And the gene to breathe underwater was not present at all in Aelish's MNA. Kaleigh's three other magical genes reflected exceptional linguistic capabilities, telepathy, and the ability to change her skin color.

Kaleigh's linguistic gene was even more complicated than Aelish's and the remaining two magical genes in her MNA, consisting of telepathic capabilities and the ability to change her skin color, were both similar to her parents. While Kaleigh's language abilities were already apparent to her family and teachers, until Isabela conducted further research, she would be unable to determine when Kaleigh's telepathic and skin-changing capabilities would emerge.

Kaleigh's DNA was more similar to Isabela's DNA than to either of her parents. Aside from only three unique genes within her DNA, Kaleigh was Human. Her DNA was as simple as

Isabela's. And in this case, simple worked for Isabela, as Kaleigh's DNA held the key, the code for life, of how Humans could survive the ravages of the climate crisis. If Isabela were able to replicate just two of Kaleigh's three unique DNA genes, Humans would be able to breathe the toxic air enveloping the Earth as well as not succumb to any type of present or future disease.

Isabela concluded that Kaleigh's third unique DNA gene involved longevity. It was similar but not identical to Aelish and Thagar's longevity gene. But Isabela felt focusing on extending the lifespan of Humans, at this point in time, would be superfluous. Unless she could alter the DNA of Humans to be able to breathe in the toxic air of Earth and not succumb to current or future diseases, Humans would never be able to attain the lifespan provided by Kaleigh's longevity gene. So, she concentrated her research on just two of Kaleigh's three unique DNA genes.

To Isabela, replicating any aspect of Kaleigh's DNA did not violate medical ethics because her DNA was predominantly the same as any other Human. Isabela considered Kaleigh's ability to breathe toxic air and not succumb to Human disease akin to her own genetic code that created her genius. Every Human had genes which made them unique in one way or another. And since Kaleigh's MNA was irrelevant and not required for Humans to survive the climate crisis, Isabela felt she was within the boundaries of medical ethics.

Isabela was fascinated by the DNA gene that prevented Aelish and Kaleigh from contracting any Human disease because it contained a mutation. Thagar's ability not to contract any Human disease was exhibited in his *MNA*, not his DNA. Isabela inferred that this trait was in his MNA strand because he'd inherited the gene from his magical parents, like all other DARlings. However, Isabela was slowly coming to the conclusion that all Earth born DARlings might have the same genetic mutation in their DNA as Aelish and Kaleigh.

Isabela believed Aelish had passed on a germline mutation to Kaleigh. DNA germline mutations came from tissue derived from reproductive cells, egg or sperm, which then became incorporated into the DNA of every cell in the body of the offspring. They could be passed on by either parent.

Isabela had already begun analyzing the genome of the mutation. She discovered it emitted a protein, initiating a protective immune response against the Yersinia pestis bacterium, the same bacterium responsible for causing the bubonic plague. Isabela deduced that because Earth born DARlings were exposed to various viruses and bacteria during their time on Earth, a genetic mutation ultimately developed in their DNA, granting Earth born DARlings an immunity from all Human diseases. This could potentially mean that any Earth born DARling, male or female, could produce a next-gen Human offspring like Kaleigh, making those with lavender skin even more powerful in the magical world—more powerful than any Yasteron. And by altering Human DNA to reflect Kaleigh's genetic code, Humans could survive the devastation of climate change wrought against them by Yasteron. Perhaps Yasteron wouldn't win in the end.

Isabela was reminded of a lecture in one of her early classes on genetics. The professor discussed a study which demonstrated how Tibetans had inherited a high-altitude gene variant from ancient Humans known as Denisovans. While there continued to be debate about the cause of the Denisovans' extinction, her professor provided references indicating that it occurred soon after they began mating with the ancestors of Europeans and Asians about 40,000 years ago. Yet regardless of the cause of their extinction, this was the first time a version of a gene acquired from interbreeding with an archaic Human had been shown to help modern Humans adapt to their current environment.

Researchers had been perplexed by how Tibetans lived and worked at altitudes above 4,000 meters, or 13,123 feet, where the limited supply of oxygen ordinarily made most people sick. Tibetans adapted by having less hemoglobin in their blood. Scientists believed this also helped them avoid serious problems such as blood clots and strokes, which can occur when blood thickens with more hemoglobin-laden red blood cells.

In 2010, researchers discovered Tibetans had several genes which helped them use smaller amounts of oxygen efficiently, allowing them to deliver enough of it to their limbs while exercising at high altitudes. Most notable is a version of a gene called EPAS1, which regulates the body's production of hemoglobin. Research bore out that the Tibetans inherited the entire gene from the Denisovans. Tibetans were able to retain the gene as part of their evolution since the variant was favored by natural selection; it helped them adapt to life in their environment. Therefore, over time it spread rapidly to many Tibetans and did not mutate or break up.

Isabela also considered Kaleigh's microbiome, which had been used as the template to create the LECCS vaccine. Over thirty percent of her microbiome contained ancient, powerful pathogenic killer microbes. If Humans took the vaccine, their microbiomes would then mirror Kaleigh's and would also contain these ancient pathogenic killers.

If she could modify Human DNA, by replicating the genetic sequence that prevented Aelish and Kaleigh from contracting any Human disease, coupled with their receiving the enhanced microbiome from the LECCS vaccine, Humans could potentially no longer experience illness or disease of any kind.

While Kaleigh's third unique gene determined her longevity, perhaps without acquiring any illness or disease, Humans might naturally evolve to live longer lives. The possibility of that was nothing short of astounding.

Although Isabela was keen to research the longevity gene in Kaleigh's DNA, she primarily focused on the gene which explained why Kaleigh had survived the carbon monoxide poisoning. Both Aelish and Kaleigh had the exact same gene in their DNA. She knew this would give Kaleigh the ability to breathe the thinner air in DAR as well as in the entire magical world. If Isabela could modify Human DNA to include this same genetic sequence, Humans would be able to breathe the noxious polluted air on Earth, in perpetuity.

However, the idea of this was fraught with political ramifications. It would grant permission to the fossil fuel industry to continue polluting the Earth, despite the fact that their actions would continue to cause the extinction of species within the natural world as well as destroying fragile ecosystems.

Yet regardless of how the fossil fuel industry might exploit her modification of the Human genome to include the code of what Isabela called the "breathing gene," her concern for the millions of Humans she predicted would die from asphyxiation overrode any apprehensions she had about the political machinations of the fossil fuel industry.

Humans who lived close to Antarctica, Greenland, the Eastern Siberian Arctic Shelf, and Arctic areas like Norway and Denmark could potentially suffer asphyxiation from abrupt melting of the permafrost and ice in these geographical locations. Abrupt melting would release high concentrations of the greenhouse gas methane, stored in the ice and permafrost. If high concentrations of methane, which had the power to displace oxygen, were to leak into household plumbing vents and air ventilations systems, people would simply die in their sleep.

Isabela pushed the fossil fuel industry out of her mind and

focused on the fact that she had, indeed, found definitive proof that Kaleigh could breathe in DAR. Isabela had mixed emotions about her discovery. While she hoped it would be more than enough reason for Aelish to forgive her, she couldn't imagine them all returning to live in DAR; she would miss them so much. But she'd been selfish and cruel to Aelish for too long. Isabela had every intention to bestow the fact that Kaleigh could breathe in DAR with a full and joyous heart. She planned on telling Thagar later tonight after she finished working.

"Doctor Torres," interrupted David. Isabela was so lost in her own thoughts about Aelish, Thagar, and Kaleigh returning to DAR, for a moment, she forgot where she was.

"Yes, David," she replied.

"Drew Devereux is on line three for you."

"Oh, okay," said Isabela. "Could you please find out when would be a convenient time for me to call him back? Please tell him I'm in personal protective equipment and don't want to go through scrubbing up again for at least another four hours."

"Will do."

"Thank you, David."

Isabela had spoken to Drew only once since leaving the psychiatric hospital, and while she still remained somewhat guarded with him, she was curious as to why he was calling so early in the morning on a Friday. She took a deep breath and returned her focus to the images emanating from the microscope.

Jennifer A. Doudna and Emmanuelle Charpentier developed the CRISPR-Cas9 technology in 2012, winning the Nobel Prize in Chemistry in 2020. Isabela had been fascinated by their discovery and knew that, one day, her scientific work would lead her into gene-editing technology.

But even before the two women had won the Nobel Prize in 2020, a five-year moratorium had been placed on the use of this precise gene-editing tool for cutting and customizing DNA in Human eggs, sperm, and embryos. And while the moratorium had technically ended about a year ago, scientists were still hesitant to resume exploration of this incredible discovery to prevent offspring from inheriting genetic disorders from germline DNA because of one scientist.

In 2018, Chinese scientist, He Jiankui, used the technology to yield the world's first gene-edited infants. The experiment on the embryos of twin girls was widely condemned as irresponsible and unethical because how CRISPR-Cas9 affected cells was still poorly understood. Dr. Jiankui was arrested and found guilty of conducting illegal medical practices in China and was sentenced to three years in prison. He was released in April 2022 and immediately began attending medical conferences. Intent on relaunching his career, Dr. Jiankui set up a lab in Beijing to work on affordable gene therapies for rare diseases such as Duchenne muscular dystrophy or DMD.

Isabela understood quite clearly that unless the DNA of Humans was altered, climatic events such as severe fluctuations in temperatures, Humans trapped in floodwater for extended periods of time, severe hurricanes like the Perfect Storm, wildfires, and even frigid weather caused by a polar vortex would strain the Human immune system, crippling its defenses. These cascading climate events, happening one after another or all at the same time, had the potential to unleash new viruses or turn peaceful bacteria that lived inside of Humans against them.

There was no way to predict which peaceful bacterium would go rogue and turn against their host. It would be very similar to LECCS with one major difference: due to the numerous cascading climate events, there wouldn't be enough time to develop a vaccine. As the climate continued to degrade, the only option to assist Humans alive today was to modify their DNA to reflect Kaleigh's genetic code.

As she stared at the images of the specimens conveyed by the microscope, she imagined using the CRISPR-Cas9 system. The system consisted of two key molecules that could introduce a mutation, or a change, to DNA. The first was Cas9, a molecular enzyme produced by the CRISPR system, and the second was a small piece of predesigned RNA sequence, called guide RNA (gRNA), which "guided" Cas9 to the exact point in the genome.

Theoretically, the guide RNA was supposed to only bind to the targeted sequence of the genome and to no other part of the genome. By following the guide RNA, Cas9 then acted like a pair of molecular scissors that cuts across both strands of DNA, or both sides of the ladder in the double helix of Human DNA, at a precise location. Bits of DNA could then be added or removed. This was how removal of existing DNA and insertion of Kaleigh's replicated genetic code would occur. Cutting out existing Human DNA and customizing that same section to include the two unique parts of Kaleigh's DNA—her immunity from Human disease and her ability to breath the noxious air of Earth—was the only way for Humans to continue inhabiting an Earth that was rapidly becoming uninhabitable. Humans had to be genetically modified.

Gene editing had always conjured images of scientists playing God, with little or no concern for ethics or unintended consequences. But what other option existed? There was no other Earth. Despite making the discovery of Kaleigh's life-saving code for life, Isabela felt defeated by the lack of progress and ethical dilemmas which had stopped CRISPR research in its tracks. There was a paralyzing timidity within the scientific community, as well as the world at large, to alter the natural trajectory of Human evolution.

But in Isabela's humble opinion, that was exactly what was

needed if Humans had any chance of surviving the toxicity already enveloping the Earth. Yet she recognized how improbable a solution it was. If policymakers prohibited the modification of Human DNA to mirror Kaleigh's code through the technology of CRISPR, which was eons behind where it should be, Humanity would ultimately go extinct.

‡‡‡‡

Isabela listened on the landline phone in her office as Drew's phone rang and rang. Everyone had left for the day, and she chided herself for not calling him back sooner and for not asking David if the number he had given her was Drew's personal cell phone or his corporate headquarters in San José, California. She picked up her cell phone to review the numbers she had for Drew in her contacts, but her search was interrupted when a woman's voice answered.

"Mr. Devereux's phone, may I help you?"

"Yes, this is Doctor Torres at the LECCS lab in Tennessee," said Isabela. "I'm returning an earlier phone call of Mr. Devereux's."

"Hold on one moment, please," said the female voice. But before she placed Isabela on hold, Isabela heard a small piece of what the woman said to Drew, "Got her, Drew."

For some odd reason, Isabela felt a pang of jealousy toward the woman who'd obviously answered Drew's personal cell phone. She tapped her fingers on her desk impatiently, waiting for him to pick up.

"Isabela, hello! Sorry for the hold time," said Drew. "Some of my staff and I were just about to go into a meeting. I sent them on their way so we could speak privately for a few minutes. How are you doing?"

"I want to apologize for not taking your call earlier," said Isabela, "but I was heavily involved in Aelish, Thagar, and Kaleigh's DNA and was wearing all of my PPE. I'm sorry I blew past the time where I could've stopped and removed it to return your call. I really need to work on my time management."

"Well, did you make the discovery you were looking for?"

"I actually did, but it's way too involved to discuss on the phone."

Isabela didn't know why she decided to shut down the conversation on Kaleigh's DNA, but she was still irritated by a woman answering his private cell phone. She was also anxious to know why he had originally called in the first place. "So, why were you calling me at eight in the morning, Pacific Time?"

"I was hoping I could take you and your parents to brunch this Sunday in Nashville. I know it's very last minute, but I hesitated to bother you sooner than today, as I knew you were hard at work on the DNA project over the last couple of weeks."

"Why on Earth do you want to have brunch with my parents?" she asked.

"Well, what I want to discuss with you and your parents are the plans already in place for our worldwide tour to promote the vaccine. I thought since you might be away for three or four months, they'd be interested in knowing about the details of our tour."

"Three or four months!" Isabela exclaimed. "Oh, my God!"

"It's a big world, Isabela. And our worldwide vaccination rate is only at fifteen percent. And the overall global temperature is hovering very close to the 1.4°C threshold. Time is of the essence, Doctor Torres. So, are you ready to help save Humanity with me?"

His optimism was infectious and Isabela finally began to relax. She started laughing at how confidently he spoke about the LECCS doomsday temperature, which was no more than six months away. DAR's Scrubber 13 fleet was working around the clock, pulling greenhouse gases out of the air, in an effort to buy her more time to convince people to get inoculated. But he was right; it was a big world and they were nearly out of time.

"I think Sunday brunch with my parents sounds wonderful," she said. "I know they will both be very excited to see you again. Especially my mother, who is incredibly grateful for everything you've done for our family, with regard to getting Abuela to her final resting place."

"I'm so sorry for your loss, Isabela. It's a tough one to bear."

"Thank you," she said, softly.

"So, what do you say we go back to the place where we first broke bread together with Hector, down in the Gulch at that lovely hotel? I checked the brunch menu and they have lots of chocolate-infused breakfast choices."

"Wow, I didn't realize how hungry I was until you mentioned chocolate," said Isabela, laughing.

"My driver will pick you and your parents up at noon. How does that sound?"

"Will we be meeting you at the hotel?" she asked.

"Yes, just like last time. I have a meeting in New York on Monday, so this will work out great. See you Sunday, then?"

"See you Sunday, Drew. Take care of yourself."

"Bye for now, Isabela."

"Bye," she said.

She'd forgotten he always ended their telephone calls or computer conferences that way. Isabela smiled, began packing up her stuff to leave, and then realized she needed to tell Thagar about Kaleigh.

Using her cell phone, Isabela called Thagar. After one ring, he picked up. "Hi, Isabela, how are you?" he asked.

"I'm doing much better, Thagar, thank you for asking. I'm calling because I have some important news for you."

"Is it good news or bad news? Because I could really use some good news today."

"You can take Kaleigh to DAR. She will be able to breathe with no problem, Thagar."

There was a moment of silence, and then he asked, "Are you certain, Isabela?"

"Obviously, any self-respecting scientist will always leave room for a small percentage of error. But if she were my daughter, I would feel confident she would not be in harm's way heading to DAR. I have further information on her DNA, but I will share that with you at another time. It's all good, so don't worry, but I knew you were anxious to hear about her breathing. It's why she didn't die from the carbon monoxide poisoning, Thagar."

"I simply can't believe it. I never thought I'd hear this in Kaleigh's lifetime. Wow! I think I need to hang up now so I can begin processing what you've just told me. Be well and stay in touch, okay?"

"You do the same. Oh, and Thagar?"

"Yes?"

"Thank you for what you did for me at the psychiatric hospital. I will never forget it."

"I love you, Isabela. I hope you never want to harm yourself again. Stay well, okay?"

Isabela wiped away a tear. "Okay, Thagar. Bye for now," she said, trying out Drew's expression. She decided she liked it very much.

8

UNEXPECTED SUPPORT

THAGAR SAT STUNNED with his cell phone still in his hand. Having just finished dinner, he continued to sit at the kitchen counter in disbelief over what Isabela had just told him: Kaleigh could breathe in DAR. How he wished he could share this news with Aelish. Every day without her was becoming more and more difficult. And to not be able to share this incredible discovery with her really drove home the fact that she might never return.

His heart was in agony. The first tear came and it pushed open the dam for all the ones to follow. With his elbows on the counter, he put his face in his hands and began sobbing. Kaleigh had gone to a friend's house for dinner and Drummond was upstairs cleaning, so he sobbed with abandon. March 11th would mark two months since he'd last seen his beloved's face.

While he was hard at work trying to formulate a plan to rescue Aelish from Yasteron, he'd hit a wall and felt utterly defeated. Despite having a few options for a team, Melanthia cautioning him not to discuss any rescue plans with Sartaine and his former colleagues at the POD, left him isolated and alone.

It was a monumental task to devise a way to secretly enter a kingdom known for its impenetrable detection grids. But even if he could gain access, how would he know where to find her? Where was she being held? The loneliness was almost as unbearable as his inertia in devising a rescue mission. And Isabela's news just broke open the floodgates for all his feelings of frustration and impotence that he'd experienced during the last six weeks.

"Sir, what has happened?" asked Drummond.

Startled and embarrassed that Drummond had caught him crying, Thagar immediately stood up from the stool at the counter and went into the tree-house room, wiping his face. He sat down on one of the couches and saw Drummond had followed him into the room. "All is well, Drummond. Forgive me, I'm sorry you had to witness such a pathetic sight."

Drummond's tiny frame stood in front of the couch where Thagar sat drying his eyes. "Sir, I think sometimes ya' forget how strong and powerful ya' are."

"Is this what strong and powerful looks like, Drummond?" asked Thagar, scoffing.

"You commanded legions of DARlings durin' war and durin' peace."

"But Yasteron always seems to win, don't they?"

"It may seem like that in this moment, but I think their time is at an end."

"What makes you say that?" Thagar stared at him perplexed.

"An arrogant king like Cardissius is goin' to fall. He forgot the first lesson in bein' a sovereign—loyalty: make sure yer subjects love ya', make sure they aren't plottin' against ya', and make sure they would die for ya'. He reached too far takin' Aelish, sir. To me, he's nearly at the height of his reign and will not die in his bed of old age.

"Because ya' love her, ya' only think about how Cardissius

is hurtin' her. But ya' forget, just like he does, why Aelish is a Livin' Legend. There has ne'er been a magical bein' like her, and by capturin' her in the middle of a peace mission, he's about to find out exactly why she's a legend. Ya' wouldn't wanna be him, sir. He's about to lose it all."

Thagar weakly smiled at the miniature being in front him, speaking words of a giant. "I wish I had your confidence, Drummond. I'm envious that you truly believe what you are saying."

"I believe it because I lived with Aelish in her cottage in DAR. If ya' recall, she gave refuge to Seratus, the Deputy Minister of Security for Komprathia, along with his family as well as the family of drone rats he found hiding in his own garden in Komprathia. Seratus was a bein' of great integrity. He refused to leave the family of drone rats behind, when he escaped to DAR, as he was fiercely opposed to King Gidius' treatment of them. I tended to both families for months, and I learned so much about Komprathia and so much about Aelish."

Thagar sat back further onto the couch as he listened to Drummond.

"I was terrified of what Aelish and I were doin,' sir. Harborin' an enemy of DAR we were currently warrin' with, whilst the drone rats were spreadin' the plague on Earth. I knew Aelish would never give up either family. And as the weeks went by, she gained the trust of Seratus. She went against every tenet of DAR to save those two families because she's cunnin' and about the smartest bein' I have ever known. She's a leader, like yerself, but she operates quite differently from what we normally think of as a commander.

"She schemes and she plots but always with a moral outcome she'd give her life for. Ya' know firsthand how loyal I am to Aelish. After she was imprisoned, I did as she and I had planned all along. If she were to die or be captured, I was to hide the two families where no bein' could ever find them. I refused to give them up because she told me not to."

"Yes, I remember," said Thagar, smiling. "Whilst you were doing that, my deputy commander and I were being interrogated and tortured for this information."

"I'm sorry about that, sir. But I would do it all over again—for Aelish. That's the kind of loyalty a king should inspire in his subjects. But Cardissius is greedy and selfish and doesn't care about any bein' or anythin' other than himself. And that will be his downfall. Despots, dictators, and fascists always meet the same end. The evil that lives within them propels them to reach too high, and they fall off a cliff of their own makin'. They always lose in the end."

Thagar took a deep breath. The little male's words had the desired effect on him. He felt better. "You are quite knowledgeable about the thirst for power, Drummond. How did you gain such insights?"

"When yer as tiny as I am, the world offers a different perspective; its clearer. I'm not up in the boughs of the high trees with the rest of ya.' I'm near the ground and see it all."

"Well, I think the least I can do is share with you why I became so upset. Isabela has scientifically examined the makeup of Kaleigh and has determined that she'd be able to breathe in DAR—all this time."

Drummond fell into a sitting position on the floor. "Now that, I didn't see comin', sir."

Thagar started laughing. "That makes two of us."

"After all that ya' and Aelish went through to give Kaleigh life, now we find out we could've stayed in DAR?" Drummond deeply exhaled on the floor and shook his head from side to side, making his conical hat fall to the floor.

Thagar burst out laughing. Drummond always offered comic relief in the most dire of circumstances. Thagar reached for the conical hat and handed it to Drummond. "Your hat, sir?"

"Thank you, sir," he said, placing his hat back on top of his head. He stood up and extended his arm toward Thagar to help him rise from the couch. "Up, up, sir. It's time to pick up Kaleigh at her friend's house."

"Ah! I almost forgot. Thank you, Drummond."

Drummond nodded. "Please let me know when ya' will be takin' Kaleigh to DAR, and I will assist in any way I can. I think it's time ya' take her home, sir, at least for a visit. Let's make sure she really *can* breathe in DAR before makin' any plans for the future."

"You're just chock-full of wisdom tonight, aren't you?" Thagar reached for Drummond's tiny hand as he stood up from the couch. He let go of it after rising about a foot off the couch.

"Always at your service, sir." And with that, Drummond aspirated out of the room and returned upstairs to resume cleaning.

Thagar aspirated into the garage and left to pick up Kaleigh with a smile on his face.

‡‡‡‡

Thagar was wrapping up a meeting in the Climate Refugee Intake Center's conference room. Since the establishment of the first three CRICs located in Tennessee, Ireland, and England, all three had always been filled to capacity. Climatic events were displacing Humans faster than Thagar could make accommodations for them. So, he'd already begun working with Drew to build new intake centers within the U.S. and around the world. The Devereux Trust was also acquiring land in new geographical locations for the never-ending surge of climate refugees who needed to permanently resettle elsewhere.

Like the settlement sites built after the Perfect Storm, up and down the Eastern Seaboard of the U.S. as well as in Ireland and England, the sites reflected the architecture of the surrounding cities. They were constructed out of the same magical material developed in DAR, so the refugees' new homes could never be destroyed by another climate event. Devoting his life to the refugees was the only reason why Thagar had maintained his sanity in Aelish's absence.

Elle buzzed the intercom on the phone at the head of the table where he was sitting. He was in a bit of a rush, as he had a four o'clock parent-teacher conference with Kaleigh's English and Social Studies teacher. He excused himself from those who continued on with the meeting, turned his chair away from the table, and answered the phone.

Elle told him Kaleigh's English and Social Studies teacher was on the line. Kaleigh was fine, nothing to worry about, but she wanted to ask him a quick question. "Put her through please, Elle."

"I hope I'm not disturbing you, Mr. Carrigan," said Kaleigh's teacher, "but I was wondering, since you are my last conference of the day, how would you feel about meeting around the corner at Kent's Koffee Shoppe? I've barely had time for lunch today and was wondering if I could buy you a coffee while we discuss your incredible daughter."

"Oh, okay, that sounds great. I haven't taken the time for a proper meal all day, and I could use a nice latte. Are we still on for four o'clock?"

"Absolutely."

"Okay, then. I will meet you at Kent's Koffee Shoppe at four this afternoon."

"Awesome. See you!"

"See you later," said Thagar. He hung up the phone and rejoined the meeting but was distracted. He'd only met Kaleigh's teacher two other times, but it was hard to forget what Brooke Thompson looked like. She was very tall with porcelain skin and had long, straight, jet-black hair, along with dazzling blue eyes. She looked more like a model or a television star than a teacher, but it was her manner he remembered most. Both times he and Aelish had previously met with her, she demonstrated the boundless energy of a Human in their early twenties, and she was always enthusiastic and excited to talk about Kaleigh.

He reminded himself to stick to the fictitious story about Aelish that he and Kaleigh had come up with for VMP Academy. When he first learned Aelish had been captured, he'd gone to the school to explain why he'd now be the one to pick up and drop off Kaleigh. He lied and said Aelish was away on a long assignment at one of their refugee centers in Africa. That was why Brooke Thompson called him directly and knew he would be coming alone. And due to the parent-teacher conferences, Kaleigh would not be attending the after-school program all week and was dismissed from school earlier than usual. Today, the mother of Kaleigh's friend, Joanna, would be picking the girls up from school, and Kaleigh was also staying at their house for dinner. Both Joanna and Kaleigh whined for a sleepover but were told, "Not on a school night."

After hanging up the phone, Thagar realized he was actually quite hungry. He was looking forward to having one of Kent's Koffee Shoppe's famous sandwiches as well as one of their amazing lattes. The meeting wrapped itself up, and he decided to go home and shower before the parent-teacher conference.

Thagar got on his new Harley LiveWire motorcycle. As he strapped on his helmet, he looked into his rear-view mirror and was unfortunately flooded with the memory of Isabela trying to take her own life with a shard of mirror. He was glad she was feeling well enough to finally return to her lab, but he was forever changed by it. To witness such a violent act, by someone he loved as much as Isabela, was not something he would ever forget; it haunted him. Whenever the memory resurfaced, he'd remember how he'd magically flung the shard out of her hand before she could cut her other wrist. Perhaps he'd saved her life, but her level of suffering and mental anguish was a horrible memory. And all of it stemmed from Aelish's capture by Cardissius. Would the pain from this being and his horrific kingdom ever cease in his lifetime?

As he began riding, he knew he was definitely going too fast, but it felt amazing and helped him forget. The bike always gave him a sense of freedom and, today, he really needed it. Between the memory of Isabela and the absence of Aelish, he felt himself near a breaking point. Thagar didn't know how to prevent it from coming, but apparently, being a bit reckless with his own life provided him with a temporary relief.

He pulled into a space right in front of the coffee shop and noted a sushi place he'd never tried, right next door. He laughed inwardly, reflecting on the fact that DARlings from the N.E. Quadrant had practically invented sushi; he'd grown up eating raw fish. He considered stopping there after his meeting to get some takeout for dinner.

The jingle of the coffee shop bells rang as he opened the door. He looked around and did not see Kaleigh's teacher, so he went to the counter and ordered himself a sandwich and a latte. He found a nice table by the window near the rear of the shop and sat down facing the door.

When Brooke Thompson entered the shop, every person inside turned their heads to stare at her. She was in a word: voluptuous. It was hard not to stare when she entered any room. Her jet-black long, straight hair was in direct contradiction to her flawless skin which was so white, it was nearly translucent. He could feel his body responding to the shape of hers, but her dazzling blue eyes brought him right back to her face.

She waved at him and gestured that she was going to place her order at the counter. As he waited for her to join him, Thagar still could not understand why she'd gone into teaching instead of becoming a model or an actress.

As she approached the table, Thagar stood up to help her with her tray of goodies. They both sat, and she began stirring her coffee and immediately began talking about Kaleigh.

"I have never before encountered a child, who is not even seven years old and can read in both English and Spanish at a third grade reading level," she said. "In fact, that's what I wanted to talk to you about. We are starting an advanced-level reading and writing program in multiple languages, during the same time period as the after-school program. Since Kaleigh is almost at a fourth-grade-reading level, I thought she'd be perfect for the program.

"It will be on Mondays, Wednesdays, and Fridays, and I think it would be a much better use of Kaleigh's time than the after-school program. We are also planning to incorporate the culture and geography of the countries that speak the languages we are planning to teach. This way, the kids can be exposed to new geographical locations around the world, which we hope will encourage them to be more equitable and inclusive in their lives. We are even going to introduce foods from each individual country, so the kids will receive exposure to different culinary pleasures. What do you think?"

For a moment, Thagar wondered if Brooke Thompson was a magical being, as he found himself so entranced, he barely heard any of the particulars of the new program. He immediately recognized his loneliness for female companionship and tried to snap out of it.

"I think the program sounds like it was specifically designed for my daughter."

"Right? That's what I was thinking." She began laughing, and once again, Thagar found himself drawn to her. He began laughing along with her.

Four o'clock turned into six o'clock and the two were still talking and laughing like they'd known each other for years. Thagar finally looked away from her gorgeous face and saw Jorge at the counter waving at him to come over. Irritated by the interruption, he graciously excused himself. "I see an old friend at the counter. Let me just say a quick hello and I will be right back."

"Take your time," said Brooke. "It will give me chance to visit the ladies' room."

Thagar got up and walked over to the coffee shop counter. Jorge walked slightly away from it, forcing Thagar to follow him toward a small nook by the kitchen.

"Hi, Jorge, is everything all right?" asked Thagar.

"Who is that woman you are sitting with?" asked Jorge. For the first time in their relationship, Thagar wanted to tell him it was none of his business. However, he remained polite and simply said, "She is one of Kaleigh's teachers. We decided to have our parent-teacher conference here in the coffee shop instead of at the school."

"Whose idea was it to meet here instead of at the school?"

Thagar thought that was an odd question, but he replied, "Hers."

"And did you ever stop to wonder why she wanted to meet with you outside of school?"

Thagar didn't know how to respond to this insinuation about Brooke's intentions. "I don't think she had any ulterior motives, Jorge, if that's what you're implying. We both had very busy days, with little time to eat, so she thought it would be nice if we had coffee and a bite to eat together whilst we discussed Kaleigh's progress in school."

"How long have you been here?" asked Jorge. He looked at his watch and showed the face of it to Thagar. "It's nearly seven o'clock, Thagar. Most parent-teacher conferences I've ever been to last for about thirty minutes. What time did you two meet up?"

Thagar was genuinely shocked it was so late. He hadn't even noticed the sun had gone down and it was pitch black outside. And then he felt it, the inkling of betrayal to Aelish. His loneliness and ineptitude in orchestrating a rescue mission to save the love of his life had resulted in a three hour "date" with Kaleigh's teacher. He was horrified by his own behavior. But he was also angry with Jorge, who forced him to examine his feelings, when he'd finally been able to forget them for a while.

"Forgive me, Thagar. I know you are angry with me, but you have to trust me. Pursuing the beautiful teacher will only lead to regret and unhappiness. Marisol was sick for so many years. Don't you think I recognized myself in your behavior at the table? You were probably not even aware of what was happening because it felt so good to feel normal again, even for a few hours. I never cheated on Marisol, but I came very close, and it ended very badly for me and a fellow employee. This is not a road you want to go down, my friend. Please believe me. She has nothing to lose. I assume she is not married?"

Thagar deeply inhaled. "It never came up," he said, softly.

"Why don't I give you the perfect excuse to get out of here? Tell her I've invited you back to my house for dinner."

"Wait, what time is it again?" Thagar began to panic. He was supposed to pick up Kaleigh at seven-thirty.

"It's seven-fifteen."

"I have to go and get Kaleigh." Thagar looked down at the floor. He was too ashamed to meet Jorge's eyes. He had never come so close to jeopardizing his Commitments to Aelish.

"It's all right, Thagar. I understand and this will stay between us."

Finally, Thagar lifted his head. "Thank you, Jorge. I have a lot to think about, don't I?'

"You'll work it out, and I'm always here for you if you want to talk, okay? I'll wait here while you say your goodbyes, and we can walk out together."

Thagar went back to the table while Jorge watched him extricate himself from what could have been a bona fide disaster. When Thagar returned to the counter, Jorge patted his back and the two walked out of the coffee shop together. Jorge waited alongside the motorcycle until Thagar had ridden away.

After pulling into the garage, Thagar situated the motorcycle and immediately got into the SUV to pick up Kaleigh. He had always promised Aelish to never let her ride on the bike. So, even though he was going to be late, at least he hadn't broken one promise to Aelish tonight.

As he drove to Joanna's house, Thagar decided he needed to leave Earth for a while. He was ready to take Kaleigh to DAR. He planned to discuss taking her flying with him before she went to bed tonight. She might have to miss a few days of school, but maybe it was for the best. He knew he was running, but he didn't care. His desperation over Aelish had nearly caused him to forget to pick up his daughter. And if he was being completely honest with himself, if Jorge hadn't interrupted them, something untoward would have happened with Brooke Thompson.

9

DANGEROUS MANIPULATIONS

AELISH WAS DESPERATELY missing Thagar and Kaleigh. She could feel a panic episode coming on, as she'd been without the use of her magic for nearly two months. Her fear of developing Magical Interruption Syndrome was becoming more and more difficult to control.

She longed to be held by Thagar, safe and secure in his arms. He always knew exactly what to do and what to say to calm one of her episodes. She closed her eyes and tried to control her breathing. She imagined Thagar right next to her and tried to hear the sound of his voice in her head. She pictured his beautiful face, tried to feel his tender lips, and imagined nestling against his muscular chest, his chest hairs tickling her face. Aelish remembered how he would gently kiss her neck and climb on top of her, protecting her with his strength. He would hold her like that for as long as it took to calm her. Sometimes, they'd make love afterward and sometimes, they'd perform the Rapture. But most times, he just held her. My God, how she missed him!

She never felt more abandoned in her life, bereft of her family, her Oraculi, and Isabela. Now, the only life she had was the imaginary one inside her own mind as she lay alone at night in the darkness. It was unbearable. Would she ever see the morning sun again?

Aelish began to rub her abdomen so the heir in her belly would illuminate the room with his magical glow. Storm stirred at the foot of the bed. Sensing his mistress' discomfort, he jumped off the bed and walked over to the side she was closest too. He took his big, furry head and placed it on her abdomen and began softly moaning. She had no idea how the dog knew she was carrying a life inside her, but he'd always known from the first day she'd met him. Aelish had named him Storm as he was completely white, like the snowstorms of her childhood in Ireland. She began petting his head and stared at the ceiling, illuminated by the heir's magical glow.

Aelish remembered the first day Captain Eli of the Great White Mountain Hund Division brought the dog to her. Captain Eli wore a distinct uniform from other members of Yasteron's military, reflecting his division of dog handlers. Upon meeting her, he removed his cap out of respect, extended his hand to shake hers, and she immediately sensed he was a kind being. His brown eyes held a steady gaze and instilled an immediate sense of trust. She imagined the dogs he trained also experienced this, which was why he was in charge of all the trainers.

He gave her protective eye equipment to wear, which he also used, during all their training sessions. The dog's ability to blind a perceived threat, while simultaneously making them mute, was a danger to be taken very seriously. Captain Eli told Aelish that she was a natural at training this ferocious animal. He thought it was her female voice that calmed Storm, as well as the life she carried within her. Aelish loved their training sessions because she had something meaningful to do, and she greatly enjoyed the company of Captain Lane. She was sorry when they ended, but now, she had complete control over Storm.

Chief Minister Stannon detested the dog and that was reason enough for Aelish to love the animal. Stannon was furious the king had given her such a powerful creature. He compared the breed of the Great White Mountain Hund to Yasteron's mythical horses, which freely roamed the part of Yasteron that bordered Hentoria. Hentoria's mountainous terrain was their natural habitat. The horses were either grey or white with a mane of silver hair. They rode on the wind and could shoot fire out of their mouths. Katrina explained to her that many in Yasteron felt the horses were the descendants of dragons, which had disappeared long ago.

Storm was the only reason Aelish had been able to endure her panic episodes, which were becoming more and more frequent. Mostly, he'd lay his head upon her abdomen. But there were other times when he'd lay beside her. She would then worm her way underneath him. His weight of one hundred fifty pounds reminded her a bit of Thagar, and she'd begin to calm.

Whenever he'd lay his head upon her abdomen, the heir's magical glow would grow very bright. The heir adored the dog, and the dog adored the heir. She tried to harness their magic, but it was to no avail. She could not obtain any magic of her own. While she knew the answer to the question she repeatedly asked herself during a panic episode, she asked it all the same: why hadn't she listened to Thagar and returned to Earth with him after the Commitments Ceremony?

Once she learned that Cardissius refused to sign the Peace Accord if she wasn't present, there was no doubt in her mind that she'd go to Yasteron. She would never have missed the opportunity to free the DARling soldiers, the Komprathian drone rats, as well as stop Yasteron from making more of the LECCS bioweapon, the DARling Draft, and their newest bomb. And Yasteron signing the Peace Accord meant they would destroy all existing stockpiles of the three weapons, as well as bring home all of their covert operatives on Earth who continued to perpetuate the climate crisis. How could she not go? But her decision had cost her too much.

Once she provided him with a male heir, the king continued to promise her that he would honor all the conditions and stipulations of the Peace Accord. But in her heart, she did not believe him. She was at an extraordinary disadvantage, locked away in this prison, alone for hours on end, without the use of her magic.

As Aelish lay there petting Storm's head, she recalled something Thagar had told her centuries ago. Finding it impossible to get over the grief of her parents, after they'd died of plague, he suggested she find a new goal to help make her loss easier to bear. While Storm moaned on her abdomen, as if the dog were speaking to the heir, an idea began to formulate in her mind. Perhaps if she did extensive research on Yasteron, she could find some strategy to use against Cardissius. She was aware Yasterons hated to read, but she wondered if he'd care if she did. She began to hatch a plan to educate herself about every aspect of Yasteron, from the beginning of the kingdom to present day.

By educating herself, she might discover some way to gain her freedom. While she had learned their language centuries ago, and knew how adept they were at detection capabilities and evil magic spells, she'd never really studied the essence of the kingdom. How long had it been in the magical world? Who was the first king? Until she'd performed the Endeavor with Cardissius, she hadn't even known how they procreated.

Now six weeks pregnant, with a being who was half Yasteron,

she wanted to learn all about its gestation. The king had said a Yasteron gestation was three months, exactly the same length as a DARlette. But she wanted to read about it with her own eyes. So far, her pregnancy had been uneventful with the exception of experiencing the magical glow. Rubbing her hands on her abdomen did calm her and made the glow much larger, but why did that happen?

Aelish didn't really understand this kingdom, which in some ways was astoundingly beautiful. Why did the nobles behave the way they did? Why did they keep the lower-orders in a prison of illiteracy and servitude? Why did they behave so demonically toward Earth? She would read, she would study, and she would learn. And ultimately, she would come up with some way to free herself. She had to or she knew she would die here, in this room, so far from home in DAR and Earth.

‡‡‡‡

The first thing Aelish decided to learn was how Katrina and other lower-orders got in and out of the suite of rooms. Since no magic worked within the suite, with the exception of Cardissius' magic, how were they afforded the freedom to come and go?

One day, Aelish was very daring. Storm was outside being walked, and she decided to follow Katrina to the back door of the suite. Katrina did not realize she was behind her. She watched as Katrina gently knocked three times on the back door. The door did not open. Once again, Katrina tried knocking three times. Finally, the door opened and twelve of the King's Guard had their weapons trained on her. Katrina screamed, not understanding what she had done wrong. But then, Katrina heard them loudly threaten, "Back up, Director Aelish, or we will kill the both of you. Do it now!"

Katrina turned around and saw Aelish a foot away from her. "M'Lady, what are you doing here? They will kill us both. Please, go back inside."

Aelish nodded and retreated to the living area. She took out her notebook, where she logged various observations, and wrote down that Katrina could exit the suite of rooms by gently knocking three time on the back door. She also noted that all twelve guards in the back hallway were male.

Katrina followed her into the living area. "M'Lady, why did you follow me? Now, I may be relieved of my duties."

"That will not happen, Katrina. Don't worry."

"You don't know that!" yelled Katrina. Realizing she was yelling at Aelish, Katrina began rubbing her face in frustration and sat down on the floor. "Were you trying to learn how the lower-orders get in and out of the suite of rooms?"

"Yes," replied Aelish.

"Since I will be relieved of my duties, anyway," she said, "I might as well tell you. All of us, with the exception of the nobles, have been through a myriad of security clearances, prior to being assigned to you. The King's Guard has our handprints, our fingerprints, our retinal scans, and any and all information about our families. If we betray the king in any way, the Guard will kill us on sight as well as our entire families." Katrina began sobbing.

"Please," said Aelish, "do not be afraid. Nothing will happen to you or any member of your family. I will simply tell the king that I was foolish and forgot to give you something on your way out. I went to find you, and I inadvertently observed you performing your signature knock on the door for the Guard."

"But I never perform my signature knock *two* times in a row," argued Katrina. "If you tell the king that in front of the Guard, they will know you are lying, as you watched me perform my signature knock *twice*. Lady Aelish, you've completely compromised my security clearance."

Knowing she only had minutes before the King's Guard were going to enter the room, Aelish ignored Katrina's sobs and pressed for further information. "So, after you perform your signature knock, the King's Guard magically peer from behind the door and ascertain it is, in fact, you, and then they open the door, correct?"

Katrina shook her head in disbelief at Aelish and asked, "Lady Aelish, are you displeased with my work? Do you wish to be relieved of my services?"

"Of course not, Katrina. Please, forgive me for compromising you. I've been imprisoned in this room for nearly two months, and I simply wanted to learn how you and the other lower-orders enter and exit the suite. I knew you would never tell me, so I admit, I used you to discover how the lower-orders come and go. Please, forgive me and don't cry." Aelish sat down on the floor beside Katrina and began rocking her.

"M'Lady, you should not be on the floor with me," Katrina said softly, wiping her eyes.

Suddenly, Stannon burst into the room followed by six members of the King's Guard.

"Do not move," Aelish whispered to Katrina before standing.

Aelish couldn't determine whether Stannon was more horrified that she was rocking Katrina on the floor or that she'd violated one of the lower-order's security clearance. She decided it was the former, which was then confirmed by his next outburst.

"The King Mother never sits or lays upon the floor, and she most certainly never touches a lower-order!" he exclaimed. "I have never in my life!"

"I would like to apologize to the King's Guard for my behavior," said Aelish. "And for putting my lower-order-in-waiting in such grave danger." Stannon glared at here, seeing that she was not going to apologize for being on the floor nor for hugging Katrina. "This is all a simple misunderstanding."

With his weapon aimed at Aelish, a King's Guard said, "You remained behind the lower-order as she performed her signature knock *two* times. We did not see you address her or signal to her that you were behind her, which leads us to believe you planned this together."

Katrina kept silent and continued to sob on the floor.

"Not at all," said Aelish. "I'd simply forgotten to give Katrina something before she left."

"Then, why didn't we see you try to hand her anything?" questioned the same Guard.

"Because I could not understand why she was knocking to be let *out*, when most beings knock to be let *in*," replied Aelish. "I was simply confused for a moment. By the time I understood she was knocking to be let out, she'd already knocked a second time. And then, you became extremely aggressive." Aelish suddenly grabbed her abdomen and began moaning.

"What is it m'Lady?" asked Katrina, who immediately got up from the floor and came over to help Aelish onto the settee. "Is it the heir? Are you all right?"

Aelish continued moaning and saw Stannon beginning to panic.

He turned toward the King's Guard and said, "Lady Aelish has offered a reasonable explanation for what has happened. Please return to your station in the hallway, and advise the headquarters of the King's Guard that nothing is to be done to the lower-order-in-waiting or her family members. Leave us! Now!"

Aelish continued moaning, and Katrina suggested, "I think she needs to lie down, Chief Minister. May I assist her to the bedchamber?"

"Yes, yes, of course."

Aelish continued moaning and could not stand up straight, demonstrating great pain.

"I think we should summon the king, Chief Minister," suggested Katrina. She helped Aelish lie down and began covering her with blankets. Storm, who'd returned during all the commotion, began fiercely growling at the chief minister. The dog stood in a threatening manner between Stannon and the bed, where Aelish was now lying.

"Fine, I will send for the king," said Stannon. Aelish detected fear in his voice and made a mental note to give Storm extra treats tonight.

Katrina said, "I will stay with Lady Aelish until King Cardissius has arrived."

After everyone had left, Katrina said to Aelish, "I am so worried, m'Lady."

"Don't be," said Aelish, smiling. "It worked, didn't it?"

Katrina looked confused and then understood the discomfort Aelish had been exhibiting was a ruse to clear the room of the King's Guard and Chief Minister Stannon. She began laughing and sat down on a chair near the bed. "How did you know it would work?"

"Please, males are so easily manipulated. Can you imagine what's going to happen them all once the king learns their weapons were trained on his heir apparent? You have nothing to fear about your duties or your family, but they do."

Katrina deeply exhaled and stared at Aelish as if she were seeing her for the first time. "You are quite cunning, m'Lady."

"Males assume we are weak, especially in a kingdom like Yasteron," said Aelish. "I simply fed into their preconceived notions."

Suddenly, Cardissius burst into her bedchamber and came

over to Aelish. "Are you all right, dearest?" He sat on the edge of the bed and began massaging her abdomen. The magical glow appeared as large and as bright as ever. "What a relief!" he exclaimed.

"I think the heir became upset after Stannon and the King's Guard burst into the room with their weapons aimed right at him," explained Aelish. Out of the corner of her eye, she saw Katrina trying to stifle a laugh.

"They did *what*?" exclaimed the king.

Aelish began crying. "It was all a misunderstanding. Before I could explain anything, they were in the room with their weapons trained on me. I don't know why they had to frighten the King Mother like that, when I'm in such a fragile state."

"And they will all be relieved of their duties this hour," said the king. "With regard to Stannon, I will deal with him privately."

"Thank you, Your Highness," said Aelish.

"Thank you for being so devoted to Lady Aelish, Katrina. Do not be worried for your position or for your family," assured the king. "You may leave us and retire for the evening."

"Yes, Your Highness, if you are certain Lady Aelish doesn't need me anymore."

"I will stay with her tonight until she falls asleep," said the king.

"Yes, Your Highness," said Katrina, who curtsied. "I will see you first thing in the morning, m'Lady. All will be well."

Aelish genuinely teared up at the turn of phrase Katrina had used. She missed Lady Antonia so much.

"I'm feeling rather tired now, Your Highness," Aelish said to the king. "Would you mind if I closed my eyes for a few minutes?"

"Go to sleep now, Aelish," said Cardissius. "We must make sure the heir is unharmed. I will send a team of doctors to examine you tomorrow. It's time for your first scanner appointment anyway, as you are now at six weeks of gestation."

Aelish chided herself for not knowing that Yasterons referred to the medici as doctors, and she was also unaware there was a mandatory scan at six weeks of gestation. But then, she remembered her appointment with Valdia and Kimber, when she first discovered she was pregnant with a Human.

They had indicated a magical scan was required at five weeks to determine if there were any magical anomalies. She wondered why the scan was at six weeks in Yasteron. Aelish had forgotten about the tests required to determine whether the fetus had any magical anomalies and began to get anxious. Something odd or dangerous could potentially be discovered tomorrow, like the first time she'd conceived—something that could get her killed.

Distracting herself from this new worry, she remembered her plan to educate herself about Yasteron. "There is something I would like to discuss with you, Your Highness," said Aelish. "Could we discuss it tomorrow after the doctors have examined me?"

"Of course, dearest. You may ask me anything," said the king.

He's certainly behaving differently toward me.

Aelish nodded and closed her eyes. She felt the king's lips upon her forehead. For the next hour, he held her hand and stroked her arm. She had no idea he was capable of such tenderness. The words of Lady Antonia came into her head, *'When it comes to their offspring, the male reaction is absolutely unpredictable.'* Apparently, this applied to male Yasterons as well as male DARlings.

Based on his current tenderness, Aelish decided to use her pregnancy to push Cardissius into giving her things she wanted or needed. At the very least, today she learned how beings got in and out of the suite of rooms. And the King's Guard lined the exit hallway of the back door with six male Guards on either side.

Each lower-order or noble had a secret knock they used on the back door, from inside the suite of rooms, to exit. On the other side of the door, the King's Guard magically confirmed who they were, based on their specific knock. And she was certain, if anything like this ever happened again, they would kill her on the spot. And then, they'd kill Thagar and Kaleigh. But at least now she knew.

‡‡‡‡

The next day, four medici entered her room with medical equipment, accompanied by the king. Storm had been taken outside by one of the trainers in the Great White Mountain Hund Division. The medici were all male and wore the same white coat as Isabela. Aelish felt a desperate longing for her and nearly began crying. But she forced herself to focus on the incredible similarities between Yasteron and Earth. The medici were dressed exactly like all of Thagar's doctors on Earth.

"Your Highness," said the eldest medicus, "we will begin with a magical scan over Lady Aelish to determine if the size of the fetus is normal. Then, we will perform various tests to make sure there are no magical anomalies."

"Thank you, Doctor, that sounds fine," said Cardissius.

Wait! Magical scans? In this room? How is that possible?

Aelish watched the medici set up an examining table, which they magically conjured in the living area. She had no idea how the medici were able to use magic in the suite of rooms. Even Katrina had to go outside to send Aelish's food to her family. Was Cardissius capable of disengaging the spells that blocked all magic except his own? Would she be able to test out her magic today? She was desperate to try, right then, but she controlled the impulse out of fear.

Sitting on the settee, her heart began racing as she remembered all that had happened to her and Thagar when she was pregnant with Kaleigh. She knew if there were any abnormalities or if the fetus presented as Human, the king would kill her.

"If you would please get up onto the table, Lady Aelish," said the eldest medicus, "we can begin the magical scanning." Aelish stood up from the settee and the king unexpectedly embraced her. She pulled out of the hug, smiled at him, and walked over to the table.

"May I stay dressed as I am?" she asked.

All four medici nodded their heads. The youngest of the four extended his hand to help her up onto a small booster step that had just appeared. As Aelish lay on the table, she prayed all would be well for both her and the fetus. The two medici she considered the second and third oldest, situated the scanner over her body. They began magically running the machine. The whole process took no more than fifteen minutes.

"We are finished scanning, Your Highness," said the eldest medicus.

The eldest medicus extended his arm to help her sit up. The king approached the table and Aelish held her breath. "The fetus is a bit smaller than we would like to see at six weeks of gestation, however, it appears healthy," he said.

"Why is it smaller than normal, Doctor?" asked the king.

The medicus nervously cleared his throat. Aelish kept her eyes solely on the king.

"Your Highness, I mean no disrespect," said the eldest medicus, "but the living arrangements for Lady Aelish are not providing her with exercise and many nutrients she needs for a healthy gestation. Most especially, she is deprived of sunlight."

Ha! Told you!

The king asked, "Do you feel if she continues living in this manner for the entire duration of her gestation, the heir will be compromised?"

"In all likelihood, the heir will be born healthy," said the eldest medicus. "But if he is to have a normal birthweight of two pounds upon delivery, his present size is a bit concerning."

The king nodded. But Aelish realized two pounds was nearly the size of a DARlette!

"We will continue on now with the magical anomaly testing," said the eldest medicus.

Since Aelish had never given birth to a magical being, she'd never experienced the next test. The second and third eldest medici asked her to perform three of the simplest of spells. It was as if she were back at Brólaigh Castle, having her very first magical lessons with Lady Antonia.

Aelish looked at the medici and said, "I am unable to use my magic in this room." She heard the eldest medicus angrily exhale. But the king interrupted before any of the medici could comment on what she'd said.

"You may only test what is asked of you, Aelish," cautioned the king.

The medici pressed various equipment against her abdomen and told her she could begin. Aelish closed her eyes and felt her magic return as she performed the three simple spells.

Oh, thank you, God!

She put her face in her hands and began crying. She knew the king was going to be furious with her, but she couldn't help it. The relief she felt knowing that she was still magically adept was cathartic.

The medici were reviewing the results of her magic on the fetus. The youngest medicus exclaimed, "He really enjoys his mother's magic! Look at the movement!"

She lifted her head from her hands and wanted to kiss

the youngest medicus. While she knew he was going to be admonished for speaking out of turn, she was grateful he'd provided information about how the fetus was responding; it was healthy.

The eldest medicus glared at the youngest and turned toward the king. "Your Highness, by depriving the fetus' mother of all her magical abilities, you are compromising the heir's development. Based on the tests, I can clearly and definitively say the fetus would thrive and be of normal size if his mother were able to experience the world and her own magical abilities."

"So, you are certain it is a male?" asked Cardissius, ignoring everything else he said.

"Yes, most assuredly, Your Highness." Not used to having his medical advice ignored, the eldest medicus asked, "Would you consider what we have suggested today, Your Highness, and perhaps allow the heir's mother to experience the sunshine and her own magic?"

"I will take it under advisement," said the king. "Are you finished with the magical anomaly testing, then?"

"We are finished with the six-week scanning and testing. Lady Aelish will need an additional scan in four more weeks or at ten weeks of gestation. We need to ascertain whether she will have a healthy delivery at twelve weeks."

"Very good," said the king. "Why don't you go and lie down, Aelish, whilst I bid the doctors farewell."

Again, the youngest medicus grasped her hand to assist her while she descended the small booster step in front of the table.

With his hand in hers, she sent him a telly: *Please help me. I am imprisoned here.*

He responded: *We know. We are so sorry. The king will have us killed if we help you.*

Aelish stepped down from the table and shook the hands

of the other three medici. "Thank you," she said. "I will rest easier knowing the heir is predominantly healthy under the circumstances."

The king aggressively grabbed her arm and escorted her to the entrance of her bedchamber. With an icy chill in his voice, he said, "I will return as soon as they have left."

Based on his reaction, Aelish knew the king was aware she and the youngest medicus had telepathically communicated. She lay down on the bed and massaged her arm, which was already swelling. She listened and heard the medici packing up their equipment. There was no further conversation, other than their goodbyes, as they exited the room.

The king entered her bedchamber. "And *that* is why you will remain locked in this room until you bear me the heir! Did you think I wouldn't know you sent a telly to the young doctor? Are you so untrustworthy? I am furious with you, Aelish. How dare you betray my trust? If it were not for the heir you carry, I would banish you to a part of the magical world even DARlings know nothing about.

"You defy me, when today was to be joyous! How are we to rule together if I cannot trust you? What did you think the doctors would be able to do for you with a small army of the King's Guard several feet away?"

He sat down on a chair in the bedchamber and untied his ponytail, letting his blond locks fall around him. He ran his hands angrily through his hair.

Aelish expected his anger, but in this moment, she didn't care. She was thrilled she'd been able to use her telepathic capabilities. Her magic was still there! Who knew when she'd be able to test out her magic again?

"Are you certain the doctors would even *want* to help you?" he accused. "Perhaps they are agents of Queen Saia, who wants nothing more than for you to disappear so she may return to my arms. You still do not understand. There are those in the kingdom who wish to harm both you and the heir. Those chosen to care for you have been thoroughly vetted by our intelligence agency and would never cause you any harm. Why do you still see me as the enemy?"

Oh, I don't know. I'm imprisoned, I haven't seen the sun, I can't go outside, I can't use my magic, and I've been raped multiple times to provide you with an heir.

What was the use in saying any of it aloud? Aelish had never dealt with a being who exhibited psychopathic tendencies, coupled with a twisted version of what he perceived was love. She decided to be mostly truthful with him, as trying to understand his mind would require a very long education in psychiatry.

"Forgive me, Your Highness, if I have caused you upset on this joyous day. Based on my surroundings, I knew the doctors had knowledge of my imprisonment here. They are not blind and have, in fact, told you how unhealthy it is for me and the heir. You know I suffer from anxiety over acquiring Magical Interruption Syndrome. I needed to test out my magical capabilities with a telly, and I was also testing out the loyalty of the doctors you chose to be in charge of my care."

"And what is your assessment of their loyalty?" asked the king.

"I believe they conducted their responsibilities with great competence, but I also believe they live in fear of you. You heard what the youngest doctor said to me in the telly. If your subjects, both the educated and the non-educated lower-orders, live in fear of you, how do you know what's real in your own kingdom? How can you trust any of your subjects or ministers to truly have your best interests and the best interests of Yasteron at heart? They serve you out of fear, not out of genuine loyalty. A king should inspire loyalty in his subjects. They should be willing to die for you."

"I am on edge, Aelish," said the king, frustrated. "We need to be married as soon as possible. Whilst the doctors have been sworn to secrecy about the heir, we must marry so the heir can properly succeed me. He cannot remain a bastard."

"I have told you, Your Highness, I am already mated. And you demanding I marry you, is causing me great internal conflict with regard to my religious beliefs."

"Thagar was supposed to be dead so we could marry free and clear. Do I have to kill him, Aelish, to get you to marry me?"

Aelish suddenly sat up in the bed. What if she'd pushed Cardissius too far and he decided to kill Thagar because she'd consistently told the king that she was already mated? She had to rectify this situation immediately. She gingerly got up from the bed and walked over to where he was sitting. She gently pulled his head against her breasts. She heard him deeply exhale.

"No, Your Highness, you do not have to kill him. My life on Earth is over and I am making peace with defying my religious beliefs. Whilst we disagree on many things, I think once we make our Commitments to one another, things will go much smoother."

"Commitments?" he asked, looking up at her. "Do you mean marriage?"

"Yes, I apologize, Your Highness. I'm still not in the habit of using the term marriage."

The king said, "I am in the process of divorcing Queen Saia and it is very stressful. And besides that, my mother wishes to meet you."

It would never cease to amaze Aelish how terms and phrases used in Yasteron were the same as those on Earth. And English was now their predominant language, making it all the stranger. In DAR, divorce was referred to as disassociate, but here, they used the Earthly term of divorce.

The king continued, "Saia comes from royal blood and understands my need for a male heir for succession. But she is making things very difficult for me. And I don't know if you are ready to meet my mother. She is not a nice being."

Aelish began laughing inwardly; Cardissius was under stress. The medici had admonished him for his treatment of the heir's mother, his current queen was giving him a hard time about disassociating, and his own mother, whom he apparently disliked, wanted to meet her, and he was very worried it wasn't going to go well. Imagine having everything you ever wanted and it's still not enough. He was entirely aggravated. She saw the opening and she took it.

She gently asked, "Do you remember me telling you yesterday there was something I wished to discuss with you after the medical examination?"

"Yes. Do you wish to discuss it with me now?"

"I'm not ready to be Queen of Yasteron. I want to learn more about this kingdom, to better understand you and this beautiful place. Then, I'll feel competent to perform my duties."

"What is it you are asking of me, Aelish?"

"Do you have a Master Keeper?" He looked at her perplexed. "A Keeper . . . a librarian? A being who fully understands the history of Yasteron and can explain it to an outsider, like myself, who is about to become queen."

"Ohh, you wish to read?" The king groaned. "I find reading utterly boring and a complete waste of time."

"Well, I adore reading and I love being educated. Is there someone in this kingdom who could provide me with an education on your kingdom before I become queen?"

"I will send Oba to you," said the king.

"Oba?" asked Aelish.

"Yes, he is very old and nearly finished with his life. He is the most knowledgeable being in all of Yasteron with regard to its history. Is that what you are seeking?"

"Yes, Your Highness. Oba sounds like the exact tutor to teach me how to be queen."

"Obviously, we must marry before your coronation, Aelish. I am scheduling our wedding for next week. It will be held in front of the Ministers of Marriage and Succession. I will send all the appropriate dressmakers and stylists to create a beautiful wedding ensemble for you."

Aelish sat down on his lap. "You've made me so happy today, Your Highness." She gently kissed his cheek. "I'm greatly looking forward to our wedding next week, my education from Oba, meeting your mother, and ultimately becoming Queen of Yasteron. But let us not lose sight of the most important thing that happened here today. We are expecting a healthy male who will, one day, rule this beautiful kingdom. You have no reason to feel stressed. You are getting everything you've ever wanted."

"Do you think it's possible you could ever truly love me, Aelish?"

"Of course. But I would like to be able to call you by your first name," she said.

The king began chuckling at her. "Let me here you say it."

"I can't wait to be your wife and queen . . . Cardissius."

The king looked at her and smiled. He pulled her closer and deeply kissed her. "You've made me very happy today, Aelish. But you must promise to never hold my mother against me."

"She will love me," said Aelish, chuckling.

"I must return now to Legislative Hall," said the king. "I will bring my mother in two days' time to give you a chance to select a proper gown and decide how you wish to wear your hair. You must be on your very best behavior with her. She is very difficult, Aelish."

"I will not let you down," said Aelish.

"Thank you, dearest. I will see you tomorrow," said Cardissius.

When the king had left her bedchamber, Aelish went into her bathing room, looked in the mirror, and promptly threw up. How she'd kept it down that long was astonishing. After she cleaned herself up, she went over to her bed. She knelt down, reached under the mattress, and pulled out her crucifix and her amethyst Commitments necklace from Thagar. She decided to wear her crucifix again in gratitude for a healthy fetus and to beg forgiveness for the sin of bigamy she was about to commit.

Sitting on the floor, with her back against the bed, she pulled her knees to her chest. As she began crying, she put her lips against the amethyst stone and said, "Forgive me, my love."

10

FLYING

THAGAR FELT CONFIDENT that he'd done all the necessary calculations to ensure a safe flight for him and Kaleigh to reach DAR. Only the Directors of the POD, Experimentation, and Head Council Chairs knew the difficult and obscure way to avoid the Portal and enter the magical dimension from Earth. By avoiding the Portal, facial recognition was not required nor were the Gatekeepers aware of one's entry. Thagar had done it several times, when he'd returned to DAR after he and Aelish had first moved to Earth. Sometimes, he just didn't feel like having his presence announced. And bringing Kaleigh through the Portal was fraught with problems, as the Gatekeepers had no record of her existence, making facial recognition impossible.

He'd never even told Aelish there was a way to enter DAR without going through the Portal. When he became Director of the POD, he'd taken the oath of secrecy and had never broken it. Flying to DAR using the Portal avoidance route, required flying above the magical dimension and then looping back downward. The entry point into DAR was on a mountaintop in the N.W. Quadrant. From there he'd transport to their home, the Artist's House, in Bencarlta.

It made the trip very long. Since DAR was 60,000 feet above sea level on Earth, in order to go above it and make the loop downward, he had to reach 80,000 feet. But in all the centuries he'd used the route, he'd never once encountered another being, any sort of detection grid, or any magical realm that prevented his entry—most especially, Yasteron.

Thagar was well aware Human life was not possible above 50,000 feet without a pressurized suit, similar to what Earthly astronauts wore. He magically created a suit for Kaleigh that would provide the protection she would need at such high altitudes. While Isabela believed Kaleigh could breathe with no problems, he could not take the risk of harming her physically. Even if she could breathe, her skin and internal organs would experience tremendous pressure climbing to an altitude of 80,000 feet. He remembered Aelish telling him how disoriented Kaleigh had become transporting to Ireland, so he was taking every possible precaution not to cause her any harm. By the time he reached the Artist's House in Bencarlta, even he felt fatigued using the Portal avoidance route. So, he anticipated that Kaleigh would feel a whole lot worse.

While their flying adventure was predominantly to test out Kaleigh's breathing capabilities, Thagar was also formulating a plan of how to gain entry into Yasteron. The kingdom was so well fortified with detection grids and protection barriers, thus far, no being or realm had ever been able to enter it, undetected. But if he were going to rescue Aelish, he had to find a way. And if he were successful in developing a point of entry into Yasteron, it would mean disclosing the Portal avoidance route to the other team members he had yet to choose. But he felt rescuing Aelish would be the best reason to divulge his long-held secret.

"Daddy, I can barely walk in this suit," said Kaleigh, her voice muffled by the face mask.

Thagar began smiling. She was so brave, just like Aelish. "That's all right, sweetheart. For the most part, you will be magically attached to my back. So, you won't need to walk in the suit. But you sure do look beautiful."

"It's hot in here."

"Well, where we are going will be very cold, so the inside of the suit is set to seventy-four degrees. It also allows air to come in and out so we can test your breathing capabilities."

Drummond walked into the kitchen and burst out laughing. "Are ya' puttin' on a bit of weight, then, Kaleigh? You seem puffy." Kaleigh began laughing.

"Before yer departure," said Drummond, "I made an extra special breakfast. I've set it up in the dining room."

"The dining room?" asked Kaleigh. "We could've eaten right here in the kitchen, Drummond."

"Not today, my sweet. Today is a special day, and I want ya' to feel that way from the first bite ya' take. But I think ya' better take off the suit before ya' try eatin' in it." Ya' will smash all the glasses and dishes." Drummond began spinning around with his arms outstretched, imitating Kaleigh in her suit. This, of course, made Thagar and Kaleigh start laughing.

Thagar said, "Let me see how well you can take the suit off by yourself." Kaleigh began untying clasps and ties, which Thagar had specifically chosen because they wouldn't freeze. It took her ten minutes to get out of it. When she was finally out, she let out a loud exhale and Thagar and Drummond began clapping.

"Now, as we eat," said Thagar, "I want to hear you tell me all about what happens to Humans at various altitudes."

"Daddy, I'm not in school. Why do I have to take an oral test?"

"Because I want to make sure you studied all the materials I gave you," said Thagar.

"Of course, I did." Kaleigh began walking toward the dining room, reciting facts and figures. "At 30,000 feet, the oxygen percentage is at 6.3 percent. Somewhere between 30,000 feet and 40,000 feet, the pressure around Humans becomes too low to push oxygen molecules across the membranes of our lungs. At 40,000 feet, we would die without a pressurized mask.

"Humans cannot survive for any length of time at elevations above 26,000 feet, or 8,000 meters, without regular oxygen. Between 30,000 and 40,000 feet, a Human must use pressurized oxygen to push oxygen into their lungs. Above 50,000 feet, Human life is not possible without a pressurized suit, like the one I was just wearing, and like the ones astronauts use. When people are on an airplane and they are flying above 30,000 feet and the cabin pressure changes, they have nine to fifteen seconds to put the mask that drops down from the ceiling, over their nose and mouth before they become unconscious. The oxygen saturation level of 87 percent must be maintained for survival. Did I cover everything, Daddy?"

"At what elevation is the magical world of DAR?" asked Thagar.

Kaleigh replied, "DAR is at 60,000 feet above sea level, but we will be flying to 80,000 feet because we are going to make a downward loop and enter DAR in the . . . I forgot the name of the quadrant."

"We will land on a mountaintop in the N.W. Quadrant of DAR. Then, you and I will transport to our home, the Artist's House, in Bencarlta, which is in the S.E. Quadrant."

"Why do we call our house the Artist's House? Does an artist live there, too?"

Thagar started laughing. He came over to Kaleigh and gave her a big hug. "You did great with all the information, honey. And I will tell you all about why your momma and I call our house the

Artist's House once we've arrived in Bencarlta. Now, let's eat."

He ushered her over to one of the dining room chairs, and Drummond began serving them all sorts of special foods that he'd made for this auspicious occasion. "This really is beautiful, Drummond," said Thagar. "Thank you."

"Thank you, Drummond," said Kaleigh, echoing her father.

‡‡‡‡

Before they left, Thagar hadn't told Kaleigh they'd be flying over Mount Everest.

"Daddy, are we almost at the first stop and where is that going to be?" asked Kaleigh.

"We've just begun flying, Kaleigh," said Thagar, chuckling. He turned his head slightly so she could hear him better. "Are you already asking me, are we there yet?"

Kaleigh began laughing. "It must be incredible to fly. Am I very heavy to carry on your back?"

"Not at all, sweetheart. Okay, the first place we are going to stop is Ireland. We should be there in about two hours. We are flying three times as fast as an airplane—"

"Which means we are flying at 1,800 miles per hour," interrupted Kaleigh. "How is it possible I can see everything so clearly and it doesn't feel that fast?"

"I have magically altered how the speed affects us. I wanted you to be able to see the world as we fly across the Earth to our special destination."

"Where is that? You still haven't told me," said Kaleigh.

"How would you like to go to Mount Everest, Kaleigh?"

"Oh, my gosh, Daddy, really?"

"Really," said Thagar. "We should be there in about six hours, including a rest stop in Ireland. If you feel like you have to pee, just go in the suit. Let me know and I will magically clean you up. Same thing with number two, okay?"

"How do magical beings pee and poop when they are flying?"

Thagar started laughing. "We magically clean ourselves up and the waste just disappears."

"That is so cool."

"How are you feeling, sweetheart? Do you feel like you normally do? Are you queasy or does your stomach feel sick? And are you having any trouble breathing?"

"No, I feel just like I did at home. While the suit felt bulky in the house, when we're flying it doesn't feel that way. It just feels like I'm wearing a blanket. It's awesome."

Relieved, Thagar said, "Good, sweetheart. That's how it's supposed to work. The suit can also deliver pressurized oxygen. Just let me know if you feel goofy or weird. Well, goofier than you normally are."

"Daddy, you're bad." Thagar started chuckling.

"If you feel tired, Kaleigh, close your eyes and try to sleep. Once we start going up very high, it will make you tired. So, after our rest stop in Ireland, try to get a little more sleep once we resume flying on our way to Mount Everest, okay?"

"Okay."

They stopped for a quick rest in a forest in Ireland. They ate some food Drummond had magically packed in Kaleigh's suit, and then they resumed flying. A short while later, Thagar heard Kaleigh's breathing change as she had fallen asleep. The suit was created to automatically supply pressurized oxygen, should she need it, but he continued to listen and monitor her rhythmic sleep breathing, just in case.

"Oh, my gosh, Daddy! Look at all the climbers on the mountain!"

While Kaleigh slept, Thagar had been observing the Humans making their ascent to the summit of Mount Everest. Now that she was awake, they got to share the experience together. He'd seen it many times before and felt nothing better exemplified the Human spirit than those attempting to conquer the highest mountain on Earth. They never failed to impress him.

He noted the Sherpa of Tibetan culture and descent. They were indigenous to Tingri County in Tibet, known as the Autonomous Region of China. They were also native to the most mountainous regions of Nepal and the Himalayas. The Himalayas either abutted or crossed five different countries including Bhutan, India, Pakistan, Nepal, and China. Mount Everest, located in the Khumbu region of Nepal, shared its peak with Nepal and Tibet. The mountain was viewed as a symbol of the relationship between the two countries.

The Sherpa's superior climbing skills and endurance for high altitudes remained unrivaled. And after Isabela explained the genetic mutation they carry, which affords them with the ability to climb and breath under such harsh circumstances, Thagar began to better understand the DNA of his own daughter. The Sherpa People had lived in Nepal's high altitudes for generations and had long-served as guides and porters to tourists needing their expertise to get up the mountain.

"One day, I want to climb Mount Everest," said Kaleigh. "Would you come with me?"

"I would love to come with you, Kaleigh. We wouldn't need oxygen, regular or pressurized. So, we'd kind of be cheating a little bit, like the Sherpa guides of Tibetan descent, who can also breathe at very high altitudes."

"That's so cool. And they can do it without magic—like me!" Thagar laughed at her.

As they approached the summit, Thagar lowered his flying speed and hovered over the peak. It was breathtaking and reminded him so much of the mountain peak in the Sanctuary of DAR. The Sanctuary Learning and Educational Workers, or the SLEWs, devoted their lives toward the protection of endangered mythical and magical beasts found in both the Human and magical worlds. Originally, they created the Sanctuary for all forms of magical and mythical creatures that were mercilessly hunted and were either nearing or had actually become extinct.

Since the climate crisis had caused the extinction of so many species on Earth, known as the Sixth Mass Extinction, Thagar had worked tirelessly with the SLEWs, bringing species from Earth to the Sanctuary in the S.E. Quadrant of DAR. Not even Aelish knew about his Earthly conservation work. He tried to save as many species as he could, so, one day, they might be able to return to Earth. But for that to happen, the climate crisis would have to end.

Human complacency about causing the extinction of so many species in the natural world deeply upset him. He was very proud of his conservation work and often wondered how Humans would react if they knew the lost species on Earth could be found thriving in the Sanctuary of DAR.

"All right, my sweetheart, are you ready to fly high?" he asked Kaleigh.

"I'm ready. I already made a pee and poop, so you'd better clean me up before we get started."

"Okay, sweetheart. It's already gone and you are all cleaned up."

"I wish I could do that. Thank you."

"Okay, we are going to begin our ascent now, Kaleigh. You must tell me if you feel anything weird in your body or with your breathing. I will be flying slower to give you time to acclimate to each additional 5,000 feet. Ready?"

"Ready!"

As they began climbing, Kaleigh was squealing with delight. She was pointing out clouds and airplanes and said, one day, she wanted to go to space. Right now, Thagar would be satisfied if she just made it in one piece to DAR.

At 80,000 feet, she said, "Daddy, I feel like Abuela is with us. I don't know why, but I feel her so close to us. And I can hear her in my head."

Thagar quickly wiped away a tear before it froze, saying, "It's very special this high up."

"I feel like we are close to God and heaven," said Kaleigh. "I'm not sure whether there is a God or a heaven, but if there is, it would definitely be close to where we are now."

Kaleigh had never expressed any doubts before about her belief in God or heaven. Thagar was genuinely shocked. He just assumed because she was Human and had been raised with an organized faith, she would automatically believe in what she was taught. He wondered if Isabela had influenced his daughter's questioning. It didn't bother him, as it demonstrated great intelligence to question everything she was taught. She had the makings of a real leader. However, he knew Aelish wouldn't be too happy to hear Kaleigh's doubts. But very few beings, magical or Human, had the ability to have such a strong blind faith, like Aelish.

"Okay, honey, we are about to make the loop downward now to 60,000 feet. Do you feel okay? Do you want me to go slower?"

"I feel fine, but don't go slower—I'm hungry!"

Thagar burst out laughing and said, "All right, Kaleigh, here we go!"

They reached the mountaintop of DAR in the N.W. Quadrant with no problems at all. When Thagar gently landed, Kaleigh began applauding the way Humans do after a pilot safely lands a plane. He started laughing at her and immediately began to magically untether her from his back.

"Now, before I remove the suit, tell me how you are feeling. Can you breathe okay?"

"Yup! Just starving."

"Okay, honey. I am going to begin unclasping and untying the suit. You must let me know if you feel anything out of the ordinary." Kaleigh nodded and patiently waited to be free of the suit. Thagar peeled it off slowly and kept his eyes on her. She did not appear to be in any distress. Even though he was witnessing it with his own eyes, he could not believe it—Kaleigh was breathing normally in DAR.

They rested on the mountaintop for thirty minutes, and then Thagar decided they were ready to transport to the house in Bencarlta. "Whilst we could stop within the capital city before heading to the house, I think you're going to feel tired from transporting, even though it's not too far away."

"And thirsty! I remember Momma had lots of bottled water for me and Izzy."

"Okay, I have already placed an order for food from one of my and Momma's favorite restaurants, and I've magically placed a case of bottled water on the kitchen table."

"Don't forget the suit, Daddy. We'll need it for the ride home."

He picked up Kaleigh and the suit and transported to the Artist's House. They arrived in the observatory. "Ohh, I feel a little woozy," said Kaleigh. "Can you please get me some water, and oh, my God, what is that beautiful building behind our house?" She was, of course, referring to the Great Rotunda of Peace whose nighttime lights were already on, casting a magical light into the room. So many memories came flooding back. But in this moment, he could not believe Kaleigh was in DAR, staring at the Great Rotunda, in the house where she was conceived.

As he brought water to where she was sitting on the floor, he said, "I will take you there tomorrow, sweetheart. It's where the Head Council meets, where all the laws of DAR are voted on, and where all the big decisions for the commonwealth are made."

"So, it's like the Capital of the United States in Washington, D.C., right?"

"Yes, very good analogy, honey."

"Oh, I can't wait to see it."

The doorbell rang to the house and Thagar said, "That must be the food."

"Oh, good," said Kaleigh. "I'm starting to get starving again, and I don't feel woozy anymore. Do you have money to pay the delivery person?"

"We don't need money in DAR, Kaleigh."

"What? No money is needed in DAR!"

Thagar started laughing. "And the food is being magically delivered, directly from the restaurant. No one in DAR is relegated to serve unless they wish to, like Drummond."

Thagar left Kaleigh with her mouth open as he headed toward the front door. He grabbed the food and aspirated into the kitchen. He began magically placing all the food onto plates, which came flying out of the cupboards, and he hadn't noticed that Kaleigh was in the kitchen.

"That was so fun, Daddy! Why we don't we do that at home? Magic is awesome!" She was doubled over laughing, and Thagar severely regretted Aelish missing Kaleigh's first magical experience in their home in DAR.

"Momma and I try to keep things as normal and Human as possible for you in our house on Earth. We felt it best you didn't see magic like that every minute of the day."

"Why not? I love it!"

Thagar picked up his daughter and began kissing her face all over. He plopped her down into Aelish's chair at the kitchen table, which faced the valley below. The lights in the valley houses had all turned on. She began voraciously eating, and Thagar took his first deep breath since Aelish had been captured. If there was a God, Kaleigh was surely one of the greatest gifts ever bestowed. Thagar was so grateful they had made it safely to DAR and that she was happily eating dinner in the Artist's House. He couldn't believe she was here.

11

THE VOTE

FRIDAY, MARCH 6, 2026 9:00 AM

THAGAR AND KALEIGH transported directly to the front doors of the Great Rotunda of Peace. She expressed a desire to begin their tour of Bencarlta, starting with the building she'd spent the night staring at. Kaleigh refused to leave the observatory, bewitched by the magical light from the enormous structure, and fell asleep on the floor.

Thagar wasn't up for meeting citizens in town, who would recognize him and ask endless questions about who the DARlette was. So, he took Kaleigh directly to the Great Rotunda. Standing in front of the great wooden entrance doors, she began reading the inscription right above the doors.

Those Who Choose Not To Accept And Respect
The Differences Of Others
Doom Us All To A Life Without Dignity

"Wow! Who wrote that? It's so true!"

"The leaders of DAR, sweetheart, many centuries ago," said Thagar.

Suddenly, the doors began to open and six soldiers on each side of the double doors emerged in full military dress. While they displayed no emotion, they all saluted their former Director of the POD. Kaleigh watched as Thagar returned the salute with her mouth agape. She had no idea how important her father was in DAR.

"Why did they salute you, Daddy?"

"It is a sign of respect to those who have served in the Protection of DAR. I was the Director of the POD for many years, honey."

Kaleigh reached up for a kiss and said, "I'm so proud of you."

Thagar began chuckling at his daughter, but her admiration penetrated his soul. For the first time in a very long time, he too felt proud of his service to DAR.

"Okay, Kaleigh, let's go inside."

Upon entering the Rotunda, Kaleigh began looking up and around as if she were searching for something. "Where's the high dome? I don't see it."

Thagar reached for her hand and said, "It's through these doors."

"Oh good, I can't wait to see it." Thagar chuckled inwardly that she'd walked right past the enormous statue of her mother slaying King Gidius—the same sculpture placed inside the Artist's House, giving the home its moniker.

The double-wooden doors of the interior Chamber began opening, and the Rotunda Guards all began to salute Thagar. Kaleigh smiled at him as he returned the salute, and they entered the Chamber. What he had not anticipated was a contentious, packed-to-the-hilt Head Council meeting taking place. Ordinarily, the Rotunda Guards sealed the entrance to the Chamber once a meeting of the Head Council had begun. But they had opened the doors out of respect for his position. Had he known a meeting was in progress, he would never have stepped foot inside, but it was too late.

The citizens and the Head Council all turned toward the doors to see why they had been opened in the middle of a meeting. The previously boisterous room became completely silent. The attention Thagar had been desperate to avoid had morphed into the worst possible exposure. Thagar heard a female voice let out a startled scream. He followed the sound to a standing Lady Antonia with her hands over her mouth. Once she recovered, she gestured for Thagar and Kaleigh to come sit next to her, as two beings had given up their seats out of respect for Thagar.

Melanthia sent Thagar a telly: *I suppose you have some news to tell me about Kaleigh. What a delight to see you both here in DAR. She is beautiful, Thagar. It is beyond fortuitous you are here, in this moment, on this day. The Earth born DARlings have, indeed, forced my hand and the Head Council will be voting today on whether or not to war with Yasteron because of Aelish's abduction. Sit and watch; by the meeting's end, you may get what you've wanted all along.*

Thagar replied in a telly: *Please forgive me for not keeping you apprised on the developments about Kaleigh. The news is very recent. Further, I had no idea a Head Council meeting was in progress, especially one of this importance. Kaleigh was desperate to see the dome, so we came directly from our house to the Rotunda. Again, I greatly apologize for the intrusion.*

He saw Melanthia nod and she sounded the magical gavel to bring the meeting back to order. While the Head Council Members resumed the discussion that he and Kaleigh had interrupted, they situated themselves in the freed-up seats next to Lady Antonia and Quentin. Thagar thanked the citizens who had so graciously given up their seats and shook both of their hands. Mercifully, the seats were on the aisle, so they didn't create a further spectacle by climbing over multiple beings. Thagar let Kaleigh sit on the aisle so she could see better, and finally, they were ensconced in their seats.

Lady Antonia looked at him in disbelief as she reached across him and squeezed Kaleigh's arm and blew her kisses. Thagar managed to reach across Lady Antonia's lap to shake Quentin's hand who was seated to her left.

"How is it possible Kaleigh is in DAR?" asked Lady Antonia. "How can she breathe?"

Thagar whispered, "Once Isabela got out of the psychiatric hospital, she went back to her lab to study the makeup of Kaleigh. Isabela wanted to determine why Kaleigh had not perished in the carbon monoxide poisoning event that took the life of her grandmother."

"And . . . is she a magical being?" pressed Lady Antonia.

"She is not a full-fledged magical being, but she has certain traits that are unique to Humans, like her ability to breathe thin or noxious air. That's why she didn't die along with Abuela."

"Incredible! So, she's like a . . . what is she like, Thagar? I don't have the words."

"I will need to discuss this with you in much greater detail, but you should look upon Kaleigh as a next-generation Human. I simply can't believe it, either."

"And you discovered all of this whilst Aelish is imprisoned in Yasteron? You are an incredible male, Thagar. When we were in Ireland, I told Aelish you are the strongest male I have ever known. I'm so glad I got the chance to tell you that, to your face, in DAR, with Kaleigh sitting right beside you!"

Thagar started laughing at her.

While Lady Antonia and Thagar were talking, Kaleigh was engrossed in the meeting. She understood quite clearly that the Head Council Members were in disagreement with each other about whether or not to declare war on the kingdom holding her mother captive. She also noticed the Council Members with the same color skin as her mother were the ones most adamant to go to war.

"Thagar, you know Aelish will survive," said Lady Antonia. "I have never met a being who can survive confinement, like Aelish. She is so strong. She will come home!" And then, Lady Antonia began quietly crying. "I simply can't believe how Cardissius tricked her. Aelish spent years working on the Peace Accord in earnest. And he kidnaps her during a peace mission? I hope the Head Council declares war today. They are despicable!"

It was refreshing for Thagar to hear her agree with him. She was an Earth born DARling, after all, and was aligned with the others who had lavender skin. Quentin asked Thagar a question, making him lean toward Lady Antonia. By the time they were finished speaking, Thagar turned to check on Kaleigh only to see her walking down the aisle toward the area in front of the Arc of Leadership. He immediately got up to stop her, but a telly came into his head.

Melanthia: *I see her coming. Let her be. Let's see what she does.*

Kaleigh was finally standing underneath the enormously high dome of the Great Rotunda. She saw the rendering of Aelish on the dome ceiling. She turned toward the Head Council, who'd once again gone quiet along with the audience. "That's Momma!" She pointed toward the ceiling and was spinning in a circle, examining the art work. "It looks just like her!"

As the citizens began to realize the DARlette with Thagar was actually the Human child Aelish gave birth to nearly seven years ago, the Chamber erupted in buoyant chatter. Melanthia let it go on for a few minutes as each citizen began to realize who the small being before them really was. Her black curls were the same as her father's, but her light brown sugar skin was very different from her mother's.

Finally, Melanthia sounded the magic gavel to restore the meeting to order. "Citizens of DAR, I assume by now, you have figured out that the small being in front of you is the Human child born to Director Aelish, Policy Director for Earth, and Director Thagar, former Director of the POD. How she is able to breathe in DAR is still a mystery to me, but I'd like to request that you and the Head Council Members indulge me as I go off-agenda at this most important meeting. I would like to ask the offspring of these two renowned directors whether she wishes to speak on her mother's behalf." Low murmurs could be heard throughout the Chamber; this was unprecedented.

Lady Antonia grabbed Thagar's hand, just as she had centuries ago, when Aelish began her thesis about Komprathia in front of the Head Council while still a student. Thagar held his breath. He was terrified Kaleigh might insult the citizens or the Head Council, as she did not know the protocol of how to behave at a Head Council meeting.

The citizens began clapping and the Head Council Members all nodded their heads in unison, indicating they approved of Melanthia asking Kaleigh if she wished to speak on her mother's behalf. Melanthia then asked, "Kaleigh, do you understand what we are discussing here today at this meeting? And would you like to say something on behalf of your mother?"

Kaleigh stood very straight with her hands clasped in front of her floral dress. "Good morning, Council Chair, Head Council Members, and citizens of DAR. My name is Kaleigh Grace Carrigan, and I am the daughter of Aelish and Thagar. This is my first time in DAR. I never thought I could come to the magical world, a place Momma longed for every day. But Daddy took me flying, and we discovered I can breathe in the magical world.

"Daddy wanted me to see where he and Momma used to live, before they went to Earth for my birth. Momma tried to hide how much she missed DAR, but I always knew this was her real home. She was always having meetings with the Head Council from our house. I recognize so many of you from the television screen in her office."

The audience stood up and applauded Kaleigh's bravery to speak in such an intimidating venue at such a young age. When the crowd naturally quieted, Kaleigh continued, "Momma doesn't know I can breathe here, as she hasn't been home for . . ." Kaleigh paused and began counting on her fingers. "Almost two months. I really miss her."

Thagar watched as some of the citizens and Head Council Members wiped away tears from their eyes. He let out a breath he'd been holding since Melanthia had asked Kaleigh the first question. He couldn't believe Kaleigh knew how to properly address Melanthia, the Head Council, and the citizens in the Chamber. She must have watched Aelish do it from their home in Tennessee. He was shaking his head in disbelief.

Kaleigh wiped away her own tears and continued. "One night, Council Chair, I couldn't sleep. I got out of bed and found Momma. I told her I was worried about something we were learning about in school called the climate crisis. Momma told me she was working on something called the Peace Accord to stop one of the kingdoms in the magical world from making the climate crisis worse on Earth. I didn't really understand why a magical kingdom would want to hurt the Earth.

"But Momma spent hours in her office working on the Peace Accord. She hoped it would help stop the climate crisis on Earth, where she was also born. Many times, I wanted to play with her or go shopping. But she'd tell me her work was very important, and suggest we go another time. I was always angry when she told me that, but she's gone now, and I wish I hadn't acted like such a brat. One day, I got very mad and had a temper tantrum. She sat me down and quietly explained that she was trying to stop a war from breaking out between DAR and a magical kingdom which was trying to hurt the Earth.

"Momma told me something I will never forget: war is never the answer. She felt it was very important to be able to discuss problems with our enemies, whether they were at school, or in a magical world, or were destructive leaders on Earth. I asked her if she felt war would ever happen on Earth because of the climate crisis. She said climate refugees might cross borders into other countries because they were trying to escape flooding, wildfires, or they had no food. And this could cause a war to break out. Daddy helps so many climate refugees in his work. I hope because of his work, war will never happen on Earth because I'm afraid of it."

Melanthia nodded at Kaleigh and asked, "So, if we were to declare war on Yasteron, the kingdom holding your mother captive, how would you feel about that?" Thagar thought Melanthia was taking an incredible risk. Kaleigh might tip the scales away from the outcome Melanthia wanted, which was *not* to war with Yasteron.

The Chamber was as quiet as a tomb.

"If Momma were standing before you today, she would definitely tell you *not* to declare war against this place, which I can't ever remember the name of. Don't go to war in Momma's name, or on her behalf, because she wouldn't want it. She takes her Oath of Peace very seriously. I wish everyone on Earth took an Oath of Peace. Sometimes, I hear Momma and Daddy arguing about their Oath of Peace."

Kaleigh's honesty about her parents arguing about the Oath of Peace rippled through the audience, causing the Chamber to erupt in laughter.

"Please find another way to get Momma home because I miss her so much. I don't know if I will ever see her again."

Thagar saw Kaleigh was about to lose it and aspirated from his seat to where she was standing. When the audience saw him, they all stood up and gave him a standing ovation. He graciously acknowledged the citizens, Melanthia, and the Head Council, who were all standing and applauding. He was genuinely shocked at the outpouring of love and respect. He'd forgotten why he served DAR, but today, he remembered.

"Thank you, Kaleigh, for speaking with us today," said Melanthia. "The Head Council will discuss what you've shared with us. It was a great honor to have the daughter of DAR's Living Legend address the Head Council. Your mother is greatly revered by all of us on the dais and by all the citizens in the audience."

"Thank you, Council Chair. I hope to see you all again soon," said Kaleigh.

Thagar picked Kaleigh up and said, "Thank you, Council Chair, Head Council Members, and citizens of DAR for allowing my daughter to speak with you today. We will not disrupt these proceedings any further."

The audience began chanting Kaleigh's name as Thagar carried her back up the steep aisle. The Rotunda Guards magically opened the double-wooden doors of the Chamber so they could exit. Lady Antonia and Quentin left right after them.

While Lady Antonia, Quentin, Thagar, and Kaleigh were at a

café eating sweets in the shopping district of Bencarlta, news alert after news alert was being sent from the Rotunda. "Well, you've caused quite a commotion here today, Kaleigh," said Lady Antonia, hugging her.

"I know! I can hear them all in my head," said Kaleigh. And that was the moment Kaleigh's telepathic abilities appeared.

"You can hear the news alerts, Kaleigh?" asked Thagar, shocked.

"Yes, Daddy. They are talking about me, Momma, and you, too. It's just like the news at home, but it's inside my head."

Thagar shook his head in disbelief.

Quentin suggested, "I think whilst you are in DAR, Thagar, you might want to have Kaleigh partake in some telepathic communication classes at the Institutum de Magicae. She's ready to learn how to send and receive a telly."

"This day is incredible!" exclaimed Lady Antonia.

"I would love to go to school here," said Kaleigh. "Can I go for a little while before we go back home?"

Thagar had no words. He looked at his beautiful daughter and just said, "Sure, honey."

"Yay!" exclaimed Kaleigh.

Thagar would always believe her telepathic abilities emerged on this day because she was immersed in a magical environment. But whatever the reason, it made the day even more memorable and remarkable. Lady Antonia began kissing Kaleigh all over again.

Suddenly, a live broadcast from inside the Great Rotunda began. Kaleigh, Thagar, Lady Antonia, and Quentin could now telepathically hear a commentary on how each of the Head Council Members were voting.

'Head Council Members Marina and Safia, who lost their entire experimenter families after the bombings in the N.W.

Quadrant, have both voted, yes, to war with Yasteron.

'Head Council Member Neya, a former Keeper at the Breanon, has just voted, no.

'Head Council Member Lisette, whose mother Amara is a Master of Agriculture in the S.W. Quadrant, has voted, no.

'Elida, whose renowned family of professors at the Institutum de Magicae, has voted, no.

'Zetian, who is the youngest Earth born DARling to ever serve on the Head Council has just voted, yes, to war with Yasteron.

'Earth born DARling Fatoumata has echoed her fellow Earth born member's vote of, yes, to war with Yasteron.

'Cheswick, the youngest DAR born DARling to ever serve on both the Head Council and the Alliance of Magical Dominions, has just voted, no, to war. That was a shocking vote, as she was part of the delegation in Yasteron for the peace mission, when Director Aelish was abducted. I don't think any citizen saw a no vote coming from one of our most revered Head Council Members, who worked so closely with Director Aelish. What a surprise!

'The vote is now a tie: four votes in favor of war and four votes opposed. It will be up to Council Chair Melanthia to break the tie. Here is what the Council Chair is saying:'

'Never before in the history of the females' leadership on the Head Council of DAR, have the members been so evenly divided on the next course of action. Today's vote is historic, and I do not take my vote lightly. I believe in upholding DAR's Oath of Peace, even when we are tested by such an unbelievably callous realm, with no regard, whatsoever, for the lives of DARling citizens and for other beings throughout the magical world. If DAR is no longer the harbinger of peace within the magical world, I believe our world will be embroiled in war for millennia. Therefore, in accordance with the tenets and principles of our *beloved commonwealth, I cast my tie-breaking vote of, no, to war with Yasteron.'*

'And there you have it, the Head Council of DAR has voted not to war with Yasteron. Thank you for being part of our live broadcast today.'

Kaleigh began jumping up and down. "Momma would be so happy!" She looked at the disappointed faces of Lady Antonia and her own father and said, "Oh, my God, you both wanted to go to war."

"I didn't," said Quentin.

"Well, thank goodness. At least there's somebody else, besides me, who agrees with Momma. She gave up everything to try and create the Peace Accord. How could you both be against her wishes? I'm so confused." Kaleigh began crying.

"You know what, sweetheart," said Thagar, "you're just as smart as your mother and you're right. War with Yasteron will never bring about peace. It has to be done a different way."

"I think we got schooled today by a six-year-old, Thagar," said Lady Antonia. "You're a beautiful being, Kaleigh. Don't ever lose hope that you'll see your mother again. I see her strength, her honor, and her integrity in you, sweetheart. She will come back to you again." Lady Antonia reached for Kaleigh and put her on her lap. She wiped her tears and hugged her tightly.

Just then, Amelia arrived at the café. "Amelia!" yelled Kaleigh, jumping off Lady Antonia's lap. "I'm so happy you're here!"

"Well, my mother sent me a telly that you were in DAR. There was no way I was staying in class another minute whilst you are here in DAR. I sent Charles a telly, and he told me he'd see everyone later, when his training at the POD was finished for the day. He's quite the sturdy soldier, Thagar." Thagar smiled at Amelia.

Lady Antonia turned to Quentin and said, "I told you we should have waited until Amelia was finished with class before we told her Kaleigh was in DAR."

Quentin just shrugged. "Honestly, I think this is more important than any of her classes today, Antonia." Lady Antonia punched him in the arm. "Ow!" he bellowed. And everyone started laughing. Kaleigh dragged Amelia away from the table and the two of them began chatting and laughing together.

"Antonia, speaking of Amelia's education," began Thagar, "I was wondering if I might bounce something off of you, but it must be held in the strictest of confidence." He looked at both Lady Antonia and Quentin. He would have preferred to speak privately about this with only Lady Antonia, but Quentin had always been trustworthy. He also knew Lady Antonia was never going to keep what he was about to ask her a secret from him anyway; nor should she have to.

"Of course, Thagar. What is it?" asked Lady Antonia.

"I have received permission from Melanthia to orchestrate a clandestine rescue mission for Aelish."

"Oh, my God," she said. "But what does a clandestine rescue mission have to do with Amelia? She's only twelve Earth years old and is still in school at the Institute."

"He's right," said Quentin.

Lady Antonia stared at Quentin. "How do you know he's right when he hasn't even asked me anything yet?"

"Because Thagar said Amelia and then a clandestine rescue mission; it all makes sense," said Quentin. "Amelia has inherited amazing evil magic skills from her father. She's years ahead of her peers in school. It's as if she were born to run DAR's first clandestine agency. Department 427 has done a great job, as a start, but what's really needed in our commonwealth is a Department of Clandestine Investigations and Operations."

Thagar had been thinking about Amelia's skills for weeks. He couldn't believe his greatest ally was Quentin. But then, he remembered how much Quentin had helped Amelia recover from her mental health issues after her father suicide and the bombings in the N.W. Quadrant.

Further, it was Quentin who had given Aelish a piece of stealth fabric he'd invented centuries ago. Aelish had magically created a protective suit from the small swatch and wore it every time she covertly entered Komprathia. It allowed her to secretly penetrate the detection grids in DAR, as well as those Yasteron had installed in Komprathia. He should have expected it.

"With your permission, Antonia," said Thagar, "I would like to discuss my preliminary plans with Amelia. If you and Quentin wish to be present, that's fine with me, but it would have to remain a secret between the four of us. No one else can know anything about it, not even Charles." Thagar knew Lady Antonia would ultimately accept Amelia's destiny. But she was going to have great difficulty with Amelia's future at the outset.

"As her mother, Antonia," said Thagar, "I don't want you to be unbearably worried. Dealing with Yasteron is always dangerous. But I believe Amelia's skills will keep her safe from harm, even whilst orchestrating a clandestine mission in the kingdom."

"Agreed," said Quentin, nodding his head.

Lady Antonia deeply exhaled. "I just witnessed Kaleigh address the Head Council today, with the grace of an experienced diplomat. She's not even seven years old. So, whilst Amelia is only twelve Earth years, I think she'll be able to handle anything required of her. After all, I was only sixteen Earth years myself, when my testimony about King Henry turned the Head Council in DAR from a patriarchal one to a matriarchal one. And that was nearly five hundred years ago!

"I won't stand in her way, Thagar. I know her skills are extraordinary and exceptional. And whilst I will be nervous every day for the rest of my life, I believe she was born to be a spy. If rescuing Aelish is her first mission, well, I can't think of any mission more worthy of Amelia's talents. You have my permission and my prayers."

"Thank you," said Thagar.

12

THE OGRE

KING CARDISSIUS ENTERED Aelish's bedchamber. She was fussing with her hair and there were various ensembles all over the dressing area. Katrina was doing her best to calm down Aelish, but she was flustered and agitated.

"What is it, dearest?" asked the king.

"I just can't seem to get my hair and a proper ensemble together to greet your mother. I know how important this is, but you've told me so little about her that I don't feel prepared. Hence, my agitation. Won't you please tell me more about your childhood?"

"You may leave, Katrina," said the king.

"Yes, Your Highness," said Katrina, who left them alone.

"My mother is furious with me that you are bearing the heir. She is, and always has been, against me on everything. And Komprathia won't stop bombing us, and the noise is irritating her." The king walked over to a simple grey skirt suit paired with a beige silk blouse that tied with a bow at the neck. "This is perfect for my mother. It matches the ominous grey cloud which sits above her head at all times."

"It looks more like an outfit for a funeral," remarked Aelish. The king smirked as if to say, exactly. "Good God! She can't be that bad."

"Oh, but she can. Cassandra is a particular form of horrible which confounds our greatest writers to politely describe. They've been working on her obituary for decades and are still struggling to make her sound as though she was at all likeable."

Aelish loudly exhaled. "Was she always this way?"

"My two older brothers died in the infamous Proelium. She had delivered my father, King Nevuna, both an heir and a spare. However, both were killed by DARling soldiers. She has never forgiven your commonwealth for killing her sons who were heirs to the Yasteron throne. This meant she, yet again, had to conceive an heir for my father's succession. And that would be where I come in."

"What were the names of your brothers?"

"Cameron and Cain." Aelish inhaled sharply at the name Cain. She couldn't believe one of Cardissius' brothers had the same name as Thagar's eldest brother. "I assume you spell Cain with a -C- and not a -K-, correct?"

"Yes, of course," said the king. "Centuries ago, it was the custom in Yasteron to name offspring with names that incorporated the first two letters of their mother's first name, which in this case is Cassandra. Therefore, we were all given names beginning with the letters -C- and -A- for Cameron, Cain, and Cardissius."

Aelish made a mental note for her discussion with Oba, the Master of Archives, to ask him if other magical realms within the magical world used this same custom as those in Yasteron and

DAR. She was shocked that one of Cardissius' brother's names was the same as Thagar's.

"The Proelium was a horrible battle," said Aelish, thinking of the death of Thagar's mother.

"Yes," agreed Cardissius. "We may lose the battle, but Yasteron always wins the war. Why do you think we've held DARling soldiers captive since the Proelium? It's in retribution for the loss of the heirs to the Crown of Yasteron. It was all my mother's idea."

Aelish was stunned. "But that battle was 666 years ago!"

"Cassandra is capable of holding a grudge until she dies," said the king.

Aelish shook her head. "Have *you* wanted to free the soldiers, Cardissius?" She used his first name to see if he would accept the new shift in their relationship. They were to make Commitments with each other tomorrow, and she'd only called him by his first name twice.

"I've wanted to free the soldiers many times, Aelish. But each time the King Mother found out about my intentions, she made life unbearable for everyone in Yasteron."

Now, this, was valuable intelligence.

"I've never been good enough for her," said the king. "I've never measured up to her memories of both my brothers. It's been very difficult living in their shadows."

"But she expresses some warmth toward you, yes?"

The king scoffed. "Cassandra has never been physically or emotionally available to me."

"But she gave you hugs and kisses when you were little, right?"

The king burst out laughing. "My mother has never held me or kissed me, Aelish. I was raised by nursemaids and lower-orders. My father was pretty much the same, except for the occasional pat on the back."

"Oh, my God! It's as if she blames you for the deaths of her sons, but you weren't even born yet. I recognize, centuries ago, parents were not as outwardly affectionate as they are today. But to have never been held or kissed by one's own mother is a form of parental abuse."

"Agreed," said the king. "I've tried to be affectionate with all three of my daughters, but I'm sure my measure as a father has fallen short. But I'm greatly looking forward to showering our son with the affection withheld from me."

Well, this explains a lot. No wonder he doesn't want be physically intimate with me.

The king said, "Why don't you finish getting ready so I can give you the Cassandra seal of approval before she arrives. It's nearly one o'clock."

"All right." Aelish went into her dressing area and donned the grey suit with the beige silk blouse, which tied into a bow at the neck. She put her hair into a proper bun and wore very little makeup. She wore pearl earrings Cardissius had given her for the occasion. She looked like she was going on a job interview at a bank or a law firm on Earth. She put on grey pumps, took a last look in the mirror, and shook her head at her appearance. She joined Cardissius in the living area, where he was waiting for her on the settee.

"Ta-da!" she exclaimed, as she entered the room.

The king stood up and began clapping. "Perfect! And now, I must leave you, Aelish. I will return this evening, where I hope to find you in good spirits. I think I've prepared you for the female you about to encounter; she's a cold, heartless being."

Aelish walked over and embraced the king. As much as she despised him, for the first time in her life, she actually felt sorry for him. She'd finally discovered why he was the way he was.

While his mother couldn't take all the blame for his ruthlessness, she certainly seemed to deserve a lot of it.

As she watched him leave the room, she sat down on the settee in the living area and awaited the King Mother. While there were no clocks in the room, she knew at least an hour had passed and wondered if she wasn't coming. Or perhaps, making her wait was all part of the King Mother's machinations.

Suddenly, Katrina entered the room and announced, "The King Mother, m'Lady."

Aelish stood up and deeply curtsied. "It is my distinct pleasure to meet you, King Mother. Please, come join me in the living area, where refreshments will now be served."

Aelish nodded at Katrina to bring in the tray of drinks and refreshments. The king had advised Katrina on all of his mother's favorites, in an attempt to stop her from complaining about what was served. However, he did say she'd probably find a way to fuss, regardless.

Aelish determined the King Mother was somewhere in her mid-sixties, in Earth years. She wore her thick grey hair pulled back severely in a bun. She wore no makeup and no jewelry, with the exception of a crown made of sapphires and diamonds. She wore a beige gown with a high neckline made of taffeta. While taffeta was a luxurious fabric, Aelish felt it was better suited for curtains than an afternoon gown; it was dated, most likely, just like the King Mother. Aelish surmised her future mother-in-law was stuck somewhere between 1350 and 1550.

"So, you're the slut the dark prince has chosen to be his new queen."

And there was the first shot across the bow. Aelish was so stunned by her remark that she remained quiet. Her face gave away nothing about how she inwardly felt.

"Why he'd choose to mate with a being from the most horrible realm in the magical world is simply incredible to me. DAR should have been absorbed by our kingdom centuries ago. But to mate with an *Earth born* DARling, with grotesque lavender skin and hair the color of a demon, defies all logic."

King Gidius of Komprathia was the last being who referred to her red hair in the same manner an hour before his death. She could only hope this female's life was nearly at its end. She didn't want her anywhere near the heir. Sensing her agitation, Storm came over to the King Mother and began sniffing around the bottom of her gown, which obscured the chair she was sitting on. The King Mother was unaware of the dog until it started growling.

"What is this hideous beast doing inside? Shoo! Get away from me, you vile creature."

Storm began growling louder. Aelish was genuinely afraid he was going to kill her.

"Storm! Go to your bed! Now!" Storm looked at Aelish, aggrieved. As he started to walk away toward the bedchamber where his bed lay, Aelish said, "Good boy! Now, stay there."

"You seem quite confident you can handle this dangerous breed. Did my son give you this dog as a pet? They'll kill you in the blink of an eye. They have no business being inside a dwelling and should only live in the wild."

"I've received extensive training from Captain Lane. I am not afraid of him."

"You should be. I've seen a Great White Mountain Hund attack its owner after owning it over twenty years. I would never let the heir near this animal. So, when can we expect the heir's grand arrival?"

Aelish marveled at how the King Mother continued a conversation with her after first, calling her a slut, second, criticizing DAR, and third, insulting her appearance. She didn't have a care in the world for Aelish's feelings. She was an ogre.

"The heir is expected to arrive in another six weeks. I am halfway through my gestation."

"Well, hopefully, he won't inherit any of your unfortunate looks. Out of all the DARling skin colors, yours is the most hideous. Truly, I don't know what my son is thinking. He's distilling the purity of the line of succession to the Crown of Yasteron. It's disgraceful!"

Aelish asked, "Perhaps you would have preferred he sired an heir with someone who had brown or black skin?"

The King Mother stood up and smacked Aelish hard across the face.

As Aelish massaged her jaw, she asked, "I'll take that as a no, then?"

"You are an impudent, brazen, shameless DARling. I don't know how I will get through the marriage ceremony tomorrow, but it has to be done. It's bad enough the heir might look anything like you, let alone be a bastard on top of it. He will always be a bastard, but at least the rest of the kingdom won't know about it. You should carry great shame bewitching my son like this. You will befall many curses for what you've done. I have seen to that; you can be sure."

So, in the ten minutes they'd spent together, Aelish could also include being physically assaulted and assured that a sorceress had been engaged to bestow curses upon her. The King Mother was precipitously close to getting Aelish's Irish up. She took some deep breaths and Katrina entered the room with a cart filled with drinks and refreshments. Katrina took one look at the welt on Aelish's face, which was already turning black and blue, and began shaking but said nothing.

"Thank you so kindly for preparing this tray for us, Katrina."

"Leave us, lower-order!" bellowed the King Mother.

Katrina made a dash for the door as gracefully as possible.

After she'd left, the King Mother glared at Aelish. "You should *never* use the name of a lower-order! They must always be kept in line and remember that their one purpose in life is to serve the nobles of Yasteron. And whilst you may be a DARling, I am aware of your noble birth on Earth, so you ought to know better. Despite it being the most disgusting place in existence, please behave accordingly. I can't wait until the Earth burns itself up and takes those vile Humans along with it."

Wow! This female is insane! She's filled with nothing but hate and intolerance. Is there anything worse than a cruel mother? No wonder Cardissius is the way he is. He never had a chance growing up with this lunatic.

"Once the heir is born," said the King Mother, seated once again, "I have arranged for proper nurse maids and nannies for his care. You will be too busy serving as queen to tend to your child. Besides, it is not the way we do things in our kingdom."

"Hmm . . . " said Aelish.

The King Mother raised her eyebrows.

"With all due respect, that's not for you to decide," said Aelish. "I am his mother, and I will, in fact, be nursing him myself. And whilst he may have a nanny, Cardissius and I will be raising him together in a happy, loving environment."

"That will not happen, my dear, but you can keep deluding yourself with these fantasies. If necessary, I will rip the child from your arms. You are in my kingdom now, and you will do as I say. Do we understand one another?"

A thousand thoughts were going through Aelish's mind: spells to terminate the King Mother's life, calling Storm in here to blind her, or simply strangling the female with her own two hands. But she had no magical abilities and would be killed on the spot by the King's Guard were she to attempt any of these things. So, instead, she just smiled at the King Mother.

"You're an insolent female," said the King Mother. "You are nothing like Queen Saia and the citizens will hate you for it."

"Perhaps, but your son loves me more than any other female he's ever known, including you. And with his love, I will be able to accomplish many things in this kingdom. You might even find we agree on some of the changes needed to happen here."

"Changes? What changes?"

"You will see soon enough, King Mother. But for now, I bid you farewell. I have grown fatigued, and it is time for me to rest. Nothing is more important than the health of the heir. Thank you so much for coming, and I look forward to seeing you at the wedding ceremony tomorrow." Aelish stood up and curtsied, indicating their time together was over. It was completely rude and exactly what she intended.

"Well! I have never in my life met such a despicable being!" exclaimed the King Mother.

"Likewise," said Aelish.

Astonished, the King Mother stood up, turned on her heel, and stormed out of the room. After a few minutes, Katrina came in with an ice pack for her face. "M'Lady, what happened?"

"I met the devil who created the king," replied Aelish.

"I think we should ice your face whilst you lie down, m'Lady," said Katrina.

"Quite right, Katrina."

Aelish discarded the ridiculous grey suit and put on a bathrobe. "Burn these clothes."

"Yes, m'Lady. I will do so at once."

"Please make sure I am awake before the king arrives this evening. I can't imagine what tonight is going to be like."

"Especially after he sees your face, Lady Aelish. I am so sorry this has happened."

"Thank you. I so appreciate you, Katrina."

"And I, you," said Katrina. She wiped tears from her eyes as she gathered up the clothes to set them on fire. "I will see you later, m'Lady."

"See you."

‡‡‡‡

When Cardissius saw the bruise on Aelish's face, he nearly dropped the ornate jewelry box he was carrying.

"My mother did that to you, didn't she?"

Aelish massaged her jaw. "Did she physically harm you when you were a child?"

"It was the only way she ever touched me—by striking me."

"Good God! How did you endure such treatment?"

"I became the way I am, Aelish. But I hope with your love, I can change and finally find some happiness in my lifetime."

"I don't know how you haven't killed her—purely out of self-defense."

"Believe me, there were many times I plotted and devised all sorts of spells that wouldn't leave a trace of murdering my own mother. But I can't do it, no matter what she does. I think there's a part of me that still hopes, one day, she will love me. And if she were dead, that hope would die as well. Please don't hold my mother against me, Aelish. We cannot choose our parents, our place of birth, or our station in life."

Aelish shook her head. "No, but we don't have to live with what was chosen for us. We all have the capacity to change the circumstances of our lives."

"Your ability to say that tells me with certitude you were deeply loved as a child. Only someone who experienced love growing up would ever believe such a hopeful thing."

"But you hold great power, Cardissius. You can make this kingdom into any vision you desire. You are the king! And even your mother cannot defy the king's orders. So, if you want to really get even with her for all she did to you growing up, begin changing the kingdom and improve the lives of your subjects, especially the lower-orders. You have the power to do what no one else can."

The king smiled at her. "I have never met a being like you in my entire life, Aelish. I feel like your presence has already begun to change me. And in order to change my kingdom, first I have to change, correct?"

"Correct. And I believe you are capable of change, and you are also capable of changing Yasteron for the better. It is a beautiful kingdom filled with art, music, architecture, and the genius of so many creatives. Just imagine what you could create, and it will be so. Instead of conquering and destroying, build and grow your kingdom into something unrivaled in the magical world."

"Will you help me do this as my wife and queen?"

"Of course, I will help you."

Aelish wanted to believe she was seeing some redeeming qualities in the king. And she finally understood where his psychopathic tendencies came from—his mother. He was an abused child, who in DAR or on Earth, would have been removed from her care. Was there anything worse than a cruel mother? She didn't think so. Cassandra had turned an innocent child into a cruel and ruthless king. She'd made her son into what he was; a male who considered imprisonment and rape as a form of love. He was completely demented, but now she knew why. And she could work with this knowledge to hopefully free herself one day. But even more than her own freedom, she was determined to free the lower-orders of Yasteron. They were as oppressed by their station in life as their own king; if they only knew.

"So, would you like to see what I've brought for you to wear tomorrow at our wedding?"

"Yes, show me," said Aelish.

Cardissius handed her the most beautiful jewelry box she had ever seen in her life. The box was in the shape of a carriage, with hand-painted scenes in oval circles surrounded by gold. The wheels of the carriage were also made of gold, and the top of the carriage ended in a peak with jewels of all kinds. She opened the roof of the carriage and inside were two boxes.

"May I open the boxes?" she asked.

The king smiled and nodded.

She opened the larger box first. It contained a necklace made of teardrop diamonds that came to the center with an enormous emerald, encrusted with more diamonds. It was an elegant design and would lay right above her breasts. It paired beautifully with her Commitments gown.

"May I open the second box?" The king nodded.

The smaller box contained emerald earrings. The top of the earrings had small emeralds encased with diamonds in a teardrop shape. The top joined the bottom of the earrings, which were also teardrop shaped, but the emeralds at the bottom were much larger and also had diamonds surrounding the jewel. They were exquisite.

"I chose emeralds to match your beautiful green eyes. I hope you like them, Aelish."

"They are beautiful. Thank you." Aelish put on the necklace and earrings, saying to the king, "I'm going to see how they look in the dressing room mirror." She walked into the dressing area and gazed into the mirror. Unfortunately, the bruise on her face overshadowed their beauty. But she knew she could hide the bruise with proper makeup.

The green of the emeralds went beautifully with her gown. The top portion of her sleeveless gown was made of a gold-textured fabric, which hugged her body and waist. The heir was so small, her pregnancy would not be revealed by the gown.

Right above her hips, folds of gold satin hung nearly to her knees. The folds then gathered on both sides of her hips to create two satin-shaped roses. The folds of satin parted in the front, exposing the bottom of the gown. It matched the gold-textured bodice with additional lace fabric sewn over it, making the front of the dress hang beautifully.

The folds of satin in the front, expanded toward the back of the dress in voluminous pleats, ultimately creating a ten-foot train. Her veil was a gold tuille fabric. She planned to wear her hair in an intricately braided bun. The veil attached above the bun and hung down only to her hips. Since white was not worn as a wedding gown color in Yasteron, she'd chosen gold, having been inspired by Naz' Commitments Ceremony gown. It surprised her that an Earthly white wedding gown had not yet been adopted in Yasteron.

Aelish returned to the living area. "They are all beautiful, Cardissius. It was very thoughtful of you to choose a jewel that matched my eyes. And since it is bad luck for you to see the gown before the ceremony, I will just say the emeralds match perfectly with the color I've chosen."

"Wonderful," remarked the king. "Then, you are pleased with what I've chosen for you?"

"I am, indeed."

"Do you have any makeup to cover the bruise my mother inflicted?"

"I do. Don't worry, I will hide it completely."

"I'm so sorry you had to endure being physically harmed by her. Why did she hit you?"

"It doesn't matter. Try and stop thinking about it. It's over and I will be fine. I'm just grateful she didn't punch me in the stomach, which could have harmed the heir."

Cardissius shook his head and Aelish noticed his right fist

was clenched. She sat down on the settee with him. She reached for his hand, gently unclenching his fist.

"I wasn't even aware my hand was in a fist," he said. "Forgive me." The king appeared as though he was keeping something from her, as he was becoming agitated.

"What is wrong, Cardissius? There's something you're not telling me," said Aelish.

"How do you know me so well already?" He lowered his gaze. "You're right. There is something I need to tell you." He looked up and said, "We must perform the Endeavor on our wedding night to consummate our marriage."

Aelish was furious he had not told her this earlier. She was caught off-guard and tried not to show her anger. She deeply exhaled.

"You are angry with me now," said the king.

"As long as you are certain it will not hurt the heir, what can I say, Cardissius?"

"I am certain it will not hurt the heir, Aelish. I'm sorry you still find performing the Endeavor with me so repugnant."

Aelish lied and said, "It is not that. I was simply worried for the heir."

"Are you certain?" he asked, looking deeply into her green eyes.

She smiled and tried lying more convincingly. "I am certain." She felt so tired.

"All right, then. I will see you tomorrow at noon for our wedding," said the king. "At the ceremony, I will present you with one final piece of jewelry for our marriage."

"I look forward to receiving it," she said.

"Till tomorrow, then."

"Till tomorrow."

After he'd left the room, Aelish laid down on the settee and reviewed all she'd been through and all she'd learned about the king and Yasteron. She felt utterly exhausted. Katrina suddenly entered the room and came over to her. She knelt down so her face was even with Aelish's.

"Is everything all right, m'Lady?" asked Katrina.

"Katrina, do the lower-orders know about my impending marriage tomorrow?"

"They do, m'Lady."

"And how do they feel about it."

"Honestly?" asked Katrina.

"Yes, honestly."

"The lower-orders have always loved Queen Saia," said Katrina, "as she tried to bring about change for the lower-orders. It failed, but nevertheless, she tried."

"What did she try to do?" asked Aelish.

"She felt every being in her kingdom should be literate. She wanted the lower-orders to be able to read and receive an education. However, she hit a roadblock with Chief Minister Stannon, the King Mother, other ministers, and the king himself. They fear us, Lady Aelish, but Queen Saia never has. Therefore, there is somewhat of a loyalty to her."

"Are there leaders within the community of lower-orders?" asked Aelish. She saw Katrina grow frightened. "I'm not asking for their names, Katrina. I'm merely asking if there are leaders within the community who could help implement changes, were they to occur."

"What do you mean?" asked Katrina.

"If Queen Saia had been successful in getting the royals and nobles to allow the lower-orders to learn how to read and receive an education, are there leaders within the lower-order community who could ensure the policies were implemented?"

"You mean leaders who could make sure Queen Saia's ideas

were carried out?"

"Exactly. There must be those within the community of lower-orders who can lead."

"There are, Lady Aelish. Sometimes, they frighten me as they wish to go against the king and other nobles, which would endanger our lives."

"I understand," said Aelish. "Well, I have some ideas of my own, Katrina, just like Queen Saia, for the lower-orders. Do you think you could arrange to give a letter to one of these leaders who does not cause you fright? Perhaps one whom you trust to act responsibly?"

Katrina dropped her head. Aelish tried to reassure her and said, "It will simply be a letter, Katrina. You will watch the leader read it, and then you will burn it afterward to destroy any trace of its existence."

"All right, m'Lady. There is a being whom I trust."

"Good. After the wedding, we will discuss this further. Say nothing to any being, as you must protect us both, all right?" asked Aelish.

"All right, Lady Aelish."

"Can you please bring me some extra makeup tomorrow morning? I don't think what I have will suitably cover this bruise, and it must be covered before the wedding."

"Of course, m'Lady. I will bring you a variety of options. I'm so sorry this happened to you the day before your wedding."

Aelish smiled at her. "All will be well, Katrina." Just saying the phrase made her think of Lady Antonia, and it gave her courage.

After Katrina left, Aelish continued to lie on the settee. She was ready. She was determined to find out every single thing about this kingdom, while at the same time, try to convince the king to stop the oppression of the lower-orders. She could get through the ceremony and marry him tomorrow, because it could lead to so much more. She would smile at Chief Minister Stannon and the King Mother, the only two witnesses invited to the wedding, as she was planning a lot of surprises for them. Aelish was going to upend their kingdom or give up her life in the process. Either way, one day, she would be free again.

13

THE LECCS TOUR

I SABELA WAS NEARLY finished packing for the flight on Drew's plane to the United Kingdom. As she hung the last of her skirt suits into her garment bag, she began chuckling; her mother had been right. When they went shopping together to buy suitable clothes for the worldwide tour to promote the LECCS vaccine, Isabela thought she'd need at most two suits and four dresses. When Isabela told her mother this as they were shopping, her mother burst out laughing. They ended up purchasing twenty suits, including both pants and skirt suits, as well as fifteen dresses and fifteen blouses. Isabela had already worn seventy-five percent of the clothes purchased and she and Drew had only been gone for ten days. Why was her mother always right?

Only a few of the items still had tags on them. She knew the U.S. leg of the tour would be the most intense, with a non-stop schedule, but Isabela never thought she would need so many outfit changes. They did one television interview after another, and she couldn't be wearing the same outfit in each one. Drew felt she shouldn't wear her white coat, as he felt it might be off-putting. But it would've made dressing a whole lot easier, and she missed her coat.

The makeup and hairstylists who traveled with Drew and Isabela were lifesavers. Between the rain in one destination, the humidity in another, and the constant temperature fluctuations they incurred from traveling cross-country—it all wreaked havoc with her hair. She always wanted it straight and shiny, but her thick Mexican hair was uncooperative with the variety of weather conditions. Mercifully, the hairstylist, José, understood, as he was also Latino. He knew exactly which hair products to use in each location to keep it straight and shiny.

Isabela was still a bit of a novice, when it came to makeup on a day-to-day basis. But she didn't have a clue as to how to do her makeup for television lighting. That's where Maggie came in. She was not only a makeup artist, but she was also a fashion stylist. Without her skills, Isabela would have despised her appearance on the back-to-back interviews. They were scheduled one after another, from national, to cable, to local news, and each had different studio lighting. She needed a pro to prevent her from looking washed out or exhausted. Drew had offered to have Maggie accompany her when she went shopping with her mother. But naturally, Isabela had refused, telling him she didn't need her services. While she'd chosen some nice outfits, she realized now what a difference it would have made if Maggie had accompanied her.

Isabela heard a knock on the door of her hotel suite. She opened it to the smiling face of Drew. "Have you finished packing or do you need some help?"

"No, I'm all set," replied Isabela.

She had never known such an even-tempered person. Day in and day out, Drew's temperament was consistent. He was patient with his staff, gave precise directions to his six-member security team, and rarely got irritated with schedule changes or things which greatly annoyed Isabela, like traffic or horrifically rude people. He let her take the lead during all the interviews and immediately sensed when she needed him to jump in, especially when she got tongue-tied or was tired. He was a gentleman first and foremost, and without Drew, she could've never kept up the pace of their schedule.

Drew stepped inside the suite and sat down on the couch in the main area. Isabela sat down in a chair across from him. "I will send Sawyer up to get your bags as soon as I leave. The 405 is already bumper-to-bumper traffic—your favorite," he teased. "Are you hungry?"

"I'm always hungry," replied Isabela.

Drew chuckled. "I had Sawyer pick up your favorite chocolate croissants as well as two hot chocolates, in case you were hungry on the ride to the airport."

"Oh, awesome," said Isabela. "I can't wait until we are in France and I can try some real croissants. I'm so curious to see if I like them more or less than those made in America."

"You're going to love them. We'll only be in England for two days, so the French pastries await! Helene just informed me that while we're in the U.K., we'll be meeting with the Prime Minister, the Chief Executive Officer of the National Health Service, and she's awaiting final confirmation about afternoon tea with the King of England. Maggie has already contacted some shops in London with your measurements to procure a proper outfit, should they confirm. We men have it so much easier. I can get away with wearing an elegant suit—unless—do you think I should wear a top hat and tails?"

Isabela started laughing. "I have no idea how to behave when meeting a member of the British royal family."

"Don't worry, Doctor Torres. Helene has all the reading materials you'll need, in order to prepare yourself with the necessary protocols for an audience with the king. Even if we don't get to meet him, she was informed we'll most likely be receiving England's highest civilian award for performing a great act of heroism."

"The George Cross," said Isabela, nodding.

Drew began clapping. "So, we really need to be on our game for that event. But we'll have the plane ride over to prepare, so we Yanks can impress."

"Drew, you are a descendant of Sir Robert Devereux, the 2nd Earl of Essex. I don't think you have to worry about impressing anyone in Britain." She shook her head at him.

"True, but my mother was French, whom the Brits are often not very fond of."

Isabela started chuckling. "I told my brother we might be meeting the King of England. Javi was not impressed, but he did say, 'Can you tell him it's high time England had a proper baseball league and to knock off all this cricket crap.' I believe that was the direct quote."

Drew laughed. "Javier does have a point." He stood up and said, "Okay, I will see you in the car, Isabela. Take your time but not too much time."

She walked him to the door and then returned to her luggage. She zipped up her suitcases, grabbed a bottle of water from the minibar, and pulled the trench coat off its hanger in the closet. She looked at the beautiful coat Aelish had given her for her sixteenth birthday. Isabela had either worn it or had it on her arm before every event. She'd brough a little piece of Aelish with her for luck and to give her hope that the LECCS vaccine would become more widely accepted, by the time the tour was over.

Isabela put on the coat and remembered the moment she'd been given this gift from Aelish in the coffee shop, with Lady Antonia watching. It was one of her favorite memories. A trench coat designed and created in the magical world of DAR. If the people interviewing her only knew—now *that* would be a much bigger story than the LECCS vaccine. She slung her handbag over her shoulder, left her suitcases for Sawyer, and closed the door to the hotel suite.

✠✠✠✠

Isabela situated herself in one of the luxurious seats on Drew's plane. She looked up the aisle and saw Drew speaking with the pilots. She closed her eyes and reflected on all they'd accomplished over the last ten days.

The Communications Department at Devereux Enterprises was comprised of top-notch professionals. Isabela was in awe of their ability to arrange television interviews for her and Drew, within the U.S., on every major cable and national news network, to say nothing of coordinating their local town-hall-style meetings with the local television stations. If there were any hitches, it was not on the part of Drew's comms staff, it was the fault of the news networks.

Isabela had some previous experience being interviewed for both print and television when she announced the discovery of the Lancaster E. Coli Climate Syndrome. But that was more than two years ago and her skills were rusty. Since then, she'd worked on developing the LECCS vaccine, served as Principal Investigator of the clinical trials to test the vaccine's efficacy, and was partly responsible for overseeing the worldwide distribution of the completed vaccine. But all of this had collided with the unprecedented climate event of the Perfect Storm as well as her own perfect storm of mental illness.

She'd greatly matured as a scientist and as an individual, but she was still in a fragile mental state. Her parents and Javier were concerned the worldwide tour might cause a mental health setback. They weren't wrong; the pressure to convince the vaccine hesitant was simply incredible. But she diligently took her medications and even had a telemedicine appointment with her psychologist. So far, she felt stressed, but she also felt strong.

For the most part, the news interviews were scripted by the communication team, which made them a whole lot easier than the town hall meetings. The town hall meetings were led by local media professionals, similar to local political debates, and were televised by the local news network. Isabela read a brief scripted introduction, usually seated next to Drew on a stool. The local media person served as moderator. After Isabela spoke, the moderator instructed the public on how they should behave and then opened the meeting up to questions from the public. Despite being asked to refrain from making inflammatory comments and to stay on-topic, there were always at least two or three people who came out just to upend the meeting with their own agenda.

Isabela found the town hall meetings in the U.S. incredibly stressful. She constantly worried there were covert operatives from Yasteron in attendance. The security issue had plagued her from day one to day ten. There was no way for DAR's Department 427 to vet those in the audience; there simply wasn't enough time.

Drew and Isabela had both suffered injuries during her presentation at the World Health Organization on May 15, 2024. And while the town hall meetings were held in far less intimidating venues, like college auditoriums, the threat and fear she experienced felt closer. Those in attendance were often no more than ten or twenty feet away from her. And despite all the security done prior to the events, many of the states they visited had open-carry laws and guns were permitted inside the venue. The gun culture of the U.S., with a mass shooting nearly every day, only intensified her fears. She couldn't discuss this with her mother, as her mother worried constantly that Isabela was still a target of assassination, like she was at the WHO.

Isabela often calmed herself about the gun issue, knowing Yasteron could bypass any and all security measures, anyway. Despite feeling continuously nervous and on edge, she realized it was all completely out of her control. She was thrilled the U.S. leg of the tour was over, as she'd never been able to fully relax and was now having trouble sleeping.

Oftentimes, they encountered vitriol from attendees. America had been severely polarized over the last ten years. And persuading the average person to believe in the vaccine hit the same roadblock time and again; despite the devastation of the Perfect Storm, people still didn't believe climate change was real. So, convincing them that a deadly syndrome, like LECCS, would emerge from the climate crisis, just fell flat. Too many Americans believed that climate change was fake news.

That belief, coupled with their innate distrust of science, often resulted in citizens screaming at both Drew and Isabela. The opioid crisis was still raging, and the mistrust of the pharmaceutical industry was widespread. Many yelled, "Science can't even cure cancer by this time. Why should we believe anything you say?" And this was when Isabela shined and calmed the audience.

She would tell the audience what it felt like to be only ten years old and learn your mother was diagnosed with a deadly cancer. She explained how it changed the entire course of her life. This was when her age worked to her advantage. Isabela garnered sympathy from angry citizens, and she agreed wholeheartedly with them that there should be a cure for cancer by now. And despite her mother surviving because of an experimental trial, her entire family had greatly suffered because of the disease.

When an audience made the connection that Isabela was the sister of the famous L.A. Dodgers' pitcher, Javier Torres, it helped bridge the divide between herself and those expressing rage at her and Drew. She learned how to communicate with those opposed to her vaccine and the climate crisis. And she, in turn, listened to their pain and even graciously suffered their implicit bias and prejudice about her Mexican heritage.

When they were in states where farming was the number one industry, Isabela finally encountered those who believed the climate crisis was real. Farmers had experienced firsthand the ravages of climate change on their soils, their crops, and their livestock. And the constant water shortages or flooding were inhibiting their ability to earn a living. Despite the fact that many were about to lose their farms, as they hadn't had a decent crop for three years, they were polite and gracious. Isabela observed how the farmers were able to convince their non-farming neighbors to take the vaccine, making those the most successful town hall meetings.

Overall, the anger and hatred she and Drew encountered demonstrated just how broken America was, and it was very sad. But every now and then, a member of the audience would come up to her afterward and tell her that she'd convinced them to take the vaccine. Isabela often cried because she knew she'd directly saved a life that day; it made the whole process worth it. Some even thanked her for her dedication in trying to save humanity from the looming mega-death event predicted once the overall global temperature hit 1.4°C.

Isabela was maturing from the direct exposure to her fellow Americans, as well as from her interviews with the media. And while she was thrilled to finally be leaving the U.S., heading to England and Europe on the next leg of the tour, she'd acquired a deeper understanding of her own country; it was a complete and total mess.

Drew stood in the aisle next to her seat on the plane and handed her a folder entitled: **Protocol for Meeting with The King of England.** Isabela looked down at the folder and up at Drew.

"So, we're on for afternoon tea, then?"

"We are, indeed. Helene just informed me." He sat down in a seat across from her. "Maggie is hard at work securing several outfit options for you, so there's no need to worry about what you'll be wearing. Are you excited?"

"All I can think about is how much Aelish detests any monarchy, especially when she has to curtsy. I guess I'm going to have to work on that. I hope I don't fall flat on my face."

Drew started laughing. "It's kind of unbelievable these customs still exist. You can practice curtsying in the aisle and use the seats on either side to help you balance. So, the U.S. leg of the tour is over. Did it alter your opinion of our country?"

"When my Abuela and Abuelo came here from Mexico, they were so unbelievably grateful. They had a shot at the American dream, and they had a wonderful experience here. Since that time, I don't know how it's all gone so wrong. This isn't their same adopted country."

"It's amazing to see the average citizen up close, like we did, from the red states to the blue states," said Drew. "I feel like we've been in an uncivil war of words for a very long time. I don't know what it will take for Americans to be united again in their beliefs and ideals."

Drew had a calming influence on the townspeople at the meetings. Isabela thought he was a great unifier and was exactly the type of politician America needed. But she also knew, once someone stepped their toe into politics, the process immediately began to change them. If Drew could skip all the campaigning and just be seated in the Oval Office of the White House tomorrow, she knew he'd make an amazing president. The man was adept at handling anything without getting ruffled. During the last ten days, his influence had calmed her more than once. And calming down this Latina was no easy feat.

The plane hit its cruising altitude and the flight attendants brought over their respective breakfasts. They both began eating in peaceful silence. Wiping her mouth with a napkin to remove remnants of her hot chocolate, Isabela said, "I'd like to tell you now about the events which precipitated my mental health crisis. Would that be all right?"

Drew smiled at her. "Of course. Thagar once told me your story was not his to tell, and I have respected that ever since."

"Did Thagar tell you that on the day I encountered your bodyguards standing outside his office at the Climate Refugee Intake Center?"

"That is the exact day."

Isabela deeply sighed and began fiddling with her hair. She put it up in a ponytail.

"I'm so sorry I ran away from you like that," she said. "I was such a mess back then, Drew. I hope in time you can forgive me for all of my abhorrent behavior toward you for nearly two years. Most especially, my avoidance of you."

Drew reached across and patted her arm. "Of course, Isabela."

"Well, I'd need to start at the beginning, when I was twelve years old and Aelish came to my bedroom. I opened my bedroom door after taking a shower and there was this tall, beautiful, lavender-faced being leaning against my bed in a white, sleeveless, billowy nightgown. Her lavender feet were bare and her long, red hair was pulled to one side in a fishtail braid."

"That really must have been a life-altering moment, Isabela. I think I would have . . . well actually, I'm not sure what I would have done."

"At first, I thought I might be dreaming. So, I pinched my arm and gave myself a nice bruise. But she was real, and it was terrifying and exciting all at the same time."

Drew smiled at her. "I was a lot older than twelve when

Aelish suddenly appeared on my helicopter. But I have to tell you, first, I thought I had died from being shot at the WHO, and then I thought I was hallucinating from the anesthesia. We were mid-flight!"

Isabela and Drew both started laughing. It was the first time they'd ever laughed together about the incident which had so alienated Isabela from Aelish.

Wiping laughter tears from her eyes, Isabela continued. "So, Aelish starts telling me about where she's from and that the Head Council of DAR had chosen me to, one, be the first Human made aware of their world, and two, assist them with regard to the climate crisis. I remember telling Aelish that, one, I was starting a new school tomorrow, and two, my mother was dying of cancer, so I was a little busy at the moment."

Drew burst out laughing. "What a comeback, Isabela. Did she laugh?"

"No, she didn't laugh. She just kept explaining why my assistance was essential. Keep in mind, at this point in my life, I knew I was smart but not *this* smart. So, I told her if she could go into my parents' bedroom and cure my mother, right then, I would work with her. She was totally prepared for that reaction, which was really annoying, as I was getting irritated by the entire encounter. Then, she explained how magical beings were unable to cure Human illness, and if they were able to, she would've stopped her own parents from dying of plague."

"Oh, my God. What did you say to that?"

"I felt like a brat. I told her I was very sorry and went over to the bed to comfort her because she'd started crying. I needed this now? A crying, magical being in my bedroom asking me to commit to helping the leaders of DAR because of my scientific aptitude? I had just met Hector Rios on a bike ride, that day, and hadn't even had a class with him yet. But Aelish sealed the deal when she spoke about my mother's upcoming clinical trials and how she could apply No Pain spells that would help my mother endure the treatments. And it was those No Pain spells that, in fact, allowed my mother to survive and go into remission, when so many others died."

"I know you would have done anything to help your mother. I felt the same way when my mother got sick with cancer. But you were only twelve, and I was already in graduate school. It's a horrible, helpless feeling. I would have done whatever Aelish asked of me if it could have helped my mother."

"Exactly! And that's what I did." Isabela paused and took a deep breath. "Shortly thereafter, I was walking home from school and this boy my brother befriended at Greatest Hits, an indoor baseball training center, stopped his expensive SUV and asked me if I wanted a ride home. His name was Glen. I often tagged along with Javi to the batting cages while he and Glen would practice, and I would do my homework. But the second I met him, I fell in love. He was gorgeous, sweet, funny, and very kind to Javi's kid sister. He looked exactly like Robert Redford in *The Way We Were*, only younger, of course."

"Redford was quite the looker in that movie. Even I fell in love with him."

Isabela started chuckling. "Well, what I didn't know at the time was that Glen was a covert operative born of parents who were also covert operatives from Yasteron."

"No! What are the chances that a covert operative from Yasteron would be living so close to you on Earth? Did his family intentionally choose to live so close to your family? Also, I never knew Yasterons liked or were talented at baseball."

"Well, Glen certainly was talented. He was a great hitter and he loved the sport. When I found out he was from Yasteron, I also originally thought Glen and his family had targeted me, but they hadn't. And this was confirmed in Thagar's interrogation of Glen. Our meeting literally happened by chance."

"Incredible," remarked Drew.

"It truly was. Glen was my first love and my first lover. I thought we'd get married one day. I kept him all to myself for a long time, but Aelish kept pestering me to meet him. Finally, I gave in. I discovered Glen was from Yasteron at the dinner party Aelish threw for us."

"At this point in time, did you know about the evil doings of Yasteron?"

"Oh, yes. As Aelish put it, 'They're the ones you never see coming.' And, oh boy, did I never see him coming."

Drew shook his head back and forth, listening to every word.

"Aelish had just learned a new evil magic spell. Simply by touching a Yasteron, she would feel a current go up her arm. This would only occur when encountering a being from the Kingdom of Yasteron. By the time she shook Glen's hand, upon entering her house—she knew.

"Not only did Aelish have to be the one to tell me, but she also only had minutes to get me and Kaleigh out of the house before Glen had a chance to kill us. She asked me to come into the kitchen to help her open a bottle of wine. I thought, seriously, can't she just use magic already? But I went into the kitchen and it was just the two of us. She told me Glen was from Yasteron. Then, she told me to take Kaleigh and go directly to my house and under no circumstances was I to go to my lab. My head was spinning, Drew. I didn't want to believe it was true, but I knew Aelish would never lie to me. I did as she instructed and dropped Kaleigh off at my parents' house, and then I made a terrible decision."

"You went to your lab, didn't you?"

"You know me too well. All of my research was in there. But more importantly, my mother's biological samples were at the lab.

My mother was already exhibiting the early symptoms of what I now know is LECCS. I almost made it out of the lab when I felt something strike me on the head. I fell unconscious and when I woke up, I was magically bound and gagged. However, the Yasteron soldiers sent to steal all of my research from the lab were too slow. It cost me plenty, but prior to them kidnapping me, I managed to secure everything in a magical vault Aelish had created for this exact type of scenario."

"How old were you when all of this happened?"

"Sixteen."

"So young! This is a fantastical story, Isabela. Definitely worthy of Nanny Marie. But I don't think even she could have come up with something this incredible. You poor thing."

"The spells the soldiers used on me were horrible, Drew. They created a terror that was unimaginable. I kept looking for the duct tape or zip ties preventing me from moving or speaking. But it was all invisible—they only used magic.

"Aelish rescued me, posing as one of the King's Guard from Yasteron. She knew it was the only position females could fulfill in Yasteron's military, and the King's Guard surpassed the soldiers in rank. She wore the uniform, had blond hair, porcelain skin, and pulled off one of the best cons I've ever seen. She told them to leave the prisoner, meaning me, with her and ordered them to go after the high value target, meaning her, at the Nashville football stadium.

"The soldiers disagreed with her assessment. So, she threatened them with death upon their return to the kingdom if they did not comply with her orders. Ultimately, they left me with her. But in that moment, I didn't know the female was Aelish. I thought she was going to be crueler to me than the soldiers. But then, Aelish spoke to me in her beautiful voice. At first, I thought it was a ruse. Sensing my doubt, she told me something only she would know about my childhood so I would trust her. She magically transported us to the Parthenon in Nashville, unbound me, and put all sorts of protective spells around us, in addition to both of our houses. I went back to her house, where she took care of me for a few days before taking me home."

Drew deeply exhaled and stared at her.

"Needless to say, that was the beginning of a long downward spiral for me. Thagar had taken Glen to an underwater bunker, in the N.W. Quadrant of DAR, to be interrogated. Yasteron bombed the underwater bunker to kill Thagar and his team, but their real target was their own spy. They didn't want Glen disclosing secrets, so they destroyed it all. When I learned Thagar was most likely killed along with Glen after the bombing, I lapsed back into the same condition Aelish found me in after I was captured by the soldiers.

"I didn't start to recover until Aelish brought back the bioweapon vials from DAR. Thagar had given the last remaining vial from the dinner party to a very brave soldier during the interrogation. Before the underwater bunker was bombed, the soldier had left the interrogation and was on his way to the Director of Experimentation in DAR, when he was struck by one of Yasteron's bombs aboveground. His name was Lancaster. He lost his life, but he saved the vial."

"Oh, my God," said Drew. "That's why you named it the Lancaster E. Coli Climate Syndrome? Why didn't you name the syndrome after yourself?"

"Because it was actually Yasteron that identified the bacterium I had been searching for in my research, and Lancaster was the DARling soldier who saved the vial, which led me to where I am now sitting."

"You have some level of integrity, Isabela. An eponym is a huge deal in medicine. Although, I personally never understood why a scientist would want an incurable disease or condition named after them."

"Because to find it, to identify it, is as important as the cure," said Isabela. Drew nodded at her. "But after all this, Glen had one more surprise for me."

"Now what?"

"When I was analyzing the genome of the bioweapon in the replicated vials Aelish returned with from DAR, I realized something. While Yasteron experimenters had created it, the foundation of LECCS came from *Human* E. coli. Where did Yasteron get a Human commensal strain of E. coli to create the bioweapon vials Glen had brought to the dinner party?"

"No way."

"Yes, way. Glen stole a commensal strain of E. coli right out of my body."

Drew's mouth was agape.

"He not only stole my biological matter and all of my research over the years, but he also broke my heart into a million little pieces. That kind of betrayal is very hard to get over because it involved the essence of who I am and my dedication to science, you know? He was my first love and he wasn't even Human. Nobody caught it—not Aelish, not Javi, who is so protective of me—no one!"

Drew shook his head in disbelief.

"And knowing Glen was brutally killed was of no comfort. It was even more upsetting because I still loved what I thought we had. You see, I never personally saw the evil side of him; Aelish only *told* me he was a Yasteron. I never experienced it firsthand. And that same night, the soldiers kidnapped and tortured me in the place I loved the most—my lab.

"I had begun to heal, but after my assassination attempt by Yasteron at the WHO, where they shot you as well, I began to unravel. I couldn't believe the person who'd helped me attain so many of my scientific dreams, had almost been killed by Yasteron. That was what was going through my mind as I assisted with your operation on your helicopter.

"I hadn't even had time to process that you'd almost died, when Aelish made the decision to tell you all about the magical world. I was still in shock from having my bodyguard at the WHO, lying dead on top of me. And the fear was still with me that it was Yasterons who'd carried me to the roof to your helicopter, not your security team. It all became jumbled in my mind, morphing into one epic traumatic event which pulled me farther and farther away from Aelish. And I never got to repair my relationship with her before she was kidnapped by King Cardissius. It's just endless for me with Yasteron. I can't even let myself think about what they are doing to her; I will go insane."

Drew unstrapped his seat belt and got up to sit in the seat next to Isabela. He embraced her and simply said, "I am so sorry." She cried on his shoulder for some time and finally pulled out of the embrace, wiping her eyes.

"I love Aelish so much, and I don't know if I will ever get to see her again to tell her that. Please, forgive me if I have hurt you, Drew. You did nothing wrong. Since the assassination attempt, coupled with what Glen did to me before that, I became so mentally ill."

"I understand," said Drew. "But you are incredibly strong, Isabela. Most Humans would never have been able to overcome all you've just described to me. Especially, at such a young age."

"I tried to kill myself, Drew. Without Thagar intervening, I would most likely be dead."

"Don't carry that event in your life like a shroud of shame you must wear at all times."

"But I am ashamed. How could I do that to my family and to Aelish?"

"You were sick. Just as sick as your mother was with cancer. No one takes mental illness seriously. It's always treated like the *other* illness, like something we should be ashamed of. When they told you about Aelish, you finally broke. You'd already experienced years and years of trauma. Your mind lost the ability to process all the mental anguish. You wanted the pain you experienced, as well as the pain you thought you'd caused, to stop. I totally understand. But you need to realize something: that one event does not diminish you or any of your accomplishments. It's just part of your life story. And I truly believe you will see Aelish again, Isabela. And I hope from this point forward, your life will only get better. Thagar was right—this really wasn't his story to tell. Thank you so much for sharing it with me."

Isabela nodded and wiped the last tears off her face with the back of her hands.

14

MASTER OBA

A ELISH SAT ON the settee in the living area. Storm had been taken outside by one of the dog handlers. For some reason, she was nervous to begin her education about Yasteron. Once the information was presented to her, there was no going backward, and she was worried for her son.

Katrina announced, "King Cardissius and the Master of Archives, Lady Aelish."

Aelish stood up and turned to see a being who was not even five feet tall. He was completely bald with the exception of a white moustache and goatee that came to a point at the base of his chin. He was quite rotund, dressed in a white, muslin kaftan, and had a smile as bright as his clear blue eyes. His porcelain skin was surprisingly smooth for his age, and he immediately made her feel at ease.

Katrina left the room and Cardissius said, "Lady Aelish, may I present Yasteron's Master of Archives, Oba."

Oba reached for her hand, lightly kissed it, and deeply bowed. "Lady Aelish, it is my honor to meet you."

Aelish did a small curtsy. "It is my pleasure to meet you, Master Oba."

Cardissius smiled at her saying, "I hope you enjoy your lessons. I will bid you both farewell, as I need to get to Legislative Hall."

Aelish nodded and watched the king leave the room. She was unsure what to do next, but Oba lead the way. "Why don't we sit together at the dining table?" he suggested. "I did not bring any archives with me, as I needed to first determine what it is you wish to learn about."

Oba sat down in one of the chairs. Aelish followed him to the table and sat down in the chair directly across from him. He smiled at her and said, "Before we begin, I would first like to apologize for my kingdom. I know everything that has transpired since your abduction into this prison."

"Thank you so kindly," said Aelish.

"Did you know, at one time, there were many DARling soldiers imprisoned in this suite of rooms? Of course, it did not look as it does now. In each room were fifty to one hundred soldiers. They had to take turns sleeping on the floor, as there was barely enough space for them to stand." He gestured with his arms toward the entire suite and said, "The irony is DARling soldiers built it all."

Aelish gasped. "Are you referring to the DARling soldiers imprisoned after the Proelium battle in 1360?"

"No. The soldiers imprisoned in these rooms were involved in another horrific battle that occurred sixty years before the Proelium, in 1300. Many are still being held captive today."

"Since 1300?" asked Aelish, shocked.

Oba nodded.

"Good God! I had no idea," said Aelish.

"Yasteron has a nasty habit of never freeing its prisoners of war. It's reprehensible."

She had been alone in the room with Oba for no more than ten minutes, and he had already provided her with so much intelligence. She could not understand why Cardissius would ever allow such a learned and forthright Master to meet with her.

Oba smiled. As if reading her mind, he asked, "You are wondering why the king would ever allow me to meet with you, correct?"

"Yes, that's exactly what I was thinking."

"Those who refuse to read are destined to a life of ignorance. And often, this ignorance becomes dangerous and deadly. The king is unaware of the knowledge I plan to share with you. It's been his choice for centuries not to read. And you having the knowledge which he has chosen to ignore, will give you an advantage over your captor, Lady Aelish."

"You may simply call me Aelish, Master Oba. There's really no need."

"There is a need, Lady Aelish. I know I am sitting with DAR's Living Legend."

Realizing Oba had information not even the king possessed, Aelish became worried Cardissius would halt her lessons on a whim. She decided to make the most of her first lesson and dove right in with her first question. "Could you please tell me why females are so oppressed in this kingdom and whether the community of lower-orders has always existed?"

Oba leaned back in his chair. "At first, you will not believe what I'm about to teach you. But in order to understand this kingdom, we must start at the beginning and go back in time, two million years."

"Two million years?" asked Aelish. "That's quite a long time ago."

"Not really, when it comes to studying the history and evolution of the beings in a particular dominion within the magical world. We live in a very ancient place, Lady Aelish."

"I understand."

"So, in the beginning, there were no Yasterons. There were only DARlings who evolved into Yasterons."

"What?" exclaimed Aelish. "Yasterons evolved from DARlings?"

"Indeed."

"That cannot be true. We are completely different in so many ways."

"All Yasterons originally came from the N.W. Quadrant of DAR. There was no war; the DARlings simply left and settled here, two million years ago. Since they all hailed from the N.W. Quadrant, it explains why Yasterons have porcelain skin, blond hair, and blue eyes. To this day, those are the predominant characteristics of a DARling within the N.W. Quadrant."

Aelish suddenly remembered something Thagar had told her after his return from the N.W. Quadrant, right before they were to attend her first Gala for DAR in 1665.

'It truly is amazing how their appearance is the most similar to us out of all the magical realms. They could easily pass for DARlings, with the exception of them all having pale, beige skin and yellow hair. Their spies have infiltrated and escaped the N.W. Quadrant so many times, we've lost count. They take our newest spells with them and can execute the stolen spells with the same precision. They care nothing about our tenets and principles of peace nor our devotion to protect Humanity. Yet they assist a barbaric kingdom like Komprathia. I believe they do it just to play with us.'

Aelish began thinking about all the DARlings she'd known from the N.W. Quadrant. Most of them had porcelain skin, blond hair, and blue eyes. They were also some of the most intelligent beings in DAR, functioning as experimenters, artists, musicians, and medici.

Oba remained quiet while flashes of recognition changed her facial expression.

Aelish looked up from the table and asked, "But if this were true, why weren't we taught this at the Institutum de Magicae? How could the Head Council not be aware of this? More importantly, how do the Keepers in the Breanon not have this information? They are some of the most devoted and brilliant scholars of history within the magical world."

"Over the millenniums, Keepers who tried to maintain records about this part of DAR's history were killed, and the records were either stolen or destroyed. The DARlings who'd left for Yasteron returned to murder the Keepers. They wanted no record of their provenance being of DAR. They wanted to start anew and erase all history of their origin."

Aelish shook her head. "But why did these DARlings wish to leave the N.W. Quadrant? Why did they want to break off from DAR and create another dominion of their own?"

"Before I answer the why, let me finish the how," replied Oba. "How could there be no record of such a monumental event?"

Aelish began to stutter. "It . . . it . . . it seems impossible."

He continued, "As the millenniums passed, beings in the magical world who tried to keep a written record of the diaspora of DARlings leaving the N.W. Quadrant, to settle the land now known as Yasteron, eventually died. In DAR, this piece of history became a myth or a conspiracy theory. DARlettes at the Institute are taught if they ever hear about this, don't believe it; it's a fabrication and not true.

"You see, Lady Aelish, if words are not written down and read from one generation to the next, ignorance spreads like a wildfire and burns knowledge into ashes. The written word is more powerful than any weapon or evil magic spell ever created because it is the truth, and the truth is divine.

"When actual history can be turned into a lie or a conspiracy, the truth is lost forever. And whoever is in power at the time, can claim ownership of what was once the truth. Falsifying the truth is permitted by those being ruled, as those being ruled *choose* to remain ignorant. To be literate, to be able to read, especially about history, is dangerous to those in power. Always beware the ignorant, Lady Aelish."

"Do any records of this still exist?" asked Aelish.

"I see you require physical evidence to prove what I'm teaching you is the truth."

Aelish vigorously nodded her head.

"A sign of true intelligence and exactly why history must remain preserved intact. I have the last remaining record in existence. If you insist, I will bring it to you at our next lesson. It's so old, it is kept in a special vault under numerous protective spells to ensure its safety."

"I need to see it, Master Oba. I don't want to endanger the record, but I must see it with my own eyes."

"I assumed as much, Lady Aelish."

"Can we please return to the subject of why these DARlings left to settle Yasteron?" asked Aelish, who'd become quite agitated.

"Of course, Lady Aelish." Oba deeply sighed and continued. "In modern day, DAR has accepted and embraced the fact that a female's magical capabilities far exceed their male counterparts. Millions of years ago, male DARlings were painfully aware that the magical abilities of the females were far superior to their own. Armed with this level of magic, they predicted the females would ultimately rise up and wish to rule over DAR, which is exactly what happened. But the male DARlings of yesteryear refused to accept it.

"In order to prevent them from ever being ruled by females, they left DAR to create a new dominion. This was when the oppression of DARling females began in Yasteron. Once the males had settled into their new dominion, they suppressed the magical abilities of the females. They kept them magically uneducated, repressed, and subservient. The females were censored, muted, and restricted from educational attainments afforded only to males. It explains why the Yasteron female of today seems magically stilted and stunted; they are."

Aelish shook her head in disbelief. "Did the lower-orders also evolve from DARlings?"

"The lower-order caste system was created by the males to allow the females to rule over a specific segment of the population in this new dominion. The caste system's intent was to give the females the illusion that their station in life, whilst not as high as the males, was infinitely higher than the lower-orders. DARlings in the N.W. Quadrant who had intermarried with beings from other magical realms, decided to accompany those who were departing. They were completely unaware that the purebred DARling males planned to turn them nearly into slaves.

"The males corrupted the exquisite freedom of a DARling's ability to mate with another magical species. They used the diluted purity of the mixed-magical being against them. To me, the lower-order caste system represents one of the greatest crimes perpetrated by one magical being against another. Creating the caste system of the lower-orders was a heinous act and should have been punishable by banishment. But at the time, there was no Alliance of Magical Dominions. Who was going to stop the tyrannical reign over the lower-orders when the males had manipulated the females to also be complicit in this crime?

"In order to continue the lower-order caste system, the males became obsessed with keeping their Yasteron lineage pure. They wanted to clearly delineate who was a Yasteron and who was a lower-order by the attributes of porcelain skin, blond hair, and blue eyes."

"But why, then, would Cardissius ever choose to mate with an Earth born DARling, like me?" asked Aelish. "That makes no sense at all."

"The idea of creating a lineage of preeminent magical beings did not originate with King Cardissius. It began a long time ago. However, he is the first king who has ever dared to tinker with the purity of Yasteron. He is rapacious and has a greater aspiration. The king is well aware the female DARling has had centuries to evolve their magical exceptionalism. And the female *Earth born* DARling's capabilities exceed even those of the females born in DAR.

"He has seen and suffered firsthand from your own exceptionalism. The female DARling was born to lead, as they are smarter, kinder, and possess the ability of critical thinking. Males simply react, whereas the females utilize an intellectually disciplined process of skillfully conceptualizing, analyzing, and evaluating information as a guide to their beliefs or actions."

Aelish sat and stared at Oba with her head resting on the back of her hands.

"Let me ask you something, Lady Aelish. Do you often find yourself in great turmoil over whether or not to war with Yasteron?"

"Ahh . . . how could you possibly know that, Master Oba?"

"Because a DARling's desire to war is part of their essence. Do you think the males in DAR, two million years ago, were peaceful? They were not. DAR was as horrible as Yasteron is today, if not worse. And the males incited war aplenty with other realms. Before the females came to power in DAR, the endless wars between DAR and Yasteron derived from the origins of the male DARling. And it takes two to make a war, correct?"

"I always thought my desire to war came from my Human traits," said Aelish.

"No, it is from your DARling provenance. The Earth born

feel it more profoundly, as it is coupled with the unfortunate trait of warring from their Human ancestry. But the female DARling possesses the ability to reason with this innate desire and can overcome it. That is how, over the last five hundred years, the female leaders in DAR were able to institute an Oath of Peace for all citizens and maintain it, in the face of one of the most aggressive kings in the history of Yasteron. War is never the answer, with only one exception: propelling a civilization to depose a tyrannical ruler is considered an ethical use of war. And that's exactly what you did in Komprathia. And remember, Lady Aelish, I also evolved from DARlings."

That she could easily believe. Aelish was in awe of the knowledge emanating from Oba. How she wished she'd known him during the most difficult times in her life. His study of history kept him completely honest and truthful. And while he appeared like a soothsayer or a prophet, he was simply educated and guided by the truth.

Aelish needed guidance on how to manipulate the king. "You are aware the king abducted me on a peace mission and has forced me to procreate a male heir with him for his succession, correct?"

Oba nodded and remained quiet.

"As of late," she said, "I've felt as though I'm seeing a kinder side to the king. He's exhibiting characteristics that appear contradictory to how he's always presented or conducted himself within the magical world."

"And you're wondering if you can effect change in him as his new wife and queen and by bestowing him with a male heir. I'm fairly certain you are trying to determine if you could convince the king into freeing the lower-orders and make Yasteron a fairer kingdom, yes?"

"Yes, exactly," said Aelish. "I'm growing more and more confused about his recent tenderness toward me, and I'm worried for my son who will, one day, be king. I have met the King Mother and I believe I've found the reason as to why he became the way he is. She is unbelievably cruel and physically assaulted me the first time I met her. Am I misguided in my thinking?"

"You are."

Aelish exhaled loudly in frustration.

"But just because you are misguided doesn't mean you are defeated, Lady Aelish."

"As of late, his kindness and tenderness seemed genuine," said Aelish.

Oba remained quiet.

"Are you saying, Master Oba, that he is incapable of change?"

"I am."

"So, I will be unable to effect any change in my new roles here?"

"I did not say that."

Aelish stared at him confused.

Oba continued, "I said, despite what you think you're seeing from the king, he is incapable of change. And blaming his mother, who treats the lower-orders exactly as the original DARling males intended, is also not an accurate assessment. The king is the way he is from centuries of male evolution in this patriarchal kingdom. You'll need further information to understand my assessment of the king."

"I feel like there is no hope, Master Oba," said Aelish.

"You are a captive here, Lady Aelish. But you have more power than any other captive in the history of Yasteron. You cannot fall maudlin to your feelings of despair. You must work around them to conquer not only your feelings but also the schemes of this treacherous king."

"I have no magical abilities in this prison, Master Oba. I am powerless to conquer anything."

"No, Lady Aelish, that is not true."

"But if I cannot effect change within King Cardissius, I will be unable to stop the proxy wars that have been going on between DAR and Yasteron since the females came to power."

"DAR and Yasteron are like two members of a family who simply can't get along. They have been at war with each other, in actuality or philosophically, since Yasteron's inception. The reason they detest one another, with such vitriol, is because they share the same origin, like siblings. The fundamental aspects of their nature are the same. Yasterons have become dark DARlings, but DAR and Yasteron are two sides of the same coin."

"That is horrible! I don't want to share traits with Yasterons!"

"But you do, because DAR is where Yasterons came from. And this kingdom is exactly what DAR would have become, if not for the prodigious wisdom, abilities, and guidance of the females. The female DARling saved DAR from a ruthless patriarchy, and all of their remarkable magical abilities keep it in check. I imagine there is great strife in DAR, at the present time, over whether or not to directly war with Yasteron because of your abduction."

"You are most likely correct, but I have no knowledge of anything happening in DAR."

"Trust me," said Master Oba, "there is great division, as this is what Yasteron does best. They sow discord and chaos to keep themselves in power. They are cunning and they are merciless. After two million years, the DARlings who evolved into Yasterons are despicable.

"With regard to King Cardissius' new tenderness toward you, keep in mind how powerful a female DARling you are. For the first time in his life, the king is allowing himself to be influenced by an evolved female DARling. He's susceptible to you because his DARling origins still live inside of him. Your influence over the king and his reaction to it are genuine. However, he is incapable of lasting change. He's in a moment, but soon the years of Yasteron's evolution will kick in. His twisted mind will take your son and your kindness, and he will use them to make his kingdom even more powerful. Do not be fooled by this king, Lady Aelish. I imagine he's also dangling the promise of signing the Peace Accord in front of you."

"He has said repeatedly that once I bestow a male heir, he will honor the accord."

"He is lying!"

That was the first time Oba had raised his voice.

"He is using the heir to further his long-term vision for his reign and his kingdom. He needs the heir's magic, which will come from you, to begin his lineage of preeminent magical beings. Ultimately, the king wants to gain control of the DARling females' magical capabilities, thereby controlling DAR, so he can rule over this one and only matriarchal dominion within our world. He's going to use his son's abilities, inherited from you, to do so. He wants the females' magic, but he refuses to cede any of his own power to attain it. His ultimate goal is to rule over the entire magical world. The kindness and tenderness you see emerging from him are nothing more than a means to an end. He is seeking magical domination like any other megalomaniac."

Aelish sighed and said, "Whilst I was unaware the Peace Accord was being used as a vehicle by which to capture me, I had always considered Cardissius a megalomaniac, who wanted to rule over the entire magical world. After I mastered a highly destructive evil magic spell created by a male DARling, I could have destroyed this entire kingdom. I grappled with using it for a long time. Should I have used it? I feel like I should have, and because I didn't, the result will be endless war in the magical world until we self-annihilate."

"Why didn't you use the evil magic spell, Lady Aelish?"

"Because there are innocents who live here! They have no power to overthrow this despot. And if we directly war with Yasteron, they will all be killed. And if the lower-orders were brought to Yasteron in the manner you've described, their entire existence as mixed-magical beings has been used against them for generations. And if DAR and Yasteron directly war with one another, the lower-orders will die as collateral damage. Or as you said earlier, they will die because two members of a family simply can't get along."

Aelish stood up from the table feeling utterly defeated. Oba remained quiet as he watched her ruminate over all the information he had taught her. After a few minutes, she sat down again.

Aelish asked, "Are you certain I am unable to influence the king? His mother is an abomination to motherhood. I've heard everything you've said about our mutual heritage and how the male DARling evolved into a Yasteron over the last two million years. But I can't help but feel his mother is responsible for what he became. Why am I wrong?"

Oba nodded. "Because you're ignoring centuries of evolution. You may feel small victories with the king, Lady Aelish, but you will lose in the end. You must trust me on this. I know all about his mother's cruelty. But I'm certain the king has never told you about his aunt."

"His aunt? No, he has never mentioned an aunt."

"Of course, he hasn't," said Oba. "His aunt was the sister of his father, King Nevuna. Her real name was Nell, but everyone called her by her middle name of Charlotte. Lady Charlotte doted on the king when he was a child, showering him with both love and physical affection. No one knows what happened to Lady Charlotte. One day, she was simply gone. But on the same day she disappeared, over one hundred DARling soldiers, from the room we are sitting in, also disappeared. No one has ever heard from her or the soldiers again. I believe she escaped this kingdom and went to Hentoria, but there's not one shred of proof to support what I'm saying."

"Oh, my God, Hentoria!" exclaimed Aelish. "I've never learned of any magical being who's been able to enter this dominion. They are killed before they ever reach the top of their steep mountains." Aelish paused for a moment. "So, you're saying the king *did* experience physical affection as a child? He told me the only affection he ever received as a child was when his mother struck him." Aelish began rubbing her jaw, remembering the King Mother's blow.

Oba scoffed, "He's an adept liar. Lady Charlotte spent years doting on her nephew. They were inseparable. She loved him more than any child could be loved. Yes, it's true, the love he experienced did not come from his mother. But sometimes, a stand-in mother is even better. The King Mother had very little to do with his upbringing, but once Lady Charlotte disappeared from his life, it was like a light went out in young Cardissius' eyes. And despite all of Lady Charlotte's love, he became who he really is, regardless."

"But maybe if she had stayed, he would have ended up kinder," said Aelish.

Oba knowingly smiled at her. "Lady Charlotte and I were friends. One day, she told me a story which I believe was, in part, why she disappeared. When King Cardissius was about ten years old, she caught him torturing a small animal. I believe it was a kitten. He wasn't using magic, just his bare hands. She gingerly approached him and asked him why he was hurting the animal. He said, 'Because it's fun. I like when it screams and then it stops, as only I can make it stop.' Lady Charlotte was terrified he would become exactly like her brother, Nevuna. She would not only have to live under the reign of her brother but also under the reign of his son. I believe the episode with young Cardissius was a turning point for her.

"When Lady Charlotte told me the story about King Cardissius torturing the animal, she disclosed that she'd caught her brother doing the exact same thing when he was the exact same age. She told me she could no longer live under either of their rule and would rather die. A week after her disappearance, King Nevuna produced a body and said it was his sister. But the corpse was severely mangled and had been burned. There was no way to positively identify that it was Lady Charlotte. To this day, I do not believe the corpse was her.

"There was a state funeral held in her honor. But afterward, she was never discussed again, except by the lower-orders who adored her. You remind me of her, Lady Aelish. She was emblematic of the outstanding kindness and empathy that females from DAR exhibit. Lady Charlotte had endless hope, similar to what I see in you. But ultimately, she knew her dreams for the kingdom could never become a reality with her brother as king and her nephew to succeed him. So, I believe she escaped. And in a last act of altruism, she took one hundred DARling soldiers held captive from the battle in 1300 with her. If what I just said were ever spoken aloud by anyone in this kingdom, it would result in a hanging in Shamalaya Square."

"So, I truly am going to bear the child of a psychopath." Aelish began crying.

"Do not cry, Lady Aelish," said Oba. "You are the child's mother. You have no idea if he will end up like his father or his grandfather before him. I see a crucifix around your neck."

She instinctively grabbed the crucifix Lieutenant Commander Stavros had carved for her.

Oba said, "My full name is Obadiah, which means servant of God." He reached inside his white muslin kaftan and pulled out his own crucifix. "Do you think I could have survived in this kingdom, for all these years, without my faith?"

"Ohh . . . Master Oba, thank you." She held her crucifix and he held his.

"You are never alone when you have your faith—never."

Aelish nodded. "The male DARling who made me this crucifix, with his own hands, once told me the exact same thing."

"You have learned life-altering lessons today, Lady Aelish. I will return next week for your next lesson, and I will bring the record I spoke of earlier, which clearly states that DARlings created Yasteron. If you require me to bring anything else, send word through your lower-order-in-waiting. Do not underestimate Katrina; she can be of great value to you."

Oba stood up. He came around the table to kiss Aelish's hand, bowing in front of her. Aelish stood up and responded with a small curtsy. "Until we meet again, Master Oba. Thank you so kindly for speaking the truth. I am so honored to have met you."

"As am I, Lady Aelish, as am I."

15

A Long-Lost Relative

AMELIA LANDED HARD on the snow-packed mountain peak. She looked across at the other mountain peak she landed on the first time she entered Hentoria. Nestled between the two peaks was a valley, which contained a small village. As she gazed down into the valley, she saw lights emanating from the dwellings below. Her spell had worked twice now. She'd been able to directly transport from the S.E. Quadrant to where she now stood.

Amelia wrapped her cloak tightly around her body and lifted up the hood. It was freezing up here. She touched the invisible face shield she wore to protect her eyes, nose, and mouth from their poisonous venom. The venom was not magical. It was simply part of their makeup, similar to a Komprathian whose upper half was king cobra. And it was just as deadly.

She began walking down the mountain toward the high walls that encapsulated the village below. Her invisible shield also protected her face from the severe cold. As her boots crunched through the snow and ice, she was on alert for any sudden movements within the forest.

After about fifteen minutes, she saw them coming toward her. Some were standing and others were on all fours. Those standing were enormous; they stood seven to nine feet tall. Even those on all fours were about four feet high and their speed was incredible in this position.

Their entire body was covered by the armor of their exoskeleton, just like the external skeletons seen on grasshoppers, cockroaches, and crustaceans, like crabs and lobsters. On Earth, they would be part of the phylum of Arthropoda invertebrates known as arthropods, which included insects and spiders. Their bodies were segmented with an external skeleton and jointed limbs. The Hentorians were amazing climbers of the steep mountain ranges found in Hentoria. They often walked on all fours, using their arms and legs to climb. Their feet resembled the structure of squirrels and could grasp almost anything. Their ability to crawl with amazing alacrity and speed worked as a defense mechanism, as they could crawl surreptitiously in the brush or up the steep side of a mountain.

Their color was brown like the rich soil of this land, but when the mountains were covered in snow, their entire exoskeleton changed to white. Again, a brilliant defense capability to protect them from invaders. No magical being had ever made it up the steep mountains; they were killed long before they reached the top. Those who tried to explore Hentoria had never made it back, so no one knew what magical creatures lived within this dominion. Eventually, magical beings just stopped exploring here.

The Hentorians had large almond-shaped eyes, no visible nose, and they consumed food similar to the way an anteater does. They had a toothless, tube-shaped mouth, which was barely visible, and inside their mouths was an elongated tongue that actually rolled up at the back of their cranium and attached to their sternum. They killed by shooting their venom from their elongated tongues into the eyes, nose, or mouth of their enemies; their height giving them an excellent advantage for aiming their venom. Their tongue ejected and retracted so quickly, it was impossible to see whether they had, in fact, emitted their venom until their victim was blinded and paralyzed, dying within seconds.

The pattern of their exoskeletal chest indicated whether they were male, female, or both. Their eye color changed with age. When they were young, their eyes were jet-black. But as they aged, their eyes became translucent.

Amelia knew they were going to capture her. In fact, she was counting on it. As they approached from a distance, she continued walking as if she were unaware of their presence. This provided them with the illusion that they were in control and she was not a threat. When they were ten feet away, she pretended to see them for the first time. Being only twelve Earth years worked to her advantage. To them, she was a small being who could cause no harm.

Amelia froze where she stood and said in English, "I'm so lost. Please don't hurt me. I wandered away from the village below and got lost in the snowstorm. I'm just trying to find my way back to the village."

The Hentorians were now no more than five feet away from her. Amelia was unafraid as she knew any one of the five spells she'd created would kill them all. But she hoped it wouldn't come to that, as she wanted to engage with these mythical creatures.

They surrounded her in a circular formation. Up close, they were magnificent. Amelia dropped to her knees and put her face in her hands, pretending to cry. She continued acting terrified until the tallest female spoke to her in accented English.

"Do not be afraid. Climb onto my back and we will take you to the village."

Amelia did as she was told and climbed onto the hard shell of the female's exoskeleton, wrapping her arms around the creature's rigid neck. Finally, she was going to penetrate the walls of the village which had repelled all of her spells.

‡‡‡‡

Kaleigh had been dropped off at school, Drummond had already gone to bed, and Thagar was rushing to make a 9:30 meeting at the Climate Refugee Intake Center when the doorbell rang. Realizing he was never going to be on time for the meeting, he texted Marisol to start without him and went to open the door.

Thagar looked at the face of the male standing before him and felt like he was going insane. It was like looking in a mirror, four hundred years into the future. Thagar was staring at his own future face. This was what he would look like, when he was in his early fifties, in Earth years. The male had a head of long, salt-and-pepper curls, the same golden eyes, the same bronzed skin, and he was the same height and build. He wore a smile just like his own.

"Hello, Nephew."

Thagar continued to stare and said nothing.

"You can believe your own eyes, Thagar. It is me, your Uncle Thurrock, younger brother to your mother, Ka."

Thagar shook his head in disbelief and kept opening and closing his eyes.

"I think it's time you invite me inside. I was told to tell you Amelia sent me."

Upon hearing Amelia's name, Thagar shook his head and ran his hands through his curls.

"You've grown up to be a fine male DARling, Thagar. I'm sorry I've missed your entire life, but I hope I can make that up to you now."

Thagar stood to the side and widely opened the door. "Please, come inside."

Uncle Thurrock stepped inside the hallway. Thagar closed the door and began walking toward the living room. When they were both seated across from each other, on their respective couches, Thagar realized he hadn't even offered his uncle anything to drink. He stood back up and said, "Forgive me. I'm in a bit of shock. I haven't even offered you a refreshment."

"If you have, a whiskey would be wonderful."

Thagar went over to the home bar and poured two glasses of whiskey. For the most part, he continued to abstain from any spirits, but he knew what was coming was going to be very difficult. He could not believe his uncle, killed in a fierce battle in 1300, was sitting in his living room. All he could think about was how much his mother had adored her younger brother. She mourned him until her own death in 1360, in the Proelium battle, when he was ten Earth years.

He walked back over to the couches and handed his uncle the glass. Uncle Thurrock said, "Cheers," and clinked his glass against Thagar's.

"Cheers," echoed Thagar, who sat down again.

The two males drank in silence for a few moments, and Thagar was able to compose himself. "So, you're alive. I assume you will tell me how that came to be? And I assume you had a reason for not telling your sister who died in the Proelium in 1360?"

"I know you've been without her for nearly your entire life. I'm so sorry for your loss and for the fact that I never saw her again before she was killed. I truly am, Thagar."

Thagar could feel his temper rising. To this day, he missed his mother and was furious his uncle had allowed her to think he was dead until the end of her life. "So, tell me."

"I was captured in the battle of 1300 and was brought to Yasteron where I was imprisoned. They never informed DAR that we were taken. I don't understand why DAR never identified us as missing in action. The magical identification implants inserted into our necks were still sending signals, indicating we were alive, until Yasteron removed them.

"As you know, there are many DARling soldiers and Komprathian drone rats still being held captive. But the soldiers imprisoned with me were like a test run for how Yasteron planned to use all their prisoners of war. We were made to work as slaves, we were experimented on, and we suffered unbelievable indignities from our accommodations. Whilst I was not killed in the battle of 1300, I might as well have been. My life was over and there was no way to get word to your mother."

As a former Director of the POD, Thagar felt the same guilty feelings he experienced during his interrogation of Glen in the underwater bunker. Why had DAR missed the fact that Yasteron had stolen their soldiers? Why had he not known that Komprathian drone rats were also imprisoned? He felt the same sense of failure he'd disclosed to Aelish in his darkest hours.

Obviously, Yasteron had violated every rule of engagement when it came to prisoners of war. But why had DAR ever trusted them to honor a bilateral agreement in the first place? He was staring at one of the earliest soldiers taken prisoner, who was treated horrifically, and he was a member of his own family. His anger at his uncle fell away completely, replaced by despair.

"Yasteron always seems to outwit us, Nephew. I know you were Director of the POD. Do not waste your time wondering how DAR missed it all. I was simply questioning why because the suffering was immeasurable."

Thagar felt like it just never seemed to end with Yasteron. They had personally caused him so much mental and physical anguish; he didn't know how much more he could take. Seeing his uncle alive should have been a joyous occasion, but instead, he felt only sadness.

Interrupting his sorrowful contemplations, Uncle Thurrock said, "I know where Aelish is, Thagar. I know where she's being held."

Thagar exhaled loudly, his expression changing from sorrow to shock.

Uncle Thurrock smiled and said, "I'm here to help you rescue her."

Thagar put his head in his hands and began weeping.

Uncle Thurrock got up from where he was sitting and sat down next to Thagar, embracing him. "We will bring her home, but it will not be easy."

After several minutes, Thagar composed himself and stared at his uncle. "How could you possibly know where she is?"

"Because I was one of the DARling soldiers who built the prison where she's being held captive. Yasteron wanted a prison built where only the king's magic would work. We worked on it for decades, and I'm sure after our escape, they continued to work on it. It was extraordinarily difficult to construct a facility that accommodated only the king's magic. Magic keeps evolving, which was clearly evident by the talents of young Amelia."

"Wait! Aelish is unable to use her magic in this prison?" Thagar stood up and began furiously pacing. "Aelish is terrified of getting Magical Interruption Syndrome. She was imprisoned once before without the use of her magic and has suffered with the fear of losing her magic ever since. I can't even let myself think about how she is coping with this."

"I imagine, Thagar," said Uncle Thurrock, "this is but one of many things she is coping with. I'm certain she's had to contend with very difficult circumstances, both mentally and physically. You must prepare yourself for whatever condition we find her in. You must be strong for her."

Thagar sat back down on the couch next to his uncle and put his head in his hands. He realized, as desperate as he was to rescue Aelish, he was completely unprepared for what condition he might find her in. After several minutes he asked, "How did you ever escape?"

"We built tunnels."

At the mere mention of the word "tunnels," Thagar mentally went back in time to the 1500s and 1600s. He and so many others had tried to dismantle the tunnel spells used to create the secret tunnels for the drone rats of Komprathia, so they could bypass the Portal and spread the plague on Earth.

So much of what had happened to him and Aelish was because the POD could never figure out how to deconstruct the tunnel spells created by Yasteron. "I'm curious, did you use spells to create the tunnels, or did you and the other prisoners manually construct them?"

"Oh, no manual labor was involved," said Uncle Thurrock. "We used complicated spells piled one on top of the other, like a layer cake. The tunnels were kept magically secret, as this was how we planned to escape. It would take centuries to understand and be able to replicate the spells we used to devise the tunnel system."

"Like about three or four hundred years, give or take?" asked Thagar.

"Why are you so interested in the tunnel spells, Thagar?"

"Because Yasteron built secret tunnels that ran along the same route as the Portal to Earth, during the reign of King Gidius of Komprathia. Yasteron allied themselves with this kingdom and created tunnels for their Komprathian drone rats, which King Gidius sent to Earth to spread the plague with abandon. Biologically, the drone rats and the rats on Earth are mirror images of one another.

"So, during a naturally occurring outbreak of plague on Earth, Gidius sent hundreds of drone rats through the tunnels on a daily basis to create pandemic conditions. He detested Humans and wanted to kill as many as possible through the weapon of the plague. The Humans didn't stand a chance. Aelish lost both her parents to plague, in 1563, during an outbreak in London, England. It changed the course of her life and, subsequently, mine as well."

"He weaponized his own beings?" asked Uncle Thurrock.

Thagar nodded.

Uncle Thurrock said, "I'm certain Yasteron ultimately decoded our spells in order to build the tunnels for the drone rats. But to this day, they've never broken through the final spell."

"Where do the tunnels lead?" asked Thagar.

"They lead into the dominion of Hentoria, and only the Hentorians can disable the final spell of the tunnel system. When the tunnels end, there is an illusory wall of rock and soil, constructed of more magical spells, which has never been breached. Using extremely complicated spells, the Hentorians sealed the wall, which leads to a passageway through the mountain range. I'm sure once Yasteron deconstructed the tunnel spells, stealing the magical technology we created, they experienced severe frustration. They've never been able to penetrate the illusory wall of rock and soil, leading into Hentoria."

"That's where you've been all this time? Why didn't you come home?" asked Thagar.

"The conditions of our sanctuary in Hentoria were actually negotiated by King Nevuna's sister, Lady Charlotte. She was fascinated by what we were constructing, and it was later on that I learned why. She, too, wished to escape the reign of her brother and the future reign of his son, Cardissius. So, as we simultaneously built the prison and the tunnels, she would venture into the unknown and dangerous dominion of Hentoria. She was desperate to escape. Sometimes, I think she was even more desperate than we were. Being of royal blood, no one ever questioned her watching us for hours on end. And it was during this time that she and I fell in love.

"The imprisoned DARling soldiers were assisted by mixed-magical beings who were treated horrifically by the nobles in Yasteron. I forget the term they used to refer to them. But they had magical attributes which were very helpful in constructing a prison facility that would allow only the king's magic to work inside of it. And they were enormously helpful in creating the secret tunnels to Hentoria. They wanted out just as much as we did. Their lives weren't even worth living. That's how badly they were treated.

"It was the mixed-magical beings who convinced us to build an escape route right under the prison facility. They believed hiding it in plain sight would guard its secrecy. There is a trap door in one of the larger areas of the prison, which I'm sure Aelish has walked over many times. The trap door leads to the secret tunnels and ultimately to the passageway, inside a rugged mountain range in Hentoria. But only the Hentorians can unlock the spells of the illusory wall at the end of the tunnel system. It must be magically decoded from the Hentorian side.

"One of the mixed-magical beings who helped us was a shapeshifter. She accompanied Lady Charlotte on her trips to Hentoria, posing as a Hentorian so they wouldn't feel threatened. Eventually, Lady Charlotte befriended a group of female Hentorians and learned all about their customs and even learned their language. They grew very fond of her. Lady Charlotte is why Hentoria ultimately gave us asylum. But they had two stipulations once we were ensconced there—we could never leave, and secondly, if Yasteron were ever responsible for creating a war amongst all the realms in the magical world, we would be expelled.

"Hentoria wants nothing to do with the magical world; they are peaceful beings who wish to live in seclusion. But they are also acutely aware of the barbaric rule of King Nevuna and his son, Cardissius, who succeeded him. They learned of the barbarous reign of the father and then of the son, from several nobles who also escaped with Lady Charlotte, as well as from the mixed-magical beings who helped us construct everything.

"We live in a small community, protected by some of the most powerful spells in the magical world. Even Amelia could not penetrate the spells inside the walls which surround our village. The wall of spells was created by the Hentorians for our protection. And despite Yasteron's discovery centuries later of the tunnel system we created, they never did figure out how we all escaped since the tunnel system dead-ends at the illusory wall. And to their knowledge, no magical being has ever set foot inside the dominion of Hentoria."

Listening to his uncle, Thagar felt his failure to deconstruct Yasteron's tunnel spells finally lift from his chest. DARlings had created the spells—not Yasterons! While they'd tormented him for what felt like an eternity, knowing DARlings had created them gave him a renewed sense of confidence and hope.

"So, where did you find a DARlette with the capabilities of Amelia?" asked Uncle Thurrock.

Thagar nodded in agreement. "I know, she has amazing abilities."

"She is so young!" exclaimed Uncle Thurrock. "I know she is the daughter of Aelish's Oraculi, Antonia. She is truly gifted, Thagar."

Thagar said, "As a former commander and Director of the POD, I learned a long time ago that finding those capable of executing the most impossible missions is, in itself, a gift. Whilst I was personally incapable of discovering where Aelish was being held, I knew if anyone could obtain this information, it would be Amelia.

"Her father, Roger, was an Earth born DARling and was exceptional at spy craft and evil magic spells. She's inherited these abilities from her father. And her mother was responsible for transforming DAR from a patriarchal commonwealth to a matriarchal commonwealth. Her mother, Antonia, is also extraordinary. So, when you combine the talents of both her parents, Amelia hit the jackpot of inherited magical capabilities."

Thagar sat in wonderment of Amelia. How had she figured out that DARling soldiers had escaped to Hentoria hundreds of years ago? How did she remain fearless in the face of so many unknowns, entering a dominion where no magical being had ever returned from alive? Her bravery rivaled that of Aelish. And if they were successful in freeing Aelish, Thagar had a sense a new Living Legend was on the rise.

Uncle Thurrock said, "Amelia told both me and my mate, Lady Charlotte, all about Aelish. Of course, I call her Charlotte when we are alone, but I still love to use her noble title." Thagar smiled at how similar he and his uncle were. Thagar also adored calling Aelish, Lady Aelish, if only just to teasingly irritate her. "Charlotte and I cannot wait to meet the Living Legend of DAR."

"I can't believe you mated with King Nevuna's sister," said

Thagar, shaking his head.

"I can't wait for you to meet your aunt who is, indeed, Yasteron royalty."

Thagar could not even fathom having a member of Yasteron's royal family in his own. "So, theoretically, once we rescue Aelish, we would escape to Hentoria?"

"Correct," replied Uncle Thurrock. "Since Aelish's abduction, Komprathian bombs have come precariously close to Hentoria. Amelia explained to the Hentorians as well as to our community that Komprathia feels a loyalty to Aelish because she freed their kingdom from tyranny. Amelia also explained that Yasteron has been holding Komprathian drone rats captive for hundreds of years, experimenting on them to create bioweapons to use against Humanity on Earth.

"Therefore, whilst the Hentorians understand why Komprathia is tactically dropping bombs on Yasteron's military installations, they do fear a war involving all the realms within the magical world is on the horizon. Amelia explained to all of us why Aelish went to Yasteron in the first place. And her being abducted whilst trying to secure a Peace Accord with Yasteron had a profound effect on the Hentorians. They believe in peace above all else and already respect Aelish for trying to stop the endless wars between Yasteron and DAR.

"We have always lived in peace amongst the Hentorians and they trust me. But their patience is growing thin because the bombings continue. They want the bombings to stop, and Amelia explained to the Hentorians that rescuing Aelish would be an excellent first step."

Thagar asked, "Do you serve as the leader of those who escaped centuries ago?"

"I would say more like an ambassador," answered Uncle Thurrock, smiling.

Thagar chuckled at his uncle's modesty.

Uncle Thurrock said, "We cannot disavow Hentoria of their belief that King Cardissius' act of kidnapping Aelish will cause a war involving all the magical realms. After listening to Amelia's explanations, we now understand what is actually happening. And we agree with our asylum hosts—we feel a magical world war is inevitable.

"You see, Thagar, our community is as insulated as the Hentorians. But we can no longer live in ignorance of the severity of what has transpired. The Hentorians and our community have decided we must take decisive action to try and stop the escalation toward an all-out war. I simply could not believe it was *your* mate who'd been kidnapped, triggering this series of events. But Yasteron should have expected repercussions after stealing a Living Legend.

"So, I suggested to the Hentorians that you and I create a rescue plan as well as a rescue team. They offered two Hentorian warriors to be included in the team. I will, of course, be there alongside of you. Further, I have been authorized to inform you, it is acceptable to the Hentorians if you wish to include two other team members of your choosing.

"Additionally, you may bring Aelish and your family to Hentoria and receive sanctuary there until things can be sorted out. They've offered you and your family the same refuge they gave us so many centuries ago. But you are free to leave the dominion once it is safe. However, our community will remain. Again, they trust me.

"But remember this, Thagar, we have to perform a non-magical rescue through tunnels we hope are still functional and escape through a mountain passageway which is very rough. We'll need Human weapons, as no magic will work in proximity to where she's being held."

Uncle Thurrock reached across and grasped Thagar's arm. "We will get her out, and she will come back to you. On my life, I promise this to you."

Thagar looked into the golden eyes of his uncle, which were so like his own.

"We must begin planning immediately," said Uncle Thurrock. "It will take weeks to develop such an intricate rescue, where any number of things can go sideways. We have to plan for every contingency. Are you ready, Thagar?"

Thagar replied, "I am, Uncle. Thank you for everything you've done."

"Thank me when she's home," said Uncle Thurrock.

16

THE LECCS TOUR CONTINUES

ISABELA WAS NOT happy. The Russian Federation had requested they move up their scheduled visit from early April to today. She and Drew had planned to go from the United Kingdom to France, where the chocolate croissants awaited. But with this schedule change, she found herself staring at the Kremlin, freezing at an outdoor café.

"I know it's a little brisk to be eating outside, but I thought we could use some fresh air before the ceremony today," said Drew.

Isabela said nothing. She picked at the ptichye moloko, known as bird's milk cake, which was one of Russia's most beloved desserts. It was a delicious cake famous for its reverse cake-to-filling ratio. The thick but exceptionally light soufflé layers of silky custard were separated by a thin layer of sponge cake and then topped with a rich chocolate ganache glaze.

Drew handed her one of the two cups of tea he was holding. "Seriously, Drew? Not even a coffee?" she asked.

"Muscovites prefer tea to coffee," said Drew, smiling. "But did you know, eighty-five percent of Russians prefer instant coffee to coffee beans?"

Despite her rotten mood, Isabela burst out laughing. "Do you know the story of Thagar and Aelish regarding tea and coffee?

"Tell me."

"When Thagar first discovered coffee and all its iterations in America, he went home with a covered cup in his hand and asked Aelish, 'Why have I been drinking disgusting tea for six hundred seventy-two years when I could have been drinking *this*?' Thagar went nuts for all forms of coffee: latte, Frappuccino, espresso, Turkish coffee, Irish coffee—if it was coffee, he loved it. He single-handedly sought out the seeds for the two main types of coffee trees, the Arabica and the Robusta. He is the reason you can find any type of coffee in DAR. I will never forget Aelish telling me that story."

"I know he loves his coffee. So, how's the cake? But before you yell at me, I know, it's not a French croissant. However, there are millions of people living here who really love it. Does it the pass the Isabela test of approval or not?"

"Yeah, it's pretty good," said Isabela, wiping some of the chocolate ganache glaze off her mouth. "But this tea is disgusting."

"So, you prefer British tea to Russian tea, then? Preferably served with the King of England himself, yes?"

"That event was so much fun. I so wish Aelish could have been there invisibly and watched the entire production. And yes, British tea, also known by the Brits as tea, at least has some caffeine in it. This tea tastes like it was made from boiled potatoes."

Drew spontaneously spit out his tea, laughing at Isabela. "You are too much, Isabela."

"Yes, so I've been told," she replied. Drew was trying hard not to laugh. "Drew, you do realize what's about to happen to us at this next ceremony, right? We are going to be presented with awards, certificates, and medals from the President of the Russian

Federation, better known as the cousin of King Cardissius of Yasteron. He's a Yasteron for God's sake!"

"I'm well aware, Isabela," said Drew. "But if we left Russia off our itinerary, it could cause an international incident and jeopardize our efforts in getting people vaccinated here. And they really need to get vaccinated here because of the melting permafrost, the rising Arctic temperatures, as well as the Eastern Siberian Artic Shelf, which contains the methane time bomb. Furthermore, the war the Russian president initiated against Ukraine caused seven of the eight members of the Arctic Council in 2023 to *pause* their work. They simply could not cooperate with Russia, and the planet lost the council's important work.

"Canada, Denmark, Finland, Iceland, Norway, Sweden, Russia, and the United States are the eight countries which comprise the Arctic Council. The council was supposed to serve as a reminder that multilateral partnerships could thrive despite global discord, like Russia's invasion of Ukraine. The whole point of the council was to foster collaboration in areas such as scientific research and the challenges posed by the climate crisis. Friends and adversaries were supposed to be able to sit down, talk, and find common ground. That's why we're here, Isabela. To serve as a reminder that a mega-death event, like LECCS, supersedes disputed military conflicts.

"And lastly, don't forget, there are over one hundred members of the United States Congress who've expressed skepticism about the role Humans have played in the climate crisis as well as the purported value of limiting emissions. I would imagine many, if not all, are from Yasteron. The U.S. is just as guilty of allowing Yasteron covert operatives to infiltrate their government as Russia. The Russian president just happens to have a bit of panache. Oh, and did you forget our own orange-haired president—the other cousin of King Cardissius? That's why it is dangerous to point fingers, Isabela. Before doing so, you need to make sure your own house is in order."

Rolling her eyes, Isabela said, "You forgot to mention that during the pause, temperatures continued to climb in the region and declining sea ice opened new shipping routes and expanded opportunities to exploit oil, gas, and other critical minerals in the Arctic. Russia took full advantage of these new opportunities. And despite the entire country being corrupted by Yasteron's covert operatives, I never agreed with the pause. Keep in mind, no one else knows about Yasteron or their infiltration of Earth, and by stepping back because of Russia's actions against Ukraine, the council lost the chance to expose Russia's perpetuation of the climate crisis.

"The Arctic is one of the planet's last wildlands. Since Norway took over the leadership of the council in 2023, they've tried to reinvigorate it by focusing on its original mission: divorce themselves from contentious military issues and seek common ground. This has been its modus vivendi since its founding in September of 1996. Conflicting parties on the council were supposed to exist peacefully, either indefinitely or until a settlement could be reached.

"But once Russia invaded Ukraine, the council lost its ability to remain isolated from geopolitics. And the most important element of the Arctic Council, trust, was lost. Russia makes up half the Arctic. How can you have an Arctic Council without Russia? Well done, Yasteron!

"Oh, and lest we forget, Russia has nuclear capabilities and are behaving as if their nukes are like this cake—lots of fissile filling on a foundation of reckless policies—they're toying with a nuclear catastrophe. And Yasteron continues to raid rare Earth metals in Afghanistan because the Peace Accord was never signed since it was used merely as a ruse to kidnap Aelish. Yasteron is just baiting the Alliance of Magical Dominions to attack them and are risking a magical world war. How can I even look at this Yasteron president? I'm so worried about Aelish."

"I know you are, Isabela. But Aelish is tough and determined, like someone else I know."

Isabela smiled at Drew. "All right, Drew. Let's get this party started and head over to the Kremlin. I will receive the Meritorious Doctor of the Russian Federation medal, and you will receive The Order of Friendship, Russia's highest honor awarded to a non-Russian citizen." Isabela stuck her finger in her mouth, pretending to vomit. "Yasteron almost killed both of us at the WHO, Drew. Good God!"

Isabela knew she was trying Drew's patience, but she felt comfortable with him and could really be herself. She'd experienced this feeling somewhat with Glen but not like this. Drew was patient and kind during her outbursts and rants, like Aelish or a family member.

When the ceremony had concluded and they were on their way back to the hotel, Isabela begged Drew, "Can we please just get on your jet and fly to France—now? I'll shower when we get there. I just want to get out of here!" And to make her happy, that's exactly what they did.

‡‡‡‡

Sitting at an outdoor café in Paris, Isabela felt the exact opposite of how she'd felt sitting at an outdoor café outside the Kremlin. And she'd made her decision: French chocolate croissants were infinitely more delicious than any made in America; they were decadent. She and Drew were sitting with a view of the Seine River, and Isabela understood why they called Paris the City of Love. There was just something about it. The Parisians were a bit pretentious, but they were also a lot of fun. Once Drew translated things for her, she realized they had a great sense of humor. She indicated to Drew that she could see herself living in Paris one day.

Isabela knew he was relieved she was happy again. He'd become the guardian of her mental health, and she began to trust him when he suggested she do or not do something.

"Helene just sent me an email," said Drew, looking at his phone. "Tomorrow, we will both be receiving the Légion d'Honneur, the highest civilian award given by the French Republic for outstanding service to France, regardless of the recipient's nationality."

"Vive la France!" exclaimed Isabela.

Drew started laughing at her.

"The ceremony will be held at the Palais Bourbon, where the French Parliament meets, in the 7th arrondissement. Both chambers will be present, the upper Senate and the lower National Assembly, and both the President and Prime Minister of France will be there."

"The president is a higher position than the prime minister, right?" asked Isabela, drinking a hot chocolate.

"Yes, after the president, the prime minister holds the second-highest position in France. The president appoints the prime minister, and the prime minister is responsible to the French Parliament; the prime minister is not elected."

Isabela said, "I'm very familiar with France's dedication to the GFATM, or the Global Fund to Fight AIDS, Tuberculosis, and Malaria. They were one of the founders, and I think they are the second largest monetary contributor since the Global Fund's creation in January 2002."

"Correct, Doctor Torres. France is demonstrating enormous respect for you and your work on LECCS. You should be very proud."

"Our work," corrected Isabela.

Drew chuckled and said, "So, tomorrow we will be in the 7th arrondissement, but the day after that, I want to take you to Montmartre in the 18th arrondissement. It might just be my favorite section of Paris."

"Tell me why," said Isabela, smiling.

Drew said, "I love walking the streets where some of the world's most famous painters lived and developed their art like, Claude Monet, Pierre-Auguste Renoir, Pablo Picasso, Mary Cassatt, Camille Pissarro, Henri de Toulouse-Lautrec, and of course, Vincent van Gogh.

"I also hope we'll have time to visit the Musée d'Orsay, which has one of the best collections of the impressionists and post-impressionists in the world. When I was young, I used to hang posters in my room, replicating some of their most famous works. I never thought I'd ever see the originals, which can be viewed in the Musée d'Orsay."

"I didn't know you loved the impressionists," said Isabela. "Now, I'm excited to visit Montmartre. What other sights are there?"

Drew replied, "The Sacré Coeur de Montmartre, otherwise known as the Basilica of the Sacred Heart of Paris, dedicated to the Sacred Heart of Jesus. Yes, I am a raging papist. My mother, Juliette, won the war of the Protestant Reformation against my father, Robert, who was Church of England all the way. In my house, it was like living through the actual wars that took place because of these two religions."

Isabela thought of Abuela and made a point of being respectful to Drew's faith. "While you are aware I am an atheist, my Abuela was also a raging papist. I, too, was raised Catholic, so I'm excited to see the French version of my family's religion at the Sacré Coeur. I didn't know your mother's name was Juliette.

What a beautiful name."

"My father affectionately called her Jules unless he was annoyed with her. Then, it was strictly Juliette. I still miss her so much."

"Cancer harms not only its victims but also the families who love them."

"So true, Isabela. When my father remarried, it was not even two years after my mother's death. At the time, I was angry. But now that I'm grown, I'm glad he found happiness again. Her death hit him so hard. My father, my stepmother, Miranda, and their fraternal twins live in Surrey, about thirty miles outside of London. My God, my half brother and sister will be ready to start college in a few years. Time goes by so fast and yet so slowly. Do you know what I mean?"

"I do," replied Isabela. She reached across the café table and patted Drew's hand.

"Let's go see the Eiffel Tower," suggested Drew. "You've seen the lights of the tower at night from our hotel, but it's amazing to see Paris from the top."

"Please make sure you show me all the sights in Paris, Drew, because I will be very sad to say goodbye to this city."

"We still have a few days. Then, I have a surprise for you." Isabela's eyes opened wide.

‡‡‡‡

As they climbed the large hill in Paris' northern 18th arrondissement, Isabela thought about all the artists who had lived there. They were headed to the Sacré Coeur, with its white-dome, at the top of the hill. There were stores filled with artwork. Some featured replicas of the original impressionists, while others featured new visionaries.

"Oh, let's first stop in this shop, Isabela." Drew veered left off the hill, onto the sidewalk, with Isabela following behind him. He entered the shop and said, "Bonjour," to the shopkeeper.

"Bonjour, ça va?" asked the shopkeeper.

"Oui, monsieur, ça va aujourd'hui," replied Drew.

Drew walked to the back of the store as Isabela tried translating the colloquial greetings. When she finally found Drew, her mouth opened wide. "Wow! That painting is positively gorgeous!"

"Très bien!" exclaimed Drew. "I knew you would love it."

"It looks exactly like the beach where Javi and I learned to surf in California. And the artist meticulously captured the light of the sunset. I could stare at this painting and feel relaxed no matter how stressful my day was. The sheer size of it mirrors the grandeur of the Pacific Ocean." Isabela sat down on a bench in front of the painting unaware that Drew was busy with the shopkeeper.

When she finally pulled herself away from the painting to find him, she noticed he was standing in the front of the store. She caught up with him, and he turned to her and said, "The painting will be delivered to your parents' house sometime in the next week. A little gift from me to you, to help you remember—even when you're away from home, you can always find something to remind you of home."

"You bought me the painting? Oh, my God, Drew!" She leaned in closer to him and whispered-yelled, "It's too much money; it was 50,000 euros!"

"Wherever you want to place it will become a Zen-zone and worth every euro. I saw it the other day and couldn't believe how much it reminded me of the beach you and Javi showed me when we were in California. I had to get it for you."

Isabela shook her head and felt a tear roll down her cheek. Drew was so generous not only with his vast wealth but also with the kindness that emanated from his heart. It was the same reason he'd supported all of her LECCS research, the building of the lab, and the wing at Wainbridge Medical Center; he believed in what it all stood for. He had both the will and the generosity to make the world a better place. And in the case of the painting, he was determined to have Isabela remain mentally well; he knew it would calm her when she needed it most.

"And to celebrate," he said, "I'm taking you someplace very special for dinner. Let's get to the basilica before it closes."

Isabela gave Drew a heartfelt hug. "Thank you so much for everything."

They waved goodbye to the shopkeeper and headed to the Sacré Coeur.

‡‡‡‡

As they exited the Sacré Coeur, Isabela said, "I think my soul has been infused with a raging hunger after viewing this incredibly beautiful church. Or it could be, the church reminded me so much of Abuela, now I'm longing for her cooking. Where are we going for dinner?"

Drew began chuckling. "Well, if you're not too tired, we can walk from here."

"Oh, okay, let's walk. This part of Paris is like a village within a huge city. I love it."

"Me, too, and someone else also loves it here."

"Who?" asked Isabela, intrigued.

"Come." Drew took hold of her hand and began slowly running in the direction they were headed. After a few blocks they arrived at a gorgeous, older, pink house. It was three stories high with wrought iron balconies. Drew climbed the few steps leading to the front door from the sidewalk and began knocking on the front door.

Shocked, Isabela asked, "Drew, who lives—"

The front door opened and a woman in her late sixties began hugging and kissing Drew's face all over, saying, "Bonsoir, ma chérie!" The smell of something delicious wafted toward Isabela, who was still on the sidewalk. "Allez, allez," said the woman to Isabela, furiously gesturing for her to come inside.

And then, it hit Isabela; she knew exactly who this woman was—it was Nanny Marie! She walked to the front door and embraced her, asking, "Nanny Marie, oui?"

Nanny Marie started laughing and began hugging and kissing Isabela, just like Abuela used to do. Isabela felt herself begin to cry and hugged Nanny Marie even tighter. "I'm so happy to finally meet you," she said. "Drew has told me so many stories about you and by you."

Drew saw Isabela crying and instinctively knew it had to do with the loss of her grandmother. Abuela and Nanny Marie were about the same age, and he imagined they shared a similar temperament, which landed hard on Isabela's heart. Nanny Marie ushered them all inside. They sat together in the front room while a younger woman, dressed in a maid's uniform, served them hors d'oeuvres and drinks.

Isabela caught bits and pieces of what Drew and Nanny Marie were talking about and was lost in her own thoughts, gazing at the artwork and furnishings surrounding them.

In heavily accented English, Nanny Marie asked Isabela, "You love Paris?"

"Oui, beaucoup," replied Isabela. "Your home is so lovely."

Nanny Marie suggested, "Drew, give Isabela a tour of la maison, while I check with Cosette to see how dinner is coming along. Make sure you take her to the rooftop."

Drew stood up, reaching for Isabela's hand. They walked through a variety of tastefully decorated rooms and climbed the staircase up to the rooms on the second and third floors. Finally, they reached the door to the rooftop. Drew opened the door. Isabela had a clear view of the Sacré Coeur. "Oh, my God," she said, stepping onto the rooftop deck. "This is incredible."

"Wait until it gets dark. The lights are amazing."

Isabela wandered over to get a closer look at the basilica. Staring at it, she reflected on how Drew and Nanny Marie were more like mother and son. She wanted to share this with him but was afraid of denigrating his relationship with his deceased mother.

Joining her, he asked, "What is it?"

Isabela was becoming more transparent to Drew. It was a bit unnerving. "Nothing."

"It's something. Tell me, don't be afraid."

"You interact with Nanny Marie more like . . . she's your . . . "

"Mother?" asked Drew.

"Yes, but I hope I haven't disparaged your relationship with your mother. I didn't mean it in a bad way. It's beautiful to watch the ease you have with one another."

"I was close with my mother, but as I told you a long time ago, my parents were always off doing this or that; we didn't spend much family time together. So, Nanny Marie."

"I understand," said Isabela. "This house must have cost a fortune based on its location. And she has a maid. I didn't know Nanny Marie was so wealthy. Was her husband wealthy?"

Drew gently laughed. "No, Isabela. Nanny Marie's husband was a welder, and they lived way outside of Paris when she worked for my family, both here and in England. She only went home once a month. But they still managed to have two children, a boy and a girl, and now, she has four grandchildren who also live in the countryside of France. Her grandchildren love to come to Paris to visit and be told stories, like Nanny Marie used to tell me."

"But then, how could she . . . ohh . . . *you* bought her this house. And you pay for the maid, and you purchased all the artwork and tasteful furnishings. I'm so stupid."

Drew came over and put his arm around her shoulder. "After all she gave me, this was the least I could do for her after her husband died. She accompanied my family when we'd visit our pied-à-terre in Montmartre. And from the time I was a boy, I knew how much she loved the art scene and the village feel here. I promised myself I would always care for her as she cared for me. I love coming to visit her. We could stay the night in the guest rooms upstairs, and we might even be lucky enough to hear one of her fabulous stories. What do you say?"

"I don't have any clothes or anything with me, but I would really like to, Drew."

"She has things for you to wear. And tomorrow, my helicopter is picking us up to take us somewhere very special."

"I thought tomorrow we were beginning the next leg of the tour in Italy, Greece, and the Balkans. Where are we going?"

"I had Helene reschedule some of our tour so we could have a little rest on my yacht."

"You have a *yacht*?" asked Isabela.

Drew nodded. "And it has a helipad, which can accommodate a single engine helicopter. So, tomorrow we will leave from the heliport, here, and use my smaller chopper to take us to Monaco, where the yacht is docked. I thought it would be fun to have a few days off there. We can use the jet skis onboard to take us to the hotels for meals or to just lie on the beach. And if you get bored with that, the yacht also has a swimming pool. Then, I thought we could take the yacht and go to Italy, Greece, and other countries that can accommodate its size so we can continue the tour. This will allow you to see things from a totally different vantage point. I want you to see as much of the world as possible,

Isabela, before it's all gone."

"So, we will travel the next leg of the tour by boat?"

"Exactly," said Drew, smiling.

"I am a bit tired," said Isabela. "When I started crying after meeting Nanny Marie, I could hear my shrink in my head telling me I needed a rest. How did you know I needed a rest?"

"I could tell. It's been a lot, Isabela, and we have so much left to do. Let's have a little downtime before we keep on going, okay?"

"That sounds incredible, Drew. And let's stay at Nanny Marie's for the night. Oh, but what about our things at the hotel?"

"Not to worry. I will have Sawyer bring everything to the heliport tomorrow. Let's just relax, have a delicious home-cooked meal, and hopefully hear a great bedtime story."

"Whew," said Isabela. "Now that I know we can rest for a while, I suddenly feel exhausted. Thank you for knowing I needed to rest. It will really help me maintain my mental health. I so appreciate you, Drew."

"You're so welcome, Isabela. You've been under a lot of pressure."

Isabela nodded. Drew put his arm around her shoulders, and they headed back inside the house for dinner.

17

PLANNING THE RESCUE MISSION

UNCLE THURROCK BROUGHT a warmth back to the house. Drummond highly respected him and Kaleigh was enamored by him. Her great-uncle was more like a grandfather figure and helped ease the loss of Abuela and the longing for her mother.

Uncle Thurrock had learned quite quickly how to drive, utilizing Thagar's best efforts at a forged driver's license. He picked up Kaleigh for Thagar after she was finished with her new advanced-level languages program, as well as her after-school program. Not only did this help Thagar when he needed to work at the Climate Refugee Intake Center, long past Kaleigh's pickup time, but it also helped him avoid seeing the beautiful teacher, Brooke Thompson, who was co-teaching the advanced-level languages program.

Thagar would often return from work and find Uncle Thurrock on the floor of the tree-house room, playing checkers and other board games with Kaleigh. She was happier than he'd seen her in months. It was a shame his uncle had not been blessed with offspring because he was a natural at parenting.

Thagar had begun preparing Marisol to serve as Acting Director of the CRIC while he and Uncle Thurrock were away in Hentoria, practicing the rescue mission. Kaleigh would be staying with Marisol and Jorge while they were away, as he didn't want to take his daughter until all the kinks and glitches were worked out of the mission.

His uncle had obtained permission for Lady Antonia to come to Hentoria; however, Quentin had to remain behind for security reasons. Despite Quentin not being allowed to accompany her, Lady Antonia was thrilled Thagar had asked her to come, as she was aware Amelia and Kaleigh would both be there awaiting Aelish's rescue. Thagar knew Lady Antonia and Amelia's presence would help Kaleigh cope with the anxiety of waiting to see her mother. And he also knew Lady Antonia would ensure everything would be ready for Aelish.

When Lady Antonia suggested Medicus Clove from DAR be available to Aelish, Thagar understood she was erring on the side of caution. However, he and Amelia disagreed with this idea. Thagar had decided the rescue team would include only himself, Uncle Thurrock, and the two Hentorian warriors; the less beings who knew, the better. He couldn't take the chance they'd be discovered in Hentoria, and Amelia completely agreed. Eventually, Lady Antonia stopped pushing. While he agreed Aelish should have access to a proper medicus, he didn't want to risk compromising his family's secret hideaway and Uncle Thurrock's community. If they were able to pull off the mission, he knew the fallout was going to be enormous.

Thagar and Uncle Thurrock set up a training center on the back acreage of the house. They magically hid everything under an invisible tent. Thagar hadn't done military exercises in some time and was profoundly feeling all of his injuries from the bombings with renewed pain. His uncle was devastated to watch his agony but was impressed by his perseverance. The months of recovery at Wainbridge Rehabilitation Center were the only reason he could continue training.

Thagar had kept in touch with some of the American veterans he'd met there, and his relationship with them was about to become useful. Since the assumption was no magic could be used inside the tunnels or the prison where Aelish was being held, they planned to bring Human military-grade weaponry.

It was Uncle Thurrock who explained to him how Human weapons could be used against magical beings. And Thagar learned why he'd never been magically damaged from the underwater bunker bombing. The part of a DARling's brain that controlled their magical capabilities as well as the core of their life force was in the thalamus. In Humans, the thalamus was an egg-shaped structure near the middle of the brain. It's known as the command center for all incoming motor and sensory information, like hearing, touch, taste, and sight, but not smell. It was the mind-body connector and Humans could not live without their thalamus.

In magical beings, it was nearly identical. The thalamus of a magical being controlled all of their magical abilities as well as their life-force core. The two subdural hematomas Thagar had endured from the steel door of the underwater bunker hitting his skull had never injured his thalamus, so his magical abilities remained intact as did his life-force core.

Thagar was intrigued by how his uncle knew so much about this. One night, they sat together in the tree-house room sharing a whiskey. Uncle Thurrock explained that he participated in an autopsy of a DARling soldier who'd become severely ill after their escape to Hentoria. Another soldier, a trained medicus, remembered a rock had struck the deceased soldier's head as they went through the Hentorian mountain passageway. In the moment, he was fine. But he died less than two days later. The medicus soldier wanted to open his skull and determine why he had died. Upon examination, every part of the deceased soldier's brain was intact except for the egg-shaped thalamus. It looked like a broken yolk, with matter spilling out onto other parts of his brain. The autopsy demonstrated how an injury to a magical being's thalamus could kill them. It also illuminated how one magical being could kill another without magic.

Human bullets could stun magical beings, but only bullets that penetrated their thalamus would kill them. Even with protective spells, various Human bombs could injure magical beings. But unless there was a direct hit to their thalamus, they could theoretically survive, as magical beings were immune to radiation, with the exception of Komprathians and Trelveland's trees.

Thagar and Uncle Thurrock met with two veterans who'd been in Wainbridge Rehabilitation Center at a local restaurant. Despite the plethora of Human weaponry available, they determined one of the most effective weapons would be a Taser. In close combat, if the Taser's current was aimed at the base of the magical being's skull, the current could travel to the thalamus and kill them. But even if it didn't, it would stun them long enough to buy time.

Thagar and Uncle Thurrock climbed into the van of one of the veterans who'd lost both of his legs and an arm to an improvised explosive device, or an IED, in Afghanistan. His van was equipped with all the necessary alterations enabling him to drive. Uncle Thurrock was fascinated this was possible without magic.

Aelish had warned Thagar in the rehabilitation center to never discuss his military experience and he hadn't. His obfuscation led the veterans to believe he was involved in some form of espionage, so they never pried. Upon meeting Uncle Thurrock, they simply assumed working in espionage ran in the family.

The disabled vet took them to the home of another former soldier who basically had an arsenal in his barn. He had night-vision goggles, or NVGs, with 360-degree vision. Thagar had never seen anything like it. Wearing the goggles meant they literally had eyes in the back of their head. The former soldier had one of the newest weapons created, favored by SWAT officers. It was a gun that could bend at a 90-degree angle. It could shoot around a corner, so the intended target never even saw the gun.

Inside the barn was every type of rocket-propelled grenade launcher, or RPGs. Thagar and his uncle chose the RPG-27 and the RPG-7. They chose the RPG-27 for its maximum armor penetration and its simple flip-up sights. The flip-up sights allowed the user to line up both sights and position the firearm in such a way that accuracy of hitting the target was assured. The RPG-7 was chosen for its versatility, as numerous rockets were developed for this lightweight weapon. To date, the RPG-7 had brought down more helicopters than most man-portable air defense systems, or MANPADS. While it was currently being phased out by most modern militaries, due to its limited effectiveness against modern battle tanks, it was perfect for their mission.

When they finished paying the former soldier in the barn for the weapons, the disabled vet drove them back to the restaurant so Thagar could retrieve his SUV. Once inside the SUV, Thagar said to Uncle Thurrock, "Now, I'm going to show you something you won't believe."

Thagar drove Uncle Thagar to an outdoor sports equipment store about fifteen minutes from his house on Bunker Hill Road.

Next to the camping gear was an entire wall of weaponry. There were 9mm pistols, revolvers, rifles, Glock and Ruger handguns, tactical rifles, semi-automatic hunting rifles, as well as Tasers and other stun guns. The state of Tennessee did not require a permit to own or carry these electric weapons, like the Taser, for self-defense.

Uncle Thurrock stared at Thagar in disbelief as he watched the average American shopping for weapons on a Sunday afternoon. "And this is all legal?" asked Uncle Thurrock. Thagar nodded. Uncle Thurrock watched Humans make their selection and walk out of the store with a new weapon. "This is madness. We train for years at the POD for all forms of weaponry."

Thagar said to him, "Ask Kaleigh about active shooter drills at her school."

"At her *school*?" asked Uncle Thurrock, shocked.

Later that night, Uncle Thurrock asked Kaleigh if she'd ever participated in an active shooter drill at VMP Academy. Kaleigh began crying and said she hated them and tried not to think about them afterward because they made her feel so afraid. Uncle Thurrock put a spell on her to make her forget their conversation and tucked her into bed.

He came downstairs into the kitchen where Drummond had made coffee and biscuits. Thagar was sitting at the counter, munching on a biscuit. He took one look at his uncle's face and asked, "You asked her about the active shooter drills, didn't you?" Uncle Thurrock told Thagar about her reaction and that he'd put a spell on her to make her forget, prior to tucking her in.

"How can you live in a place like this?" asked his uncle.

Thagar replied, "When I first learned of the mass shootings that occur nearly every day in America, I told Aelish I wanted to leave and go to another country. I was not going to have my Human child murdered at her own school. Obviously, we didn't move. So, Kaleigh leaves for school every day with a protective spell around her to prevent any type of firearm from injuring or killing her. And now, I'm thinking about bombs, accidents, and her thalamus being injured."

"Sorry," said Uncle Thurrock. "But what about the Human children who don't have magical parents who can envelop them in a protective spell?"

"Aelish and I put the Impenetrable spell around the entire school," said Thagar.

Uncle Thurrock nodded. "Well, at least that's something. But Thagar, I'm horrified non-military Humans have access to these kinds of weapons."

All Thagar could say was, "Right," and shook his head.

In the end, they concluded the venom of the Hentorian warriors would probably be the most powerful and effective weapon they'd have. Their venom was not magical and caused death within seconds. The warriors could take out a squadron of magical beings in less than a minute. When shooting out their venom, their aim and its velocity was precise and quick. And its lethality was completely quiet.

‡‡‡‡

The night before Thagar and Uncle Thurrock left for Hentoria, Marisol made dinner for everyone. She and Jorge were very excited to meet Uncle Thurrock and they immediately hit it off. Despite Isabela being away on her worldwide tour with Drew, it was a fun-filled evening, and Kaleigh seemed relaxed.

When it was bedtime, both Thagar and Uncle Thurrock tucked her into bed, in her second home. She looked at them and asked, "Are you going to use the Portal avoidance route?"

Thagar had finally broken his oath of secrecy and told

Uncle Thurrock about the route. They both started laughing at how easily Kaleigh had given away one of DAR's most historic secrets. "Yes, sweetheart," said Thagar. "I'm really going to miss you on my back."

"Me, too, Daddy. But I understand why I can't come. Do you promise that you will both come back to me?"

Thagar and his uncle nodded, and they simultaneously said, "We promise."

"Okay, good." And with that, Kaleigh gave them each a hug and a kiss goodbye and fell soundly asleep before they'd left the room.

Uncle Thurrock looked at the sleeping angel with the light brown sugar skin and black curls.

"She's so beautiful, Thagar, both inside and out."

"Just like her mother," said Thagar.

"And a little bit like her father, I think."

Thagar started chuckling and Uncle Thurrock slapped him on the back. They went back to the dining room to thank Marisol and Jorge for dinner and told them Kaleigh was sleeping soundly. As they got ready to leave, Marisol said goodbye to Thagar with tears in her eyes. She tightly embraced him and kissed him on the cheek. She also hugged Uncle Thurrock and whispered, "Please take care of Thagar." Uncle Thurrock nodded to her. Then, Jorge came over to shake both of their hands and wished them a safe trip.

Once in the SUV, Uncle Thurrock remarked, "They are such nice Humans. You are so lucky to be able to entrust your daughter's well-being to such kind and competent Humans.

"They are like her backup parents. I adore both of them," said Thagar.

"Speaking of family," said Uncle Thurrock, "I'm very excited for you to meet my mate, Charlotte. I think you're really going to like her."

"I'm sure I will," said Thagar. "I'm looking forward to it."

After they finished packing up their gear for the trip, the two males went to bed and rose before the sun was up. Drummond had prepared them a feast, which he magically packed with their gear. Before they left, Drummond said, "I want to wish ya' both a safe and successful mission. I hope it will be possible to rescue Aelish because I miss her so much." Drummond wiped a tear from his eye and shook the hands of both males as they departed for Hentoria.

✟✟✟✟

Even with all of his military experience, Thagar was momentarily fearful and startled by what the Hentorians looked like. But their peaceful demeanor immediately put him at ease as the welcoming committee graciously escorted them down to the village.

Opening the gate with a spell in a language Thagar had never heard before, the Hentorian leaders along with the two Hentorian warriors, conjured a door in the huge wall that encircled the village. The door had not been there a moment before. Even his uncle didn't know how to conjure the door in the wall surrounding the village. After living there for the last six hundred and fifty years, he still needed the Hentorians to gain access to his own home.

Thagar respected the high level of security. Once inside the wall, the Hentorian leaders departed. They left behind the Hentorian warriors in Uncle Thurrock's care. Thagar was astonished at how tall they were and wondered what the home of a Hentorian looked like. When they reached the door of Uncle Thurrock's simple thatched-roof cottage, Aunt Charlotte came outside to welcome them all. She gave his uncle a rather passionate kiss, which Thagar totally appreciated. He could see her young beauty had morphed into a mature elegance in her later years. Her blond hair was flecked with grey streaks, and her blue eyes were the color of the deep blue ocean found in DAR's N.E. Quadrant.

His aunt was warm, kind, and very welcoming. Since the Hentorian warriors could not stand upright in their cottage, she directed them to a structure behind the house, which resembled a barn. She told them she'd set up two pallets which would accommodate their height. There was also a dining table and the roof was at least fifteen feet high, so they wouldn't feel cramped. She also told them she would be bringing their dinner after everyone had a chance to rest.

Being warriors and used to far worse conditions than this, they graciously thanked her and went to the barn to rest. Once inside Uncle Thurrock's house, Thagar saw how simply they lived. There were no lavish furnishings, no ornate art pieces, and none of the material trappings found on Earth or even in his own home in DAR.

The cottage reminded him of Aelish's first cottage in DAR and beautiful memories washed over him. He felt relaxed and in need of a good sleep. He was finally here and was eager to begin planning and practicing Aelish's extraction from Yasteron. Being in the cottage, behind the high wall of fortified spells, Thagar did not feel the proximity of the kingdom that had tormented him for centuries. He knew they weren't more than twenty-five miles from the border of Yasteron, but it felt more like twenty-five thousand.

His aunt escorted him to one of the two guest bedrooms, which was modestly furnished. The mattress was a feather-bed of old and immeasurably comfortable. And there was a washroom right off the bedroom, which was very convenient.

"Why don't you get cleaned up," she suggested, "and then

join us at the kitchen table where we can have some refreshments. What's your favorite spirit?"

"If it's all the same to you, I'd prefer not to drink spirits during the planning phase of our mission. I would like to stay clear-headed."

"Ohh, I completely understand, Thagar. Also, I apologize if I've been staring at you. I simply can't get over how much you look like Thurrock. It's like his young self has returned to me, but now I'm an old hag." She started laughing and Thagar saw how joyful a being she was. Their simple lifestyle must have been a relief from her royal upbringing. He couldn't believe he was in the home of King Nevuna's sister. If someone had told him when he was young that this would happen, one day, he would never have believed it.

"You're hardly an old hag, Aunt Charlotte."

"Oh, my goodness, no one has called me Aunt Charlotte for centuries. How wonderful!"

And with that, she left his room. He heard her speaking quietly to his uncle in the kitchen among the clatter of crockery. Thagar sat on the side of the bed and took a deep breath. Amelia had arranged with Komprathia's military to have the squadron of drone rats arrive sometime later this evening. This way, they could all get a fresh start in the morning.

He'd never lived with drone rats and wondered what accommodations his aunt had made for them. They were coming to work as scouts in the tunnels under the prison. Thagar hoped Yasteron hadn't destroyed the tunnels, as they needed them for their escape. He doubted they did, as they still hadn't figured out where they led to.

After a good rest and a delicious dinner with his aunt and uncle, suddenly, they all heard a loud knock on the cottage door. Aunt Charlotte went to open it and there stood the Hentorian leaders. At first, Thagar didn't see them. But then, they came scurrying into the kitchen.

In total, there were five drone rats. They all stood together in a line and Thagar immediately identified the leader. Standing up on his hind legs, he spoke in accented English to Aunt Charlotte and Uncle Thurrock. "My name is Haurice. Thank you for welcoming us into your beautiful home. We wanted to present you with this." He turned toward the courtyard in front of their home. They'd magically installed a beautiful fountain resplendent with shimmering stones and water that peacefully trickled. "We hope it brings you peace and comfort."

"Ohh," uttered Aunt Charlotte. "It's absolutely beautiful. I've always loved the sound of a fountain. It faces our bedroom and will lull us to sleep, won't it, Thurrock?"

"It will, indeed. Thank you so kindly for this gesture, Haurice," said Uncle Thurrock. "It was totally unnecessary, but it is very much appreciated." Seeing all was well, the Hentorian leaders bid them all a good night and left.

Haurice said, "Most upright beings don't care for our presence inside their homes. So, if you'd prefer us to sleep outside, all we need is some thatch to create a nest."

Thagar looked at his aunt and uncle and was grateful he didn't have to make that decision. And then he realized, after all the centuries of war with Komprathia and all the plague spread by the drone rats on Earth, he'd never really spent time with them after they'd become full-fledged citizens and active members of their now-free society. He felt somewhat ashamed.

Without a moment's hesitation, his aunt replied, "You are more than welcome to stay in our second guest room. I've set up small beds for each of you, and I hope you will be very comfortable in our home. Please let me know what spirits you wish to drink, if any, and I will bring them to you at once."

Thagar was genuinely impressed by his aunt's comfort with the drone rats and that she'd planned ahead and had already prepared the second guest room. He knew Isabela worked with drone rats in her lab on a daily basis, but they were kept in cages. Being kept in cages was by their own volition, as they had volunteered to be test subjects in Isabela's clinical trials for LECCS. But nevertheless, he wondered how Isabela or Aelish would react to having drone rats scurrying around the house. He'd once received quite the reaction from Aelish in the Sanctuary, on their first outing together, when he asked her how she felt about rats in general. But Aelish had been willing to give her own life to free the drone rats from King Gidius' tyranny. He imagined she would act much the same as his aunt, gracious and welcoming. It appeared as if he were the only one with reservations.

The drone rats had their dinner in their bedroom and were off to sleep long before Thagar, Uncle Thurrock, and Aunt Charlotte. They were quiet and respectful soldiers, as were the Hentorian warriors, whom Thagar hadn't seen since they'd gone to the barn. After having a lovely chat with his aunt and uncle, he decided to retire to bed. For the first time in months, he slept through the night with peaceful dreams. Perhaps it was from the sound of the fountain.

‡‡‡‡

They reached the illusory wall at the end of the mountain passageway, which Yasteron had never penetrated. Thagar hoped the tunnel system was still intact on the other side of the wall. The Hentorian warriors began reciting overlapping spells in their native language and it took thirty minutes for the wall to disappear. Thagar had begun profusely sweating, mostly from anxiety.

Once the wall fell away, he saw the tunnels were intact and

breathed a sigh of relief. This was when Haurice and his squadron of drone rats took over. They marked each section with a small flag where magic would not work. When they reached the end of the tunnel system, Haurice came scurrying back to report that no magic worked within the entire tunnel system. The Human weapons Thagar and Uncle Thurrock had purchased would be needed after all.

When the upright beings entered the tunnels, they tried to be as quiet as the drone rats, who did not accompany them. But the rock and soil gave way from their weight and the years of non-use. They finally reached the end of the tunnels and Thagar saw a trap door above his head. It melded seamlessly with the ceiling of the tunnel. He knew once the trap door was opened, they would be inside the prison where Aelish was being held. Suddenly, they all froze upon hearing a male voice coming from inside the prison.

Thagar immediately recognized the voice of King Cardissius. The king was speaking too quietly for Thagar to hear what he was saying, but then, he heard the distinct sound of his mate's laughter. What happened to him internally must have showed on his face, as Uncle Thurrock grabbed his shoulder to keep him calm. His uncle pressed his forefinger against his own lips, indicating Thagar needed to remain completely quiet. They heard a heavy footfall retreating, and then Thagar heard Aelish's voice. She was speaking softly to someone else, and he was frustrated he couldn't use an auditory spell to clearly hear her. But she was alive!

The Hentorians motioned to Uncle Thurrock that they needed to leave. Reluctantly, Thagar followed his uncle and the Hentorian warriors back out through the tunnels. But before they could exit, an alarm began blaring. They all momentarily froze. Thagar hoped they had enough time to seal the exit before

Yasteron soldiers came into the tunnels, as they'd left behind their Human weapons. All they had was the Hentorian's venom. He and his uncle began running, but the speed of the warriors on all fours was incredible. Once outside the tunnel system, the warriors began reciting the spells needed to seal the tunnels with the illusory wall.

‡‡‡‡

"Katrina, what in God's name is that alarm?" Aelish yelled over the din.

"I don't know, m'Lady, I've never heard anything like this before."

Aelish began investigating each of the rooms and could not identify where the alarm originated. The noise was driving her insane and Storm was furiously barking on top of it. Suddenly, all twelve of the King's Guard stationed in the back hallway came charging into the room along with Chief Minister Stannon. Storm was running back and forth in front of Aelish, trying to block the King's Guard and Stannon from approaching her.

"Tell that miserable beast to move or we will kill him!" yelled Stannon.

"Storm, come!" At first, Storm did not obey his mistress, knowing she was in extraordinary danger. "Storm! Bed, now!" The dog retreated into her bedchamber but stood on the threshold at the ready.

"What is that noise?" she yelled to Stannon.

"You set it off! You should know!"

"I most certainly did not!" yelled Aelish.

Stannon scoffed at her as he began searching the suite of rooms. Aelish followed him.

"Katrina and I were speaking in the living area, when it just began screeching. Can you please turn it off and tell the King's Guard to stand down before a being is injured or killed?"

"I will fetch the king," said Stannon. He left the suite of rooms and instructed the King's Guard to remain with their weapons aimed at Aelish.

Aelish sat down on the settee with her hands over her ears. When the king finally came into the room, he instantly turned off the alarm with his magic.

"Thank God above!" exclaimed Aelish. "What was that, Cardissius?"

Stannon rolled his eyes at her after she addressed the king by his first name.

"I will need to investigate this, Aelish," said the king. He turned toward the King's Guard. "Please return to your posts. Stannon, you may leave."

Stannon glared at Aelish and she knew, right then, just how much he hated her and the heir. She felt fear run up the back of her neck. The king believed Stannon to be loyal, and he was—to the king. But when it came to Aelish and the heir, his fealty was highly suspect. Stannon said to the king, "Do you need anything further from me, Your Highness?"

The king replied, "Meet me in the small conference room in the Royal Governmental Affairs building so we can discuss what happened. I think the dog may have had something to do with it."

As Stannon left the room, Aelish became concerned the king might hurt Storm or remove him from the room. "You won't take him away from me, will you?" she asked.

"No, dearest. I'm just theorizing about what could have triggered the alarm. Were you doing any odd activities in the room?"

"Like what? Dancing? Jumping up and down? Of course, not!"

"All right, Aelish. Try to calm yourself. It's no good for the heir if you're upset."

"I hope the heir still has his hearing! How ridiculous!"

"The alarm was installed for your protection, dearest. I must ascertain everything is in order and you were not in harm's way. Try to relax now and I will see you later."

"All right, Cardissius."

‡‡‡‡

The illusory wall had been sealed. They all sat on the ground for a moment, on the other side of the tunnels, catching their breath.

Haurice, who'd been timing their inspection of the tunnels said, "You were in the tunnels for fifteen minutes. But the scouting done by my squadron took a total of thirty minutes and the alarm never went off. I feel we can draw a conclusion from this trial run that the alarm is only triggered by upright beings after fifteen minutes. This is a very tight window for an extraction."

"Agreed," said Uncle Thurrock, who looked at the Hentorians for their opinion.

One of the warriors said, "This is a very dangerous mission, Thurrock. There may not be time to rescue the DARling prisoner. We need to review some other options with Haurice."

"There are no other options without using magic inside the tunnels," said Thagar, extremely agitated. "I heard her. She is alive and she is here. If we could just transport from the illusory wall to the trap door above us, it would save time. Is this something you could fix?"

The Hentorian warrior replied, "It is unlikely. But we'd like to think about it and speak more with Haurice to discuss other options of approach."

"All right," said Uncle Thurrock, with his hand on Thagar's shoulder. He was squeezing it as if to say, remain quiet while I handle this.

When they all returned to Uncle Thurrock's cottage and barn, Thagar gave his aunt a kiss on the cheek and retreated to his guest room. He sat down on the edge of the bed. He couldn't get the sound of Aelish's laughter out of his head. He wondered why she seemed so at ease, laughing with Cardissius. He felt confused and his judgement was clouded.

Had he not known how much Aelish detested Cardissius, it would've seemed as if she and the king were romantically involved. After being in Commitments with her for nearly four hundred years, he knew that specific laugh very well, and she was not afraid.

But maybe *he* ought to be. Perhaps what awaited him beyond the trap door was going to be infinitely more upsetting than her being held captive. What if Aelish had fallen in love with Cardissius and had forgotten him? He stood up from the side of the bed and looked out the small window of his room. Had he lost his mate to this evil king?

And how were they going to get in and out of the tunnels, plus rescue Aelish, in only fifteen minutes? The whole plan seemed doomed from the start. He couldn't understand why he suddenly felt so hopeless about everything. Something wasn't right, he could feel it in his metal-plated bones. Her laugh was an intimate laugh; something he thought was reserved only for him. What was going on between Aelish and Cardissius? Right now, he felt like he wanted to die.

After about an hour, Thagar heard on a knock on his door. "Come in," he said.

Uncle Thurrock gently opened the door. "What is it, Nephew? You've been in here alone for quite some time. You're a commander. You know extractions are always complicated. We will work out the timing of the alarm."

Thagar remained quiet.

Uncle Thurrock pressed further. "I'm getting the sense something deeper is troubling you. Would you like to share it with me?"

Thagar remained on the edge of the bed. He ran his hands through his curls. His uncle sat down alongside of him. Thagar said, "At first, we heard nothing. But if she's imprisoned with others, how could it be so quiet? Then, I heard the distinctive cadence of King Cardissius' voice. I could not make out what he was saying, but I highly doubt the king would be with Aelish in the prison if other prisoners were around. I think she is in there alone, Uncle."

"That's a distinct possibility. I'm sure the prison is completely different than when I was held captive. What else is troubling you?"

"I heard my mate's laugh. I simply can't get the sound out of my head. We've been in Commitments for nearly four hundred years, and I know all of her different laughs. It was her intimate laugh, reserved only for me. Or at least that's what I always thought. She was not afraid of the king, Uncle. I fear she's fallen in love with Cardissius and has forgotten me."

Uncle Thurrock began gently rubbing Thagar's back, trying to soothe him. "Do you remember when I told you that you must mentally prepare yourself for whatever condition we may find her in?" Thagar nodded his head. "You heard the king speak and you heard her laugh. I agree, on the face of it, that's disconcerting. But we don't know what she's been coping with. We don't know what she's had to do to survive. Only those who've shared the experience of being held captive can truly understand what it takes to survive. Those on the outside cannot even imagine what a prisoner must endure. You are making assumptions from an outside perspective. Your perspective is not hers, and a rush to judgement is unfair to both you and her."

Thagar said, "I don't want to know who I am without her. I can't lose that part of me. She is my life; she is my heart. I never anticipated anything like this was even remotely possible."

"Cardissius is cunning and shrewd. He knows how to put on a good show to impress. Somehow, Nephew, I don't get the sense the Living Legend would fall for it. But she's been without her magic for months now, so she's had to adapt, and most likely finds herself desperate. But to believe she's truly in love with him, whilst still a captive, is not reality, Thagar.

"You must understand, there are no windows in this prison. You cannot see the sunlight. You don't know what time of day it is. Your reality is completely altered. So, if she's found some way to cope with it all, if you truly love her, you must be ready to let her tell you truths you may not want to hear. When I said you must be strong for her, I meant in every way. Even if you feel like your heart is breaking, she must know, in her soul, she has your unconditional love and support. And no matter what she tells you happened during her captivity—you have to bear it. Otherwise, you will lose her forever. You must trust me on this, Nephew."

Thagar was processing every word his uncle was saying. He had never been tested in this way. But Aelish had, when he was injured and in rehabilitation for two years. Could he do this?

Suddenly, there was a knock on the door. Aunt Charlotte slightly opened the door and announced Haurice was here.

"Please come in, Haurice," said Uncle Thurrock.

In a second, the drone rat was at the side of the bed, up on his hind legs, looking at Thagar and Uncle Thurrock. Thagar was embarrassed, as there were tears on his face. He quickly wiped them away and Haurice graciously did not remark on his obvious dismay.

"My drone rats and I have been in a long discussion with the

Hentorian warriors out in the barn. I believe we've come up with a way to outwit the alarm, giving us much more time to rescue your mate, Thagar."

"Please, tell us, Haurice," said Uncle Thurrock.

"We drone rats are going to smooth and reinforce the ceiling of the tunnel system with a material to hold the rock and soil in place. Once the material has been installed, we will space iron bars that the Hentorian warriors can grasp, so they can walk along the ceiling. I believe the weight of all the upright beings walking on the floor of the tunnel system is triggering a sensor, which, in turn, is triggering an alarm.

"If you go through the tunnel system on the ceiling and not on the floor, I believe we can save the entire fifteen minutes before the alarm goes off, for your exit. The Hentorian warriors also indicated they'll arrange for additional warriors to be waiting at the end of the tunnels, on the Hentorian side. This way, once you are all out of the tunnels, they can quickly apply the spells needed to seal the exit with the illusory wall. We are hoping to finish the refurbishment of the tunnel system's ceiling in two days' time and be ready for a run-through in three days' time."

"So, my nephew and I will use the iron bars upon the ceiling to reach the trap door underneath the prison, correct?" asked Uncle Thurrock.

"No. The warriors will carry all the Human weaponry on their backs. Each warrior will cradle one of you against their chest. You will be carried through the tunnels as if you were on a hammock of Hentorians." Haurice began laughing and it was a bit screechy. Even Thagar began laughing as did Uncle Thurrock. Not only was this drone rat squadron leader intelligent, he was also funny.

Haurice explained, "Unless you're used to walking on all fours, you can't acquire the coordination and speed needed to quickly get to the trap door, on the floor or the ceiling. No disrespect, but you two DARlings would slow down the mission; you have to be carried."

Uncle Thurrock looked at Thagar and smiled. "We're not up to par."

Thagar felt his mood brighten. He was relieved the mission was back on track.

"So," said Haurice, "my squadron will prepare the tunnels over the next two days and on the third day we will test out the plan. Sounds good?"

"It sounds excellent, Haurice. Thank you," said Thagar, who smiled at the tiny drone rat.

"Okay, great!" exclaimed Haurice. "Charlotte is bringing dinner to our room now so we can be up before the sun and get to work. I bid you a good night's sleep. See you tomorrow."

"Thank you," said Uncle Thurrock. "Have a good sleep."

After watching Haurice flatten himself to squeeze underneath the opening at the bottom of the closed bedroom door, Uncle Thurrock looked at Thagar and said, "That was a humbling experience." He slapped Thagar's leg and stood up. "Get yourself washed up and let's eat."

"All right, Uncle," said Thagar, smiling.

‡‡‡‡

Three days later, they tested out the new plan. They made it to the trap door in the ceiling within minutes. They all hovered on the iron bars next to the trap door, listening. Suddenly, Thagar heard Aelish crying and her footfall above him was pacing. She was distraught.

Over the last three days, Thagar and his uncle had many conversations about how he needed to prepare himself for whatever they were going to find once they opened the trap door.

He promised his uncle he'd support and love her, unconditionally. Thagar closed his eyes.

I'm right here, my love.

18

Four Unsealed Letters

A ELISH LOOKED AT the concerned faces of the same four medici who had conducted her six-week scan and her magical anomalies testing. They'd just completed the ten-week scan of the infant, and she knew something was wrong. The medici were keeping something from her.

"Will he live?" asked Aelish.

The eldest medicus replied, "Whilst most Yasteron infants weigh two pounds at birth, he is still relatively small and will have a low birthweight."

When Aelish had found out she was carrying a Human fetus, she clearly remembered Medicus Valdia and Medicus Kimber in DAR telling her the normal weight of a DARlette was one pound. She found it fascinating that a Yasteron infant was one pound larger. Since the original DARlings who'd left DAR to form Yasteron chose only to mate with one another, perhaps over time, the birthweight of their offspring had become larger.

Seeing the look of concern on her face, the eldest medicus offered, "Once he is born, we believe with the right amount of sunlight and magic enveloping him, he will thrive."

"Oh, thank God," she said.

"Why don't you go and lie down now, Aelish," said the king. "I will be in to see you shortly."

Aelish nodded and thanked the four medici, shaking all of their hands, and retreated to her bedchamber. But she did not lie down. She snuck back into the hallway between the living area and the bedchamber. She knew the medici were keeping something from her, and she wanted to hear what they were about to tell the king. The eldest medicus' voice was somewhat raised, making it easier for her to hear.

"We have not seen Magical Sunlight Deprivation Heart Syndrome for centuries, Your Highness."

Aelish gasped. She tried to remember if she'd ever heard of this syndrome in DAR. She was well acquainted with Magical Interruption Syndrome, but she definitely knew she'd *never* heard of this syndrome.

The eldest medicus continued. "Being deprived of both sunlight and their magical capabilities, prisoners during the reign of your father suffered from this fatal syndrome. It was previously called Magical Interruption Syndrome because, at first, the prisoners experienced unreliable and dangerous interruptions in their magical abilities. But because we still have so many prisoners in captivity from DAR, upon further examination, the medici concluded Magical Interruption Syndrome develops into Magical Sunlight Deprivation Heart Syndrome if the prisoners have neither sunlight *nor* the use of their magical abilities. For some, it may take years to occur. But if they are deprived of both, their hearts will eventually stop."

"My father, King Nevuna, instituted a change in the treatment of prisoners once this was discovered," said the king. "Prisoners have long-been afforded recreational time outside in the sunshine as well as three hours per day of their magical abilities in a controlled environment. Where is this lecture going?"

"I meant no disrespect, Your Highness. As you know, magical beings depend on the sunlight reflected off the Earth by our shared sun. But Lady Aelish is an Earth born DARling. The sun is much closer to the Earth than it is to DAR or Yasteron. Therefore, because Lady Aelish was born of the Earth, she is experiencing the lack of sunlight a hundredfold to those born in the magical world."

"I don't follow your meaning," said the king.

The eldest medicus deeply exhaled. "Lady Aelish has two factors working against her: she is an Earth born DARling and she is pregnant. During her months of imprisonment, she has been deprived of both sunlight and her magical capabilities, whilst at the same time, being pregnant. This has put an enormous strain on her heart, as the infant is pulling on all of her body's reserves in order to survive. Further, because she was born and raised in the stronger sunlight of the Earth, she is declining far more rapidly than a magical being born in the magical world. Haven't you noticed her lavender skin color is fading, Your Highness?"

"I have," replied the king.

"This is a warning sign for an Earth born DARling—their heart is under severe strain."

As Aelish leaned against the hallway wall listening, she remembered Lady Antonia remarking on how faint the color of her skin was after she was released from the Detention Center in the N.W. Quadrant of DAR, back in 1665.

Despite being allowed outside for one hour per day for recreational time, she did not have the use of her magical abilities for six months. The Earth born obviously suffer greater repercussions when imprisoned, as her skin had grown very faint, even then. It seemed impossible to believe the medici in DAR were unaware of this syndrome. But Yasteron had acquired this horrific knowledge because of their despicable policy of keeping

DARling soldiers captive for such long periods of time.

"Without intervention, Magical Interruption Syndrome will develop into Magical Sunlight Deprivation Heart Syndrome, and it is deadly. Yet the treatment is so simple: sunlight and being able to use one's magical abilities. Won't you consider allowing your new wife, Lady Aelish, the opportunity to go outside and use her magic, Your Highness?"

Cardissius asked, "But do you feel she will be able to deliver in two-week's time and that the infant will thrive?"

"Yes," said the eldest medicus. "But if she's kept in the same conditions after he is born, she will not survive for more than a month."

The king asked, "Will she be able to nurse the infant in those first two crucial weeks after she delivers so the heir may receive the nutrients only his mother can provide?"

"Yes, but this will put an even greater strain on her heart, Your Highness. Lady Aelish is very young, which is why she is doing as well as she is. But even her youth is not enough to provide her with long-term survival under these conditions."

"All right, Doctors. Thank you for this information. I will see you again when it is time for the heir to be delivered."

Cardissius' dismissive tone indicated to the medici that it was time for them to leave. They packed up their equipment and left. Before they'd left the living area, Aelish situated herself on her bed. As she lay there, she thought of the many centuries she'd lived in fear of the Magical Interruption Syndrome. She had no idea there was a syndrome far worse than MIS. MIS would cause her to lose her magical abilities, but Magical Sunlight Deprivation Heart Syndrome would cause her to lose her life.

Eavesdropping on the conversation between the medici and Cardissius confirmed to Aelish that he cared only about her ability to deliver his heir apparent. His declarations of love for her, as well as his recent tenderness were all lies. Oba was right, he was incapable of change. Cardissius was the same evil being she'd always known him to be. He was using her to procreate a first-of-its-kind magical being, with the coupling of an Earth born DARling and a Yasteron.

Once she'd nursed the heir for two weeks, he would no longer need her and would allow her to die in this room. She imagined after her death that he would steal other Earth born female DARlings to sire future offspring. She laughed inwardly at the relief death brought. She would never again have to perform the Endeavor with the king and betray her love for Thagar.

Cardissius truly was malevolent. She had never encountered such an evil being in her entire life. He had absolutely no redeeming qualities. He was brilliant at convincing his prey they meant something to him—that there was hope they could learn to live within their newfound circumstances. Aelish knew the king was well aware of every single fact the eldest medicus explained and, in fact, had anticipated it all. He cared nothing for her. She was merely the vessel by which to pass on her extraordinary magical capabilities to his heir.

She had wondered why, as of late, it had become difficult walking from the bedchamber to the living area. She thought it was simply because she was nearing her due date. But now, she knew it was because her heart was slowing down.

Oba hadn't been here for nearly three weeks, but he was scheduled to come tomorrow. Aelish had no more than two weeks before her son's birth to put some things in motion and leave behind a few surprises for Cardissius in her wake. Lying there, her only regret was not being able to say goodbye to her beloved Thagar and Kaleigh.

Oba entered the room accompanied by the king. She noted he did not have any archives with him and looked exhausted. Storm got up to greet both Oba and the king; the dog infused life back into the Master of Archives. He vigorously began to pet Storm and chuckled.

"I will leave you two alone for your next lesson," said the king. Aelish thought him a cold and callous being. He knew this would most likely be the last time she'd ever see Oba, but his affect gave nothing away.

"Thank you, Your Highness," said Oba. Aelish, Oba, and Storm watched the king exit the room. Turning toward Aelish, Oba said, "I apologize for taking so long to return to you, Lady Aelish." Oba took her hand, lightly kissed it, and gingerly bowed in front of her. He seemed to be in great discomfort. Aelish gently curtsied.

"And please forgive me for not bringing the last remaining written record denoting Yasterons are DARlings. After our last lesson, Chief Minister Stannon, who has never set foot inside of my dwelling, began making unannounced visits. It was very unnerving because my dwelling is where all the archives are kept. I knew things were becoming dangerous, as he was magically scanning my home for documents and information that he could use against me. Of course, I had prepared for this centuries ago. The necessary protections of the ancient archives have always been in place. Therefore, I decided it was best not to disturb any of the spells guarding the archives. Will you forgive me?"

"Of course, Master Oba," said Aelish. "Were you harmed by Chief Minister Stannon?"

"No, not directly. However, I've become exhausted from the constant state of anxiety he has put me in. I feared he might order the archives destroyed or abscond with whatever was not magically hidden to be used for some nefarious purpose. It has taken its toll on me, as I am no longer a young male."

Aelish smiled at him. "I'm so glad you are all right, Master Oba."

Oba began hobbling over toward the dining table. He sat down in the same chair as the first time they'd met. Aelish sat down across from him and Storm lay at her feet.

"I suggest we get started, as there is a lot to cover today, Lady Aelish."

"Understood. Please, begin."

"The Office of Covert Affairs, which falls under Yasteron's Intelligence Agency, enacted the policy of strategically placing covert operatives, posing as Humans, throughout the Earth. This began after you permanently broke the alliance between Komprathia and Yasteron in 1665. Their purpose was to foment overall chaos and to exacerbate the climate crisis on Earth as revenge for your actions. Originally, King Nevuna chose only males to serve as covert operatives. But once Cardissius became king, he decided Yasteron females could accompany their male-operative spouses, to allow them to seamlessly meld into Earthly society.

"As females on Earth expanded their roles in society, working in factories, canneries, and clerical occupations, Cardissius decided to send unmarried females to work as covert operatives. After World War II, Earthly females worked in fields such as mathematics, science, legal, and health services, ultimately reflecting the modern-day workforce of females on Earth.

"So, whilst female covert operatives at first infiltrated Earth by accompanying their spouses, they subsequently worked alongside Earthly females and eventually worked alongside Earthly males as well. Once they got a taste of the freedoms they were granted on Earth, they never wanted to return to Yasteron. Keep in mind, Lady Aelish, all female operatives were from noble families. No lower-orders were ever given this opportunity."

As Aelish sat there listening, she realized she'd been correct; despite all their inherent magical capabilities, the King Mother and other female nobles were stuck somewhere between 1350 and 1550. She said, "Considering how females on Earth still live and work under an exhaustive patriarchy, it seems unfathomable to me that Yasteron female operatives experienced more freedoms there than they did in their own magical dominion." She shook her head.

"Now, you understand why I stated in our previous lesson that Yasteron females are magically stunted and stilted. They haven't evolved for centuries, except for those living on the Earth as covert operatives.

"Once unmarried female operatives began working alongside Human males, and vice versa, some of the operatives fell in love with their coworkers, as well as Humans they met in social circles used to maintain their cover identities. What was not anticipated by King Cardissius or the Yasteron Intelligence Agency, was that some of our covert operatives, whether male or female, were determined to marry their Human lovers. And then, they wanted offspring."

Aelish said, "But I've always known DARlings can't conceive with Humans. Are you saying Yasteron operatives were unaware of this fact?"

"Inbreeding amongst Yasteron royals and nobles kept them ignorant of this fact. It was only after they married their Human lovers and tried to conceive with them that they realized they'd made a gross miscalculation. And the covert operatives had never disclosed to their Human spouses they were magical beings for fear of their cover being blown."

"Oh, my God! What a thing to keep secret."

"Exactly, it was not a wise decision. But no Human knew of the existence of the magical world and the covert operatives were terrified of what would happen should the Human world discover who they really were. They were also terrified the Kingdom of Yasteron would discover they were no longer covert; they would all be hung in Shamalaya Square."

"So, what did they do?" asked Aelish.

"They accepted the fact that their marriages would not yield any offspring. But then, something incredible began to happen. Both female Yasteron operatives and female Humans who'd married male Yasteron operatives, did conceive. But every pregnancy ended in a miscarriage. They simply could not bring a pregnancy to term."

"Oh my God!" exclaimed Aelish. "I can't believe they conceived at all!"

"Life always finds a way," said Oba, smiling. "Finally, the operatives could no longer bear the suffering of their spouses, miscarriage after miscarriage, so they came to a consensus: they agreed to tell their Human spouses who they really were. And the reason they decided to become *overt* had to do with a very young scientist, named Isabela, who was on the verge of discovering the LECCS syndrome."

Aelish would never be able to describe in words what it felt like to hear such a learned master in Yasteron discussing Isabela and her discovery of LECCS. But she also felt a great sadness that Glen was not one of the operatives who had genuinely fallen in love with a Human. It made his actions against Isabela even more despicable. She began to tear up.

"I know you are an Oraculi to Isabela, and I know she has suffered greatly at the hands of Yasteron." Aelish nodded but did not want to interrupt Master Oba. She was finally going to learn how Yasteron discovered the mysterious bacterium Isabela had tirelessly searched for.

"Many of the operatives married to Humans were

experimenters. Once they became aware of Isabela, who was not only a genius, but who also suspected the climate crisis was going to cause an extinction-level syndrome, they decided to help her. Most, but not all of the operatives, had long-since abandoned their desire to harm the Earth. And the covert experimenters believed they'd found a way for the Human spouses of all operatives to forgive them for lying about who they really were.

"So, despite being exposed, the covert experimenters were determined to unlock the cause of the forthcoming syndrome. I believe many of the covert experimenters joined an organization known as SOS, initiated by Isabela. I forget now what the acronym stood for."

"Scientists Organizing for Science," replied Aelish. She remembered the creation of SOS was long before Tozer began vetting scientists through Department 427. "I can't believe they were actually working to *prevent* the extinction-level syndrome."

"Indeed. And the covert experimenters also became aware of the fact that one of the youngest operatives on Earth was posing as Isabela's lover. They knew he'd stolen all of her scientific research and turned it over to the kingdom."

"The young operative's name was Glen, correct?" asked Aelish.

"Yes! Thank you for telling me his name. When you get to be my age and have studied as much as I have, it becomes harder and harder to remember small details—like names!" Oba began laughing and his white kaftan began jiggling around the middle. "After Glen turned over Isabela's research to the kingdom, experimenters in Yasteron who were politically aligned with the covert operatives on Earth and wished to overthrow the reign of King Cardissius, ultimately returned the young scientist's research to the covert experimenters. So, armed with the assistance of the experimenters in Yasteron, who were no longer loyal to the

Crown, they worked day and night and finally discovered that a commensal strain of E. coli was going to morph into E. coli O157:H7 or LECCS."

Aelish shook her head in disbelief. "So, they made one of the most important scientific discoveries in Human history because they loved one specific Human. I can't believe love was their motivation for discovering the mysterious bacterium, threatening all of Humanity. Did the covert operatives who'd married Humans receive the forgiveness they were seeking?"

"Once the Human spouses realized the Yasteron experimenters, both in Yasteron and on Earth, had unlocked the mysterious bacterium threatening all of Humanity, they forgave them for lying. And once Isabela began working on a vaccine for LECCS, the experimenters turned their attention toward discovering a successful way to procreate. From their research on the bacterium, Yasteron experimenters had become experts on Human genetics, the science of DNA, and overall genomics."

Aelish remembered how fascinated Isabela was that Yasterons were so good at genomics. She asked, "But why did the experimenters use their research on the bacterium, which led to the discovery of LECCS, to create a LECCS bioweapon if they truly loved Humans?"

"That was never their intent," replied Oba. "Chief Minister Stannon discovered the experimenters in Yasteron were working on a Human bacterium. They were simply assisting the covert experimenters on Earth, but Stannon forced their hand. So, they lied and told him they were working on a bioweapon to kill Humans.

"Lying about developing a bioweapon severely backfired on the experimenters in Yasteron. Once Stannon got a taste for bioweapons, he ordered them to take their research and turn LECCS into a bioweapon. In order to continue assisting the covert experimenters on Earth with their procreation research, they had to continue developing bioweapons to avert suspicion. Stannon still has no idea that the covert experimenters on Earth ever worked on the bacterium."

Aelish shook her head in disbelief at everything Oba was telling her.

"The Komprathian drone rats were experimented on for the Human bioweapon, but Stannon wanted more. He ordered the experimenters to create a specific bioweapon that worked only on DARlings. So, they were forced to perform experiments on the plethora of DARling soldiers, who still remain in captivity, in order to create the DARling Draft."

What Aelish would have given for Isabela to hear all of this. Still shaking her head, she asked, "Did the experimenters ever achieve the ability to procreate with Humans?"

"They did."

"Oh, my God," said Aelish. She reflected for a moment on the fact that had Glen truly loved Isabela, they could have had children together.

Oba continued, "The first Yastermans were born in rogue labs on Earth using the technology of in vitro fertilization along with a new technology that created artificial wombs."

"I assume a Yasterman is the offspring of a Yasteron and a Human?" asked Aelish.

"Correct," replied Oba.

"Wait! Artificial wombs!" exclaimed Aelish. "My God, if that existed, both Human and magical females would be free from having to endure pregnancy."

"Precisely," said Oba. "In 1923, an eccentric English biologist, named J.B.S. Haldane, created the term "ectogenesis," which means the artificial conception and complete gestation of a fetus outside of its mother's body. Artificial wombs are currently assisting Human babies born very prematurely. But to create a Human life through in vitro fertilization grown entirely in an artificial womb is years away. However, when you combine magic with science, which the Yasteron covert experimenters and their Human scientist spouses did, it became possible.

"The Human scientists and their Yasteron experimenter spouses developed this evolutionary science. These Yasterons wanted to overthrow King Cardissius for centuries. They want to destroy the DARling Draft, the LECCS bioweapon, save Humanity from climate change, and remain on Earth with the Humans they fell in love with, along with their Yasterman offspring. They are in awe of the LECCS vaccine developed by the young Human scientist."

Aelish asked, "Can the Yasterman offspring breathe in the magical world?"

"Not at this time," replied Oba. "But the experimenters in Yasteron are assisting those on Earth, by searching for the genetic code which would allow them to breathe here."

"My God," said Aelish.

"My dear Lady Aelish, unrest has been brewing in Yasteron for centuries. If the covert operatives on Earth allied with the lower-orders and could convince a noble close to King Cardissius to lead the overthrow of his reign, I believe the kingdom as we know it would end. It could thrive as an egalitarian dominion, and we could finally have peace within the magical world. Cardissius must be eliminated, or it will never be. Your son becoming the male heir will make him a target of the revolutionaries, because as of the moment, there is no true heir to the king since he only has daughters. And the nobles will never accept a female as their sovereign."

"Is Cardissius aware of the fact that so many of his covert operatives on Earth wish to overthrow his reign? And further, is he aware of the unrest brewing amongst the lower-orders, in addition to so many of the nobles?"

"If he is, the king keeps this knowledge closely guarded between himself and Chief Minister Stannon. Cardissius derives much of his power from the advice and guidance of Stannon. Stannon is the power center of the king. He encourages the king's murderous and heinous policies against the lower-orders as well as the policies against DAR and Earth. To me, Stannon is more evil than Cardissius."

Aelish's head was spinning from all of this information.

"I have one final piece of vital information for you," said Oba. "There is a noble who is aware of what I'm about to tell you, but he says he trusts you. If you betray him, Lady Aelish, he will be hung in Shamalaya Square for all the citizens to see."

"What is it you wish to tell me, Master Oba? You can trust me."

"Special Envoy Ragdon is the noble conduit between the lower-orders and the covert operatives on Earth. He is also very close to Queen Saia, who would be an excellent choice for an interim sovereign until the kingdom could rid itself of the monarchy and its nobles. He told me to tell you that what he needs to create a coordinated overthrow of the kingdom is weapons."

"Do you mean Special Envoy Ragdon who serves on the Alliance of Magical Dominions?"

"Yes."

"I cannot believe Ragdon is the conduit! Why doesn't he just ask the AMD for weapons himself?"

Oba went to speak and hesitated.

Aelish continued, "The dominions in the AMD despise Yasteron and would be more than happy to help overthrow King Cardissius. I always blamed him for my imprisonment. I assumed he knew all along what the king was planning for me, and he was a part of it."

"You are very wise, Lady Aelish. That is the exact reason why he cannot ask the AMD for help. He *was* a part of it. But he had to go along with the king's plans in order to maintain his allegiance to the Crown. Chief Minister Stannon and King Cardissius are well aware there is a noble conduit to the lower-orders. But I don't know if they are truly aware of the sheer number of lower-orders, noble Yasterons, and covert operatives who wish to overthrow the monarchy.

"If Ragdon had not arranged for you to be taken, by forcing you to accept the *one last condition* Cardissius requested before signing the Peace Accord, Ragdon was in great danger of being discovered as the conduit. But in doing so, he lost the trust of the AMD forever. He needs you, Lady Aelish, to tell the AMD or some dominion within it that trusts you implicitly, to convince them he is actually trustworthy and will help overthrow King Cardissius."

Aelish asked, "Can you get a letter out of this kingdom, Master Oba? Because if you are caught, you and I are both dead."

"I can."

"Please, wait here one moment. I will return with three letters I've spent the last few weeks composing. I never thought they'd ever make it out of this room, but I wrote them in the off-chance that they could."

"You have them ready to go now?" asked Oba, astonished.

"I do."

Oba could not hide his shock nor his admiration of her.

Aelish said, "One is for the leader of the lower-orders' community, one is for the leader of the covert operatives on Earth, and the final one is for the director of Komprathia's military. If you'd give me the name of the covert operative's leader, I can fill it in now."

"His name is Ryker."

"All right, I will be right back." Aelish went into her bedchamber and added the name of Ryker to the second letter and returned with all three letters. She placed them on the dining room table. They were not yet sealed, as she'd been waiting for the final name. She'd finally convinced Katrina to give her the name of the lower-orders' leader and had a sense he was her brother. She deduced this from the way Katrina had told her, as well as by his name, Kam, which started with the same two letters as hers.

"May I read them?" asked Oba.

"Of course, and please let me know if I need to add anything to them. Actually, let me have back the one to Commander Orión in Komprathia. I need to tell him about Special Envoy Ragdon. This way you can review what I add."

"My God," said Oba. "No wonder you're a Living Legend."

Aelish smiled and began adding another paragraph to her letter to Commander Orión. Orión and Aelish were very good friends and he greatly admired her. He once told her if she ever needed anything from Komprathia, he would make sure she received it. He was the son of Obredón, brother of King Gidus, who'd led the regime change in Komprathia. Orión was as kind as his father and trusted her completely.

When she finished adding the section about Special Envoy Ragdon to her letter, she handed it back to Oba for his review. The letter read:

My Dear Orión,

I have just learned today that Special Envoy Ragdon is the noble conduit who has been orchestrating the overthrow of King Cardissius and his ministers. Queen Saia and her daughters will most likely maintain the monarchy, like your father did, until the revolution is over and the kingdom can become an egalitarian dominion. This may take some time.

Ragdon has indicated the one thing he desperately needs is weaponry to pull off the coup. I would suggest you arrange with DAR for additional weapons, as I'm sure they have been assisting you with military supplies in continuation of DAR's proxy wars with Yasteron. Please tell Council Chair Melanthia she should trust this information as she would my life.

Ragdon will provide you with all the logistics, but I also wanted to give you the name of the leader of the lower-orders here in Yasteron. His name is Kam. And the name of the leader of the covert operatives on Earth is Ryker. Perhaps one day, the magical world will live in peace.

All my love,

Aelish

Oba looked at her and said, "This is perfect."

Aelish said, "I do have one other letter. But I didn't know if you are close to Queen Saia or if she would trust information from you."

"She most likely trusts Ragdon more, but she would definitely take a letter from me."

"All right. I will go get it in a moment. Whilst I was adding the part about Ragdon for Commander Orión, you read my other letters. Did they meet with your approval?"

Oba smiled at her. "They are all incredible, Lady Aelish."

"All right, excellent. Let me retrieve the letter for the queen. I would like you to read it as well before I seal all of them. My lower-order-in-waiting gave me the materials for a seal."

Oba nodded and Aelish went into her bedchamber to get the fourth letter she had composed to Queen Saia. This one was more personal, but she needed to know if Oba felt the queen would be receptive to it. It was very important to Aelish that Queen Saia forgive her for any pain she had caused the queen or her three beautiful daughters.

Aelish momentarily returned and handed Oba the fourth letter. The letter read:

Her Royal Majesty Queen Saia:

Please don't throw this letter away. If you can't bring yourself to read it now, save it for another time. I hope you can find it within your heart to forgive me for all the pain I have caused you and your daughters. I know you have endured endless humiliation in front of the entire kingdom because of me, and for this, I am truly sorry.

I came to Yasteron, against the advice of my mate, because I was determined to get the king to sign the Peace Accord I'd been working on for years. It has always been my belief that peace is the only bridge that will end the discord between two warring dominions. If one side merely defeats the other, the loser will always want retribution. Both sides must be willing to accommodate the other in order for there to be a true and lasting peace in perpetuity.

Whilst I was concerned King Cardissius might not honor the Peace Accord in perpetuity, I never suspected he would use this sacred document to perpetuate heinous crimes against me and against you. Raping me to procreate a male heir, who would be imbued with my magical abilities, is a crime so egregious it defies all sense of morality. This kind of evil can never be satisfied, as evil on this level is one part insanity, one part cruelty, mixed with a side of sadism, covered in a blanket of invincibility. You cannot reason with it; you have to kill it.

I have taken an Oath of Peace. My oath has caused me many hours of mental agony, wrestling with the concept of ending a life, either through murder or through war. Even after all I have suffered at the hands of the King of Yasteron, I know I'm incapable of killing him because of my oath. So, let me be clear: when I say you have to kill it, I mean the society which allows this kind of male entitlement and privilege over females. The laws governing said society must be changed. Something went awry during the evolution of the male species and females silently allowed them to enact systemic patriarchal laws of male domination. You can see it in both the magical world as well as the Human world.

Even now, when females try to grasp power within a patriarchal society, they are unable to create meaningful change and are often corrupted by that same male-dominated system. Simply replacing leaders who have breasts instead of a phallus is not real change.

A true matriarchal society is one where justice, institutions, and systems, operating within the overall governance of that society, reflect the female ideologies of peace and prosperity without the threat of war as the ultimate weapon. Warring is easy; peace is hard. To maintain peace means you have to look your enemy in the eye at a negotiating table and not through the blur of a battlefield filled with smoke and mangled bodies. After the war, always comes the peace talks. Therefore, why not start at the beginning with peace talks or a Peace Accord and save the innocents who are usually females and their offspring.

Whilst it causes me unfathomable sadness to know I will never see my mate or my daughter again, I will go to my grave in peace if I know, deep in my heart, you will take back what was rightfully yours to begin with. For you to understand how alike we are, you must seek out the sage advice and lessons that only Oba, Master of Archives for Yasteron, is capable of teaching. You will learn that within you, lies the same magical acuity the king sought within me, in order to create a lineage of preeminent magical beings or a master-magical race.

What the king does not understand is that there is no magical being more powerful than the females from DAR and Yasteron. Males are incapable of reaching our level of magical attainment. However, when females don't stop male domination, denying themselves their innate right to power and influence, they pay a horrific price.

I am dying of Magical Sunlight Deprivation Heart Syndrome, and I will never be Queen of Yasteron nor will I bear any more heirs for King Cardissius. I hope knowing you will be the last true Queen of Yasteron will bring you solace. The citizens of this kingdom love you, and I hope you will feel confident to rule when it comes time for you to do so. I hope you'll rule with kindness, compassion, and justice, ultimately abolishing the monarchy and giving power back to the citizens to duly elect their leaders. Caste systems with royals, nobles, and lower-orders never last.

Please know there are so many females in DAR who will assist you with your duties. They have longed for peace with Yasteron for centuries so the entire magical world may live in peace with one another. You can be the individual to put all of it in motion. Do not hesitate to ask for help from the females of DAR. They will be so happy to work with you to create an egalitarian society; one that will be allied with DAR and no longer at war with DAR.

Those you can trust with your own life and those of your daughters are Special Envoy Ragdon and Master of Archives Oba. They both have all the information you will need to form a new government as well as create institutions of learning so the females of Yasteron can finally become as magically talented as the females of DAR.

I wish you so much good luck and you remain in my prayers,
Aelish

Oba had tears streaming down his face as he put Aelish's letter to Queen Saia down onto the table. "You are dying?"

"Apparently. I have acquired Magical Sunlight Deprivation Heart Syndrome."

"Ohh, Lady Aelish. No one has suffered from that in centuries, as it is so easy to prevent and to cure. The afflicted merely need hours in the sunlight and the use of their magical abilities. The king knows this, but he is purposefully allowing you to die?"

"Indeed. As you said in our first lesson, he is incapable of change. I have never encountered such evil in my life, Master Oba. And now he will take my life. But I will rest easier knowing I helped put things in motion to hopefully end the misery perpetuated by Yasteron. My only regret is I will not see my mate and my daughter one last time to say goodbye."

"Would you like to give me a letter for them?"

"My love for them is so great, it would take a century to compose. If you ever get the chance to meet either one, please, tell them how much they meant to me."

Oba nodded and wiped away his tears.

"The last thing I desperately need your help with, Master Oba, is to help Katrina find a lower-order family to care for my son. As long as he lives, he will serve as a dangerous weapon for those who wish to reinstate the patriarchal monarchy. He needs to remain hidden his entire life. Perhaps in time, he could be relocated to another dominion within the magical world. Oh, and if possible, please don't forget to take Storm so they can be together. Storm loves the infant, and the infant loves Storm."

"I will do as you ask, Lady Aelish," said Oba. "Please be sure to tell Katrina I will be her contact when it comes time to remove the heir from this room. That will be the most dangerous part of all. The king has been obsessed for centuries with siring a male heir with you, in order to attain your magical abilities. I am so sorry the heir will never know his mother. But he will certainly know *of* her."

Aelish nodded and wiped away a tear.

19

Hotter Than 1.4°C

A s isabela lay on the deck of Drew's yacht, soaking up the sun's early morning rays over Port d'Hercule in Monaco, she realized the last true vacation she'd been on was in Disneyland for her tenth birthday. It was the last family vacation, prior to her mother being diagnosed with cancer, more than ten years ago when she was still a child.

What followed soon after was her mother's diagnosis, her unsuccessful cancer treatments for two years, and her mother's participation in an experimental clinical trial, which led the family to move just outside of Nashville, Tennessee. Then, she met Dr. Hector Rios, who discovered her genius, shortly after starting at her new middle school. That led to the non-stop ride of college, medical school, pursuing her MD/Ph.D., and ultimately discovering the Lancaster E. Coli Climate Syndrome and developing a vaccine. She felt a lifetime of exhaustion at the age of twenty.

Once Drew recommended they take a rest from the LECCS tour on the Mediterranean in Monaco on his yacht, Isabela experienced clinical fatigue by her own diagnosis. For the first week on the yacht, aside from meals, she didn't leave the boat and just slept and slept. Sometimes, she'd wake up to find Drew in a chair in her luxurious cabin, sitting with her as she slept.

He'd either be reading for pleasure or reviewing work materials while keeping a watchful eye over her. She'd feel his presence and fall into the deepest sleeps of her life, totally at peace. She didn't dream of Aelish, the climate crisis, the vaccine, or even her family. She slept in a far-away dreamland and remembered nothing when she woke up—it was heaven.

Seeing how exhausted she was, Drew had Helene reschedule a lot of their tour engagements and told Isabela they could stay in Monaco until she felt truly rested. And that made her relax even more. For the first time in over ten years, she didn't have to take an exam, use a microscope, develop a vaccine, or worry about the rising overall global temperature. She just turned her brain to the "off" setting.

After a week of doing nothing but sleep, she finally felt like venturing out to the various restaurants, casinos, and hotels, which were mere steps from where the yacht was docked. Port d'Hercule was a superyacht marina with the richest yachting heritage of anywhere in the world. It was the superyacht capital of the Mediterranean, surrounded by Monaco's steep hills with elegant high rises surrounding the city. It was the playground of the rich and famous, and she completely understood why it was featured in so many movies. After an evening in Monte Carlo of fine dining or winning at the blackjack table, her favorite game, she and Drew would head back to the yacht and it felt like she was going home.

Isabela had always loved the water and she rediscovered its

healing powers in the gentle rocking of the water's current while the yacht was docked. She simply loved being on the water and thoroughly enjoyed doing laps in the yacht's swimming pool every morning after breakfast. At the moment, her life consisted of eating, sleeping, and sunning herself. When they dined together, she and Drew talked about nothing important; they did not discuss the vaccine or the balance of the tour. Isabela greatly enjoyed his biting sense of humor and they spent most of their time together laughing. But it was her solitude that she enjoyed the most, when her brain was completely turned off.

One morning, she went up to the deck to wait for the sun to rise. Everyone was still asleep, with the exception of her personal bodyguard who was never too far away. The cool morning air tickled her tanned skin as she lay in a bathrobe over her swimsuit, in one of the reclining deck chairs. The slight chill in the air made her reach for a light blanket, folded neatly on the chair next to her. She fell into a deep sleep, but shortly thereafter, she felt a presence next to her. Isabela slowly opened her eyes, but it wasn't Drew in the chair next to her, it was Tozer staring at her.

"What magic it is to watch you sleep in complete peace and not be working in that horrible stuffy lab surrounded by rats," he said, with a sly grin.

"Tozer! What are you doing here, and how did you get past my bodyguard?"

"I put everyone on board this magnificent ship under a Slumber spell so we could have a nice early morning chat."

Ordinarily, this would have made Isabela nervous that Yasterons could board the yacht and put everyone under a spell. But the rest had done her good; she didn't even think about it.

Isabela continued lying on her side on the recliner and stared at this marvelous magical creature. "How have you been? You aren't going to magically seduce me again, are you?"

"Would you like me to?" asked Tozer, who began heartily laughing.

She replied, "I don't know, maybe?"

He knew she was teasing him, and he began laughing again. "No, I promised myself I would behave. Although, I must say, my dear, you look positively radiant this morning. And besides, I have some stiff competition downstairs in the master stateroom. Drew is quite the specimen, and I do admire his rather impressive attribute."

Isabela burst out laughing, knowing exactly which attribute Tozer was referring to.

"You really are a scoundrel, Tozer. Why are you looking at Drew's private parts?"

"Well, I was just wondering why, my friend Isabela, hasn't partaken in all that he has to offer. Hmm . . . ?"

"You are so unbelievably naughty. You are aware of that fact, correct?"

"I am. But I've also made your happiness my little mission in life. I like to keep tabs on you, now and again, and I was curious as to why you've decided to abstain, in light of such a grand offering."

Isabela continued laughing at this incorrigible being. "Because Drew doesn't feel that way toward me. He's just been incredibly kind and caring while we've been working together on our tour, trying to increase the world's vaccination rate for LECCS."

"Blah, blah, blah," replied Tozer. "I'm trying to think of the eyesight restoration spell. Have you been magically blinded by some other being, Isabela? Or does that genius brain of yours simply not understand what is staring you right in the face?"

Isabela smiled. "Drew could have any woman in the world, Tozer. Why would he choose to be with this run-down scientist, who feels fifty instead of twenty?"

"So, I truly am dealing with the deaf, that would be Drew in his right ear, and the blind, which would be you, Isabela. Whilst I think his money more than makes up for his lack of hearing, the burn scars on his arm, and his gunshot wounds—look at him, Isabela! His looks, his physique, his height, and his ability to be quite stiff in his nether region could be positively ruinous to a young woman's reputation. Apparently, I'm with the dumbest genius I will ever encounter. You're literally wasting your brain cells, Isabela."

Isabela began laughing again and knew she was definitely not under one of his spells.

"Drew is madly in love with you, Doctor Torres," said Tozer. "But for some reason, you simply can't see it. Why not?"

"Do you really think so?" she asked, sincerely.

Tozer groaned and Isabela started chuckling.

"I don't *think* so, I *know* so!" exclaimed Tozer loudly, as he exhaled in frustration. "Honey, you've got a filet mignon right in front of you, but in your mind, he's ground beef. Seriously, Isabela?"

Isabela began thinking of all the ways Drew had, theoretically, demonstrated love toward her. But she felt like it was just his nature and his innate kindness which propelled him to be so caring. She truly never imagined that Drew could possibly be in love with her.

Tozer asked, "Don't you feel anything toward that gorgeous piece of meat downstairs, in his sumptuous bed, other than gratitude?" Tozer exhaled a deep breath. "I mean . . . really?"

"Hmm," said Isabela. "You really think Drew has romantic feelings for me?"

Tozer let out a loud whistle of frustration. "Girl, wake up and smell the billionaire. You've got bread in the toaster that popped up a long time ago."

His incessant erection euphemisms were so funny, Isabela could not stop laughing.

"He's the one, Isabela. I know he's a lot older than you, but he's a lot younger when you factor in his wealth. Do you follow me, honey? He more than covers the spread of your age difference with cold hard cash. And you appear quite comfortable in his jet-set world and not the least bit intimidated by his vast fortune. So, I would say—lean in, Isabela."

Isabela was chuckling and said, "I honestly never looked at our relationship that way."

Tozer impatiently tapped one of his goat hooves on the deck of the yacht. "You cannot be serious, Isabela. Why can't you see how much he loves you?"

"I don't know, lack of self-esteem, maybe? To me, his wealth allows me to continue on with my work. I've never felt like he uses his fortune to woo me."

"He doesn't. That's what makes him so sexy. His money doesn't inflate his ego. He merely treats his wealth as a means to an end. He always has a virtuous reason for spending it: your research, a hospital wing, a vaccine to save Humanity, helping the impoverished, reducing illiteracy, and donating gobs of money to help others around the Earth. He's the real deal, Isabela, a true philanthropist. And you deserve that. I wish you could see what I see in you. Then, you would realize how much you deserve to be loved by a man, like Drew. He's extraordinary—like you!"

"I promise to think about what you're saying, Tozer."

"Honey, love isn't something you *think* about, it's something you *feel*. It's something that consumes you until all you want is *that* feeling. It gets its claws into you."

"I've only felt that once in my life, and we both know how that turned out."

"Okay, a first love is, of course, very special, Isabela. But eventually, even a first love can sometimes not fit anymore once you've grown up. Here's a man who shares your ideals. You and Drew think the same way and find the same things important. Sure, he has a lot of toys you never thought you'd experience in your life, but you seem quite at ease with it all. Thinking alike and having similar goals is what makes for a lasting love, chica."

Isabela had never heard Tozer use Spanish before and found it endearing and hilarious.

"He loves you, Isabela. Of that, I am certain. In fact, I've never been so sure of anything in my entire life, and I've lived a lot longer than you. Please, hear what I'm saying and open your heart. Drew will never hurt you because he adores you. And it's because you're *not* enamored by his wealth that makes him love you even more. You're as honest as he is. You appreciate what his wealth can give you, but it will never be *why* you love him. When you fall in love with Drew, it will be for the essence of who he is and not because of what his vast fortune can give you. You have a deep integrity, Isabela, but you need to start looking at your situation differently. Abre tus ojos, cariño."

Isabela burst out laughing after Tozer told her: open your eyes, sweetheart. Hearing him speak Spanish reminded Isabela of her mother, who'd told her similar things about Drew.

Isabela reached across the chairs and grasped Tozer's hand. "Thank you for always looking out for me, Tozer. I will try to open my heart and feel what you say I've been missing. Thank you for always having my best interests at heart."

"Drew also has your best interests at heart, Isabela. Even though he has billions, he's still a one-in-a million guy. And he adores you. All right, cariño, I have to get back to DAR and leave this glorious ship. Go back to sleep and dream about our talk. One day, when you least expect it—boom—Cupid's arrow will slam into your heart! And look out because a happiness you've never known will follow."

He stood up on his goat hooves and bent down to kiss her forehead. "Till we see each other again, Doctor Torres. Enjoy the ride, Isabela." And just like that, he vanished.

A few minutes later, her bodyguard came to check on her. He looked well-rested and Isabela smiled at him and began quietly chuckling. She fell back into a blissful sleep under the morning sun, and her heart felt a bit more open than it did an hour ago.

‡‡‡‡

Isabela and Drew finished the European leg of the tour and said goodbye to the yacht. They traveled in Europe to as many countries as possible by sea, sometimes using the small chopper. But when it came time to visit the Middle East, they used the jet.

Isabela found it odd that the safety net of socialized medicine in the European Union was actually causing the vaccination rate to remain static. The citizens didn't seem to appreciate the overbearing attitude of policymakers toward near-compulsory vaccination. It was having the opposite effect and causing a rebellion. Being American, Isabela and Drew addressed the issue head-on, comparing the U.S. to the EU. They discussed how the U.S. was the only industrialized nation that did not have some form of universal healthcare for all its citizens. And the subsequent repercussions were greater disparities in access to healthcare as well as unfavorable health outcomes. Despite spending twice as much per capita on healthcare, the U.S. consistently underperformed in common health metrics than other high-income countries.

Isabela tried to make a sympathetic case for governmental interference. She explained that because there was no form of universal healthcare in the U.S., it was nearly impossible to impose a policy of near-compulsory vaccination for LECCS. And the result would be a greater number of fatalities. In fact, among the industrialized nations, America had the worst LECCS' vaccination rate, despite no pharmaceutical company earning a profit off the vaccine. Americans were often suspicious of any policy forcing them to do anything because a monetary gain was usually at play. But in this case, there was no entity profiting off the situation. While Isabela personally appreciated the policy of near-compulsory vaccination, as she knew it would save many lives, she also understood that people didn't like things shoved down their throats, either.

Isabela and Drew received many honors and awards from the European nations, and she found that she enjoyed the town hall meetings very much. Despite needing interpreters, it went very smoothly, and she didn't constantly feel afraid like she did in the town hall meetings in the U.S. Isabela would explain the science of LECCS in a way that was easy for the average person to understand, and she was able to convince most citizens to willingly accept the vaccine.

Visiting the World Health Organization again, in Geneva, Switzerland, was quite difficult. But Isabela was finally able to finish a new presentation she'd created on LECCS and the vaccine. It brought back some awful memories for both her and Drew, but they got through it, and graciously accepted accolades and awards from the WHO.

When it was time to depart for the Middle East, Drew gathered his small staff on the jet and explained they were heading into a region that distrusted anything American. "After so many years of war in this region," he began, "not taking a vaccine developed in America is like wearing a badge of honor. We'll have additional security measures here, including a much larger security team.

Be aware of your surroundings at all times and err on the side of caution. We are not liked here, but our mission is still to save lives. And that's what we're going to try and do in the safest way possible. Please contact Bryce if you have concerns or feel threatened in any way during our time here."

Drew was a true statesman when it came to dealing with the current leaders of countries that the U.S. had occupied or had been at war with for decades. He'd mastered speaking Farsi, Arabic, Dari, and Pashto. Isabela had no idea he'd learned these additional languages, subsequent to their first dinner together in Nashville, when he'd first told her that he was multilingual. She observed how effective it was when he spoke with either governmental leaders or ordinary citizens in their native language. They began to open up and discussed their harsh resentment of America.

Drew would translate for Isabela, when she'd discuss how climate refugees continued to be harshly treated at the U.S. border. She also talked about what it was like to be a person of Mexican descent. She explained how she experienced prejudice every day of her life, regardless of her achievements. Despite the difficulties in getting supplies of the vaccine to certain regions within the Middle East, the governing bodies of each nation were more inclined to have their citizens become vaccinated after meeting Isabela and Drew and listening to their presentation.

When the Middle East segment of the tour was concluded, Drew said to Isabela, "This was an exhausting leg of the tour and we should probably rest."

Isabela replied, "We can't, Drew. The overall global temperature is so close to 1.4°C. We have to keep going."

"Then, let's go to the most beautiful, wild, and sometimes dangerous place on Earth."

Isabela looked at him perplexed. His use of the word dangerous, while he was smiling, said everything about how

Drew felt about the African continent and how the African continent felt about Drew. Africa was the world's second largest and second most populous continent after Asia, in both respects. And Drew was greeted in nearly every country, from the north to the south and from the east to the west, with the same high praise and warm welcome.

People came out in droves, with mile-long lines, to see Drew at town hall meetings. They weren't there to see Isabela. They wanted the chance to meet the man who'd bestowed millions of tech devices for free so they could read, write, and compose. Whether it was music, books, poetry, or short stories, the written word was so valued here it was as if it were a currency that could lift people out of poverty. And in many cases, it had.

In every nation on the continent there were those of great wealth. It was rare to see a middle class comparable to one in America, but it was beginning to happen. People were determined to rise out of poverty, and Drew had helped many to do just that, by simply improving their reading and writing abilities. But despite the differences in their wealth status, everyone shared that same beautiful African smile, which was a language all by itself.

Drew had been to these countries throughout his life as he developed and kept improving the Réciter App. In many of the countries, Drew addressed the leaders by their first names and everyone called him Drew. People he'd met as children had grown up to become leaders in their country's government or had started businesses and now had children of their own. But they all remembered the importance of reading, writing, and storytelling from the genius of Drew's creation of the Réciter App, in addition to his generosity in bestowing millions of tech devices for free through his philanthropic foundation, The Devereux Trust.

People were intrigued by the young scientist who

accompanied Drew, with brown skin a bit lighter than their own. They wondered how someone so young had achieved so much, in such a short lifespan. In every town hall meeting, Isabela stressed the importance of education, especially for girls, and especially in science and mathematics.

Isabela developed quite a fan base after visiting and receiving honors from each country, and she began to bloom. She became very confident in this magical place, with Drew by her side, which boasted wildlife she'd only ever seen in photographs. In Africa, she felt like she was visiting a bygone Earth, one that existed long before Humans had begun recklessly destroying it.

On the African continent, Isabela and Drew found a rhythm with one another and began finishing each other's sentences. The continent was falling in love with the benevolent billionaire and the genius scientist and they, in turn, were falling in love with each other. When it came time to leave what Isabela described as one of the most beautiful and underrated places on Earth, she felt great sadness. The people's smiles and hearts had captured her own.

She and Drew had begun holding hands, as of late, and at their last stop at the base of Mount Kenya, now a UNESCO World Heritage Site, she and Drew shared their first kiss in front of a multitude of cameras, reporters, and international media. It wasn't planned, it just happened.

As they bid farewell to the continent at the press conference, now touting the highest vaccination rate in the world at ninety percent, their triumph was a mutual one, shared in a passionate kiss. That was the moment Isabela felt Cupid's arrow pierce her heart, which had been broken by Glen but repaired by Drew, and she fell in love. She didn't think about it, she just felt it, exactly as Tozer had predicted.

For weeks, photos of them had been plastered on the front

pages of newspapers and magazines, and they were often the lead story on broadcast news around the world. After the Mount Kenya press conference, when the world learned that the billionaire and the scientist were actually in love, the reception they received when they traveled to Asia, South Asia, Australia, and New Zealand was thunderous. And while Isabela nor Drew could ever explain why—once the world learned they were in love, the vaccination rate began to climb.

They were the world's newest "it" couple and became celebrities overnight. And since people wanted to be them, following their every move, people wanted to imitate them and began lining up to be vaccinated. Their love story was more powerful than the science that went into creating the vaccine.

When Isabela's heart finally opened for Drew, it was as if her heart made room for all of Humanity. For years, she'd stressed the importance of the rising overall global temperature and how once it hit the threshold of 1.4°C it would flip the switch on LECCS. But it was the love story of Isabela and Drew that transcended the science and made taking the vaccine a cool thing to do. It wasn't the temperature threshold for LECCS that compelled people to become vaccinated, it was the sizzling temperature between Isabela and Drew that finally drove home the message, saving millions and millions of lives.

20

THE RESCUE MISSION

DRUMMOND WAS COOKING up a storm in the kitchen. Thagar knew it was because he was extremely nervous about the rescue mission. He was cooking all of Kaleigh and Thagar's favorite foods. He even threw in a special muffin that was Aelish's favorite, in the hopes she'd be found alive and be able to eat it.

"Drummond," said Thagar, "I really think you should come with me and Kaleigh. You are part of our family and to leave you behind seems wrong. Won't you reconsider your decision?"

"Thank ya', sir, but no. I feel my place is to keep the house in pristine condition for when Aelish returns."

"Drummond, are you afraid of going to Hentoria?'

He shrugged his shoulders, which Thagar interpreted as yes. "My uncle's community is very gracious and kind, and you would be more than comfortable there. It is peaceful, and whilst the Hentorians do take a minute to get used to looking at, they are also very kind and gentle."

Drummond remained quiet as he cooked. "I would never force you to come," said Thagar, "but I really feel it would be better if we all stayed together, as a family."

"I don't really understand why I don't want to go with ya', but it just feels like the right decision, sir," replied Drummond.

"All right, Drummond," said Thagar. "I will respect your decision. Do remember, I have received permission from the Hentorians to give you the secret location of my uncle's community should you change your mind. You will have to use the Portal avoidance route, as there is no other way to access the dominion of Hentoria in secret, as it borders Yasteron."

"I know you are trustin' me with the secret of the Portal avoidance route, and on my life, sir, I will never tell anyone," said Drummond. "Thank you for trustin' me."

"Of course," said Thagar. "Kaleigh and I will be leaving right after I pick her up from school today. They are having a little party for her, as I told them she was accompanying her parents on a climate refugee mission outside of the United States. I don't know when we will be able to return to Earth, Drummond, so please, feel free to come to Hentoria if you miss us."

Drummond wiped away a tear as he continued cooking. He looked up at Thagar and said, "I miss her so much, sir. I just hope I can see her again before I depart this life. I can't imagine never layin' eyes on her beautiful lavender face again, ya' know?"

"I understand, Drummond. And I know she misses you just the same. Don't cry."

Drummond walked over to Thagar, who knelt down and embraced the small being who had been a part of his life for centuries. "You are making me cry now, Drummond. All right, I have to go to the Climate Refugee Intake Center as Marisol has arranged a surprise goodbye party for me."

"If it's a surprise, how do ya' know about it?" Drummond asked chuckling.

"I know her too well and she would never let me leave without a proper sendoff."

"She's a good Human, like her daughter," said Drummond. "I miss Isabela so much, too."

"Hopefully, we will see Isabela soon. All will be well, Drummond. I will see you later."

Drummond nodded and Thagar shook the tiny hand of his Brownie. Then, he aspirated into the garage, got into the SUV, and set off for the CRIC.

‡‡‡‡

After the surprise party at the CRIC, Marisol and Thagar sat together in his office, which was soon to become hers, at least temporarily. "You didn't have to go through all that trouble, Marisol, but I really appreciated it," said Thagar.

"Like I could let you go on a dangerous mission without a proper sendoff? Basta!" Thagar started laughing at her. "It's so nice you hung that in your office, Thagar," she said, pointing toward a framed photo on the wall of Isabela and Drew kissing at the base of Mount Kenya. "I will never forget the day I opened the paper and saw that photo. I went screaming into the bedroom and nearly gave Jorge a heart attack, who was showering for work." She started laughing at the memory. "I think Drew really gets my daughter. He's taking this courtship nice and slow. Hopefully, one day, she will be truly happy."

"Aside from being happy for the both of them," said Thagar, "my other thought was of Aelish. If she only knew what she'd put in motion on Drew's helicopter that day, right?"

"Do you think you will be successful in bringing her home, Thagar?"

"It's an incredibly dangerous mission, Marisol, and I hate all the unknowns. I have no idea what condition Aelish will be in. I just hope we aren't too late."

"Don't think it and don't say it, Thagar. I've been lighting candles at church every morning on my way to work. Aelish just has to be okay. And she and Isabela have to be reunited. I'm going to miss you all so much." Marisol began crying. Thagar got up and came around from behind his desk. She stood up and graciously received the hug he embraced her with.

After a few moments he said, "Come, let's see how you look in my chair."

He ushered her over to his desk chair and she sat down. "This seems kind of unreal to me, Thagar," said Marisol.

"Hmm," he said. "Very impressive. You look very commanding at my desk, and I know you are more than capable of handling everything in my absence. You won't have time to miss us, as the influx of refugees just seems to be increasing every week. You're going to do great, my friend."

Just then, they heard a knock on the door. Thagar mouthed to Marisol to tell whoever was at the door to come in. "Come in," said Marisol.

Elle opened the door and couldn't hide the look of shock on her face, seeing her interim boss in her new office. "Congratulations, Mrs. Torres. I am really looking forward to working with you."

"The feeling is mutual, Elle. I have a lot more confidence taking this position, knowing you will be working right alongside of me. Thank you."

Elle smiled and said, "Well, I just wanted to wish you a wonderful trip, Mr. Carrigan. I hope you travel safely and return safely. I'm sure goin' to miss you." Elle began crying and Thagar gave her a big hug.

"I think when I return, you're going to end up preferring to work for Mrs. Torres."

Everyone started laughing, and Elle said, "You never know!"

She said goodnight to her bosses and left for the day. "Well, Marisol," said Thagar, "I'm going to leave you in your new office. Here are the keys and Elle has a duplicate copy. Also, here is the key to our home on Bunker Hill Road, in case you miss us and just feel like hanging out in the tree-house room."

"Gracias, Thagar. Thank you for this opportunity and please know you will all be in my prayers." Marisol stood up, kissed Thagar on both cheeks, and hugged him one last time before he walked out the door.

‡‡‡‡

Kaleigh was exhausted from her party at VMP Academy, and Thagar knew she was going to fall asleep as soon as they started flying. She stood yawning in the same protective suit she wore the first time they went flying.

"It's going to feel so good to listen to you sleep whilst we fly, sweetheart," said Thagar. "Are you hungry?"

"I ate so much cake and sweets, I feel like I won't need to eat again until tomorrow."

Thagar started laughing at her. Drummond came into the tree-house room to magically pack some last-minute items into her protective suit and he began crying again. "I'm going to miss ya', sweet Kaleigh."

"Me, too, Drummond." She went to hug him and nearly fell over in the suit, providing the exact comic relief everyone needed during this tearful goodbye. "Whoa! I forgot how bulky this suit is."

"Are you ready, sweetheart?" asked Thagar. "Did you pack one of your favorite bears and anything else that's precious to you?"

"I did, Daddy. I'm all set. Let's go get Momma!"

Her enthusiasm and hopefulness were just what Thagar and Drummond needed. Kaleigh was the light in everyone's life.

"All right, then," said Thagar. "Be well, Drummond, and we will all see you soon."

"Take care of yourselves!" exclaimed Drummond. He waved goodbye as Thagar magically affixed Kaleigh to his back and they transported out of the room.

‡‡‡‡

Thagar and Kaleigh landed on a snowy mountaintop in Hentoria. The welcoming committee was there to greet them: Lady Antonia, Amelia, the Hentorian leaders, the Hentorian warriors, as well as Uncle Thurrock and Aunt Charlotte. This time, there were no drone rats. As Thagar took off Kaleigh's flying suit, he said, "Remember what I told you. Momma may seem different than the last time you saw her, but she will always love you, like I will." He gave her a kiss before Lady Antonia and Amelia came running over to hug and kiss her.

Thagar embraced his uncle and gave his aunt a kiss on the cheek. He shook the hands of the Hentorian leaders and said to the Hentorian warriors, "Are you ready?"

They both shook his hand and said, "We are ready, Thagar."

Thagar had prepared Kaleigh with drawings of what the Hentorians looked like, so upon meeting them, she wouldn't be afraid. And he was very proud of her, watching her shake hands with the Hentorian leaders. The leaders and warriors began speaking to one another in their native language and Kaleigh greeted them in their native tongue.

They stepped back in shock that the tiny Human had grasped their language so quickly. They came over to Thagar and asked,

"Is she magical, then, Thagar?"

"She has certain magical traits. Her affinity with languages being one of them, but she is Human."

"Positively amazing," said one of the leaders.

Aunt Charlotte came over to Kaleigh and spoke to her in Hentorian. Uncle Thurrock looked at Thagar and said, "Females truly are superior to males, whether they are magical or Human. I still haven't been able to grasp their language." Thagar heard Kaleigh laughing and Amelia and Aunt Charlotte also started laughing. Apparently, Amelia had also learned the Hentorian language in the brief time since she'd first entered the dominion.

"Come," said the leaders. "We will open the door to the wall so you may all have a good rest before the mission tomorrow."

Thagar grabbed Kaleigh's suit and walked down the mountainside with his arm around Lady Antonia. "Well, did you scream when you first saw what they looked like?"

Lady Antonia replied, "No, but only because I would have received a strict scolding from my daughter. But inwardly, it reminded me of the first time I laid eyes upon King Gidius in his cage at the Military Detention Center. But the Hentorians are completely different. They are so peaceful and have been extremely welcoming. I hope you like what I've done to the cottage your aunt and uncle provided us with."

"I'm sure it will be lovely," said Thagar.

"I just can't wait until Aelish is in it," said Lady Antonia, with tears in her eyes.

"You and me both," said Thagar, deeply sighing.

"You're worried, aren't you?" she asked.

"I'd be lying if I said I wasn't. I'm trying so hard to mentally prepare myself for any and all scenarios, but somehow, I don't think it's truly possible to prepare oneself, you know?

"I do. I've tried to think of all the scenarios, too, and I just can't seem to calm myself without spells."

"Exactly," said Thagar.

They all reached the wall to the village, and the Hentorian leaders conjured the door, and they entered the community. Aunt Charlotte said to the warriors, "You will be living in the same barn as before, and I've also prepared the same pallets for you to sleep on. Please let me know if you need anything else. I will be bringing your dinner later this evening."

"Thank you, Charlotte," said one warrior. "You are very kind," said the other. They walked toward the barn as if they were returning home.

The Hentorian leaders said, "We will leave you now. We want to wish you the best of luck tomorrow, Thurrock and Thagar. You have our finest warriors with you. We hope the mission is a success because we are very anxious to meet this Earth born DARling who is as devoted to peace as we are." They uttered what Thagar assumed was good luck in Hentorian, and they left the village.

"All right," said Aunt Charlotte. "Antonia and Amelia, why don't you take Thagar and Kaleigh to the cottage? I have to start dinner so everyone can eat well and hopefully have a good night's rest. I will see you all later in our cottage for dinner at six o'clock. Let me know if anything is not to your liking, Thagar. And as for you, little one, I hope you like the special present I left on your bed."

Kaleigh reached up and kissed Aunt Charlotte and began pulling on Amelia' arm to lead the way. "She's simply adorable, Thagar," said his aunt. "Your uncle and I are looking forward to spoiling her." She smiled and left with Uncle Thurrock, who waved goodbye.

When they arrived at the cottage door, Amelia said, "We really hope you both like it."

Amelia opened the door and inside were so many little touches which reminded Thagar of Aelish's original cottage in DAR. The only thing missing was Drummond. There were three bedrooms: one for Amelia and Kaleigh, one for Lady Antonia, and one for Thagar and hopefully Aelish. In Thagar and Aelish's bedroom, which was the largest of the three, was a mural of Brólaigh Castle, just as there had been in Aelish's first cottage. Even the bed was similar. It was a four-poster bed with sumptuous white bedding, and the bed had so many pillows, it was impossible to count them. Billowy white sheaths of white fabric hung from the iron frame between the four posts.

"It's not an actual painting of Brólaigh Castle, there simply wasn't time. But it's a pretty good figment, don't you agree, Thagar?" asked Lady Antonia.

Thagar had tears streaming down his face. "Don't cry, Daddy," said Kaleigh. He picked her up and they both stared at the mural. "That's the castle Momma grew up in, the one we visited in Ireland. It looks just like it."

Thagar was overcome with emotion. It all seemed like yesterday when he'd first met Aelish in Brólaigh Castle; she was just five years older than Kaleigh was now. And the bedchamber was so similar to the one in her cottage in DAR. He hoped Aelish would be well enough to remember it all. He especially loved the large window on one wall, which would let in the beautiful mountain sunlight.

"Thank you, Antonia and Amelia, for all of this," said Thagar. "It's simply lovely."

"Daddy, can we go see my present now?" asked Kaleigh.

Thagar started chuckling at his daughter and put her down. Amelia took her hand, and Thagar and Antonia followed them to their bedroom. There were two twin-sized beds, separated by a small night stand in between. The bedding was also white and the two windows in the room made it very cheerful. On the bed, farthest from the door, was a large stuffed bear on the pillow.

Kaleigh immediately knew this was her bed and her present was the new bear. He was a snowy white bear, and she announced, "I will name him Henry for Hentoria." She nuzzled the bear and began bouncing on the side of the bed.

"Your Great-Aunt Charlotte made him for you," said Lady Antonia.

"Please don't let me forget to thank her, Daddy. I love him already."

"All right, sweetheart, I won't," said Thagar.

What amazed Thagar was how easily Kaleigh adapted to any environment. She had so little fear about anything new, and he wanted to believe it was because she was adored by both her parents. He was also fascinated by how Amelia, the brilliant evil magic DARling, had patience and genuine love for Kaleigh. Amelia was now the same age as Aelish—twelve Earth years— when he first met her in Brólaigh Castle. While Amelia had extraordinary magical abilities, she was still very young, and Thagar saw the deep bond between her and Kaleigh. Amelia sat alongside Kaleigh on the edge of Kaleigh's bed, and the two were chatting away as if they'd grown up together as sisters. It warmed his heart.

"Where is your bedroom, Antonia?" asked Thagar. They left the young ones alone and went across the hall. "Okay, good. This is very close to our bedroom, so you'll be very close to Aelish if she needs you."

"You can always sleep in here and I can sleep with Aelish, if necessary, Thagar."

"Ah! I like having that option since we have three bedrooms," he said. "This cottage is truly lovely, Antonia. Thank you for adding all the special touches."

"Your lovely aunt also helped. I still can't believe I'm palling around with King Nevuna's sister! She is so kind, Thagar, and nothing like what we assume Yasterons are like."

"I know. I still can't believe King Nevuna's sister is my aunt. Well, I'm going to start unpacking all of our things and Drummond's treats."

"Why didn't he come?" asked Lady Antonia.

"I don't know the real reason, Antonia. I think he was afraid to see what condition Aelish might be in. I tried to convince him. He has the information to come on his own, but I miss him."

"He's very special, Thagar. But you can't force a Brownie to do something they don't want to do, as you well know, when he wouldn't disclose the location of the Komprathian family or the drone rats they escaped with. Brownies have to come to a decision all on their own."

"I remember," said Thagar. "But it would feel more like home if he were here."

"Agreed," said Lady Antonia. "Whilst you unpack, I'm going to rest a bit. The stress is making me exhausted. I'm not doing anything taxing or difficult, yet I'm simply so fatigued."

"I'm so ramped up; I don't know how I will ever sleep tonight—even with spells."

"I understand. But you will, because you know how rested you need to be for tomorrow night's mission. I'm so scared, Thagar."

The two embraced and began crying. It was a wonderful comfort for them both, to have someone else who completely understood what was at stake.

‡‡‡‡

Dinner was delicious and everyone had a great time getting to know each other better. Aunt Charlotte instantly adored Kaleigh, and Kaleigh now had a new grandmother figure to help her continue healing over the loss of Abuela. After they returned to their own cottage, Thagar kissed Amelia and Kaleigh good night, and he and Lady Antonia had a drink together in the living area. It seemed to do the trick for Lady Antonia, who promptly went to bed afterward.

Thagar, however, could not sleep. He left the cottage and went walking along the dirt streets between the dwellings of the community. He found an open clearing and saw his uncle sitting on the ground. He sat down beside him.

Uncle Thurrock looked up and asked, "Can't sleep, either?"

"Nope," answered Thagar.

"It reminds me of the night before a huge battle," said his uncle. "Some of the soldiers fell into the deepest sleep of their lives, but me, forget it. I could never sleep before a battle."

"We are so alike, Uncle. I could never sleep, either. It didn't matter whether I was a soldier heading for the battlefield or a commander safely housed in the command center. Lives were at stake, and I always felt a profound responsibility for my sisters and brothers-in-arms during battle or for the soldiers I was commanding."

"I hope all goes well tomorrow night," said Uncle Thurrock, "but we both know there will be something unforeseen that can make the mission go sideways. It could be in the literal sense or something that mentally affects us. I want to reassure you and tell you everything will be okay, but I don't want to offend your intelligence."

"I appreciate your honesty, Uncle. I want you to know how much it means to me, to have you by my side, helping me try and rescue the love of my life. I could never express my gratitude into words."

"There's no need, Nephew. By now, you know I would do

anything for you."

"I do. Thank you, Uncle."

‡‡‡‡

The Hentorian warriors hung on the iron bars next to the trap door and listened. It was completely quiet. Uncle Thurrock pressed his foot against the trap door to the prison to see if it would give or if it were firmly affixed. It was firmly affixed. They couldn't use any of the Human tools they'd brought, as they would make too much noise. The only option they had was for the Hentorian warriors to shoot their venom along the outline of the door.

Thagar and Uncle Thurrock kept their heads turned to the side so they wouldn't breathe in or touch any of the poisonous venom. It was over in a minute and Uncle Thurrock once again pushed his foot against the trap door. This time, it gave way. It appeared as if the Hentorians' venom had also cut through something lying on top of the door. Thagar and Uncle Thurrock quietly eased open the door, flipping it backward onto the floor. They boosted themselves up through the opening and saw that the door was directly in front of a settee. The settee was placed on top of a large, elegant hand-woven rug, which had covered the door from view.

It was the same settee in the living area, where Aelish had first sat, waiting for a message from Earth to appear on a drop-down television screen. The Hentorians let go of the iron rungs and their squirrel feet grasped the edges of where the door had been. They lifted themselves up and entered the prison.

There was very little light, but Thagar and Uncle Thurrock were hesitant to use the flashlights they'd brought from Earth. The beams would be too bright and could potentially set off an alarm or alert a being. The exoskeleton chests of both Hentorian warriors began emitting a thin narrow beam of blue light. Uncle Thurrock and Thagar smiled at one another.

They all quietly walked through the living area, took note of the dining room table, and followed a hallway toward the interior of the suite of rooms. They found themselves inside a dressing area and Thagar saw female clothing he'd never seen before. They continued onward and finally found a door. They slowly opened it and saw the interior of a bedchamber. They paused at the threshold upon hearing an animal start growling.

The Hentorian warriors stepped forward without any fear as if they recognized the sound. Thagar could see Aelish lying in an enormous, hand-carved mahogany bed with an elaborate headboard and footboard. At the bottom of the bed was a Great White Mount Hund, growling. Thagar was very familiar with the breed. He knew if it felt threatened or felt a threat to those it protects, it would gaze into your eyes and blind you, while at the same time making you mute, so you couldn't even call out for help. What he did not know was that these dogs freely roamed the Hentorian mountains and the warriors knew exactly how to calm them.

The Hentorian warriors approached Storm and quietly spoke in their language. They began petting him. Storm trusted the Hentorians and became silent. The warriors motioned to Thagar and Uncle Thurrock that it was now safe to approach the bed. Thagar stood with his uncle at the foot of the bed and studied his mate. He noted her skin was no longer lavender and her hair was longer and hung loosely about her shoulders. She was extraordinarily thin, as if the bed could swallow her up. Aelish's chin was bent toward her chest. Thagar surmised that she was sleeping and gently said her name, remaining at the footboard.

"Aelish, my love."

She lifted her head slowly and gazed at him with a vacuous

look, as if she did not know him. She looked at the Hentorians, Thagar, and Uncle Thurrock and clutched the blankets against her chest. She moved slightly backward against the headboard in fear. Her fear of him broke his heart in half; she did not know who he was.

"Aelish, it's me, Thagar."

She continued to look fearfully at him and the other beings.

"Aelish, all is well. We are here to take you home, my love."

Recognition gradually crossed her face, and she whispered, "Thagar."

She dropped her head and began weeping. Thagar slowly approached the side of the bed. Uncle Thurrock and the Hentorian warriors remained at the footboard. When he bent over to embrace her, she cautioned, "Be careful."

Confused, Thagar asked, "Are you injured, my love?"

Aelish pushed the blanket aside revealing an infant the size of a newborn DARlette. Thagar jumped back, gasping, as if he'd been magically shocked. Aelish whispered, "I'm sorry. Please, forgive me. He told me he would kill you and Kaleigh if I didn't do exactly what he said. I had no choice, as I have no magical abilities in here. He is my son."

Thagar remained frozen where he stood and just stared at her. He began processing all that had taken place in this room. "He," uttered Thagar, realizing the infant was Cardissius' son, a byproduct of rape. He slowly walked back toward the side of the bed. "The infant is the heir, then. That was the whole plan—to steal your abilities by forcing you to procreate a son for his kingdom." He could feel himself strangling Cardissius with his bare hands.

Uncle Thurrock, who remained at the foot of the bed said, "Thagar, we cannot steal the heir. It will cause a colossal incident that would reverberate throughout the magical world and lead all the realms to war. We must leave the child."

"Then, leave me as well," said Aelish.

"I am *not* leaving you, Aelish," said Thagar. "What about Kaleigh?"

"Kaleigh has you. He has no one. Leave me."

"We are *not* leaving you," said Thagar. He turned toward his uncle and the Hentorian warriors and firmly said, "If she insists upon taking the infant, we will take it."

"Thagar," said Uncle Thurrock, "they will send an army to retrieve the heir. Even if we make it back to Hentoria, you will never be able to leave."

"Just leave me, Thagar. I've made my peace with it all. I am dying, anyway."

Thagar felt like his head was about to explode. He assumed Aelish meant she was metaphorically dying and was speaking like a captive who had simply given up.

Uncle Thurrock saw Thagar trying to make sense of how changed his mate was. He quietly walked over to where Thagar was standing and whispered into his ear, "Cardissius is an abomination. You must prepare yourself—what he's done to her physically will be nothing compared to what he's done to her mentally."

Thagar said, "We are taking the infant, Uncle. I will never leave her, do you understand?"

"I do," said Uncle Thurrock. "But this is a complication of epic proportions that we are not prepared for."

"I will *not* let the infant allow our mission to go sideways. We'll just have to think on our feet, then, won't we?"

"All right," said Uncle Thurrock, who retreated back toward the foot of the bed.

Thagar leaned over and saw the infant against her breast, nursing. "I'm so sorry I couldn't get to you in time, Aelish. Please, forgive me. We have to go now, and we are taking the infant."

He watched as she pulled away from him, hesitant and reluctant.

"You won't hurt my son, will you?" she asked.

Thagar looked deeply into her green eyes. "How could I ever hurt anything that is a part of you, my love? I could not—ever." He could not bear her fear of him. "I once asked you in the loaned house in London, where your parents lay dead, if you trusted me. Do you trust me now, Aelish?"

"With my life."

"Then, let me save it. For you and the infant will surely die here. This is the one time I'm going to have to insist, my love, that you do as I ask. You must trust me. We have to go now."

Aelish replied, "But Cardissius told me he would kill you and Kaleigh if I ever tried to escape. So, I promised I'd stay with the king so you both could live. He gave me his word that no harm would come to either of you if I stayed."

"Cardissius' word is worth less than the excrement on my boot, Aelish," said Thagar. "He has surrendered nothing. None of the Peace Accord has been honored, despite his imprisonment of you, forcing you to procreate with him, and whatever other lies he's told you. He isn't going to get the chance to kill anyone. You must trust me on this."

Aelish nodded in acquiescence. "All right, Thagar. But I'm too weak to walk."

"Then, I will carry you and the infant. Is there anything else you wish to take?"

"Yes, we have to take Storm." Storm immediately responded by lifting his head. "And my amethyst Commitments necklace is hidden under the mattress. Please find it for me."

Thagar reached down and lifted Aelish and the infant up in his arms. He commanded the others, "Find the necklace and take the dog. Grab anything else that looks important."

Aelish leaned against his chest with Cardissius' child between them. In the moment, he feared they'd never make it back to Hentoria alive. He also wondered how he was going to explain the infant to Kaleigh. Then, he felt Aelish sobbing against him, and the infant began gently crying. He began walking quickly toward the trap door.

"We must hurry through the tunnels, Thagar," said Uncle Thurrock. He looked even more worried than Thagar that they weren't going to make it back.

"We will make it," he said to his uncle. He turned toward the warriors. "Watch our six and make haste." The Hentorian warriors split up. One went in front toward the trap door and the other secured the rear.

At the trap door, Thagar leaned over and handed Aelish and the infant to the lead Hentorian, who was already in the tunnels. Thagar dropped to the floor and the warrior gave him back Aelish and the infant. Once they were all in the tunnels, the Hentorian warriors ran on all fours ahead of Thagar and Uncle Thurrock toward the illusory wall which needed to be sealed. Thagar saw other Hentorian warriors at the end of the tunnels and knew they were ready to seal it as soon as they had all passed through it.

The alarm never went off and they safely exited the tunnels. The Hentorian warriors sealed the tunnels with the illusory wall. They'd made it safely into Hentoria. They all began walking through the rugged mountain passageway. It was freezing and Aelish was only wearing a nightgown and the infant was wrapped in a thin blanket. Thagar was hesitant to use magic in this particular location, but he knew both she and the infant wouldn't survive in this cold. Suddenly, one of the Hentorian warriors produced the heavy blanket that had been on her bed in the prison. Thagar smiled and wrapped it around Aelish. The warrior patted Thagar on the back.

It took them over an hour to reach the wall of the village. It was snowing and the wind was fiercely blowing the entire time. The Hentorian leaders were waiting for them. They conjured the door in the wall and everyone entered the village.

The leaders heard the coo of the infant and looked at Thagar, awaiting his explanation. Bracing for trouble, Thagar firmly said, "My mate was held captive by King Cardissius. She was raped by him in order to conceive a male heir imbued with her magical abilities. Yes, I stole the heir of Yasteron, which also happens to be my mate's son. If you no longer wish to give us safe harbor, I will understand."

The leaders looked at one another. "This evil king deserves much worse than his heir being stolen. We are so proud to know such a brave commander. You may stay with us as long as you wish. The King of Yasteron will never know you are here. You will be safe."

Thagar exhaled a breath he'd been holding since he'd dropped to the floor of the tunnels from the trap door of the prison. He profusely thanked the leaders, who then left. The warriors remained with him and Uncle Thurrock, and they all began walking toward the cottage where Aunt Charlotte, Lady Antonia, Kaleigh, and Amelia were waiting.

21

THE POISON IS THE CURE

THURSDAY, APRIL 23, 2026 4:00 AM

THAGAR THOUGHT AELISH had fallen asleep under the blanket. But when he went to place her in their bed at the cottage, he saw that she was unconscious. Mercifully, Kaleigh had fallen asleep in her room waiting for them, so she did not see her mother like this. Lady Antonia, Amelia, Thagar's aunt and uncle, and the medic soldier who'd conducted the autopsy on a fellow soldier's brain after being hit by a rock, were all in the bedroom watching Thagar try to revive her. The infant was still in a sling against her and was sleeping. No one noticed the infant until the medic soldier gently lifted him up in preparation for examining Aelish.

Lady Antonia, Amelia, and Aunt Charlotte gasped when they saw the newborn. The medic soldier handed the infant to Aunt Charlotte, who looked down at him in shock. He wrapped the sling around the infant to keep it warm. "Thagar," said Lady Antonia, "whose infant is this?"

"He is the reason Aelish was abducted. Cardissius forced her to procreate a male heir for his kingdom that would be imbued with Aelish's extraordinary magical capabilities."

"Good God!" exclaimed Lady Antonia, staring at the

newborn.

Amelia stated, "So, you've stolen the heir to the Kingdom of Yasteron? Good job!"

Uncle Thurrock came over to Lady Antonia and said, "I see the fear in your face. Yes, there will be severe consequences, but you are all safe here. Please, do not be afraid."

Lady Antonia had to steady herself as she sat down in a chair in the bedchamber. She began crying uncontrollably as rage and sorrow merged together. She said through gritted teeth, "Cardissius came straight out of hell and someone needs to send him back there."

Amelia knelt down and began comforting her mother. The medic soldier whose name was John said, "Aelish is very ill, Thagar. In fact, she's dying." Lady Antonia began wailing even louder. The infant also began to cry as did everyone else in the room.

Aunt Charlotte asked John, "Have any female DARlings recently given birth? The infant needs a wet-nurse immediately."

"Let me send a message to my mate," replied John. "She can look in my records and find a suitable female." They all watched as he sent a telepathic message. Aunt Charlotte stood rocking the infant who'd begun to quiet while Lady Antonia continued sobbing.

"Mother, why don't you go lie down for a bit?" suggested Amelia.

"No! I want to know why my Aelish is dying!"

John stood in the corner of the bedroom. Thagar sat on one side of the bed, stroking Aelish's arm, Uncle Thurrock was sitting on the floor, Amelia sat on the floor by her mother, Aunt Charlotte stood rocking the infant, and Storm lay at the foot of the bed. The warriors were outside, guarding. "Aelish is suffering from Magical Sunlight Deprivation Heart Syndrome," said John. "Her heart is simply going to stop. We don't have much time.

Unfortunately, I don't have any modern scanners or Human equipment here. And she would never survive a journey to Earth or DAR, even if the Hentorians would allow it."

"So, are we just going to sit here and wait for her to die?" accused Lady Antonia.

John replied, "After I served the POD as a medic, I wanted very much to continue my studies and become a medicus. But I was imprisoned in the same prison as Aelish and you all know the rest of that story. Many of our soldiers suffered from this same syndrome because there is no sunlight where she was held captive and no magic works inside the prison."

"Dear God!" exclaimed Lady Antonia. "So, she hasn't been outside for nearly four months? And she's been deprived of all her magical abilities?"

"Precisely," said John. "I've already sent a message to the Hentorian leaders that we need to remove the roof and install a special glass over this room to allow the sunlight to enter. Whilst the sunlight will help, what is really needed is for her to use her magical abilities. However, she's reached the stage of the syndrome where she's already lost consciousness, making that impossible. I've faced these extraordinary circumstances with many of our soldiers. The only option left is to administer a potion I created from the poisonous venom of the Hentorians."

"Oh, my God," said Lady Antonia.

John continued, "The Hentorian venom kills so fast because it contains epinephrine or adrenaline. It overwhelms the heart, causing cardiac arrest, debilitating brain damage, and ultimately death. On Earth, epinephrine is often used during cardiac arrest. However, recently it's been discovered that it may also have potentially dangerous side effects.

"But when epinephrine is used on Humans in combination with other drugs, at a very low dosage, patients have the best outcome for survival with normal or limited compromised brain function. Epinephrine seems to cause less side effects when it is administered at the beginning of the cardiac event and not at the end.

"I would never suggest this unless I believed there were no other options. I perfected a potion for the soldiers afflicted with Magical Sunlight Deprivation Heart Syndrome by using a small percentage of venom, mixed with various spells, along with black or green tea. The potion is administered two times a day, using a rudimentary intravenous system I created. If it works like it did for my fellow soldiers, I believe it will not only keep Aelish's heart beating, but it will also strengthen her heart. She needs to regain consciousness so she can use her magic. She will also have to stop nursing immediately, as this is putting an even greater strain on her heart."

Thagar asked, "So, you want my permission to administer poisonous venom to my mate, correct? And if she dies from it?"

John replied, "Her death would be less painful than the trajectory she is currently on. Forgive me if that sounds incredibly harsh, but I've treated many soldiers suffering from this syndrome. The potion dosage will be adjusted to suit her frailty. I recommend we start immediately, as the Hentorians are preparing to install the special glass over this room for the sunlight. The two treatments work in tandem and will give her the best chance of survival."

Thagar looked at the medic and saw the sincerity and truthfulness in his eyes. Lady Antonia said, "Thagar, I know with certainty that she is dying of this syndrome. She has absolutely no color left in her skin. When she was released from the N.W. Quadrant Detention Center, in 1665, her skin color was very faint, but the color had not completely disappeared like it has now. We need to try or she will surely die. You know how much I love Aelish and that I would give up my life to save hers. Please allow him to administer the treatment."

Suddenly, sunlight came into the bedroom as the roof was magically replaced with the special glass. The sunlight came streaming into the room as if it were a divine sign from above.

Everyone turned their gaze upward and immediately shielded their eyes. John said, "I need to put protective eyewear over her eyes. He gently lifted Aelish's head and put on what looked like swimming goggles over her eyes. "There are spells inside the eyewear, to ensure the sunlight won't harm her vision."

"All right, John," said Thagar. "You have my permission to administer the potion. How long will it take before we know if it's working?"

"We will know in three days' time. If her heartbeat becomes stronger, hopefully, in another three days, she will awaken—so about a week from now. But she will be very weak and fragile for at least a month. Her Oraculi can work with her doing simple spells at first, to initiate her magical abilities. Her own body will heal itself until she can perform complex spells."

"If she survives, John, will she totally regain her magical abilities?" asked Lady Antonia.

"The more she works her magic, the easier it will be for her to regain her extraordinary magical gifts. Whilst she's been imprisoned for what seems like a very long time, compared to our soldiers, it has actually been a relatively short period of time. However, she's had two factors working against her: the pregnancy and the fact that she is an Earth born DARling. They are born and grow up in the sunlight of the Earth, which is much stronger than any sunlight in the magical world. These two factors accelerated the syndrome very quickly for Aelish."

All Thagar could think about was murdering Cardissius. The fact that he could do this to one of the most gifted magical beings in the entire magical world was in itself a heinous crime. But to do this to the mother of his own child, just to steal her magical capabilities, was so immoral, Thagar knew he would never be able to express his feelings into words. In actions, however, he knew exactly how to express himself: he could feel his hands squeezing Cardissius' neck as he watched the life drain from his eyes.

Thagar looked at the medic and asked, "Can the wet-nurse feed the infant in this room?"

"Yes, of course. But I'm curious, why do you feel that's important?"

"I know my mate and she will feel the infant's presence. Perhaps he can lie next to her in the bed when he needs to sleep. I believe he will provide healing powers for Aelish, and the infant will also thrive if he is closer to his mother."

John nodded his head, assessing the medical benefits of what Thagar was suggesting.

Lady Antonia stared at Thagar in astonishment. "I don't believe I've ever known a male with a more generous heart than yours, Thagar. The fact that you are worried about the welfare of Cardissius' child . . . well, I have no words."

Thagar said, "The infant is an innocent who has already been made to suffer because of his father's incalculable cruelty. It stops today."

Lady Antonia stood up and walked over to where Thagar was sitting on the edge of the bed. She leaned over and gave Thagar a kiss on top of his head. "You are the kindest male I have ever known."

Just then, Kaleigh came into the room, trying to rub the sleep out of her eyes. Before anyone could say anything, she walked over to her mother and kissed her on the forehead. "I love you, Momma. I'm so happy you're home." Storm began furiously wagging his tail. "Oh, wow! We have a dog now? He's so beautiful." She accepted Storm's kisses, tightly hugging his neck. Looking at everyone in the room, she said, "I don't know how Momma can sleep with all the noise you're making." She looked at John. "Hello, my name is Kaleigh. Who are you?"

"Hello, Kaleigh. My name is John and I am a medic. I'm here to help your mother get better from everything she's been through."

"Thank you." She stopped playing with Storm and noticed the infant in her great-aunt's arms. "Wow, I've never seen a baby that small. Where did it come from?"

Thagar stood up and took the infant from his aunt's arms. He knelt down so Kaleigh could see him more clearly. "He is your brother, Kaleigh."

"He is? Momma had a baby? But she wasn't gone for nine months. How could the baby be born already?"

"The baby is magical, Kaleigh, and it only takes three months for them to be born."

"That's so cool and way better than nine months." Everyone started chuckling. "His skin color is so much lighter than mine and he's blond. I can't wait until he's bigger."

"He will grow very fast and you will be able to hold him very soon," said Thagar.

"What's his name?" asked Kaleigh.

Thagar realized he had no idea what the infant's name was, so he picked a name he knew would have special meaning for Aelish's religious beliefs. "His name is Elijah. It means the Lord is my God," said Thagar.

"Oh, that's a beautiful name, Daddy. I remember learning something about Elijah in Sunday School. I will read more about why the name is so famous."

Lady Antonia knelt down in front of Thagar, Kaleigh, and Elijah. "If it's all right with you, Thagar, perhaps we could have a small christening for him? I know it would be very important to Aelish."

"I will leave it to you, then, to organize, Antonia," said Thagar.

"That's a beautiful idea and it would mean a lot to Aelish."

Lady Antonia gently kissed the forehead of the infant and embraced Kaleigh. "You're going to be such a wonderful big sister."

"I'm so excited," said Kaleigh. "I never thought Momma was going to come back with a baby!"

"It is a wonderful surprise," said Thagar, magnanimously.

‡‡‡‡

The next seventy-two hours were much longer for Thagar than the last time Aelish was injured, trying out the first part of Roger's evil magic spell at the football stadium near their home in Tennessee. But until she drew her last breath, Thagar would never leave her side.

He sat with her day and night, gently holding her hand or stroking her arm. He magically cleaned her up when she soiled herself and would let no other being care for her with the exception of the medic, who administered the IVs of his venom potion. Thagar did not get into the bed with her, remembering how DARlings have the ability to heal themselves but must be left virtually untouched in order to do so. As he stroked her hand, he noticed she was wearing a beautiful emerald ring encrusted with diamonds; a ring he'd never given to her. He sighed.

On the third day, John announced that her heart was stronger. For the next seventy-two hours, Thagar continued to stay with her. He was determined to be there if she opened her eyes, which she did on the seventh day. He could not believe his own eyes, gazing into her green ones.

Her first words were, "Where is my son?"

Thagar replied, "He is here in the bedchamber with a DARling wet-nurse. We were worried we might have to use a

Yasteron wet-nurse, but thankfully, we found a DARling who'd recently given birth."

Aelish said, "It matters not. Yasterons are DARlings." And she fell back to sleep.

Lady Antonia entered the room just as Aelish finished saying her last statement. "Did I hear Aelish correctly? Yasterons are DARlings? My poor Aelish, she must be delirious. I pray her brain is not damaged."

As if her subconscious were insulted, Aelish opened her eyes, located the voice of Lady Antonia and said, "I am not delusional. Yasterons are DARlings. I will tell you all about it later." And then, she fell back to sleep for the next four hours.

Lady Antonia looked at Thagar, who was shaking his head.

Thagar and Lady Antonia had dinner that night, in the cottage kitchen, with Amelia, Kaleigh, Uncle Thurrock, and Aunt Charlotte. They could not believe what Aelish had said, twice now, and were still talking about it with everyone around the table.

Amelia said, "I think Aelish is correct."

"What?" asked Lady Antonia. "That's preposterous."

Amelia replied, "I recently uncovered some information that supports what Aelish said. I need to do more research, or I can be lazy and wait until she wakes up and can tell us more."

Everyone at the table was stunned by this possibility and also quite horrified. Kaleigh innocently asked, "Well, do Yasterons look the same as DARlings?"

They all turned and looked at Kaleigh. At first, they said nothing. But then, they all burst out laughing. Talking over and around each another, Thagar exclaimed, "Aside from the variety of our skin and eye colors, they *do* look nearly identical to DARlings!"

Thagar looked at his daughter and asked, "How is it you are

so smart, sweetheart?"

"Well, it just seemed like an obvious question," said Kaleigh, who shrugged her shoulders and continued eating.

‡‡‡‡

The next day, Thagar knew he had to tell Aelish that Kaleigh was in the magical world with them. He told Kaleigh he was going to tell her mother and she should wait outside the bedchamber until he called for her. Kaleigh was so excited to surprise her.

"How are you feeling today, my love?" he asked Aelish, entering the bedchamber.

"I can't seem to stop sleeping, but I feel a bit stronger."

"I need to share something wonderful with you. Isabela was finally released from the psychiatric hospital and she went back to her lab to start some new research."

"Oh, my God! She's out of the hospital? That's wonderful news. What new research is she working on? She shouldn't overdo. I hope she's taking care of herself."

"Well, a tragedy occurred the same night I was hoping you'd be returning from signing the Peace Accord. Jorge had installed a new standby generator because of all the storms and continuous loss of power. On that Wednesday, the unit malfunctioned and began emitting carbon monoxide into the home."

"Oh, my God! Was anyone injured?"

"I'm very sorry to tell you, my love, but Abuela died from carbon monoxide poisoning."

"Ohh, Thagar! She's gone? I love her so much." Aelish began sobbing and Thagar embraced her in the bed. "Kaleigh was with her in the house as the two were preparing dinner for all of us, in the hope you'd be home by then."

Aelish pulled out of the embrace. "Kaleigh was in the house?

Thagar, what are you trying to say? Is my beautiful Kaleigh gone?"

"No, she is absolutely fine," said Thagar.

"But if she were in the house with Abuela, she would also have been killed from the carbon monoxide. Being Human, she could never have survived this. Please, tell me what is happening, Thagar. I feel so upset and confused." Aelish continued crying.

Thagar yelled, "Kaleigh, come on in now!"

"Momma! Finally, you are awake!"

"Ohh!" gasped Aelish.

Aelish looked like she was either going to pass out or burst from joy. At first, she couldn't speak, and then she asked, "How is it you are here in Hentoria, Kaleigh?" Finally, reunited with her daughter, the two began hugging and kissing one another.

Thagar let them be for some time. They were both talking, laughing, and crying all at the same time. He said, "Why don't you show Momma what you learned to do at the Institute in DAR, Kaleigh?"

Aelish suddenly began holding her head as she received a telepathic message from Kaleigh. "Oh, my God! How are you able to do that? Are you magical, like Daddy and me? How are you able to perform the complicated magic of telepathy—you're not even seven years old!"

"Did I do it well, Momma?"

"You did it perfectly." Aelish drew her in for more hugs and kisses.

Thagar said, "It was Drew who inspired Isabela to get out of the psychiatric hospital and return to her lab for one reason and one reason only: he tempted Isabela to resume her research, to determine why Kaleigh had not succumbed to the carbon monoxide poisoning. It was exactly the jolt Isabela needed to make her want to resume her normal life. She worked on nothing else for nearly two weeks after her release.

"Isabela determined that you, Kaleigh, and I have DNA and something else she named MNA or Magical Nucleic Acid. Whilst Kaleigh is not, nor will she ever be a full-fledged magical being, Isabela located specific magical genes within Kaleigh's MNA that she inherited from us. Isabela also found the genetic code, within Kaleigh's DNA, of how to alter the DNA of Humans so they'd be able to survive the toxicity of the Earth's atmosphere.

"But I wanted to make sure Isabela was one hundred percent correct, so I took Kaleigh on my back, and we went flying together. And we went all the way to DAR."

"Oh, my God!" exclaimed Aelish.

"We used the Portal avoidance route, Momma."

"You've been to DAR, Kaleigh? And I missed it?" Aelish was quiet for a moment.

Thagar knew it would only be a matter of seconds before Aelish asked him about the Portal avoidance route.

"Wait! What in the world is the Portal avoidance route?" asked Aelish.

"I will tell you about it another time," said Thagar, who was chuckling. A secret he had kept for centuries had, yet again, been disclosed.

"I love the Artist's House, Momma," said Kaleigh. "And I had a really great time speaking in front of the Head Council, like you do."

"You spoke in front of the Head Council, Kaleigh? Thagar, I have missed everything!" She began crying again, but Thagar could see she was also experiencing hope and joy.

Kaleigh continued, "I did, Momma! The Head Council was having this big meeting to determine whether or not to war with Yasteron. I told them you wouldn't want them to. After I spoke at the meeting Daddy, Lady Antonia, Quentin, Amelia, and I went out for sweets. That was when I heard the news alerts in my head about the final vote cast by the Head Council. The vote was evenly split, and Council Chair Melanthia broke the tie vote of the Head Council Members by voting, no."

Thagar said, "It was in DAR, when her magical gene for telepathy became active. It was simply incredible, Aelish. Kaleigh has been imbued with four magical genes from us: she has the ability to breathe underwater, she has incredible linguistic capabilities, she is telepathic, and she also has the ability to change her skin color. These were all found in her sparse MNA strand.

"Isabela said that based on Kaleigh's DNA compared to ours—oh, just to be clear, we all have three strands, not the usual two strands that Humans have. Anyway, whilst Isabela is not certain exactly how long Kaleigh's lifespan will be, based on her DNA, she estimates it to be at least five hundred years or more. Isabela needs to do more work on all of our genomes, but she is currently on a worldwide tour with Drew. They are promoting the LECCS' vaccine since the vaccination rates have been abysmal. But the rates are finally starting to rise because of their tour."

"Thagar, I feel like it will take me months to process all of this."

"Well, we are going to be in Hentoria for a while, so you'll have lots of time," he replied, chuckling. "When I told you in the prison that Cardissius wasn't going to kill anyone, it was because Kaleigh was safely hiding in Hentoria," said Thagar.

Aelish's face suddenly lit up. "Wait! What about Human illness? Is Kaleigh susceptible to Human disease? Can she develop LECCS?"

"In her DNA strand," replied Thagar, "it was discovered Kaleigh has the ability to breathe the thinner air of the magical world as well as toxic air, like carbon monoxide. She cannot contract any Human disease, like LECCS, and as I mentioned earlier, her lifespan is far longer than Humans. I believe we have created the first next-generation Human, Aelish."

Aelish said, "Let me make sure I understand this correctly. Is the code for how Humans could potentially be altered, in order to survive the toxicity of Earth, inside of Kaleigh?"

"Theoretically, yes," said Thagar. "But Isabela said we are quite a ways off from using the CRISPR technology—"

"CRISPR!" exclaimed Aelish. "I remember Isabela telling me about this new gene- editing technology, years ago. Oh, my God, maybe Humans do have a chance to survive."

Aelish's color began to improve as the conversation continued. She became much more animated and began to remember who she used to be. Kaleigh said, "You look so much better now, Momma. Your lavender skin is almost back to its normal color. While I don't understand all of the things that are inside of me, I really hope, one day, I can help Humans. Oh! And I wanted to tell you something else. Even though I can't fly or perform spells, like you and Daddy, I really love being in the magical world. I feel very comfortable here. I miss home and all of my friends and teachers, but I really like taking classes at the Institute in Bencarlta."

"I can't believe I'm hearing you talk about DAR, the Institute, Bencarlta, and the Artist's House!" exclaimed Aelish. "So, tell me, my angel, what did you think of the view from the observatory in the Artist's House of the Great Rotunda of Peace?"

Kaleigh replied, "I was a bit naughty and didn't let Daddy put me to bed in any of the bedrooms the first night we were in DAR. I went into the room and just stared at the beautiful lights until I fell asleep on the floor. I love that room and I love that house! Daddy finally told me the story of why you both call it the Artist's House."

Aelish realized she hadn't let go of Kaleigh the entire time they were all talking. "I'm sorry I've been holding you so tightly, sweetheart. I missed you so much whilst I was gone, and I just can't believe you are with us in the magical world!"

"Antonia had the same reaction you did when she first saw me in DAR."

Aelish started laughing and it was music to Thagar's soul. "All right, Kaleigh," said Thagar. "Why don't you go outside and play? I want to speak to Momma for a few more minutes before she takes a nice long nap. You must be exhausted from everything we've just told you."

"I am, Thagar," said Aelish. "But it's a good kind of tired, you know?"

Kaleigh said, "I'm so glad you feel better, Momma. I was really worried about you. But I've been worried about you the whole time you've been gone. I'm so glad we are all together again, and I think my brother is really beautiful. Thank you for making him for me. I know we are different in many ways, but I already love him so much. I can't wait until he gets a little bit older so we can play together."

Aelish hugged her daughter and kissed her face all over. "You are the light of my life, Kaleigh, and you are going to be the very best big sister. I'm so proud of you. I can't wait until we can talk more about DAR and your experience speaking in front of the Head Council. I'm bursting with love and pride over you, my angel."

"Thanks, Momma. I love you so much, too. Okay, I'm going to try and find Amelia."

"All right, sweetheart," said Thagar. Aelish and Thagar watched Kaleigh bound out of the bedchamber in search of Amelia. "I would have waited a bit longer to tell you all of this, Aelish, but I didn't want to cause a literal heart attack if you were to suddenly see Kaleigh entering the bedchamber."

"I did feel a bit funny in my chest when I saw her, but it has stopped now. Please don't worry," said Aelish.

"I will be worried about you until you've made a complete recovery, my love. I think you are well on your way toward that outcome, especially now that you are able to hold your daughter after so many months of being away from her. I also wanted to tell you that Kaleigh has not questioned Elijah's parentage. She assumes I am his father." Aelish nodded and deeply sighed. "I'm so sorry for all you've been through, Aelish. Please forgive me for not getting to you sooner. If I had been any later, we would not be sitting here together."

"I feel incredibly blessed, Thagar, and I am so grateful for everything. I can't believe after all we've been through that Kaleigh can breathe in the magical world. I guess we have a lot to think about regarding the future, don't we?"

"We do, but not right now," he said. "Now, you just need to rest. I am so thankful you are on the road to recovery because I am not ready to know who we are without each other." He embraced her and gently kissed her forehead. "I love you now and forever, Aelish. Try and sleep and I will check on you later."

After Thagar left the bedchamber, Aelish thought about Abuela. She began praying and speaking to her as if she were in the room. She was devastated Abuela had lost her life because of a faulty generator now necessary because of the climate crisis. Aelish silently told Abuela what she meant to her, Thagar, and Kaleigh. She fell asleep, praying that Abuela was at peace.

22

Shamalaya Square

Six weeks after regaining consciousness, practicing her magic with Lady Antonia, and spending time with Thagar and Kaleigh, Aelish finally began to feel more like herself. She was thrilled Thagar had named her son, Elijah, and was greatly looking forward to the christening they were planning for him next week. She detested the name Cardissius had given him—Lucius—as she thought it sounded like Lucifer. She knew it meant "light" in Latin, but she still hated it.

Aelish was frankly astonished at how loving Thagar was to her son. She assumed he would resent the child and Cardissius' son would come between their Commitments. But so far, that had not happened. And Kaleigh was a blessing around Elijah. She'd never questioned his parentage and was still fascinated that her mother's pregnancy was such a short period of time. Aelish knew she'd have to tell Kaleigh about his parentage, one day, but today was not that day.

Early Monday morning, Aelish woke up with a gasp. She was disoriented and thought she was still imprisoned in the room. She looked at the beautiful large window in her bedchamber in the cottage, the special glass ceiling above her, and the mural of Brólaigh Castle. She looked across the bed at the face of her beloved Thagar, who was still sleeping. Kaleigh was curled up next to her father sound asleep, and Elijah lay between her and Kaleigh.

Sensing Aelish was awake, Elijah began to stir. She couldn't believe her milk had not dried up during her convalescence and she could still nurse her son. The medic told her it was not uncommon for magical females to resume nursing after an interruption. He also assured her the venom was long since out of her system and it would not affect the infant. She turned on her side and began nursing Elijah before his hungry cries woke the others.

As he suckled at her breast, she thanked God for allowing her to survive. She couldn't believe her entire family was sleeping beside her, in the same bed, in a magical world she'd known nothing about. She began softly crying as she watched the early morning snowfall. The wind whipped the snowflakes around in no apparent direction, making it all the more beautiful. Having never lived in a mountainous place, she was surprised it could still snow in June. In the distance, she saw a snow-capped mountain. The only thing familiar from her imprisonment was Storm warming her feet. She lifted her head and looked into the dog's startling blue eyes. He winked at her, and she decided to take him for a walk before everyone woke up.

Aelish detached a sleeping Elijah from her breast and put numerous pillows around him to keep him from rolling onto the floor. She put extra pillows between him and Kaleigh so she couldn't roll over onto him. At six pounds, he was still small, but he was thriving. She kissed his soft head and checked the pillows one more time to make sure he was tucked safely in the bed.

She put on her boots and slipped on her new, light blue woolen, floor-length cloak over her nightgown. She beckoned Storm and they quietly walked toward the front door of the cottage. Aelish opened the door and a gust of wind blew right into her eyes. She began laughing. Aelish pulled the fur-trimmed hood of the cloak over her head and retrieved the gloves inside the pockets. She'd only been outside in Hentoria three other times, accompanied by Lady Antonia, Amelia, and Kaleigh. But she knew exactly where she wanted to go. She began walking towards the woods, near the last street in the community, at the base of the snow-capped mountain.

She began walking faster and faster and suddenly felt like running. Storm stayed right beside her. To be able to walk, to run, and to freely move about was an ecstasy. She was free, and she would stay in Hentoria for the rest of her life if it meant she'd never have to see Cardissius' face again. Exhausted from her jaunt, she fell to the ground and threw snow at Storm's face. He formed a small snowball with his front paws and threw it at her with his snout. She began rolling around in the snow like a small child and started laughing and crying tears of joy. Storm came over and licked the salt from her tears while she nuzzled her face in the thick white fur of his neck. He was momentarily distracted by a small animal, but he would never leave her side to go hunting.

"It's all right," she said. "Go! Go and have your breakfast!" Storm took off and she watched how easily he captured his prey. He took it behind a rock to devour it. Aelish lay on the ground and looked up at the steel-grey sky spewing thousands of snowflakes. She swore she could make out the face of God in those clouds and began praying. She gave thanks to God for her health and her freedom as tears streamed down her face.

Suddenly, a small troll emerged from the woods and walked over to her. He looked down at her and asked, "Are ya' all right there, Miss?"

Aelish sat straight up and looked into the craggy face of the troll. He reached into his pocket and took out a white linen cloth. He handed it to her and said, "I thought ya' might be hungry." His Scottish Highlands' accent was so familiar and so comforting. He reminded her of Hamish, one the Gatekeepers of the Portal in DAR. My God, how she missed DAR, and she realized how much she also missed Drummond.

"That is so kind of you," she said. She opened the cloth and saw sweet cakes enclosed. "I've worked up quite an appetite frolicking in the snow." She took a bite and instantly knew they were the recipe she'd stolen from the sweet shop in Dublin, all those years ago, when she used to visit the city with her father. They were the same lavender sweet cakes she'd made for Hamish on her first trip to Earth to meet Isabela. How the recipe could have made it into this foreign land was beyond her, and right now, she didn't care. She devoured them as quickly as Storm had his prey.

"They were so good. Thank you . . . I'm sorry, but I don't know your name."

"Liam," said the troll, as he bowed in front of her. Aelish began laughing and thought about Drummond, always bowing and dropping his conical hat. Aelish heard branches breaking deep in the woods and she looked for Storm—he was right beside her. She squinted harder and could not believe her eyes: Drummond was coming out of the deep woods.

Aelish bolted upright and began running to meet him. "Drummond! What are you doing here?" She dropped to her knees and embraced her dear friend, crying tears of joy.

"I've been waitin' here, day after day, hopin' each one would be the day I'd finally lay eyes on ya' and here ya' are!" They both began laughing and Drummond also began crying. "I knew if Thagar got you out of that horrible kingdom, this would be the spot where you'd come to pray." Aelish hugged him tighter, feeling a joy she never thought she'd feel again.

"Whilst I waited each day," he said, "I scoured the area for herbs to cook yer favorite dishes. The food here is awful. No one knows how to cook!" Aelish began laughing at him.

"But wait! Have you been eating out of the refuse from the dwellings in the village?"

"I have." He saw the look of concern on her face. "Not to worry, Aelish. And there hasn't been one bin with any decent leftovers. No wonder they throw it out; it's positively dreadful!"

"Why didn't you just come to our cottage? Why have you been out here alone, all by yourself?" she asked, stroking his face. She saw the troll, Liam, head back into the woods.

"It was good for me to find my own kind again," said Drummond. "It's been a long time. I really wanted to surprise ya' and I wanted us to be alone the first time we saw each other."

Storm came over to Drummond, laid down, and licked his entire face with one swipe of his tongue. "Drat! That's not goin' to work, big fella!" Drummond grabbed the fur around Storm's neck and lifted himself up onto the back of the dog. Let's go home, Aelish!" Storm took off at a galloping pace with Drummond screaming the entire way. Aelish was laughing so hard, she couldn't stand up. Thankfully, Storm and Drummond circled back and she decided to also get on Storm's back. The dog brought them both back safely to the cottage.

What she did not expect, upon her return, was everyone to be outside searching for her. "She's here!" yelled Lady Antonia. "What in the world, Aelish? You gave us such a fright! You can't just disappear like that after all you've been through."

"Aren't ya' even goin' to say hello, Antonia?" asked Drummond.

Lady Antonia began chuckling. "Finally, you're here. What took you so long?"

Aelish saw how deeply upset Thagar was and profusely apologized. Breaking the tension, Drummond announced, "Who wants to eat the first proper breakfast served in Hentoria?"

Everyone relaxed and began to embrace Drummond, thrilled he was here. Thagar knelt down, pulled the little male closer and whispered into his ear unbeknownst to anyone else. "You missed Aelish's illness. She is well now. She was forced to procreate with Cardissius and has a son. He is here with us and his name is Elijah. Please don't say anything about Cardissius being the father. Kaleigh has accepted he's magical and has not questioned his parentage."

Drummond's Brownie eyes opened wide and Thagar saw rage in them. Drummond said quietly, "Perhaps a nice poison fit for a king would do, then, aye?"

"Aye," agreed Thagar. "He is despicable. I'm so glad you are here. Now, the whole family is finally together."

"So, when ya' rescued Aelish, ya' stole the heir to Yasteron?" asked Drummond, quietly.

"Indeed," said Thagar.

"Good for you, sir. He deserves a lot worse than that."

Thagar nodded and everyone headed inside for breakfast.

‡‡‡‡

After a week of Drummond cooking like a maniac, Thagar began to suspect the little male was hiding something and all of this cooking was because of nervous energy. One morning, after Drummond had cooked enough food to serve breakfast to the entire community, Thagar gingerly approached him in the kitchen.

"Drummond, are you ready to tell me what is troubling you?"

Drummond got so flustered he dropped a sack of flour on the floor and began swearing. Both actions were highly unusual for the experienced chef, and Thagar had never heard Drummond swear before. They were Cockney expressions, but he understood the gist of them.

"In my entire life, I've never been able to keep a secret," said Drummond, shaking his head, angry with himself. "Amelia is playin' outside with Kaleigh. Please, find Antonia and Aelish and bring them here. Then, I will tell y'all everythin' that's happened."

"I assume this isn't going to be good news, correct?'

"Correct, sir."

Thagar deeply sighed and went to find Aelish and Lady Antonia.

They all came into the kitchen and sat down at the table. The table was covered in flour, cooked and raw muffins sat side by side, and the entire kitchen was a complete mess. Lady Antonia knew her former Brownie very well. She took one look at the kitchen and immediately sensed there was trouble. She asked him, "Drummond, are you sure this is the right time?"

"It's now or never," he said.

"What's going on, Drummond?" asked Aelish. "Is something wrong?"

"I need to tell y'all somethin' so I can stop cookin' and makin' a mess like a first-year Brownie. I can't take the stress anymore."

Aelish said, "Please, dear Drummond, tell us what is upsetting you."

Drummond stood on one of the chairs and deeply exhaled. "I was sleepin' during the day and just before I was goin' to rise, at about four o'clock, I heard the stompin' of boots above me. I magically peered into all the rooms and saw Yasteron soldiers pourin' a liquid on all of the furniture, the floors—everywhere! I invisibly went and tried to gather the most important mementos for Kaleigh, especially her collection of stuffed bears and her favorite books.

"The liquid the soldiers were pourin' was a fire accelerant. They burned our Bunker Hill home to the ground. I cried as I watched the Human firefighters tryin' to put out the flames, but the accelerant the soldiers used had magic in it, so the house burned for two days. Finally, the firefighters got it under control. No other neighbors were injured, but it's all gone."

Aelish remained completely quiet, whereas Thagar stood up, paced for a moment, and then put his fist through the kitchen wall. Lady Antonia was in shock over the news, with her hand over her mouth. Drummond said, "I know we have to tell Kaleigh at some point, but I will leave that to y'all to determine when and how. She has lost so many things."

Thagar magically repaired the wall, tried to calm himself, and sat back down at the table.

"There's more," said Drummond.

"Good God! More?" exclaimed Lady Antonia.

"I tried to write down everythin' so I wouldn't forget." Drummond pulled out a piece of paper from his pocket and began reading. "As the soldiers were pourin' accelerant all over the house, they were speakin' to one another about the last time soldiers had come to this Earthly neighborhood. The previous soldiers' target was the daughter of the Living Legend, known as Kaleigh. The current soldiers inside the house were discussin' how they couldn't believe any Human could survive the intentional carbon monoxide poisonin' event.

"Kaleigh was the target of the carbon monoxide poisonin' all along. It was all supposed to look like an accident. The soldiers were tellin' each other that King Cardissius wanted his heirs, procreated with Aelish, to be the only offspring she'd have left. This way, she'd have no desire to ever return to Earth after being abducted and forced to bear the king's heirs. With her daughter dead, and her husband useless from his injuries, she'd have no reason to miss her previous family and yearn to return to Earth." Thagar did not outwardly react to the soldiers' disparaging assessment of him, but it hurt, nevertheless.

Drummond looked at the sorrow-filled faces around the table and said, "Yasteron intentionally tried to kill Kaleigh and Abuela was the collateral damage. The soldiers never anticipated Kaleigh could breathe in carbon monoxide nor survive it."

Drummond returned to his notes. "The soldiers started talkin' about how kings should always beware the Ides of March, or March 15th, ever since the year 44 B.C., when Julius Caesar was assassinated in Rome. Two months after Aelish's abduction, on the Ides of March, King Cardissius discovered the soldiers sent to kill Kaleigh had lied to the Crown and Aelish's daughter was still alive. The king went insane and ordered the soldiers involved in that mission to be tortured for lyin' and executed for failin'. The king was furious because he'd already married Aelish and discarded Queen Saia so their heirs wouldn't be bastards and could reign. But Cardissius knew with her daughter still alive, Aelish would always want to return home to her child. Her focus would never solely be on his kingdom as his new wife and queen. Once he learned Kaleigh had survived, all the king's plans for Aelish and their future offspring went awry. After that, he no longer cared if Aelish lived or died once she'd given birth to a male heir. The mission failure of the previous soldiers changed the course of his entire reign."

Thagar now knew the ring on Aelish's finger was a wedding

ring, put there by Cardissius, while she was already mated. He wondered why she hadn't taken it off.

Drummond looked up from his notes, with tears down his face. "Yasteron and King Cardissius were totally responsible for the carbon monoxide poisonin' that killed Isabela's grandmother. We are so lucky they didn't kill Kaleigh. I don't understand how the Yasteron soldiers penetrated the Safeguard spell that was around Isabela's house as well as our own." Drummond then began sobbing.

Thagar said, "Cardissius must have spent the last four years decoding the Safeguard spell, which I placed around both houses since the night of the dinner party with Glen in April of 2022. Whilst I was in the ambulance with Kaleigh, the evening of the carbon monoxide event, I made sure the Safeguard spell was still intact around Isabela's house, and it was. I always checked to make sure the Safeguard spell was working around both houses.

"So, Yasteron learned how to remove and reapply the spell with murderous precision. They are so evil and so heinous. They worked for years decoding the spell, in order to kill our child and ended up killing an innocent older woman. And they burned down our house in petty retaliation for rescuing Aelish. I don't like that the Torres house is exposed, but it will have to wait until we can leave Hentoria. I'm so glad you weren't hurt, Drummond."

Drummond nodded at Thagar, wiping the tears off his face.

The room was deathly silent. And then, Aelish began screaming. She began violently pushing items off the table with her arms. Flour went everywhere, muffins flew through the air, and when there was nothing left on the table, she stood up. "Lies! Lies! All lies—always!" She opened the kitchen cupboards and threw dishes, glasses, mugs, and pots onto the floor. Drummond hid under the table. Lady Antonia sat at the table hysterically crying, with her face in her hands, listening to Aelish's agony.

When Aelish finished destroying everything in the kitchen, she grabbed a sharp knife and headed toward the living area. "He raped me over and over! He ripped my Commitments' necklace from my neck! He slapped me hard across the face! His mother hit me so hard she nearly broke my jaw whilst I was pregnant! Evil! Evil beings that don't deserve to live!"

In the living area she began using the knife to slash chair cushions, settee cushions, and Thagar had a flashback of Isabela using her mirror to cut her own wrists. He magically flung the knife out of Aelish's hand, intensifying her rage. She began punching walls with her bare hands and Thagar saw that both of her hands were bleeding.

"He intentionally left me to die. He never let me see the sun. I couldn't use my magic. And every single world that ever came out of his mouth was a lie! He told me he would never kill Kaleigh because she was an anomalous Human and he wanted to see what she would become. He tried to kill my Kaleigh? And ends up killing Isabela's beautiful Abuela? Abuela never hurt anyone in her entire life! She took care of everyone and now she lies in a cold grave."

Thagar had never seen Aelish like this in the five hundred years he'd known her. She went from room to room breaking anything that could be broken. She continued ranting and raving and he watched her forcefully pull the emerald ring off her finger. She violently threw it. It landed somewhere in the living area. He was terrified she was preparing to hurt herself.

While he was hesitant to render her unconscious after the Magical Sunlight Deprivation Heart Syndrome had done just that, he decided for her own safety that he needed to sedate her with a spell. He placed the spell on her, caught her before she hit the floor, and carried her into their bedchamber. He laid her onto the bed and Lady Antonia came into the room with bandages for her bleeding hands. He sent Amelia a telly and told her to keep Kaleigh and Storm out of the house for as long as possible. As Lady Antonia wrapped Aelish's hands, Thagar went through the house and magically repaired all the damage she'd done.

Thagar found Drummond under the kitchen table, curled up on the floor, crying. He reached underneath for the little male, who was shaking uncontrollably. "It's going to be all right, Drummond," he said. "She had to be told. Do not blame yourself." He sat down on the floor, embraced Drummond, and began rocking him like a small child.

When Drummond finally stopped shaking, he looked at Thagar with his soulful eyes. "I can't believe what that evil king did to Aelish, sir. How will she ever get over it?"

"With a lot of love, a lot of time, and the support of those she trusts the most, like you. Why don't you go under the cottage now to rest? No one will be eating for some time. You've told us the worst thing a parent could hear: our daughter was intentionally targeted for murder. I've cleaned up all the mess so you can rest. And now that you've unburdened yourself of all of these horrible secrets, you can start to relax again. It's a miracle Kaleigh was unharmed. It will all get better from here, Drummond."

"I've never seen Aelish like that in my entire life, sir. It scared me," said Drummond.

"It scared me too, Drummond. Cardissius caused great harm to Aelish. He imprisoned, raped, and forced her to bear his child, and marry him. He made her betray her religious beliefs."

"I wondered where that emerald ring came from, but I was too afraid to ask."

"I think we can assume it was her wedding ring, given to her by Cardissius. I can't think about it all right now, as I have to try and remain calm for her. He is the most despicable being in the entire magical world, and one day, Cardissius will reap what he has sown, Drummond."

Drummond nodded and they both stood up. "Thank ya' for your kindness, sir. I'm so sorry for all the pain I caused in tellin' y'all this story."

"All will be well, Drummond. Go and rest now, and we will see you later."

Thagar watched Drummond aspirate from the room to rest underneath the cottage. He went back to the bedchamber to check on Aelish and Lady Antonia. He sat down in a chair by the bed and stared at Lady Antonia, who remained silent. Aelish was still unconscious. He thought about Abuela. He knew, one day, they'd have to tell the Torres family how sorry they were—by simply knowing them, Abuela had lost her life.

Thagar thought about everything he heard Aelish say as she lost her mind. He marveled at how she'd survived her imprisonment, her sexual assaults, her physical assaults, and being impregnated by such a reprehensible being. Her strength was unrivaled, but when she learned the king had lied about trying to kill Kaleigh, and ended up killing Abuela instead, she just broke. Lady Antonia didn't say a word as she sat with Thagar in the bedchamber while they waited for Aelish to wake up. He nervously fiddled with Aelish's wedding ring in his pants' pocket. He'd found it in the living area, while he magically cleaned up her destruction.

An hour later, Aelish opened her eyes. She looked at Thagar. "I want you to kill him."

"I couldn't wait for you to ask," said Thagar.

"Thagar, no!" exclaimed Lady Antonia. "Drummond gave us devastating information. You are newly traumatized, Aelish. Please, try and give it some time. Thagar does not have to break his Oath of Peace."

"Yes, Antonia," said Aelish. "I'm afraid that he does. I

can't live with what's inside of me anymore. After everything Cardissius did to me, now I find out he intentionally tried to murder our daughter? He lied! Everything he ever said to me was a lie! And until he is dead, there is no hope for Yasteron or for peace in the magical world. And if he remains alive, I will personally never know peace again. I am certain I cannot kill him. I know you understand why I cannot do it, Antonia, because you are a Catholic, like me. I also can't break my Oath of Peace. But someone has to do it for me. I will not be able to go on."

"I understand, my love," said Thagar. "I will try."

"Thagar," said Lady Antonia. "You are not an assassin. To do what Aelish is asking would mean you'd break your Oath of Peace and become a murderer. That is not who you are."

Aelish pleaded, "I won't be able to live, Antonia, as long as Cardissius remains alive. Please, Thagar, free me from this nightmare. I am so tired."

Thagar remained silent for a moment. He turned to Lady Antonia and said, "We can't let anyone else know what we are attempting. We cannot jeopardize the safety of Hentoria and those who gave us safe harbor. We don't know what is happening in Yasteron since Aelish and the heir disappeared. And there is only one being who might stealthily be able to enter Yasteron. Would you permit Amelia to enter Yasteron to gather intelligence for this mission, Antonia? I will leave it up to Amelia to decide whether or not she wishes me to accompany her."

Lady Antonia deeply exhaled, looked at Aelish's face, which was in agony, and simply nodded her head. "All right, Thagar. Amelia is destined for a life of espionage and perhaps even becoming an assassin. Whilst I think I can stop it, I know I can't. You have my permission to speak with her about all of this." Lady Antonia stood up from her chair and sat on the edge of the bed and embraced Aelish. "I'm so sorry for everything that has happened to you. My God!"

‡‡‡‡

Amelia and Thagar were dressed liked lower-orders. She pretended to be his child as they sat in a tavern in the lower-order section of Yasteron. Thagar had never witnessed such a covert spell in his entire life. It allowed them to gain direct entry into Yasteron, undetected. Amelia told him she'd found the spell among her father's papers and she'd been excited to try it out. She was thrilled it had worked.

The lower-orders were getting quite drunk on ale and all Thagar and Amelia had to do was sit and listen to gather intelligence. Thagar would never forget the moment when he learned the king was dead. And he was furious he would be denied the deed. They learned it was the failed mission to kill Kaleigh that had propelled the insane machinations of the king, which had ultimately led to his death.

Cardissius truly believed that once Kaleigh was dead, Thagar could offer Aelish nothing, whereas he could offer her being the Queen of Yasteron. But when it all went sideways, the king knew Aelish would always want to return to her daughter. He amended his plans and decided to simply use Aelish to imbue his heir with her exceptional magical abilities. He convinced himself he could abduct another Earth born DARling to be his queen and bear him more offspring.

However, according to the lower-orders in the tavern, Chief Minister Stannon was tired of the king's endless scheming, to create a lineage of preeminent magical beings with an Earth born DARling. And once Aelish and the heir had disappeared, the king unraveled to the point of madness. Seizing the opportunity, Stannon slowly poisoned him, making him sicker and sicker.

It appeared as if the king were dying of grief over the loss of his beloved Aelish and the heir they'd created together. Stannon convinced the ministers who controlled Yasteron that the king had become unfit to rule. Of course, Stannon took the responsibility of ruling Yasteron upon himself. But when Queen Saia saw the dead body of Cardissius, she knew he'd been slain.

The king and queen had always had a secret code between them. If either of them ever felt like they were being targeted by a noble or even a lower-order, they were to make small cuts in their thigh each time they suspected a betrayal. When the queen lifted up the king's burial robe, she saw twenty cuts on his thigh. And one cut was engraved with an "S" on either end. She immediately knew Cardissius had sent her one final message, disclosing who was trying to kill him.

Queen Saia had Chief Minister Stannon arrested along with all the other ministers who'd supported Stannon's coup to rule the kingdom. They were now all sitting in a filthy jail awaiting execution, scheduled in two days. Saia took back what was rightfully hers, and with most of the noble ministers jailed, she put in motion Aelish's plan of reconstituting the entire kingdom.

Aelish had told Thagar, Lady Antonia, and Amelia the contents of the four letters she had given to Oba, Master of Archives. Sitting in the tavern, Thagar and Amelia learned that many of the covert operatives were already on their way back from Earth, the weapons from Komprathia were in the hands of Special Envoy Ragdon, and Kam, the lower-orders' leader, had already begun training an army. They were astonished at how the queen was following Aelish's directives to the tee. Her letter to Queen Saia was now one of the most historic documents ever written within the magical world. What Amelia and Thagar gleaned in one night, in a drunken tavern, was more important than any covert mission they could have envisioned.

Thagar turned toward Amelia and said, "Aelish put all of this in motion whilst she was pregnant, sick, and knowing she was going to die. She managed to convince a queen, whom she caused to be dethroned, to restructure an entire dominion. My admiration of her is as deep as my love for her."

Amelia nodded her head in agreement. "That is why Aelish is a Living Legend."

Thagar shook his head in disbelief of what his mate had accomplished. He remarked, "I wonder how many previously occupied positions of great power on Earth will suddenly become vacant as Yasteron's covert operatives return home?"

Amelia began chuckling and said, "Hopefully, we can soon leave Hentoria and return to Earth and find out exactly what's happened. I'm sure they calculated how to slowly evacuate their positions to make it appear more natural. But let's not forget what Aelish told us about the Humans who love their Yasteron operatives as well as the offspring they managed to create."

"Yastermans," said Thagar. "Like the Earth doesn't have enough destroying it."

"Who knows? Maybe they will end up being a good thing for the Earth," said Amelia.

"It will take me until the end of my life to ever believe there is any good inside of any Yasteron or any half-Yasteron," said Thagar. "I will most likely detest them all until I die."

"But what about Elijah, Thagar?" asked Amelia. "And what about Aunt Charlotte?"

"Hmm . . . touché, Amelia," replied Thagar, smiling at her.

Two days later, Amelia and Thagar, along with thousands of Yasterons of noble and lower-order birth, gathered in Shamalaya Square for the executions. Stannon and the ministers were in rough shape and looked as if they'd been tortured the entire time they were imprisoned. They watched as Queen Saia went up onto the scaffold. She began speaking to the crowd.

"I am your rightful queen, Yasteron, and I will rule until we can once again determine what our kingdom stands for. I loved King Cardissius, despite all that he did to me. Siring an offspring with an Earth born DARling was my ultimate humiliation. Yet, to this day, I love him. And when I learned he'd been slain, by Chief Minister Stannon along with these ministers sentenced to hang today, I knew, one day, I would restore our kingdom for *all* Yasterons, not just for those of noble birth."

The crowd began cheering for their queen, nobles and lower-orders alike.

"If King Cardissius had asked me to forgive him, I would have. And that is the lesson I want you all to take home after you leave today. Love is the only thing that lasts, and the quest for power is corrupting and leads to unimaginable crimes. We will no longer be the kingdom of hate and fear—not whilst I am your ruler. We will live in peace, with justice and an education for all. We will become an egalitarian society where any Yasteron can achieve their dreams, no matter their station of birth. We are one kingdom. Every Yasteron deserves to be educated, and every Yasteron deserves a voice in how our kingdom is run."

The cheers were so loud that Amelia and Thagar had to momentarily cover their ears.

"Good citizens, say goodbye to the old guard. Say goodbye to the King's Guard and say hello to the Queen's Guard. The Guard was always the only part of the military where females could ever serve and, now, the Guard will be *entirely* female! Say goodbye to all the males who have destroyed this beautiful dominion, for they will never rule again, not as long as I am your queen. And whilst saying that makes me a target for those wishing to return to the origins of this kingdom, I tell you here and now, that will never be. The Queen's Guard will always protect me. I will rule for *all* the beings in this kingdom, not just for the nobles. And the lower-orders will finally have an education and serve their kingdom alongside those they were forced to serve for thousands and thousands of years."

Amelia said to Thagar, "I think the queen has been infused with Aelish's passion and deep sense of justice. What I wouldn't give to read the actual letter she wrote to the queen."

Thagar nodded at Amelia and smiled.

"Aelish is simply incredible, Thagar. One day, I hope to emulate her."

"You're well on your way to becoming the next Living Legend, Amelia," said Thagar.

"We'll see," Amelia said humbly.

As each minister was hung, gasping their last breath, Thagar felt it cleanse his soul. While he had not been given the opportunity for retribution, this was close enough. And apparently, it was having the same effect on the citizens. With each hanging, they grew louder and louder and began dancing in the streets. But when it came time for Chief Minister Stannon to have the noose around his neck, the crowd quietly resumed watching. Stannon tried to speak some final words in his own defense, and the queen shouted, "Quiet, Stannon! Or I will have you drawn and quartered! Your days of telling us what to do are over. It ends *today*!"

The noose tightened around his neck and no hood was used, so he could gaze one last time at the kingdom he'd helped cruelly rule alongside the king. He had enforced and perpetuated the most heinous and longest-lasting caste system in the entire magical world.

When he'd taken his last breath and his body hung limp from the noose, Shamalaya Square erupted in song and dance. And that was the beginning of the revolution in Yasteron, and Thagar and Amelia were lucky enough to have witnessed it all.

When Uncle Thurrock learned Thagar and Amelia had entered Yasteron without the permission of the Hentorians, he was not happy. But when he realized Aelish was responsible for putting the entire revolution occurring in Yasteron in motion, he said to his nephew, "One day, maybe we'll be able to decide of our own free will whether to leave or stay in Hentoria. Your mate truly is a Living Legend."

23

A Rare Jewel

A S ISABELA GOT dressed for dinner, she was thinking about how grateful she was for DAR. Their Scrubber 13 fleet had been pumping carbon out of the Earth's atmosphere twenty-four hours a day, seven days a week. DAR had bought her precious time, so she and Drew could finish their worldwide tour before the overall global temperature breeched the LECCS threshold of 1.4°C. The Earth was simply enormous, but they were determined to try and visit nearly every country in the world, to promote the vaccine and save as many lives as possible.

China was so large that it took them over three weeks to traverse the world's third largest landmass. And from China they travelled to Canada, the world's second largest landmass. In Canada, English and French were the primary languages spoken, so they had an easier time communicating with the citizens. And the citizens in both China and Canada were very keen on taking the vaccine, which made their time on the road much more pleasurable.

Isabela couldn't believe the overall global temperature continued to hold past the month of June. She had predicted to David, her Clinical Trial Administrator, that the temperature would hit 1.4°C by April or May of 2026. She knew without DAR's assistance, the temperature would have already flipped the switch on LECCS.

She thought about Aelish every day. Isabela knew from her mother that Thagar had not yet returned to Earth from the rescue mission he was attempting in Yasteron. She took this as a hopeful sign that he'd either gotten her out and they were still in hiding or he was still trying and had not abandoned the mission. Aelish had been gone from Earth since early January.

Isabela missed her Oraculi and wanted to share her newfound feelings about Drew. After their famous kiss at the base of Mount Kenya, the reception she and Drew received was far different now than it had been at the beginning of the tour. Leaders of countries they'd yet to visit would have felt snubbed if they weren't included. And crowds now clamored to see Isabela and Drew. They were the new "it" couple, making it necessary for them to appear in larger and larger venues. While they still held a few town-hall-style meetings, most of their presentations were done in stadiums and arenas. Drew told her that when he was a teenager, he'd always wanted to be a rock star. He never thought he'd be packing stadiums and arenas because of a deadly syndrome threatening the existence of Humanity.

Their celebrity grew with each stop on the tour and the vaccination rate climbed from the original paltry rate of ten percent to a new level of seventy-five percent. And as the vaccination rate increased, it mirrored the rate of Isabela's heart beginning to open. Drew made the tour very enjoyable and took her to the most famous attractions in every country: the Taj Mahal in India, the pyramids in Egypt, the Great Wall of China, and Machu Picchu in Peru.

And like the science book collection of her youth, Drew created a history of where they'd been. Sometimes, he'd present her with the simplest gift, like a notebook, or a historic treasure, or rocks and stones only found in a specific location they'd visited. Unbeknownst to Isabela, when the tour was over, Drew was planning to create a surprise art installation for her with the help of his staff.

With each kiss, with each stroke of her face, and with every gentle embrace, Drew was unlocking Isabela's heart. And as Marisol had observed, Drew was taking his courtship with Isabela very slowly. Isabela had only just been very mentally ill, and he did not want to overwhelm her. But it was getting more and more difficult for him to reign in his love for her.

Two days ago, in Mexico City, Isabela was awarded the Belisario Domínguez Medal of Honor, the highest award bestowed by the Mexican Senate to its citizens. While Isabela was not a citizen of Mexico, she was honored accordingly and joined at least fifteen other foreigners who had historically received the award. The fact that Marisol, Abuela, and Abuelo were all born in Mexico didn't hurt, either. Belisario Domínguez was a famed politician who was also a doctor. The award, in his honor, was given to those who stood out for exceptionalism in their profession, while at the same time, demonstrating their dedication and love for Mexico.

Drew was awarded La Orden Mexicana del Águila Azteca or The Order of the Aztec Eagle. It was the highest honor Mexico bestowed on foreign-born individuals, who had done a great service to Mexico or for Humanity.

Isabela and Drew also attended an awards ceremony at the Instituto Nacional de Salud Pública (INSP), or the National Institute of Public Health of Mexico, at their main campus in Cuernavaca, forty-four miles south of Mexico City. A dinner was held for Isabela and Drew, which included Mexican dignitaries in government, health, and science.

Isabela greatly wished her parents and grandparents could have attended both these ceremonies, as they would have been so proud of her. It had special meaning for her to receive these honors from her mother and grandparents' place of birth. While she'd been to Mexico only once as a child, she came to realize how important her heritage was and promised the dignitaries she would return soon for another visit.

As they sat down for dinner in a famous restaurant called El Cardenal in Mexico City, people stood up from their dinners and both patrons and staff gave Isabela and Drew a standing ovation. Isabela was still not used to this kind of attention and always looked to Drew for guidance. He always knew the right gestures to perform and the right words of gratitude.

Drew never disappointed and always made her feel safe. Many of the diners pointed to stickers they wore, indicating they'd just received the LECCS vaccine. It meant so much to Isabela to see the importance of all her work in the form of a small sticker affixed to a recipient's clothing. She wiped away a tear and smiled at the patrons, offering her sincere thanks in Spanish. Drew shook many hands and a little girl came over to embrace Isabela. She was the same age as Kaleigh and nearly made Isabela's heart burst with longing for Aelish, Thagar, and Kaleigh. The little girl gave her a kiss and a rose taken from a floral centerpiece on one of the tables.

It was a moment Isabela would never forget. After the small reception was over and people resumed their dinners, Isabela and Drew were left in peace and began quietly chatting with one another.

"That was really lovely," said Drew.

"The little girl reminded me so much of Kaleigh," said

Isabela. She began softly crying. Drew leaned over and put his arm around her, kissing her forehead.

"We will see them all again soon, Isabela. You must have faith it will all work out."

"I keep trying, Drew. As the months go by, I wonder how changed Aelish is and how Thagar and Kaleigh will cope with those changes when it's all over."

"With our love and with our help," said Drew, smiling.

Isabela grasped his hand. She lifted it to her mouth and softly kissed it. Drew smiled back and said, "Well, I think we should just follow their specials menu for dinner. What do you think?"

He always knew how to bring her back to the moment and replace sadness with joy. She began laughing, dried her eyes, and stared at the menu. "Why don't you order for the both of us? I just want to relax and be taken care of tonight."

"Ah! Wonderful!" exclaimed Drew.

Dinner was outstanding. When it was time to order dessert, an older woman wearing an apron, who was not their server, approached the table.

"I hope you both saved room for dessert," she said in Spanish. "We have two special options tonight." She handed them each a dessert menu. "I am the mother of the owner. I was actually looking for any excuse to come over and introduce myself. I used to know your Abuela and Abuelo, Doctor Torres. My name is Lucinda González. I was wondering how they were? I haven't seen them since we were all very young. They must be so proud of you."

Isabela looked into the blue eyes of this woman and began to remember tales Abuela used to tell her about a friend she used to know who had bright blue eyes. Abuela and Abuelo used to frequent her taqueria, which specialized in tacos and burritos. It was from this taqueria that Abuela took many of the recipes for some of Isabela's favorite foods made on Cinco de Mayo. Every fifth of May, Abuela would raise a glass to her friend, Lucinda, with the bright blue eyes.

"Oh, my goodness," said Isabela. "Every Cinco de Mayo, my Abuela would make my favorite foods from many recipes that came from a taqueria owned by her friend, Lucinda, with the bright blue eyes. She made a special toast to you every year!" Isabela stood up and hugged Lucinda, feeling Abuela looking on. Lucinda was the same age and was even similar in height and weight to her beloved Abuela. It was like holding her again.

"You speak about your Abuela in the past tense. Have your Abuela and Abuelo left this life?" asked Lucinda, with tears in her blue eyes.

"Abuela tragically passed away this past January and my Abuelo passed away many years before that," replied Isabela, who started to tear up.

"Ay! I'm so sorry for your loss, Doctor Torres."

"Please, call me Isabela. Can you sit with us for a bit? Oh, and please forgive me for not introducing you to Andrew Devereux. He is my partner on the LECCS vaccine."

Drew stood up and shook hands with Lucinda. "I suppose my son won't yell at me if I sit with you both for a few minutes." Drew pulled out a chair for her and sat down again after Lucinda was situated.

"Thank you, Mr. Devereux," said Lucinda. "What a gentleman." Drew smiled at Lucinda and then looked at Isabela, who was also smiling at him. "Aside from wanting to meet my friends' famous granddaughter, I also came over because I wanted to tell your Abuela something. I can't believe she's gone. Your Abuelo and my husband, José, were also very good friends as they were both auto mechanics. José passed away several years ago. After he died, I closed down the taqueria and came to work for my son, also named José, who wanted to own a fancy restaurant. He grew up in my kitchen and is an amazing cook. Well, he likes to call himself a chef, but he's still a cook to me." Lucinda started laughing as did Isabela and Drew. "He lets me prepare certain dishes here, as well as some of the desserts. It keeps me busy."

Isabela reached across and touched Lucinda's hand. "Well, why don't you tell me whatever it was you wanted to tell Abuela."

"Did she ever mention that your Abuelo worked as an auto mechanic for a very wealthy family? They owned one of the most beautiful properties in Mexico City and were known for their philanthropy. The property was called Hacienda de San Miguel de Hernández. The Hernández family would throw a party once a year for all the people who worked for them. José and your Abuelo were invited every year, as they were their personal auto mechanics for their fleet of automobiles. And every year your Abuela would say, one day, she was going to live in a place like Hacienda de San Miguel. Saint Michael was her favorite saint and she always wore a necklace of him around her neck. She said Saint Michael was her protector and as long as she wore the necklace, no harm would ever come to her."

Isabela reached inside her blouse and pulled out the necklace of Saint Michael that Abuela had given her weeks before her death. "Do you mean this necklace?"

"Ay! That's the necklace! She left it for you after she died?"

"Actually, she gave it to me a few weeks before she died, and I will always believe she passed away because she took it off."

Lucinda began crossing herself and started crying. "That is incredibly sad."

"I know. When she gave it to me, I promised her I would never take it off, and I never will," said Isabela, also crying. Even Drew began to tear up.

"I wanted to tell your Abuela that the children of the Hernández family no longer wish to own Hacienda de San Miguel, now that both of their parents have passed away, and it is up for sale. It is very expensive, but it's one of the rarest properties in Mexico City. It seems like we are all reaching the age where we are dying off. Getting old is not easy, Doctor Torres—I mean, Isabela. Oh, I also wanted to tell you, my whole family has taken your vaccine and we are so grateful for it. Thank you for developing something that will save so many people."

"Of course! Drew and I are always so happy when people tell us they've taken the vaccine." For a moment, Isabela had a faraway look in her eyes. "Wait! Did Hacienda de San Miguel have some of the oldest and most amazing trees on the grounds of the property?"

"Yes, yes," said Lucinda. "One year, your Abuela and I had too much tequila at the annual party and José and your Abuelo couldn't find us. That's because we climbed up one of those amazing trees, shaped like an elephant. It had many branches that extended very low from the trunk. The branches were low enough to grab and climb. Our husbands were ready to kill us because the parties the Hernández family threw were very elegant. And there we were, climbing up trees and hiding from them, like we were six years old." Lucinda started laughing. "The four of us also had a weekly poker game. For weeks afterward, our exploits during the party would come up and we would laugh for hours. Of course, playing for shots of tequila always made us feel a bit giddy, but your Abuela and I never forgot that night and neither did our husbands."

"Oh, my God, Abuela did tell me that story—many times!" exclaimed Isabela. "Now, I remember it. She loved the Hacienda de San Miguel, mostly because she got to pretend that she was very wealthy. But I think the main reason was because of the fun she had that night with you. One day, I was trying to climb a small tree and Abuela told me I was doing it all wrong. She was up inside of that tree in less than two minutes. I knew from then on, I had not inherited my mother or my Abuela's love of heights. What a wonderful memory, Lucinda. Thank you so much for coming over and reminding me about how special and naughty my Abuela was. I miss her every day."

"You are so welcome, mi querida," said Lucinda. Hearing Lucinda call her mi querida, just like Abuela used to, made Isabela smile and start crying again. "Will you promise to come back and visit us, here at the restaurant, the next time you're in Mexico?"

"I promise," said Isabela.

"I'm going to bring you our two dessert specials tonight—on the house! It's the least I can do for my dear friend's beautiful and intelligent granddaughter. I hope you both enjoy them." Lucinda stood up, right as her son came over to chastise her for sitting with the patrons. He told her this was not a taqueria and she had to remember herself. He smiled at both Drew and Isabela, but Isabela did not smile back at him for scolding his mother. He suddenly realized who Isabela and Drew were and began shaking their hands profusely, thanking them for the vaccine. He told them to come back anytime and their entire meal would be comped.

Drew tried to protest, but young José would hear no more about it. Then, Isabela smiled at him and told him he was lucky to have such an amazing mother. He thanked her and left with Lucinda, leaving Isabela and Drew alone again.

"This is what I love about Mexico," said Drew. "The people are so warm and welcoming. I can only imagine what Lucinda and your Abuela were like when they were together."

"How I wish I could tell Abuela I met her childhood friend tonight. It was Lucinda's blue eyes that made me remember it all.

I wish I knew my Abuela when she was young. She must have been so much fun to hang out with."

When the desserts were served, a small mariachi band played a traditional melody Isabela remembered learning from Abuela. As the band played, she began singing while eating the most delicious dessert she'd ever eaten that wasn't chocolate. After they were finished with dessert, the band moved on to another table, and Drew took out a rectangular gilded box with an elaborate pink bow on it.

"What is this, Drew?" asked Isabela, smiling.

"Life is very interesting," he said, chuckling. "Your mother called me about some invoices at the Climate Refugee Intake Center, and I told her our last stop on the tour was going to be Mexico. She told me to show you this very special house your Abuela used to talk about owning, one day, when they all became millionaires. So, I went past the house and saw it was for sale. I bought you the Hacienda de San Miguel so you would always be able to come to Mexico, stay in your second home, and remember your Abuela and all of her exploits. I suggest you host a party there as soon as possible and invite Lucinda and her son."

"You bought me the Hacienda de San Miguel? Oh, my God! Why did you do that?"

"Mexico is a part of you, so I thought it would be nice if you owned a part of it."

"I don't know what to say," said Isabela.

"Open the box," said Drew.

Isabela began untying the elaborate pink bow and opened the gilded box. Inside was an enormous old-world wrought iron key. She lifted it up and asked, "Is this the key to the house?"

"It was, but now it only opens one of the buildings on the property. The other locks have been modernized. But the key is historic and actually does still open one of the other buildings."

"How many structures are on this property?" asked Isabela, incredulous.

"Why don't we take a ride over to your new house and find out?" asked Drew.

‡‡‡‡

The driver pulled up to the front of the property, which was completely illuminated with outdoor lighting. The grounds were enormous. The house was made of pink stucco with fieldstone accents. It had an orange-tiled roof and white pillars adorned the two-story structure of the main house. And then, Isabela saw the elephant tree. She immediately knew it was the tree Abuela and Lucinda had climbed on that infamous night.

Isabela opened the door and ran out onto the property and stood at the bottom of the tree. She looked at its incredible configuration and sat down on a stone bench in front of the tree and thought about Abuela.

By the time Drew reached the tree, Isabela was sobbing. "No, mi querida," he said. "This present is only supposed to bring you joy, not sadness."

She looked into Drew's hazel eyes and knew she'd fallen madly in love with him.

"Thank you so much for knowing what this house would mean to me. I can't wait to tell my mother what you did because it was also a part of her life."

"Why don't we walk the grounds and then go inside and take a look around?"

Hand in hand, they walked the grounds which took quite some time. Isabela adored the swimming pool area, which had a covered area at one end made of white stucco with pillars and a tiled roof. Trees surrounded the rectangular area of the pool in a canopy, providing just enough shade from the hot Mexican sun. They wandered over to an older structure and Drew said, "This is what the key opens. It's a guest house. Although there are sixteen bedrooms, perhaps some of your guests would like their own casita while they stay with you."

"This hacienda is more like a hotel than a home. Yet it does have an incredible warmth to it. I think it's because it's pink. Ah! That's why you wrapped the box with a pink bow!"

Drew started laughing at her. "You figured it out! Wait, are you a genius?"

She punched him in the arm, laughing.

When they entered the main house, Isabela just gasped. The antiquity of its Mexican heritage along with its modern touches made it truly unique and very livable. In the dining room was a fresco on one wall.

Drew said, "The fresco came out of a church from the 13th century. Unfortunately, it has since been torn down. Look at the craftsmanship of this painting, Isabela."

Isabela looked at the fresco, but she preferred watching Drew examining the fine brush strokes. The man simply loved art, and it was starting to rub off on Isabela. As they toured the house, they entered a salon containing the painting Drew had bought her in Montmartre, France.

"What is this doing here? Oh, my God, my favorite painting! I thought it was going to my mother's house?"

"It did. Marisol called to tell me there was no room large enough to accommodate it, so I told her to hold on to it until I could arrange for it to be shipped, framed, and hung in the hacienda."

"Wait! So, my mother knows you bought me this house?"

"She does," said Drew. He smiled at Isabela. "She told me to tell you she expects to visit her homeland of Mexico very soon and to tell you that she's staying at the hacienda."

Isabela burst out laughing. "Nothing would make me happier."

As they continued through all the furnished rooms, Drew said, "I purchased the seller's original furnishings and thought you could decide what to keep or what to replace. But there is one room I'd very much like to show you."

As they climbed up the gorgeous, curved stone staircase, Isabela thought of the staircase in Aelish's childhood home in Ireland. She could only hope that, one day, they'd all be together in the hacienda. Upstairs, Drew took her hand as they stood outside of a closed door.

"Ready?" he asked.

"I guess," said Isabela, tentatively.

He opened the door and inside the room was a literal museum of all the mementos Drew had collected on their LECCS tour. "Do you like it? I never want you to forget what we accomplished, Isabela. I had all the items of our tour collection installed in this room so you could come in here and relax while always remembering our trip together." He walked her over to a leather recliner that swiveled and was situated in the middle of the room. Drew gestured for her to sit down in the chair for the full experience he'd created for her.

"I suggest you call this the LECCS reflection room," he said, chuckling. "Now, along with the painting of the Pacific Ocean downstairs, you will have two places where you can relax and enjoy a Zen-zone."

Isabela stood up from the chair and began passionately kissing Drew. "You are the most generous person I have ever met in my life. Thank you for all of this, and thank you for always being there for me."

"Come," he said. "Let me show you the owner's bedroom suite."

They entered the most beautiful bedroom Isabela had ever seen. One wall was made of fieldstone, resembling the specific feature found on the structures outside, and the other walls were painted a gentle coral color. The four-poster, wrought-iron bed had white sheaths of fabric hanging from the iron frame above the bed. It reminded Isabela of the bed Aelish had described to her, in her first cottage in DAR, as well as in the Artist's House in Bencarlta. The highboy dresser was an antique from the original owners as were many of the other pieces in the room. Isabela's favorite spot was a built-in window seat on an overhang window. The window jutted out over the grounds outside and had a tufted cushion and numerous pillows.

She sat down on the seat and said, "What a place to read a really good book." She opened the casement window and smelled the jasmine in the garden. "Drew this house is magnificent."

"Well, until we depart for our respective homes, this is where we'll be staying for the rest of our trip. By the time we are ready to leave, you'll have become accustomed to all the features of the house and know which pieces you want to keep and which pieces you want to replace."

Isabela had been with Drew for so many months, she could no longer imagine herself going back to her parents' home in Tennessee. She felt more grown up after seeing the world. And now that she'd been given this house, she thought she might stay here a bit longer.

"I can see the wheels inside your head turning," he said. "You love it here, don't you?"

"I do," said Isabela. "I feel like I could stay here forever."

"Well, we'll be here until July 5th, so you have another few weeks to decide what you want to do. But for right now, I suggest you get some rest. All your things are here."

Isabela got up from the window seat and opened the dressers and closets and saw all of her clothing from the tour, neatly pressed and put away. "You have spoiled me rotten, Drew."

He came over and kissed her forehead and said, "In the morning, you will meet your household staff. We can see if the cook I hired is as good as I hoped after we eat breakfast."

"My *staff*? Drew, I'm not used to living like this and how in the world am I going to pay for staff?" She took one look at his face and knew he intended to cover all of her expenses, just like he did for Nanny Marie in France. "Oh no, Drew! I can't let you do that!

"We will talk all about it tomorrow. For now, go to sleep in the house of Abuela's dreams. Remember, she said, one day, she hoped to own this house, with the money she and your Abuelo earned from living el sueño Americano. So, as you lay your head down tonight, think of your Abuela. This was her American dream—to, one day, return to her birthplace."

"Okay," said Isabela, beaming. "I will see you in the morning."

‡‡‡‡

The next morning, Isabela met her household staff. She had two cooks, two maids, and a slew of gardeners to attend the enormous grounds. In one of the structures on the property was a security command center with a team of former American military personnel, similar to Drew's security team who travelled with them. There were computer and television screens everywhere, showing every single room in the house. During their first week at the hacienda, she'd be given tutorials on how to maintain her own privacy while using the bathroom or when dressing in the bedroom.

She looked at Drew and asked, "Is all of this really necessary?"

"Mexico is a magnificent country," said Drew. "And while Mexico City is not considered one of the thirty-one states within Mexico, and is more like Washington, D.C., the Sinaloa Cartel has a presence in twenty-two of Mexico's thirty-one states. And they also have a presence here in Mexico City." Drew saw the fear in Isabela's face. "I want you to feel safe at all times when you are visiting the hacienda, especially when you are with your family. So, I arranged a meeting with the cartel."

"Oh, my God! You did what?" exclaimed Isabela.

"I did not personally meet with them, but the American security company we are using has a very good relationship with them. They know exactly how important you are to the world, and for a small fee, they will provide protection in collaboration with our security detail. They do not want the rare jewel of Mexican descent to come to any harm, especially since you are an American citizen, which could cause quite the international incident."

"How much is a small fee?" asked Isabela, who had to sit down to steady herself.

"You don't need to worry about that. Further, we can also engage the services of DAR, unbeknownst to our own security detail, to place protective spells around the entire property. After all you've been through, Isabela, I think it's best to face any potential dangers head-on. I want you to be able to live your life freely and safely, wherever you wish to live it."

Isabela nodded and deeply exhaled.

"If you are unable to feel free living here," he said, "I will simply sell the property. But I wanted to give you the opportunity to do so. There's no need to worry about anything. You will either feel safe here or you won't. I do think you should give it enough time, though, to be sure."

"I have never known anyone like you in my short time on this Earth," she said. "Thank you for trying to give me the freedom to live my life, while at the same time, feeling safe."

After a week of getting to know all the security features, like the panic rooms installed for her protection, as well as getting to know her household staff, Isabela began to relax. She loved the house and greatly enjoyed taking walks in the late afternoon with Drew on the grounds. At the hacienda, she felt insulated from the world and was greatly enjoying not having to do anything. Her mother was very excited about the house. And her mother's excitement seemed to reassure Isabela that they could all feel safe, whenever they visited the hacienda.

One afternoon, after a lovely walk, Isabela and Drew were sitting by the pool on one of the marble benches alongside the pool's edge. Drew turned to her and said, "You are the rarest jewel in all the world, Izzy, and I want us to spend the rest of our lives together. I only want to make you feel happy and safe and for you to know I will never leave you. You are the most beautiful person on this Earth, and I fell in love with your intelligence and your passion the first night we met on a computer in Hector Rios' house. I have waited for you to grow up, and while I am eighteen years older than your young twenty years, I feel you are the wise old soul who will help me make sense of a world filled with some of the worst cruelty, yet also some of the kindest gestures I will never understand." Drew got down on one knee and presented Isabela with a black velvet box. He opened it and she saw one of the rarest gemstones in all the world: a red emerald-cut diamond, set on a simple platinum band.

"Izzy, will you help me make sense of it all for the rest of my life?"

Isabela gasped, looked at Drew's smiling face, and said, "Yes, Drew, I will." He took the ring out of the box and slipped it on her finger. It fit perfectly, like their love for one another.

She loved how he called her Izzy for the first time ever, when he proposed. He stood up, and she went flying into his arms with a joy she'd never known before. Over the last four months, Isabela had truly grown up. While she was only twenty years old, in genius years, she was a lot older than that. With the ring on her finger, she took his face in her hands and gazed into his rare hazel eyes. He kissed her so deeply that she felt reborn. He led her to the enormous owner's suite, where she'd slept alone for the last week, and they made love all night.

Drew was a generous lover, the same way he was with his wealth and his heart. There were times when he devoted himself to only her pleasure. And he experienced the most joy when Isabela was happy and sexually satisfied. She had never known a love like this before.

✝✝✝✝

On the morning of Friday, July 3rd, Isabela came out of the bathroom and said to Drew, who was still dozing in bed, "Hey, Drew, I think you're going to need to develop some biometric apps."

"Oh, why?" he asked, sleepily.

"Because the one I've been using to track my cycles is not reliable. I understand the jet lag from all of our traveling as well as my new medications have affected my normal cycle . . . but, I'm pregnant."

"*What*? Are you serious?"

"As a heart attack."

"Oh, my God, Izzy!" he exclaimed. "Your father is going to kill me!"

"To say nothing of my brother, Javi."

"How are you feeling, honey?"

"I actually feel great. I can't believe I'm a physician-scientist who got knocked up, accidentally. I always track my cycles; I never saw this coming. I'm *such* a genius!"

Drew got out of the bed and came over and embraced her. He whispered into her ear, "I can't believe my baby is going to have a baby. I'm so excited." He pulled out of the hug and stared at her. "We need to get married right away!"

"Oh yeah!" exclaimed Isabela, laughing. "And I know one person who is going to be over the moon—my mother!"

Drew lifted her up and twirled her around. "I don't think I've ever been this happy in my entire life, Izzy!"

He set her down and Isabela deeply kissed him. "I can't believe I'm going to have a baby in the same year I will finally be able to legally drink alcohol." Drew started laughing.

Isabela knew they had conceived a child the first night they'd made love after becoming engaged. She knew her mother would be more than willing and excited to plan a fast wedding for them. The locked box where she'd kept her heart had burst open from Drew's love. Never in her wildest dreams had she envisioned herself getting married so young, let alone having her first baby by the time she was twenty-one.

She couldn't believe how much she wanted it all, but it was because of how much she loved Drew. When she returned to Nashville, engaged and pregnant, Drew gave her an early wedding gift—a gift she could never repay. He'd built Isabela her very own state-of-the-art research lab, outfitted with all the latest CRISPR technologies for gene-editing research.

Drew knew Wainbridge would never allow her to genetically modify Humans in order to survive the climate crisis, using the key code found in Kaleigh's DNA. He wanted Isabela to finally be in control of her own research, without having to go through a Board of Directors and the massive administration of a huge healthcare system. He wanted her to have complete independence, and he knew her scientific ethics and integrity would never allow her to abuse it.

As they walked inside the new lab, Drew said, "I think it's time you're in control of the science the way you want to do it, without the bureaucracy of hospital administrators holding you back. Please, discover how Humans can continue to inhabit this dying planet, Izzy. I know you can do it, and even if you never finish it in your lifetime, leave the science behind, intact, for the next genius to finish it. We simply can't give up on our home, the Earth, even though it is giving up on us."

Isabela looked at Drew in shock and said, "Thank you for believing in me."

The only thing missing from this moment was sharing it with the one being who had made it all happen—Aelish—who was still missing from her life. But Isabela knew she would see her again. Isabela also knew in her heart that she would never again be hospitalized for mental illness. She would always be at risk for suffering bouts of despair and depression, especially in light of what awaited Humanity. But she'd been healed by the love of this man and her life had been forever changed. And she owed it all to Aelish.

24

IN FLUX

ISABELA HAD BEEN correct when she predicted her mother would be over the moon by the news of her engagement to Drew as well as her being pregnant. She'd made her mother a soon-to-be Abuela. Marisol had already begun planning the wedding. She hadn't seen her mother this happy since long before her cancer diagnosis. So, it surprised Isabela when she went into the kitchen and found her mother sitting at the table preoccupied and seemingly worried about something so early in the morning.

"Good morning, Mom," said Isabela. "Is something wrong? You don't seem happy like you've been for the last few days."

"Ay, Izzy," said her mother. "I need to show you something before you return to work today. I don't want you to discover it on your own without me there."

"Okay, now you've got me really worried. What is it?"

"Let's take a quick walk and I will show you," said Marisol.

"What you don't want me to discover on my own is *outside*?"

Marisol nodded.

They began walking toward Aelish and Thagar's house on Bunker Hill Road. When they reached the top of the street, Isabela asked, "Wait, isn't this Aelish's street? Why does it look so different at the bottom of the cul-de-sac?"

"Because it is different, mija," said her mother. "Come."

As they got closer and closer to the charred five acres, where the house once stood, Isabela gasped and put her hand over her mouth.

"Oh, my God, Mom! What happened to the house? It's gone!"

"A month ago," began Marisol, "I'd just gotten home from work and was inside getting dinner started. But I kept hearing so many sirens, I decided to come outside and see what was going on. The street was blocked off and there were so many fire trucks, ambulances, and police cars—it reminded me of the night of the carbon monoxide poisoning. I stood at the top of the street and just stared. As the house burned, the flames went higher and higher and the firefighters could not put out the fire. I knew Thagar and Kaleigh were not in the house, so I wondered how the fire had started.

"I stood outside for three hours, with a lot of other neighbors, and just watched how the firefighters simply could not get the blaze under control. Yet it never spread to another house. It just burned and burned for two whole days, Izzy."

Isabela and Marisol slipped underneath the CAUTION tape and began walking the acreage. It was astonishing not to see one piece of the house left—not the foundation, not a chimney— nothing. All that was left was burnt soil.

Marisol said, "I didn't want you to see this by yourself."

"Mom, do you remember me telling you there were spells protecting our house as well as Aelish's house, ever since the night of the dinner party with Glen?"

"Yes, mija, which is why I can't understand how this could have happened."

"I do," said Isabela.

"How, Izzy?"

"This is the work of Yasteron," said Isabela. "I know it as sure as I am standing here. They must have figured out how to break through the spell Thagar put around both our houses. And now I know, with absolute certitude, that Yasteron was responsible for Abuela's death."

"Oh, my God, Izzy!"

Marisol sat down on the ground and began sobbing. "Why would a magical kingdom care about Abuela? Why would they want to kill her? I don't understand."

Isabela sat down on the ground with her mother and embraced her. "I imagine Kaleigh was their intended target and Abuela just got caught in the crosshairs. I can't believe they took her away from us, Mom." Isabela began crying as well. But she did not feel fear, she felt only anger. "I also think we might be looking at this situation the wrong way." Isabela gestured toward the burned house.

"How so?" asked her mother.

"I think Thagar was successful in getting Aelish out of Yasteron, and they burned down their house on Earth as retribution. They're probably in hiding and that's why we haven't heard anything further about what happened with Thagar's mission. Wow, I never thought the powerful kingdom of Yasteron would need to send such a paltry message to Thagar and Aelish. So, now we know for sure, Yasteron killed Abuela. Well, Dad can finally stop feeling guilty about the standby generator and the carbon monoxide detector malfunctioning. Abuela didn't stand a chance against their powerful magic."

"But then, this means our house is no longer protected by a spell, right, Izzy?"

"Correct. When we get home, I'm going to send a Sylph to the magical being in DAR, named Tozer, who helped me run background checks on all the researchers who worked on the LECCS vaccine. He'll know what to do."

"I hope the little magical being who cooks and cleans for Aelish and Thagar went with them," said Marisol. "I'm forgetting his name right now."

"You mean Drummond?"

"Yes! That's it! He's so sweet and is such an amazing cook."

"He is the sweetest and is so funny," said Isabela. "I'm sure he's okay, Mom. Drummond is a survivor and has lived for a very long time. Don't worry."

"Okay, Izzy."

"Let's go back home so we can send the Sylph together," said Isabela.

"I guess that's no small thing, right, Izzy?"

"I'm so relieved I can talk with you about all of this, Mom. Everything will be all right."

"You seem so different, Izzy. I was worried about showing you the house because I was afraid it might cause a setback in your mental health recovery."

"I'm also a bit surprised by my own reaction. I don't feel fear, I just feel angry. I think the benevolent billionaire has changed me, Mom. He makes me feel so happy and so safe. And if you think spells are needed for security against Yasteron here, wait until I tell you about the security measures Drew came up with for the hacienda in Mexico because of the cartels."

Marisol's eyes opened wide. "Oh, my God, Izzy! I forgot all about the cartels! It wasn't like that when I was growing up in Mexico City. Maybe owning property there and visiting the hacienda on a regular basis is not such a good idea?"

"I think it's going to be okay, Mom. And like Drew told me, if we don't feel safe there, he will just sell the property. But you're going to have to get used to a small army patrolling and monitoring the property at all times when you come for a visit."

"Are you kidding?" exclaimed Marisol.

Isabela started laughing. "No. At first, it seemed insane to me, too. But after spending a few weeks there and learning all about the security protocols, I got used to it and felt safe. And besides, once we get a new spell to protect our house here, we can also use DAR's magical spells to protect us in Mexico City. We will be safe."

"Oh, mija. To hear you speak like this has lifted my heart. Ever since the fire, I have been so worried to show you."

"It's all going to be okay. I love you so much, my soon-to-be Abuela."

Marisol started laughing and crying at the same time. "Oh, when we get back, don't let me forget to show you the binder I've already started for your wedding. And then, we will need to plan for a baby shower, too. This is all so wonderful, Izzy."

They both stood up, embraced, and began walking home, hand in hand.

‡‡‡‡

The sound of the civil war occurring in Yasteron penetrated the insulated community within Hentoria. Some of the bombs came far too close to the border, just like the Komprathian bombs had after Aelish's abduction. So, Uncle Thurrock and Thagar called for a meeting with the Hentorian leaders. Thagar wanted to provide them with magical warcraft spells, similar to what DAR had used during their endless war with Komprathia, in order to protect life and property in Hentoria.

While the leaders at first pushed back, Thagar and Uncle Thurrock were finally able to persuade them to do so. They helped the leaders set up a modified command center to monitor the warcraft spells. As the civil war raged on, Aelish told Thagar she wanted to leave Hentoria and return to DAR. Thagar could not in good conscience leave the beings, who'd been so kind to his family, unprotected, with a war in such close proximity to Hentoria and to the community. He was also deeply concerned about his aunt and uncle's safety, as he'd grown very attached to them.

The civil war in Yasteron brought Aelish great satisfaction, knowing she'd helped put all of it in motion. However, she conveyed deep concern to Thagar about Katrina. She told him she worried constantly about her and wondered what'd happened to her after the rescue mission. Her ruminations over Katrina took Aelish nowhere pleasant and Thagar would often find her crying. He knew she imagined the worst of the worst and that Katrina had been killed.

Aelish longed to return to the Artist's House in Bencarlta and resume her position as Policy Director for Earth. Thagar and Lady Antonia worked in tandem to gently, but firmly, dissuade her of both notions. They privately discussed how she was mentally unwell and could never cope with the notoriety she'd experience in the bustling capital city or in front of the Head Council. Thagar also felt Bencarlta was not the proper place to quell her anxieties about Elijah being a target of Yasteron's civil war.

Throughout the course of the civil war, the heir remained a target of assassination by the revolutionaries and a target of abduction by the nobles. The nobles wished to reinstate the one true male heir and resume the patriarchal monarchy. Conversely, the revolutionaries, like Queen Saia, other nobles, and all the lower-orders were fighting to form an egalitarian society. They never again wanted a male to accede to the throne of Yasteron. With Elijah alive, this always remained a possibility. Even after the civil war ended, danger would still surround the heir.

For this reason, Thagar advocated for the family to stay in Hentoria, at least until the war had ceased. But when he suggested this, Aelish's reaction was so extreme and unreasonable, he knew after their third argument their discord was making her sicker. He knew she wanted the freedom to resume her normal life. She was still imprisoned in her own mind and wasn't thinking clearly about the best options for the safety of the entire family. He found it ironic that he was advocating harder for Elijah's safety than she was.

Consequently, Thagar suggested they stay on a boat in the N.E. Quadrant, near his father and brothers' fishing boats. He felt a boat would allow them to keep moving their location, hopefully, keeping Elijah safer. Thagar also felt the sunshine, warm weather, and calming effects of the ocean would provide Aelish with restorative healing.

While Aelish understood the tactical reasoning behind living on a boat for Elijah's sake, she told Thagar it would feel like living on a floating prison; she would feel trapped. He was very patient and kept gently reminding her that she'd regained the use of her magical capabilities and could escape the confines of the boat whenever she wished. But she was adamant; she wanted a house on land with space and ocean access.

Thagar recalled an incredible house in the N.E. Quadrant, situated on a hill in a private cove, close to where his family occasionally fished. If she insisted living on dry land, he felt this particular home, with steep cliffs on both sides of the house, built high above the cove, offered privacy and a good tactical location for Elijah. He preferred the boat, but he deferred to Aelish's wishes. It was very important to him that she experience happiness in their new location.

Lady Antonia agreed with Thagar that the N.E. Quadrant was exactly where the family should live next. She privately told him Aelish was in no position to resume her responsibilities as Policy Director for Earth. She also confided to Thagar that she felt Aelish was tormented by something very specific and was keeping it hidden from her Oraculi as well as her mate. Lady Antonia told Thagar she was determined to get to the bottom of it and suggested she accompany the family to their new dwelling, to discover what was deeply troubling Aelish.

Amelia, on the other hand, would be returning to her studies at the Institute and would stay with Quentin until Lady Antonia returned to the S.E. Quadrant, where she'd resume teaching at the Institute. When Amelia tried to protest about returning to school, Lady Antonia put her parental foot down, quite forcefully, and easily won the battle. Thagar was very impressed and made mental parenting notes for when Kaleigh and Elijah became Amelia's age.

Kaleigh was very excited about going to the N.E. Quadrant. Thagar framed it for her as a family vacation, when in reality, it was an intermediate step toward returning to a permanent life, somewhere. Aelish and Thagar had not yet decided whether they would ultimately return to Earth or remain in DAR. Their primary concerns were Kaleigh's education and Elijah's safety.

Kaleigh was thrilled she was going to meet all of her extended family who lived in the N.E. Quadrant. This included Thagar's father, Lomax, as well as Thagar's stepmother, Scarlett, along with their two children who now had families of their own. Additionally, Kaleigh was going to meet Thagar's three older brothers, Kane, Kaleb, and Kaden, their spouses, and their children, many of whom were the same age as Kaleigh.

After ten days of nothing but meetings with the Hentorian leaders and the community, as well as the back-and-forth conversations between him and Aelish, finally, they were getting ready to leave Hentoria in two days' time. Thagar knew his aunt and uncle would never even approach the Hentorians about temporarily leaving, in order to accompany him and Aelish. But he asked, nevertheless.

Uncle Thurrock told Thagar once the civil war was over, perhaps then, he and Aunt Charlotte could discuss relocating for a short period of time. But in the moment, things were far too tumultuous to even approach the Hentorian leaders. He told Thagar even if the leaders allowed him to do so, he could never abandon the Hentorians and his community at the present time. This, of course, saddened Thagar, who'd become quite attached to his aunt and uncle. But he graciously accepted and understood their decision, despite knowing how much he was going to miss them.

Thagar was well aware that Aelish required mental health treatment. But there were no services in DAR, similar to what he'd received at the Wainbridge Rehabilitation Center. Once they were no longer in hiding, he planned to seek out advice from Isabela. His hope was that Medicus Clove, who was very special to Aelish, might receive specific training resources from Isabela, in order to create some sort of treatment plan for Aelish.

Telling the Torres family about why Abuela died, as well as arranging for a protective spell for their home was also weighing on Thagar's mind. Additionally, he was concerned Marisol might need his support or assistance at the Climate Refugee Intake Center. He was surprised by how much he missed his work on Earth.

Thagar knew the overall global temperature was climbing ever closer toward the LECCS threshold of 1.4°C. Once the temperature flipped the switch on the deadly climate syndrome, the Earth would be in turmoil. Millions would die and Human civilization would be severely altered as it had been in previous pandemics. But this was a new scenario. Cascading climate events, like flooding, wildfires, extreme heat, and deadly storms would cause further displacement of Humans while LECCS raged around them. He hoped Isabela and Drew's tour had been successful in significantly increasing the vaccination rate. Otherwise, he could not imagine how the Earth would ever regain any degree of stability.

He also imagined Marisol and Jorge had witnessed his home on Bunker Hill Road burn to the ground. He worried for his Human friends, as he suspected the scene of the fire was very similar to the night of the carbon monoxide poisoning event. Yasteron had done a horrific thing to both families. But Thagar carried around substantial guilt because he was from the magical world, and he knew if the Torres family had never known them, Abuela would still be alive. Yasteron had inflicted great trauma on all the surviving members of the Torres family.

Everything was in a state of flux, but Kaleigh kept their spirits upbeat. Once Thagar told her she'd be attending lessons on a boat-school, established for the DARlettes of the fisher families in the N.E. Quadrant, she couldn't wait to start school. And she was greatly anticipating boat-hopping from one of Thagar's family members to another; the child simply loved an adventure.

25

UNDERWATER

A ELISH WAS LYING on a lounge chair on the rooftop deck of their new cove house. The quiet was so different from the incessant sound of Yasteron's civil war in Hentoria. She stared out past the cove, toward the deep blue ocean in the N.E. Quadrant. Thagar had taken Kaleigh and Elijah to visit his eldest brother, Kane, and his family. Thagar had the use of a small boat which could sleep six. When not in use, it was kept anchored in the ocean, close to the cove. They were scheduled to return sometime after dinner.

Lady Antonia was lying down for a nap and Drummond was asleep under the house. While the quiet brought a peaceful reprieve, Aelish could not seem to quiet her mind. She was in a state of constant agitation, slept very poorly, when she could sleep at all, and found herself irritated by things that were just a part of normal life. She knew she was mentally unwell but did not know how to help herself. She felt confused by the fact that she couldn't seem to feel any happiness, even when spending time with her beloved Kaleigh. And she was pulling farther and farther away from Thagar. She properly cared for Elijah, but his blond hair and blue eyes constantly reminded her of Cardissius' betrayal, when he lied and told her that he would never hurt Kaleigh.

Aelish began to doze in the late afternoon sun when, suddenly, she awoke with a start. She saw a Sylph hovering above her. In all her life, she'd never seen a Sylph that looked like this. She had porcelain skin, bright blue eyes, and her blond-braided hair was in an elegant updo underneath a crown of gold. She wore noble robes, accented with ermine fur, over a shimmering, formfitting, long, gold dress. She stared at Aelish, deeply curtsied, and handed her a white package with a gold ribbon around it. Aelish realized it was a noble Sylph and her heart began racing. She panicked Cardissius had found her, and he was still alive.

Aelish took the package from the Sylph and watched her curtsy once more before vanishing. She tried to steady her breathing, which had become more and more difficult to do. She was battling constant panic attacks and this delivery had set off another. She stood up and walked to the edge of the rooftop deck and stared at the ocean, trying to calm herself. She couldn't stand the way she felt and missed who she used to be. She simply could not reacclimate to normal life. She had more confidence and surety when she was held captive.

Aelish went back to the lounge chair and sat down along its edge and began opening the package. Two letters dropped to the floor of the rooftop deck and in her hands were two notebooks. One was her own notebook from the suite of rooms, which she'd kept in her bedchamber writing table. It was where she'd written down all of her observations and the information she'd gleaned from her lessons with Oba. The other notebook was leather bound with a turquoise ribbon around it. For the moment, she placed the leather bound one aside and focused on the notebook from her bedchamber. She opened it and immediately began crying, not because of what was written there, but because it felt like she'd recaptured a bit of herself. Why anything from her prison in Yasteron would bring her comfort was bewildering. She couldn't believe she'd forgotten to take it with her when Thagar rescued her.

After quickly reviewing the contents of her notebook, she put it aside and reached down to pick up the two letters that had dropped to the floor. One was addressed to Lady Aelish and the other envelope was blank, yet it was secured with an elaborate seal. She knew the entire package was from Yasteron but had no idea why there were two letters enclosed. She fought against her fears and opened the envelope addressed to Lady Aelish. Inside were beautiful pieces of parchment paper, with writing from a quill pen in blue ink. It read:

My Dear Lady Aelish,

It has been months since I last laid eyes on you and I miss you. I hope this letter finds you in good health after receiving no medical care for the Magical Sunlight Deprivation Heart Syndrome you acquired. I cannot believe you survived!

It was very difficult watching you slowly die and being helpless to do anything about it. Whilst your escape nearly cost me my life, I regret nothing. I am still in disbelief that your husband secured your rescue, let alone in time to save your life. I'm so glad you stole the heir. His absence put everything in motion that led to the king's death and Queen Saia taking control of the monarchy. I hope baby Lucius is thriving.

The king went mad knowing you had taken his son. He spiraled out of control from the very first morning, when I came in to dress you and reported to the King's Guard that you had vanished. Chief Minister Stannon walked around the suite of rooms, smiling, knowing you were gone. He made me sit in the living area and wait for the king's arrival, whilst the King's Guard kept their weapons trained on me the entire time.

I learned a lot from your bravery and courage and remained calm, despite the King's Guard surrounding me. It was quite clear that Chief Minister Stannon was thrilled you both were gone, after he exclaimed, "That wretched, bastard infant is also gone—good!"

When the king arrived, he went through each room searching for you and his son. Finding nothing, he let out a scream like I've never heard from any male in my life. And that was the beginning of his descent into madness. If your husband ever regrets not killing him directly for what he did to you, tell him your rescue was the beginning of the end of the king's sanity, his reign, and his life. Retribution belongs to your husband—he won—the king lost.

I know how hard it was for you to endure being held captive, but you set the example of how to survive. This helped me enormously during the weeks of my torture and imprisonment after your escape. Whilst I was not sexually assaulted, I was physically tortured and have lost the use of my right eye. I now wear an eye patch at all times. I wear it like a badge of honor for surviving the many days of torture and interrogation until I was finally freed because I knew absolutely nothing about your escape. My happiness for you angered my interrogators, making my torture sessions quite barbarous.

When it came time for the King Mother to question me, she was particularly brutal. She backhanded me so many times in the face that it caused me to lose the vision and ability to ever open my right eye again. But she suffered greatly watching her son go slowly insane. Ultimately, all the king's plans led him to be poisoned, murdered, and betrayed by the male closest to him during his entire life, Chief Minister Stannon.

I assume you've figured out by now that Kam, the leader of the lower-orders, is my brother. My interrogators, however, never discovered the fact that Kam is their leader. If they had, I would surely have been hung in Shamalaya Square. Whilst I was obviously not hung, I was present in Shamalaya Square when

Stannon and all the king's ministers were hung. The atmosphere was one of jubilation and hope that the lower-orders might actually be free.

I've enclosed my first lesson book from my newfound education in reading, writing, mathematics, science, and magic. I never thought in my entire life I'd be able to write such a long letter to you, as well as be able to attend school and become literate in all ways. I've even mastered the spells of transporting and telepathy. You would be so proud of me. And because of my thirst for knowledge, which you inspired, Master Oba has offered me an apprenticeship as an archivist for all the records of our kingdom. Under the reign of Queen Saia, all the archives will shortly become available to every citizen. They will be housed in a library, scheduled for construction, after the civil war has ended.

The King Mother has died of grief. It was a great privilege to be the one chosen by Master Oba to prepare the record of her life and death. She was a horrible female and is hopefully one of the last of her noble generation. The King Mother exemplified everything that was wrong with our realm and the lives lived by the highest noble females. She rotted from the inside out. She may have taken away my sight, but I gained a vision of who I could become—a female greater than her in every way. So, do not despair over the partial loss of my sight. The fact that I still have my life is a miracle.

I cannot believe I will become an archivist of the realm. The peace I find in reading and studying has brought me a joy I never thought possible. Master Oba is a good teacher and a kind mentor and has promised I will take over for him after he has passed from this life. What an honor I have been promised!

None of this would have happened without you, Lady Aelish. From our first encounter, when you taught me how to write my own name, to the first spell you recited for me, teaching me how to magically deliver the food you saved from your plate for me and my family, you showed me what my future could look like. Those two lessons will go into the archives I am now responsible for. Recording how you set our kingdom free, during your imprisonment, will be my greatest tribute to you. It will demonstrate what is possible when truth and freedom are allowed to reign, instead of a handful of male nobles.

I hope we can see each other again, as you not only changed the course of my life, but you also changed the course of Yasteron's existence. In the near future, all citizens will be truly equal in education and opportunity. I am honored to have served you and to have learned firsthand how powerful females are. My magical spells are getting easier and easier, even when executing the most difficult of spells. You, Master Oba, and Queen Saia are all responsible for that being the case. Female abilities are now celebrated, and we hope to shortly emulate the freedom that all females have in DAR.

Finally, I've enclosed a letter to you from King Cardissius. They did not formally arrest me until the third day after your escape. On the second day, the king came to see me in the suite of rooms. He was bereft that you and Lucius were gone. He believed you might contact me again, so he gave me the enclosed letter to give to you.

I wasn't sure whether or not I should send it to you. And I could not base my decision on its contents, as I would never open and read such an important piece of private correspondence. However, since the king is dead, I thought the letter might contain important information for Lucius, when he's older, which is why I decided to enclose it. Forgive me if it causes you any further pain or suffering.

The day after the king gave me the letter, I was arrested by the King's Guard and Chief Minister Stannon. The chief minister said he believed I helped you escape and that he would never believe otherwise. I was fortunate to have been able to smuggle out the king's letter, as well as your private notebook to my brother, Kam. When I was finally released, I found both items in my mother's house in my bedchamber. There was a note from my brother attached to them which said, "I've kept both items safe for you, dear Sister. I hope we see each other again, very soon." My family and I have not heard from him in weeks. Whilst I do not pray, I know that you do, and I hope you will pray for his safety. To lose him would be a loss I would never get over.

I want you to know how grateful I am to have known DAR's Living Legend and to have had you set the example of what is possible, even for a lower-order-in-waiting. Thank you, Lady Aelish. Please, do not remain saddened by what you have been through, but instead, revel in your triumph over it. Lastly, I hope to meet a male as brave and brilliant as your husband, Thagar. Please tell him that for me.

Yours always,

Katrina, Archivist-in-Training

Aelish opened Katrina's notebook of lessons and began crying. Each page marked the progression of her education as well as her freedom as a female. Katrina could finally attain the magical capabilities that lived inside of her. She could live a fruitful life, surrounded by the historic lessons of her dominion, bestowed by Master Oba, and could freely live her life.

It also made Aelish fully realize how incredible the rescue mission designed by Thagar, Amelia, Uncle Thurrock, the Hentorian warriors, and the drone rat squadron really was. And by rescuing her and Elijah, they ended Cardissius' life as well as his horrible mother's. She had to finally embrace that it was over. But she also knew, if she did not confess the shame tormenting her to Thagar, she would always remain imprisoned.

She was so thrilled about Katrina's evolution that she almost forgot about the king's letter. Before she could bring herself to open it, she decided to look through her own notebook again. The memories of her imprisonment flooded her mind as she turned page after page. She could see by her own writings how much she'd changed. Imprisoned, her notes were clearer than any thoughts she had subsequent to her rescue. She was so focused on changing Yasteron, it allowed her to survive. But now, she felt lost. She simply could not understand why she felt mentally stronger during her captivity. What was wrong with her?

Lady Antonia was still napping and Drummond was still sleeping. Aelish gathered up both notebooks, as well as Katrina's letter, and put them in one of her dresser drawers in her new bedchamber in the cove house. The bedchamber was modern and simple, but the views more than made up for its simplicity. She put on a pair of jeans, a light sweater, and a pair of sneakers. She decided to transport to the beach, near a cave she'd recently discovered, deep inside one of the steep cliffs on the right side of the cove. No one else knew of its existence. She gauged that she had some time before the tide rolled in and flooded it, to read the king's letter in solitude.

Aelish stood on the sand at the water's edge and saw the sun was just starting to drop, slightly changing the color of the water. She turned and headed for the cave whose opening was somewhat obscured by an overgrowth of wild sarsaparilla on the cliff above it.

She walked deep inside the cave and found her favorite rock. She had no idea if it had naturally formed or if someone had placed it here. It was a rectangular, flat piece of stone, which she'd laid on several times before, to try and quiet her mind. She sat down and opened the letter.

She magically illuminated a light and began to read. At the first word, "Dearest," she put down the letter unsure if she'd be able to get through it. She began crying, remembering the first time the king had ever called her that. She'd tried to kill herself with the poisoned dagger, originally intended for him. Seeing what she was trying to do, he'd magically flung the dagger out of her hand and placed a paralytic spell on her. She could hear and see, but she could not move. He had carried and placed her on the bed in her bedchamber, within the suite of rooms, and told her how her life was going to be from that point forward.

She walked back out of the cave and once again stared at the ocean for strength. Ever since Drummond had disclosed that Cardissius had ordered Kaleigh's murder, she found it very difficult to pray. She seemed to have lost her relationship with God. In the ocean, she could see a pod of dolphins interacting with one another. They were playing a game, and she wished they would invite her to participate. She knew she was procrastinating reading Cardissius' letter. She deeply sighed and turned away from the water and walked back inside the cave. She sat down on the rock, magically illuminated the letter, and once again began reading. It read:

Dearest Aelish,

The past has become my enemy. You left me with nothing, Aelish. All I do is think of you and see you in my dreams. I will never get over losing you. I can't think, I can't focus on anything, except for the fact that you and our son are gone. I am not well. I have no idea why I am ill, other than the grief you've inflicted upon me.

I underestimated Thagar's love for you, and I should have

sealed up those tunnels a long time ago. Please tell him from me, well-played! He took back what I stole. You were never really mine, but I regret none of it. I really have loved you Aelish, ever since you defied Yasteron whilst in Komprathia, in 1665. I have never met another magical being with your guile, your kindness, and your beauty. I've loved you for so long and wanted to make sure you knew that. I couldn't bear it if you ever thought otherwise.

Now that you are no longer in Yasteron, you will hear many horrible things about me. But the one thing you must never believe, no matter who tells you, is that I never really loved you— because I did, and I still do. I know you thought I was going to let you die after you finished nursing our son, in those first two crucial weeks, but that was not the case. I met with all of your doctors and we came up with a regimen to bring back your health entirely. How could I let the mother of my son perish, especially when we were married and planned to rule Yasteron together? I can't tell you how grateful I am to you for giving me Lucius. He's a beautiful boy, born under the harshest of circumstances, and I miss him terribly. It's like my heart has been ripped from my chest to have lost my only son and the only female I have every truly loved.

I thought, finally, I would find happiness, married and ruling with you as we both taught Lucius how to be a good and kind king. But I've come to realize that it doesn't matter whether I am the son of the king or the actual king, it's a misery to be king. Those closest to the Crown covet the king's power because they don't realize it's actually no power at all. So many rules, so many traditions—you never get to live your own life the way you want to live it.

When I was with you, Aelish, especially during those brief times when we performed the Endeavor, I found true happiness.

I was so looking forward to raising our son together. Ruling Yasteron, with you and Lucius by my side, would've made a lifetime of misery all worth it.

Please, don't hate me for what I did to you. No one ever taught me how to properly love or court a female. Using my powers as king was the only way I knew how to literally capture you, and I hoped, in time, I would truly be able to capture your heart.

I know you think me insane or a very evil being. But please know, I will love you until my dying day. I hope you are happy again. I will rest easier in your absence, knowing you are once again happy and at peace with your real family. I only wish it could have been with our family.

One final thing, dearest, please know that I never ordered your daughter, Kaleigh, to be killed. It was all Stannon. On the Ides of March, I discovered a mission he had orchestrated in January against your daughter. He told everyone involved that I'd ordered Kaleigh's murder. Why would they believe otherwise? Stannon was always loyal to me. I nearly had him executed that same day.

Stannon was adamantly opposed to the idea of the heir to the throne of Yasteron being half an Earth born DARling. And by killing your daughter, Stannon intended to destroy any hope of you ever loving me. He perpetrated this heinous act, so that when you discovered Kaleigh had died, you would hate me forever and never believe I had not ordered it. He concocted a fable for those involved: he stated that I wanted Lucius to be your only living child so you'd never wish to return to Earth. Stannon never wanted you to find happiness as the mother of the heir or as my wife and queen.

The stupid fool never even entertained the fact that Kaleigh could survive. And when his plan failed, he and the soldiers kept it hidden from me for over two months. I found his lying as contemptible as his actions. But when he begged my forgiveness, I foolishly gave it to him.

Do you remember when I told you during the month of March that I was under great stress? I told you a falsehood about the queen being difficult about our impending divorce. That was not the case. What Stannon did vexed me to my core. And since your disappearance, he's been practically giddy.

My mentor and father-figure has betrayed me. As I observe his happiness because you and Lucius are gone, I now know I should have executed him along with the soldiers. I plan to do so shortly. But without you and Lucius here, I've just been too unwell to order it.

Please tell the young scientist, Isabela, that I'm terribly sorry, on behalf of my kingdom, that her grandmother was killed in the carbon monoxide poisoning event orchestrated by Stannon. Tell her the soldiers were executed for doing such a thing. I remain so grateful Kaleigh did not perish; I knew all along that she would turn out to be something very special and she has.

I never told you about what Stannon did because Kaleigh survived. And whilst I warned you there were those in the kingdom who wished to harm you and the heir, and being kept inside the suite of rooms was for your safety, I never imagined my closest advisor and loyal friend was actually working against me. Forgive me for being such an ignorant king and not realizing sooner that Stannon is a viper.

I could never kill anything that was a part of you, dearest Aelish. I still believe we could've been happy together, and I love you more today than yesterday. I will love you forever, and you will always live on in my heart. How I miss you!

Yours always,

Cardissius

By the end of the letter, Aelish was sobbing so hard she could barely see the words. She folded Cardissius' letter up, put it back inside the envelope, and tucked it inside her sweater next to her heart. In the moment, she had no idea how to make sense of his letter or of anything in her life. She felt so tired, so confused, and like she would never trust her instincts again. When she'd told Oba that she felt the king might be changing, perhaps Oba had underestimated the power of her love over the king. Perhaps Cardissius could have changed and become a better male. Did she really believe he planned a regimen with her doctors to bring her health back? Unless she asked the doctors firsthand, she would never know.

Cardissius' actions tormented her ever since she discovered that he and his father had aligned themselves with King Gidius to create secret tunnels so the drone rats could spread the plague with abandon on Earth, killing her beloved parents. How was it possible that she was now mourning his death? Sometimes, an adversary becomes a part of you. And when they're gone, you lose your purpose when your lifelong fight against them ends. Is that what happened to her? Was there no one left for her to fight? Had she become too used to living in a constant state of chaos? Had she lost the ability to live a normal life? She felt like a soldier after the war was over. She'd finally put down her weapon but no longer knew how to live without the incessant, unremitting state of war around her.

She laid down on the rock and placed her right arm underneath her head. Her back was to the entrance of the cove. After reading Cardissius' letter, she didn't know how to live again for the next fifteen minutes, let alone for the next 1,500 years. She forgot all about the tide coming in and fell sound asleep on the rock, with her sworn enemy's love letter right next to her heart.

Aelish felt something cold touch her cheek and then retreat in a constant rhythm. She would fall back to sleep and once again be irritated by the coldness. Then, she saw an enormous light above her and wondered if it was her time to leave this life. She did not move and closed her eyes, awaiting death.

Suddenly, she heard a familiar, panicked voice cry out, "She's in here! Hurry!"

A being was shaking her, but she wanted to go, she was ready to leave now. Why wouldn't they just let her be? "Aelish, wake up! Aelish!"

She was suddenly very cold and wished she could return to the earlier warmth she experienced when she first saw the light. Then, she felt strong arms lift her up out of water, which had completely covered her with the exception of her face.

She heard someone scold her. "Aelish, you could have drowned! What were you doing in here all alone?" Then, she found herself back on one of the lounge chairs on the rooftop deck of the cove house and believed the letters from Katrina and Cardissius were all a dream. Someone began taking off her clothing and she heard, "What's this?" And someone else replied, "Oh, my God! It's a letter from Cardissius!" Then, a male voice strongly instructed, "Make sure the water hasn't washed away the ink. Use the Repair spell, immediately."

So, it wasn't a dream. She felt the cool night air for only a moment on her naked body. Then, she felt the warmth of a soft blanket envelop her and heat emanating from an unknown source. As she warmed, she began to fall back to sleep. It was blissful. She hadn't slept peacefully in so very long, she thought she'd forgotten how.

"I don't think she should sleep. We have to keep her awake. Make sure her heart is beating properly. She needs to wake up!"

"Aelish, my love. Can you please open your eyes for me?"

Aelish slowly opened her eyes and saw a pair of familiar golden eyes staring into hers.

"Can you see me, my love?"

She nodded her head and asked, "Why did you wake me up? I was finally at peace. You should have let me go."

She heard sobbing from a female, and then the wail of an infant. Someone opened her blanket and put the infant at her breast. At first it was uncomfortable, and then its suckling began to soothe her with its rhythm. She could feel herself falling back to sleep and hoped they would just let her go. Then, she felt a needle in her thigh. It made her cry out and the infant stopped suckling. Someone took the infant away and she began to awaken.

"No! Leave me alone! Please let me sleep!" she yelled.

"Aelish," said Thagar, "we gave you a small amount of the Hentorian venom potion in a shot. John gave it to me, in case something like this ever happened to you. You are suffering from hypothermia and it has slowed your heart down again. Won't you try to awaken now, my love?"

"Thagar," she whispered. "You came back for me, and you brought me home. Katrina wanted me to tell you how brave and brilliant you are."

Lady Antonia asked, "Who is Catríona? Catríona from Ireland?"

"No, Katrina from Yasteron," she said. "She survived my escape. I'm so proud of her."

Finally, Thagar and Lady Antonia came into clear focus. They both had tears streaming down their faces and knelt beside her next to the lounge chair on the rooftop deck. They had a magical fire going to warm her up.

"Where am I?" she asked, suddenly confused again. "I don't know where I am. Please take me home, Thagar. I'm so tired. I need to sleep more."

"You will feel better in a few minutes. Let the venom potion go into your system."

Lady Antonia asked, "Aelish, do you know how loved you are?"

"Cardissius said he loved me," said Aelish. "Do you think he really did?"

Thagar sat on the floor of the rooftop deck and ran his hands through his curls. He chose his next words very carefully. "I think Cardissius did love you, Aelish, in the only way he knew how. Be at peace with that now."

"He didn't try to kill Kaleigh, and he didn't kill Abuela, Stannon did. That male hated me from the second he laid eyes on me, the first night in Yasteron. Upon meeting me, Cheswick thought he was going to strike me across the face. We never understood why. Now, I understand why. I'm so glad Cardissius didn't lie to me about killing Kaleigh. It was that evil male, Stannon, who killed Abuela, and I'm glad he's dead. I'm so sorry I asked you to kill Cardissius, Thagar. Drummond was wrong. The king did not try to kill our daughter. Oh, my God, I'm so sorry I asked you to break your Oath of Peace for me, especially when Cardissius wasn't the one who tried to kill Kaleigh. I'm so confused about everything. I can't think straight anymore."

Lady Antonia stroked her face. "All will be well, Aelish. You just need time to recover from everything you have been through. Thagar and I are going to help you."

"How can you help me? I no longer know my own mind. And I feel so weak all the time. I wonder if my heart has really recovered or if I will always feel like this? Broken and defeated."

Thagar said, "You were in ice-cold water in the cave by the cove for a long time, Aelish. The tide came in, some time ago, and nearly drowned you. You were submerged in very cold water. After all the trauma your heart experienced from the Magical

Sunlight Deprivation Heart Syndrome, it's no wonder you feel like this, my love. Do not be afraid. You will get well, both physically and mentally. I promise you that. We will be happy again. I will devote myself to your recovery if it takes the rest of my life. Do you trust me, Aelish?"

Aelish pulled the blanket over her head, holding onto the secret she could not bear to tell him. She felt him pull it down off her face. "Do you trust me with your wounded heart, Aelish?"

She shook her head, no. In the entire time they'd known each other, even before they'd made their Commitments, she'd never indicated to him that she did not trust him. She knew she had just broken his heart in half. Why didn't she feel like she could trust him and finally tell him everything? What was wrong with her? How could she ever hurt Thagar like that? But it was the truth. In this moment, she didn't trust him. And, more importantly, she didn't even trust herself.

"I'm so sorry for everything, Thagar," said Aelish. "Please, forgive me."

Unbeknownst to Aelish, Lady Antonia whispered to Thagar, "I promise you. I will find out what is tormenting her so she can lay it down and begin living again."

Aelish began to softly weep. "I just want to feel better and I can't."

"You will, my love, you will," said Thagar, wiping tears off his face.

26

SHAME

WEDNESDAY, JULY 15, 2026 10:00 AM

A ELISH DIVULGED HER deep humiliation yesterday to Lady Antonia, who returned to the S.E. Quadrant early this morning. Her last words to Aelish before she transported home were, "You have to tell Thagar." Aelish knew she was right. If she didn't confess to him the things that were tormenting her, she would remain imprisoned in her own mind forever. It was time. She had to tell him everything. She owed him the truth, as she also owed him her life. He'd more than made up for any lack of support he'd demonstrated for her covert mission into Komprathia, all those centuries ago.

Kaleigh was staying overnight with her grandparents, Lomax and Scarlett, Elijah was sleeping in his crib for his morning nap, and Drummond was asleep under the house. Aelish sat in the living area of the cove house, near the open kitchen, which had floor to ceiling windows facing the ocean. The water was exceptionally blue today as was the sky it reflected.

She was sitting on one of the couches, facing the water. Her legs were tucked underneath her and she was incredibly nervous.

Storm lay on the other end of the couch, providing her with some comfort. Lady Antonia had trimmed Aelish's hair before she left, making it less unwieldy to put up in a messy bun. She wore no makeup, a pair of soft black leggings, and a short-sleeved top, which matched the color of the water.

Thagar came into the room and sat down in one of the chairs across from her, with his back to the water. "Elijah is sleeping peacefully," he said.

Aelish simply nodded her head.

"Aelish, do you remember when I told you about the darkness I was living in after spending two years trying to restore my broken body from the underwater bunker bombing?"

Aelish nodded her head but did not look at him.

"You helped me find my way out of it," said Thagar. "And I got stronger and ultimately did find a new purpose in my life. Please don't lock me out of what's tormenting you. Let me in. Let me help you, the way that you helped me."

Aelish remained quiet.

"You've been disappearing from our life together, little by little, every day. And if it continues, you won't remember why you ever loved me. Tell me everything. I can bear it. I am here for you."

Aelish kept her eyes downcast and remained completely still on the couch.

"For the most horrible parts, you can softly whisper them to me. You must rid yourself of all of it. Give it to me and you'll be free to live once again. We share one heart and when yours is broken, so is mine, my love."

Aelish deeply inhaled and exhaled.

"Start wherever it feels best and each day you can tell me a little bit more until there is nothing left to tell. Then, it will be finished. And we can start living again. For without you by my side, there is no living, Aelish. Do you understand?"

Aelish nodded imperceptibly. Thagar sat patiently, waiting for her to find her voice.

"When I left for Yasteron, I strapped a poisoned dagger to my thigh. I never took it off the entire time I was there until the day Stannon tricked me into going into the room. He used my greatest loves against me, by telling me there was an urgent message from Earth. I was worried something had happened to you, Kaleigh, or Isabela, who had just been admitted to the psychiatric hospital. Stavros insisted on accompanying me into the room, but I told him I needed some privacy. I sat down on the settee that was inches from the trap door you used for my rescue. I waited for the message."

Aelish kept her eyes downcast as she spoke. "When the king suddenly appeared in the room, I knew I'd been tricked. All I could think of was immediately getting out of the room. But every spell I tried, every piece of magic I'd ever learned, didn't work. It was horrible. He began telling me that he was in love with me. He explained how all the ways he'd hurt me in my life, from killing my parents with the plague to blowing you up in the bunker, were inflicted by him to simply garner my attention. I thought he was insane.

"He began telling me that he wished to create a lineage of preeminent magical beings with me, which would ultimately rule Yasteron and the entire magical world. He wanted this to be his legacy along with magical world domination. He explained how he needed my extraordinary magical capabilities to create such magical beings. I knew he intended to rape me, in order to steal my magic, which has been done so many times throughout history to female DARlings.

"When I realized I was trapped, I tried to stab him in the neck with the poisoned dagger. But he was faster than me. He magically flung the dagger out of my hand and it landed somewhere concealed in the room. As he rambled on about our future life together, I caught sight of the dagger. I stealthily walked nearer to it. I knew killing myself would be my last chance to stop him from carrying out all his plans for me. Before I tried to stab my own neck, my last thoughts were of you and Kaleigh. But again, he was faster than me. He magically flung the dagger out of my hand. I lunged at him screaming, and he used a paralytic spell on me. Being defenseless against his level of magic was absurd."

Thagar shifted in his chair.

"Trying to save myself, I committed two acts against my faith—attempted murder as well as extermination. And I broke my Oath of Peace. I was already losing myself."

Thagar deeply exhaled.

"After placing the paralytic spell on me, Cardissius carried me into the bedchamber. I was unable to speak or move, but I could see and hear. He called me *dearest* for the first time as he mapped out how I was going to spend the rest of my life.

"I planned to use the terminate spell to destroy any life he put inside of me. But lying there immobile on the bed I realized, without the use of my magic that would be impossible. He clearly told me if I didn't do exactly what he wanted, he would kill you and Kaleigh. If I hurt the offspring we created, he would kill you and Kaleigh. If I tried to escape, he would kill you and Kaleigh. And if I tried to kill myself, again, he would kill you and Kaleigh. He used the two beings I loved the most against me. I'd already committed two acts against my faith and had broken my Oath of Peace. I felt no more fear and tried to accept my fate."

"Would you like some water, my love?" asked Thagar.

Aelish lifted her head and finally looked at Thagar. "No, I'd like to just keep going."

Thagar nodded and faintly smiled at her.

"That Wednesday night, as Abuela lay dying and you were with Kaleigh in the hospital, I never went to sleep. I remained fully clothed and had no perception of time. I wondered if I'd ever see the sun again. Cardissius left me alone that first night. The next day, I met my lower-order-in-waiting, Katrina. She was very kind. Later that day, she brought in a peignoir set I was instructed to wear for the king for my first rape. It was so calculated, so menacing, and so unbelievably cruel, I will never again wear a nightgown of any sort. Forced to wear something for his pleasure, as I awaited to be defiled, was completely heinous.

"I prayed for hours for some sort of deliverance, prior to him coming into the room. Finally, I received a sliver of salvation."

Aelish knew Thagar was imagining the entire scene in his mind. His eyes grew dark.

"Before we lay in the bed together, he asked, 'Would you like to keep your robe on during the Endeavor or just the gown?' I looked at him totally confused. Then, he began laughing at me and asked, 'Did you think we were going to have relations like Humans, which would require we completely disrobe? Aelish, we aren't farm animals; we are evolved magical beings! Now, come and lay down beside me.' And he got into the bed with all of his clothes on.

"In that moment, I had no idea what the Endeavor was, but I was so grateful to God for this deliverance—Cardissius would never be inside of me. He was not planning to physically touch my body the way you do when we make love. I almost sank to my knees in gratitude to God, but he was waiting for me to get into the bed. We lay side by side, just like you and I do before performing the Rapture.

"Cardissius told me to close my eyes and that he would magically take care of everything. But he was having trouble. Something was blocking his magic. I opened my eyes and saw his frustration turn to rage. Then, he ripped my Commitments necklace from my neck and tossed it across the room. The stone you gave me was emitting some form of magic, preventing him from performing sexually. I will always believe our love was in that stone, stopping him."

Aelish took a deep breath and grasped the amethyst necklace that she, once again, wore around her neck alongside the crucifix from Lieutenant Commander Stavros.

"Once the necklace was removed, he tried again. It felt like the beginning of the Rapture. I saw your beautiful face and believed I was with you. Our love was so strong, that even under the spells of his magic, I saw only your face the entire time. As the Endeavor receded, I was trying to understand how it was nearly identical to the Rapture. But before I could finish my analysis, he slapped me hard across the face. He screamed, 'You are never to think of him again whilst we are together! Do you understand me?' I thought he was going to kill me right then.

"Seeing the bruise he inflicted upon my face, he apologized. I could see he was embarrassed and displeased by his own behavior. It was as if he were an inexperienced lover who really didn't know what he was doing. At the time, I couldn't imagine how he and the queen had managed to procreate three offspring."

"Did he hit you more than once?" asked Thagar.

"No. The next night, which was Friday night and the day after Abuela died, we tried again. I knew if I didn't see his face during the Endeavor, he would probably kill me. I could tell his frustration was getting the better of him. And as king, it was humiliating he could not properly perform."

Tears began rolling down Aelish's face. She put her face in her hands and began crying. Thagar remained where he was, giving her space.

After some time, Aelish composed herself. "You see, he'd told me that once I conceived, he would leave me alone. If I became pregnant, I would no longer have to perform the Endeavor with him. So, I began to weigh my options. If I allowed his desire to permeate my mind, I might be successful in procreating. I would be done with it until the next time he wanted an infant. He planned on siring three per year with me, like I was some sort of breeding animal."

Thagar deeply inhaled and exhaled.

"The second time we performed the Endeavor I betrayed our Commitments and felt sexual pleasure. My body broke faith with my mind and allowed me to experience sexual arousal from Cardissius. After he left that night, I went into the bathing room and threw up at the sight of my face in the mirror. I wanted to exterminate myself, but I couldn't even attempt it because I had no magic. Of course, there are other ways to do so without magic, but I remembered what he told me: 'If you try and kill yourself, I will kill Thagar and Kaleigh.' I was certain that he would. Therefore, I was trapped.

"I had to live with my self-loathing and the humiliation of experiencing pleasure at the hands of my sworn enemy. I'd experienced sexual pleasure by the being who had murdered my parents. I never wanted to die so much in my life. And this went on night after night until I saw the magical glow on January 21st when he finally left me alone. I betrayed you, Thagar. I betrayed our Commitments, but more importantly, I betrayed myself. I let this king experience sexual gratification off me, a being I've hated my entire life. I am so ashamed, and I am so sorry." Aelish began sobbing.

Thagar got up and came over to the couch. He embraced her as she cried. She leaned into him, feeling his strength. "Do not cry, my love," he said. "All you've told me has not decreased my love for you. In fact, it's made me love you even more. You know the power of the magic in the Rapture—it can create life.

Imagine how he altered the magic to harness its power with a being who had no magical capabilities, whatsoever. You have no idea what spells he put on you. You were defenseless. There is no shame, Aelish."

Aelish pivoted on the couch so she could look directly into his golden eyes. "He forced me to marry him so the infant would not be a bastard and could reign. I told him many times I was already mated. He explained that blowing up the bunker had a two-fold purpose: killing Glen and killing you. Then, I would be free and clear to marry him and become his queen.

"When I kept protesting the idea of marrying him, he asked me point blank if he had to kill you to force me to wed him. I began to panic that I'd pushed him too far. I believed he was going to have you killed. So, I backed off and lied about wanting to marry him. I used my Catholic faith and the sin of bigamy as the reason why the idea was so abhorrent to me. I was trying to steer him away from my devout love for you.

"He'd been planning all of this for so many years, Thagar. His obsession of wanting me to be his wife and queen goes back hundreds of years. After he learned of my covert mission into Komprathia, which led to the end of King Gidius' reign and the freedom of Komprathia, he fell madly in love with me. He was in awe of my mission and my defiance of DAR's tenets. He felt I was his equal. And after Komprathia, he wanted no other. He begged his father, King Nevuna, to allow him to marry me, but his father refused. So, he waited until his father's death to put all of his plans in motion. But all the while, he'd been preparing my prison for centuries.

"Cardissius kept upping the level of magic in the prison to match my own. He explained that he'd determined I became more magically adept and powerful with each new level of grief I experienced. So, he decided to ramp up my grief and casually told me how he picked which family members of mine to kill, as well as Isabela. He said all the things he'd perpetrated as ruler of Yasteron were done to keep me fixated on him and his kingdom. All the horrible events that occurred over the centuries, to so many I have loved, were all my fault because he loved me. I thought he was morally reprehensible and his mind was irrevocably twisted.

"But as the weeks of my captivity passed, I learned more about his life. I thought I'd finally discovered what had caused him to become the way he was—I met his mother. In all my life, I have never met a more monstrous female than the King Mother, Cassandra. She was a horrid being and was extremely cruel to Cardissius for his entire life. She never told him that she loved him, she never held him or kissed him, and she always made him feel like he didn't measure up to his two older brothers who died in the Proelium battle. Cassandra had born the heir and the spare, but after they were killed, she once again had to birth an heir for Nevuna. Cardissius was the result, and she seemed to never forgive him for having to create another heir for the Crown."

"Was she cruel to you?" asked Thagar.

"Yes. Cardissius warned me that his mother was not an easy being. But I, mistakenly, thought I could win her over. Within the first fifteen minutes upon meeting her, she disparaged my Earth born heritage, the color of my skin, and accused me of bewitching her son. She told me she laid curses upon me for all that I had done to him.

"When I asked her if she'd prefer her son mate with those who have darker skin, she struck me so hard, I thought she'd broken my jaw. I was goading her, of course, but I knew within minutes that Cassandra was one of the most despicable beings I have ever met. I also knew Cardissius loved me more than his own mother, which I decided to tell her. And she was forced to watch me marry her son the next day. I walked away bruised, but I won the battle."

Thagar began softly chuckling at her last comment.

"But with Cardissius, there was always one more landmine. When he saw my face, he knew his mother had inflicted the bruise. He was livid but was powerless against her. Cassandra was such an evil mother that I believed she caused him to be the way he was. Later in the day, as I was icing my face and preparing for our wedding the next day, Cardissius informed me that, whilst pregnant, I would have to perform the Endeavor to consummate the marriage. I was livid, but what could I do—nothing.

"I had experienced a reprieve from betraying my love for you, for weeks, and now it was all going to come back. All of my self-loathing returned. Afterward, I tried to distract myself by learning more about the kingdom I was preparing to rule as queen. That was when I asked Cardissius if I could meet Yasteron's Keepers or librarians. He looked at me confused. It really is true, Thagar—Yasterons hate to read. Why the king ever let me near Oba, Master of Archives, I will never understand. For centuries, the king had access to the same information bestowed upon me by Master Oba. But Cardissius chose ignorance over knowledge, a long time ago. During my lessons with Master Oba, I learned all about the history of how DARlings created Yasteron. To accept that Yasterons were originally DARlings from the N.W. Quadrant—my God—I couldn't sleep for days."

"Did Master Oba tell you anything with regard to Cardissius?" asked Thagar.

"Yes, he did. I'd convinced myself that his mother, Cassandra, had molded him into the psychopath that he was. But then, Master Oba told me about Lady Charlotte—Uncle Thurrock's wife. I still can't believe your uncle is married to King Nevuna's sister."

"Neither can I and neither can Antonia," said Thagar.

"Anyway," continued Aelish, "after I'd convinced myself that Cassandra, the King Mother, was entirely to blame for Cardissius turning out the way he had, Master Oba challenged me and asked me if the king had ever told me about his aunt? Of course, he had not. So, Master Oba began telling me about Lady Charlotte, who was a friend of his.

"Lady Charlotte showered young Cardissius with love and affection until she caught him torturing small animals when he was about ten years old. She was horrified because she'd caught her brother, Nevuna, doing the exact same thing at the exact same age. Father and son were both defective. Despite her love for her nephew, after catching him torturing small animals, she decided to escape from Yasteron. And you know the rest of that story."

Thagar got up from the couch. He pulled the chair he'd been sitting in earlier closer to the couch so he could face her directly. He asked, "But there was a part of you that still believed Cardissius was redeemable, despite what Master Oba told you. Am I correct?"

"Yes, you are."

Thagar continued. "When Drummond told us what the Yasteron soldiers were saying as they burned our house down, with regard to Cardissius ordering the Living Legend's daughter killed, you reacted as if Cardissius had lied and betrayed you. During your captivity, had he ever discussed Kaleigh with you?"

Aelish replied, "In the first hours after my abduction, as Cardissius described choosing which beings in my life to murder in order to ramp up my grief and propel my magic to become even stronger, he told me he would never harm Kaleigh because she was an anomaly; she was Human and he was too curious to see what she would become. I believed him. But when Drummond told us what the soldiers had said, I broke. I began to no longer trust any of my own instincts with regard to Cardissius.

"Whilst I'm still unable to trust my instincts, I'd been trying to come to terms with his betrayal about Kaleigh. But then, I received the letter Cardissius wrote me the day he discovered I'd been rescued. You found the letter on me when I nearly drowned in the cave by the cove. Did you read it?"

"I would never do such a thing without your permission, Aelish."

"Then, let me retrieve the letter, and you will understand why I am the way I am."

Aelish got up from the couch and went into her bedchamber. She opened the bottom drawer of her dresser. Before she'd left, Lady Antonia told Aelish that she'd magically repaired the letter, maintaining its legibility, and had put it in the bottom drawer of her dresser. Aelish had never read the letter again nor had she ever opened this drawer before. Alongside the letter, she saw her emerald wedding ring from Cardissius. She realized Thagar must have found the ring and put it here next to Cardissius' letter. Seeing the ring for the first time since she'd violently thrown it in their Hentorian cottage, she became instantly nauseated. As the memories came flooding back, she nearly began crying, but her rage about being forced to marry Cardissius kept the tears at bay. She retrieved the letter and slammed the drawer shut.

She came back into the living area and handed the letter to Thagar. "I insist you read it now. You're not going to get the chance to tuck it against the side of your chair, like you did with my student thesis about my covert mission into Komprathia."

Thagar wryly smiled at her thinly veiled dig at him. "You're right. Despite you asking me to read your thesis, prior to your presentation to the Head Council, I never did. If I had read it, I certainly would've stopped you from presenting it to the Head Council. As a commander, I knew the disclosure of your Komprathian mission would've resulted in your detention.

"Had you never been imprisoned for six months, in the N.W. Quadrant Detention Center, you would have never been denied the use of your magical capabilities. This, in turn, would have prevented you from developing your lifelong fear of acquiring the Magical Interruption Syndrome, or MIS, which we now know is the sister-syndrome of the Magical Sunlight Deprivation Heart Syndrome that nearly killed you. One day, I hope you can truly forgive me, Aelish. I hope you can finally internalize that my miscalculation in not reading your thesis never meant I was careless with your love or that you couldn't trust me with your life, even back then." He deeply sighed and turned his attention back to Cardissius' letter.

Aelish huffed as she sat back down on the couch. She watched Thagar read the letter. She imagined it was extremely difficult for him to read another male's love letter, especially one from Cardissius, whom he detested. While he tried very hard to conceal his emotions, there were moments when she physically felt the pain he was experiencing while reading it.

When he finished, he put the letter down on his lap and did not look at her. After a few moments, he took a deep breath and looked up. "Amelia and I watched Chief Minister Stannon hang in Shamalaya Square. He incurred Queen Saia's wrath when he tried to speak some final words. It appears as though Stannon was more diabolical than Cardissius. This was the minister that both you and Cheswick thought was going to strike you upon meeting him for the first time in Yasteron, correct?"

"Correct. Stannon's hatred of me was right on the surface from the second I met him."

"So, Cardissius' letter completely confused you, with regard to what Master Oba had said and with regard to what Drummond overheard the soldiers say. You'd begun to accept that Cardissius was a liar and had committed the ultimate act of betrayal against you, by ordering Kaleigh's murder. But in reading this, you discovered that was not the case. What did it mean for you,

Aelish? Had you fallen in love with the king and did his letter now restore that love?"

Aelish never expected this to be Thagar's reaction. She was ill-prepared for such a direct question about her feelings for Cardissius. She tried to speak but began stuttering. She took a deep breath and cast her eyes downward.

Thagar said, "When we tested out the rescue mission in the tunnels, there was a moment when we were right beneath the trap door of the prison. Although I could not clearly hear what he was saying, I heard the cadence of Cardissius' voice. Then, I heard you laugh and realized you were together in the prison. The laugh I heard you emit was an intimate laugh, one I thought was reserved only for me. I wanted to stay and listen further, but the team said it was time to exit the tunnels. On our way out, an alarm began blaring—"

"Oh, my God! You and the rescue team set off the alarm? Katrina and I were held by the King's Guard with their weapons aimed at us whilst Chief Minister Stannon accused me of setting it off. I didn't know what he was talking about and neither did Katrina. When the king finally arrived, he immediately shut off the alarm, dismissed everyone in the room, and was completely flummoxed. What caused the alarm to go off?"

Thagar replied, "If too much pressure was applied to the floor of the tunnels for a prolonged period of time, the alarm would go off. The drone rat squadron determined we only had fifteen minutes before the alarm was triggered. That was why Uncle Thurrock and I were carried by the Hentorians, on their chests, as they traversed through the tunnel, grasping iron rungs inserted by the drone rat squadron mounted onto the ceiling."

"My God, what a brilliant solution," said Aelish.

"But you haven't answered my question, Aelish," said Thagar. "Do you remember laughing with the king, in the prison, a short time before the alarm was triggered?"

Aelish closed her eyes, trying to remember. But it was so long ago, she remembered nothing. However, she didn't want it to appear as if she were hiding something, so she was completely honest. "I really can't remember anything specific, Thagar, I'm sorry."

"But by this time, you were no longer afraid of the king, correct? You were already married, getting ready to deliver the heir, and preparing to become Queen of Yasteron, yes?"

Aelish wasn't certain, but it appeared as if Thagar were trying to mask feelings of jealousy. She'd never seen him jealous during all the years they'd been together.

She spoke very calmly. "You are correct. By this time, I was no longer afraid of the king. I'd made my peace with being his mate and was determined to use his love for me to try and begin altering his kingdom so that DAR and Yasteron could peacefully coexist. I wanted him to begin honoring parts of the Peace Accord, as well as free the lower-orders, so they could become literate and receive an education."

"Were you in love with him, Aelish?"

Aelish began fidgeting. "Never like I was with you, Thagar. I was his captive. I was trying to survive. Perhaps, momentarily, I thought I was. Perhaps I still do. I'm so confused."

"Okay," said Thagar. "So, it *was* an intimate laugh that I heard. But now, I understand the context of your laugh as well as your feelings for the king. My uncle was right."

"What was he right about?" asked Aelish.

"Let me start at the beginning so you clearly understand what my uncle explained to me."

Aelish sat up straighter on the couch. She knew their next exchange was going to determine the course of their Commitments, one way or the other.

"You are an extraordinary being, Aelish. And your ability to love and forgive, even a being as evil as Cardissius, is why I am and will always be in love with you. If there were ever a being that could change Cardissius into a better male, it would be you."

"So, you feel my instincts were correct? Do you agree that Cardissius might have been changing for the better and could've become a kinder and fairer king to all of his subjects? I'm aware that with his mother and Chief Minister Stannon working against me, it would have been extremely difficult for him to make real or meaningful changes, most likely, for centuries. But I felt him wavering, Thagar. I know I did."

"I understand," said Thagar. "But after reading his letter, where he professed his undying love for you, do you believe your escape led to his death, which you now regret? Do you feel like you abandoned him by coming with me, Aelish?"

"I'm . . . I'm . . . not sure," she stammered. She began fidgeting again. "After my lessons with Master Oba and eavesdropping on Cardissius' conversation with my doctors about the Magical Sunlight Deprivation Heart Syndrome, I thought he was simply going to let me die. I no longer believed he loved me.

"But now, after reading his letter, I see that he learned of Stannon's betrayal on the Ides of March, two weeks before he met with my doctors for my ten-week scan and four weeks before my delivery on April 16th. Stannon's betrayal most likely caused the change in his behavior toward me. And he was most likely concerned that Stannon was planning to hurt me and the heir. He'd often told me I was kept inside the prison for my own protection, as well as for the protection of the heir. I never believed him until I read his letter. Obviously, those closest to the Crown were averse to what he was trying to do. They deeply opposed his desire to create a lineage of preeminent magical beings with an Earth born DARling, as well as making an Earth born DARling Queen of Yasteron.

"I truly believed I could influence the king into changing his kingdom because of his love for me. But once I felt he no longer loved me and was going to let me die after the heir was born, I took another route to change his kingdom. That's when I wrote the four letters to try an instigate a revolution. I realized I was dying and had very little time left to try and effect real change in Yasteron. But now, after receiving Cardissius' letter, I remain completely confused by his feelings for me and my feelings for him. And Master Oba's assessment of the king still pollutes my mind. I'm so befuddled."

"I understand why his letter left you unable to trust your own instincts," said Thagar. "Would you permit me to deconstruct his letter? I think it might help you to move forward."

Aelish felt herself becoming defensive. She shifted uncomfortably on the couch, crossing her arms over her chest. She did not want to continue this conversation with Thagar.

"There's no need to feel defensive, Aelish," said Thagar. "When I share with you all that Uncle Thurrock explained to me after the night I heard you laughing with Cardissius in the prison, things might become clearer and hopefully bring you some peace."

Begrudgingly, Aelish nodded her head. "All right, Thagar, go on."

"Cardissius was always in control. He had his own timeline for everything. You need to stop questioning yourself for feeling a shift in the king's love for you. After reading his letter, now you feel like you misjudged him, and the shift was because of Stannon's betrayal. But you will never truly know what was going on inside his mind, and you can't ask him because he's dead. His letter left you utterly confused and feeling as though you may have betrayed his love."

Aelish slightly nodded.

"No, Aelish. He was a master of deception. Especially, to those with a good heart."

Thagar leaned forward on the edge of his chair.

"Could the fact that he didn't order Kaleigh's murder make up for all the horrific actions he took against so many, for centuries, both in the magical and Human world? Because he kept his word *once*, is that enough for you to forgive him for everything he did, as well as develop feelings for him again?"

Aelish went to speak, but she didn't know how to answer Thagar's question.

"How could he ever be forgiven?" asked Thagar. "He coerced you into procreating his male heir, as well as marry him, or else he would kill me and Kaleigh. And just because he didn't order Kaleigh's death whilst you were imprisoned, doesn't mean he wouldn't have done so at a later date. He held her life and mine above your head at all times, in order to make you do things you would never do. That's not love, Aelish, that's control.

"How could a real love ever come from what you endured? Especially, after all the trauma he was responsible for in your life, including killing your parents, trying to kill me, and trying to kill Isabela. Isabela nearly killed herself, Aelish. She became mentally damaged after the soldiers kidnapped her and even more damaged after Cardissius ordered her assassination at the WHO. Imprisonment warps the mind and distorts reality. Uncle Thurrock explained that a captive has to find a way to cope and live through it. But to believe anything that happened during your imprisonment was just or fair, or that you grew to truly love him, is simply not reality, Aelish.

"Look at the physical and mental recovery I went through because of Cardissius' decision to bomb the N.W. Quadrant, as well as the underwater bunker, where I was interrogating *his* spy. His spy sent to kill you, me, and Isabela, leaving Kaleigh an orphan. Cardissius' spy broke Isabela's heart, stole all of her research, and she ended up being institutionalized in a psychiatric hospital, where she tried to kill herself. The existential crisis that Isabela and I both went through, by examining our entire lives, is exactly what he's doing to you now.

"He placed a wedge between us and tried to destroy your love for me, Aelish. You told me the other day that during your captivity, Cardissius told you that I didn't really love you. He said I was careless and reckless with your love and allowed you to be exposed to grave danger, by your covert mission into Komprathia and by you going to Yasteron to sign the Peace Accord.

"Cardissius said the reason you didn't tell me about your mission into Komprathia was because you didn't truly trust my love for you. He enjoyed taking serious events in our life together, out of context, to sow doubt in your mind about your feelings for me. He was trying to ruin your love for me, Aelish.

"When a being won't let you live freely and forces you do things against your will, the mind becomes distorted—first, to just survive and second, to try and find some semblance of happiness. But it's not reality. It's forced circumstances under coercion.

"In the hours after your abduction, you tried to kill yourself. A being who really loves you doesn't drive you to the point of wanting to kill yourself. But he did. That was one of the last times you were in touch with reality. You wanted out, and you were willing to die in order to get out. That could never be the beginning of a real love, Aelish.

"He mentally raped you as much as he physically did. He took your beautiful, clearheaded mind and confused you to the point where, as you say, you can no longer think. My uncle shared many things with me about his own imprisonment. He explained what a toll it takes on you not only physically but also mentally. Your reality is survival. And any feelings of love that come out of trying to survive, is an imprisoned love. It would never happen in the real world. Do you understand what I'm saying?"

Aelish did not respond but was looking directly into his eyes.

"In his twisted mind, I'm sure he believed that he truly did love you, Aelish. But it was a sick, abusive love that tortured you. And in my opinion, that is no love at all. It was simply power and control over you. It was a love on his terms and his terms alone.

"You are so powerful and so extraordinary that you probably did make him start to think differently. But forcing you to perform the Rapture, or the Endeavor, or whatever you want to call it, in order to save the lives of your daughter and your mate, is about the sickest thing I've ever heard. How cruel and sadistic was he? In my opinion, very.

"Your mind has been altered by your captivity. You've lost the ability to think rationally. You're still thinking like a captive. But after some time has passed, you will come to understand that what he did to you was a crime against your soul."

Thagar ran his hands down his face and smoothed his beard.

"He put the love of his life in a cage, because if she were free, she would never have loved him back. And he knew it. And that's not real love, Aelish.

"I'm so sorry for everything he put you through. But you will get well. It will take some time, but you will remember who you once were, and you will be strong again. I promise you— deep down inside—you are still Aelish. I promise you this on my life. You belong to me and to no one else, and I belong to you and to no one else. And no other being will ever change that," said Thagar.

Aelish stood up from the couch. She began pacing the room. She stopped, pivoted, and looked at Thagar sitting in the chair. "Don't you understand? I will never forgive myself for experiencing sexual pleasure with Cardissius, Thagar. I betrayed you each and every time it happened. How could I be your mate any longer? Look at all the ways I betrayed our Commitments—marrying him, preparing to become his queen, giving birth to his heir. I died a little more each and every day in that room. I am not the same. He broke me, Thagar."

"No, he hasn't, Aelish."

"Yes, he has! Everything has changed! Another male has given me pleasure. I have born his child. I married him. My God, Thagar! Don't you see? Even our love can't conquer my shame."

Thagar shook his head. "When we took our vows, Aelish, we always knew our devotion to DAR could interfere with our love. But I am still your only mate. A forced marriage is not real. And I will never stop loving you, and I will never give up on us, Aelish.

"Cardissius may have warped your mind during the Endeavor, but he never reached or touched the essence of you. That is something only you and I have ever shared. And if it takes me the rest of my life, I will make you feel that love again. Because it will restore you not only to yourself but also to me."

"I'm not the same being I used to be. I've lost the ability to pray and my relationship with God eludes me. I've lost my faith, Thagar, and I don't think I can go on living anymore."

"If you wish to exterminate yourself, then I vow to do so as well. We will die right here, right now, together in this room."

"No, Thagar! Kaleigh needs you! No!

"You don't get to leave me, Aelish. Not after everything we've been through. We will raise your son and the four of us will be a family. Or we can both die, right now, in this room, as I will never be apart from you again, Aelish."

"How could you possibly still love me after everything I've told you? After everything that's happened to me? I am not the same, Thagar."

"I will love whatever part is still left of my Aelish. I will love whatever part remains of the beautiful soul I've loved for centuries and will continue to love until I cease to draw breath."

Aelish shook her head. "I am permanently soiled by Cardissius, Thagar. There is nothing left of me for you to love."

"Don't you understand, Aelish—there is no shame. You are not soiled. My estimation of you is higher than it ever was for the suffering you endured and the sacrifices you made to save my life and Kaleigh's life. You are still alive; you survived it all. And you will find your faith again. You are not alone, my love."

Aelish collapsed onto the couch in great distress.

Thagar got up from his chair. He stood before her and took a knee. He bowed his head in reverence. When he lifted his head, he gently took her hand, kissed it, and said, "M'Lady, I love you more in this moment than I have every loved you before. You are my mate, and I hope we die in each other's arms. I cannot express into words how much I admire and respect your determination to survive your captivity. You sacrificed everything to save the life of your daughter as well as the life of your mate, to say nothing of the sacrifices you made for DAR. You never stopped trying to make peace with Yasteron. You gave up so much in the hope that there would finally be peace in the magical world."

Thagar stood up and sat across from her on the couch. "You were pregnant, sick, and dying but had the wherewithal to put in motion, through four hand-written letters, a revolution in Yasteron that was long overdue. How did you find the strength, my love? For I know with certainty, I will never possess that kind of strength."

Thagar moved closer to her. He tightly embraced her with tears running down his face. Finally, she hugged him back and began sobbing. Thagar had broken through the wall.

27

THE NAUGHTY SELKIE

AFTER LADY ANTONIA left the N.E. Quadrant, she wrote to Isabela and told her about everything Aelish had endured. Isabela was devastated by the news. She wrote back to Lady Antonia, promising to send treatment resources for Medicus Clove in DAR. Isabela also told her she was engaged and pregnant with Andrew Devereux's child, which made Lady Antonia squeal with delight. Then, Lady Antonia sent Isabela a confetti-balloon Sylph. The Sylph had to make certain Isabela was in a secure place for magic before releasing multi-colored-confetti and balloons out of a teeny tiny cannon. Isabela knew who'd sent the celebratory Sylph, even before she'd read Lady Antonia's note of congratulations. The back-and-forth Sylphs gave them both a lift after discussing Aelish's dire condition.

After speaking with Lady Antonia and receiving mental health resources from Isabela, Medicus Clove had been to the cove house twice to meet with Aelish. Even though Clove was now a medicus and always conducted herself professionally, when she saw Aelish for the first time, she couldn't stop herself from bursting into tears. Their first appointment consisted of a full day of walks and meals on the beach while discussing everything Aelish had been through. Clove informed Aelish that she'd wanted to venture into the field of psychology after learning about Thagar's mental health treatments at the Wainbridge Rehabilitation Center.

Once Clove had discussed her forthcoming treatment plan, Aelish suggested DAR create a mental health treatment center for the soldiers and drone rats who would, one day, be returning from their imprisonment in Yasteron. Once again, Clove found herself in tears because the Aelish she had known before her captivity was still there; she was still the same beautiful soul she had always been. It was so like Aelish to take her own misfortune and transform it into a method of helping others. By the second appointment, Clove knew it would take some time, perhaps even years, but Aelish would find her way back and fully recover.

After unburdening herself of the shame she lived with to Lady Antonia, Thagar, and Clove, Aelish began to feel a weight lifting off her chest. She could breathe easier, and she stopped crying all the time. And while she still couldn't imagine being intimate with Thagar, she hoped, one day, in the near future, she might be able to do so.

Clove had suggested lots of exercise to help with her anxiety and despair. So, Aelish had begun taking morning swims in the cove while Kaleigh was at boat-school and Elijah napped. Sometimes, she would take Elijah with her and sometimes, she would go alone. Thagar was very attentive to her needs, but she also noticed he seemed to be working on something. She didn't have the strength to ask him about it yet and let him go about his business. Whatever he was involved in was bringing him joy, and she was happy for him.

Since their arrival in the N.E. Quadrant, Kaleigh had missed most of Aelish's torment. She was hardly ever home and greatly enjoyed spending time with her newfound extended family. And they, in turn, adored her. It gave Aelish the respite she needed, to internalize the mental relief she experienced after disclosing her shame. She felt more optimistic after her initial treatments with Clove and no longer wished to end her own life. Occasionally, she even caught herself smiling. But her relationship with God remained dormant.

Aelish tried not to dwell on anything upsetting and worked hard on restoring herself through her sessions with Clove, swimming in the ocean, going to the hot springs in the N.E. Quadrant, and taking quiet walks with Elijah wrapped against her chest. Occasionally, Kaleigh and Thagar would accompany them, walking beside her at dusk, which was Aelish's favorite time of day on the beach.

When she took Elijah swimming, she'd magically strap him against her. She loved floating on her back with Elijah resting on her chest. He loved the water and had become a brawny male, weighing in at fifteen pounds. Aelish was relieved he was thriving. He was a joyous and beautiful male that never complained, except when he was hungry or needed changing. His smile could light up a room, and Aelish had stopped comparing his outward appearance of being porcelain-skinned, blond, and blue-eyed with Cardissius. She'd finally begun to see him for himself.

Today was a beautiful day. The sun was shining and the water was still, just like Aelish's mind. She could finally think again and even experienced moments during the day when she'd forget about everything that happened to her. When she'd remember, it still brought back a sinking feeling in her stomach, but finally, she had stretches of time with no traumatic thoughts or memories. She was learning how to just be again.

As she floated in the water, with Elijah on her chest, she was thoroughly relaxed. Suddenly, a seal emerged from the water. Aelish stopped floating and pulled Elijah closer to her breasts. It swam to shore and galumphed over to the rocks at the base of the steep cliffs on the right side of the cove. She observed how the seal shed its skin and shape-shifted into a beautiful naked Selkie. Her long, red hair partially covered her breasts and reached her knees. The Selkie left her skin on the rocks, dove into the water, and swam over to Aelish.

Ever since Thagar's brothers had told her about Selkie Island, during the search for him after the underwater bunker bombing, Aelish wondered if she'd ever encounter a Selkie now that she lived in the N.E. Quadrant. Knowing she was not near Selkie Island, she was fascinated this magical creature had wandered so far from home. She found it hard to believe it had travelled all this way just to see her.

After the brothers described the powers of the Selkie, Aelish read a lot about their legend. The legend states that the Selkie belong to the collective emotional pool of the ocean, signifying all the longings of both Humans and magical beings. They often save the lives of small children or fisherfolk who fall into the ocean.

The Selkie are highly sensitive and their messages lie deep within the ocean. One must hear the call of one's own heart and be honest with themselves before a Selkie would ever approach. Aelish had been in such recent turmoil, she knew a Selkie would never come near her; she'd been harboring too many painful secrets. But she'd begun healing and found it a positive sign that a Selkie had emerged so close to her.

The Selkie quickly swam in circles around her and Elijah, her long, red hair matching the color of Aelish's. She had expressive eyes that penetrated the soul, and Aelish was careful not to let the

Selkie bewitch her. The circular movements of the Selkie made small waves around them, which made Elijah start laughing. He seemed captivated by the feeling of the ebb and flow of the water and appreciated its volatility. He was completely unafraid of the increasing current nor of the Selkie.

"Hello," said Aelish.

"You are very beautiful," said the Selkie.

Aelish smiled at the creature. "Do you wish to tell me something?"

"Why do you hold the child so closely to your chest?" asked the Selkie. "Let him stretch out in the water. No harm will come to him. Extend his arms, like this." The Selkie gestured with her arms that Aelish should hold Elijah away from her body, by grasping his forearms. Since Elijah could now hold his head up, Aelish began to do as the Selkie instructed and Elijah smiled at his mother.

"You, see? He likes it," said the Selkie. "Now, spin him around in circles."

Holding onto his forearms, Aelish began gently spinning Elijah in a circle. Not wanting him to get dizzy, she then began spinning him in the other direction. He loved this new game.

"Elijah, come," beckoned the Selkie.

"He's too young to swim on his own," said Aelish, fearfully. "He could drown."

"Or he could swim," said the Selkie, smiling.

Aelish was becoming frightened of the Selkie, but before she could pull Elijah back to her breasts, the Selkie dove underwater and came up between Aelish and Elijah. She grabbed one of Elijah's arms and pulled him toward her.

"No!" yelled Aelish.

The Selkie put her forefinger against her mouth telling Aelish to remain quiet. Then, she gestured for Aelish to follow them.

But the Selkie dove underwater with Elijah.

Panicking, Aelish dove underwater to keep Elijah in her line of sight. As she began running out of air, she saw the Selkie begin to surface with Elijah.

The three of them surfaced together and the Selkie held Elijah close to her naked breasts. "Give me my son, this instant!" yelled Aelish. "He could have been killed!"

"Ah! But he wasn't. Because like his father, he can breathe underwater."

"*What?*" exclaimed Aelish. "No Yasteron can breathe underwater and neither can I!"

The Selkie gently returned Elijah to her arms. "He is not a Yasteron. He is a son of the ocean and the grandson of Lomax. His father is your mate, Thagar. He is a beautiful and gentle soul. Go back in time, Aelish. You will see that your mate did not properly perform the Prevent spell the night of the Commitments Ceremony for Sartaine. And you were too drunk to notice!" She began maniacally laughing and broadly smiled at Aelish. "Congratulations, Aelish! You are free!"

The Selkie then dove under the water and swam back over to the rocks where she'd left her seal skin. Donning her skin, she shape-shifted back into a seal and vanished underwater.

"Oh, my God!" cried out Aelish.

Her heart felt like it was going to explode out of her chest. She looked at Elijah and for the first time saw the face of her mother, Saoirse. Her mother had blond hair and deep blue eyes, as did her two brothers who died before she was born. Elijah's blond hair and blue eyes came from her, not Cardissius. And like Kaleigh, Elijah's ability to breathe underwater came from Thagar—Elijah was Thagar's son.

Aelish began to count back the dates to the early morning of the day after the Commitments Ceremony, which was January

11th. She and Thagar had made wild passionate love, followed by the Rapture. She held on tightly to Elijah, swam to shore, and from the beach decided to travel back in time.

She stood in her bedchamber in the Artist's House watching Thagar make love to her. It was so beautiful; she began to remember who they were together. Then, Thagar began to recite the Prevent spell and she clearly saw how he'd forgotten the most important part of the spell. He had, indeed, prevented nothing. She stood there and watched the last time they'd performed the Rapture and the joy on their faces as they both came out of it. She looked down at Elijah. He'd transported back in time, to his own conception, quite well. She kissed the top of his soft head.

"You are *our* son," she said softly, kissing him with tears running down her face. "Oh, my God." She wouldn't have believed any of it, had she not gone back in time to witness their lovemaking, Thagar's Prevent spell mistake, and their performance of the Rapture. She longed to stay back in time before she ever went to Yasteron to sign the Peace Accord. It felt magnificent in the past. But she was concerned about the effects of staying too long on Elijah.

"We have to go back now, sweetheart," whispered Aelish. "Are you ready, my angel?"

Elijah smiled at her. She tightly held him in her arms and transported back to the present. She felt the sand beneath her feet and opened her eyes. She was in the N.E. Quadrant again.

She took Elijah swimming again, and this time, she did let him go. She watched as he began to swim on his own and he went underwater. She saw bubbles on the surface and followed them until he ultimately resurfaced. She took hold of him against her chest and cried tears of joy. The Selkie had given her back her life. Cardissius was becoming a memory. She'd seen how to make love to her mate again and was ready to try. She'd been reborn in the water, baptized again by God, and internalized the fact that both God and Thagar had forgiven her.

As she swam back to shore, with Elijah swimming alongside of her, for the first time in a very long time, Aelish began praying. She rediscovered her relationship with God and felt born again; her heart began to open.

The next thing she intended to do was send a long-overdue letter to Isabela. In it, she would enclose clippings of Elijah's blond hair along with a cheek swab. Before she told Thagar anything, she wanted to make sure Isabela could match Elijah's DNA to Thagar's. She couldn't wait to get home and write the letter.

‡‡‡‡

Upon entering the cove house, she noted Thagar was still not home. Aelish prepared a bath for Elijah. She carefully clipped a lock of hair from his head and placed the clipping in a sealed bag. Then, she gently swabbed the inside of his cheeks and put the swab into another sealed bag. She nursed and changed him and then put him down for his nap.

Aelish magically cleaned herself up and sat at the desk in the living area. She found a few sheets of paper and began writing at a feverish pace. She wanted to get the letter delivered to Isabela without delay. She would never tell Thagar that Elijah was his son without scientific proof from Isabela.

Dear Isabela,

Enclosed are clippings of hair from my son, Elijah, along with a cheek swab. I would be ever so grateful if you could run a DNA test on his hair and saliva and compare it to the information you've gathered on Thagar's DNA. I've recently discovered that Elijah is not Cardissius' son but is actually Thagar's! I went back in time to the night of Elijah's conception and clearly saw how

Thagar messed up the Prevent spell, causing me to conceive.

A DARling has up to three weeks from the Rapture to potentially conceive. We performed the Rapture in the early morning hours of January 11th and the magical glow of conception occurred on my abdomen on January 21st (your birthday) whilst I was imprisoned in Yasteron. So, it was ten days later, placing me in the window of conception of a DARlette.

I must have scientific confirmation before I tell Thagar, as he has been through so much. I must be 100 percent positive. Please, hurry the results as fast as possible and forgive me for asking you to do me a favor before I've even said a proper hello. I guess we can say that you and I have been on some journey. I truly hope we can see each other again, very soon.

I know from Lady Antonia, as well as from Thagar's correspondence with your mother, that you are expecting a child and planning a quickie wedding to conceal the pregnancy. Congratulations, sweetheart! I cannot believe what you and Drew have accomplished together—not only by discovering your love for one another, and creating a new life, but also by increasing the vaccination rates on Earth. Well done, Isabela! I hope by this time, you've forgiven me for telling Drew about DAR without having a long discussion with you beforehand. I have questioned my impulsive decision to do that for so very long. But perhaps now, I can begin to forgive myself for inflicting so much pain and confusion upon you.

After my rescue from Yasteron, Thagar told me about your release from the psychiatric hospital. He also told me you were on a worldwide tour to promote the LECCS vaccine to Humanity. Hearing this was the first time I felt any true, unbridled joy in a very long time. And learning that you are expecting a child and planning to marry has brought me unmitigated happiness for both you and Drew. I have known for some time that Drew was in love with you, as did Thagar and your mother, but I suppose we have to discover things on our own for them to be truly meaningful. They cannot be forced or rushed if we are not ready.

Thagar also told me that you and Marisol both figured out that Yasteron caused Abuela's death. I haven't even had time to properly mourn her, but I did want to apprise you of something. It was actually not King Cardissius who ordered Kaleigh's murder, resulting in Abuela's death, but it was, in fact, his chief minister who ordered it. Further, the king did not order the soldiers to burn down our house on Earth. The king was already dead by the time our house burned down. Again, it was Chief Minister Stannon who ordered it. He hated me from first moment he laid eyes on me, Isabela. I will tell you the whole story when I see you.

Discovering that Elijah is Thagar's son has finally freed me from the prison in my own mind. We've both shared being mentally unwell, and I cannot thank you enough for providing Medicus Clove with resources for me. We've already had two sessions and are scheduled to have more shortly. I hope to fully recover so I can be there for my family.

At the moment, I do not know what we will do with the property that is in ashes on Bunker Hill Road. Perhaps I will turn it into a park for the community. Now that you've given me the ultimate gift, by discovering Kaleigh can breathe in the magical world, Thagar and I are unsure if we'll be returning to Earth to live since we now have one Human child and one magical child. I really can't think about it all at this moment, but soon, we will decide.

Thank you for researching the DNA and MNA of DARlings! Something tells me this information will be very useful in the not-too-distant future. I also need to tell you more about Yasteron when I see you, but I'll leave you with this teaser: Yasterons were originally DARlings!

Yes, it's true! You can read that line over and over. I still have not internalized this fact, but I'm getting closer to it. I miss you so much, Isabela. You have no idea how I've longed for you. During my captivity, thinking about our relationship helped me to retain my sanity. I pray you are no longer angry with me because I love you with all of my heart and hope you will let me be a part of your life again. Please give my warmest regards to your mother, your father, and Drew. When we return to Earth, I promise to visit the final resting place of your beloved Abuela. How you must miss her. I am so sorry that by knowing me and the magical world's existence, you lost someone so important in your life. There is no way I can ever make that up to you. Please forgive me and forgive DAR.

Please send a Sylph as soon as you've had a chance to analyze Elijah's hair and cheek swab. I pray you are feeling well in your first trimester and it is nothing like mine was with Kaleigh. By the way, having a DARlette is so much easier! The labor took twenty minutes with slight cramping. We have so much to catch up on, but in the meantime, please take care of yourself. Don't overdo and remain healthy and happy for your new baby! I hope to see you soon!

All my love always,

Aelish

Aelish immediately called for a Sylph and the letter and DNA samples were gone in an instant. Further, she was relieved the Sylph looked nothing like the one from Yasteron. Orange hair and violet eyes with a swirling floral dress was more to her liking.

‡‡‡‡

Three days later, on July 23rd, a Sylph fluttered above Aelish's face, waking her up. It was very early in the morning and the sun was about to rise. The Sylph gestured for Aelish to remain quiet and pointed to a sleeping Thagar and a sleeping Elijah in his crib in their room. Kaleigh was asleep in her own room and she could hear Drummond beginning to prepare breakfast. Storm began to stir and Aelish gestured for him to remain quiet. He laid his head back down on the bed and resumed sleeping.

The Sylph handed Aelish a letter, which she knew was from Isabela. The Sylph smiled and vanished. Aelish's hands were shaking as she quietly opened the letter. It contained one line:

Elijah is Thagar's son! I am 1,000 percent positive! Love you, Isabela.

Aelish rested the letter against her chest and thanked God for her deliverance. Never in her wildest dreams did she believe this could be possible. Thagar began to stir next to her.

"Is everything all right, my love?" he asked.

"Everything is 1,000 percent all right, Thagar," she replied.

He rolled over and lifted one eyebrow at her response and asked, "What is going on?"

"Nothing, go back to sleep."

"Okay, now I'm up. What is it, Aelish?"

"I have something to tell you, my love. Perhaps alone in our bed, with our son sleeping in his crib beside us is the perfect time to tell you."

"All right, I'm listening."

The fact that her use of the words "our son" did not alert Thagar to anything unusual was the exact reason why she was so happy to finally be able to tell him. He had never treated Elijah as anything different than his own son. And the fact that he believed Elijah was from a being he despised more than any other said a lot about his character and integrity. He had always been a noble being, no more so than right at this moment.

"I have a surprise for you, Thagar. A surprise you deserve so very much."

Thagar smiled and looked inquisitively at her. "Are you going to tell me?"

"Elijah, whom you named, is your son."

"Of course, he is my son. I promised you that I would always raise him as my son."

"No, Thagar. He is *biologically* your son. We created him together the night of Sartaine's Commitments Ceremony. You messed up the Prevent spell and I was too drunk to notice. I think you wanted to make sure I took a piece of you with me before I left for Yasteron. Thank you, my love."

Thagar sat straight up in the bed. He stared at Aelish as if she were speaking another language. He stuttered, tried to speak, and finally said, "I messed up the Prevent spell?"

Aelish burst out laughing. "That's your takeaway from what I just told you?"

"I actually can't believe what you just told me. How do you know this to be true?"

"Your brothers warned me that the Selkie can be very naughty. I encountered one in the ocean a few days ago. She basically seized Elijah, dragged him under the water, demonstrating how he could not only swim at three months but could also breathe underwater, like his father and his sister, Kaleigh—not his half sister, his full sister.

"And it was the Selkie who told me he was a son of the ocean and the grandson of Lomax. She instructed me to go back in time to the night of Sartaine's Commitments Ceremony, which I did with Elijah by the way, and I watched us making love. Then, I watched you incorrectly recite the Prevent spell before we performed the Rapture. You left out the most important part and prevented nothing!

"I suspected he was yours because of his ability to swim and breathe underwater but witnessing the mistake in the Prevent spell confirmed it. However, before I told you anything, I asked Isabela to run his DNA and compare it to yours, to be absolutely certain. This was her response, just delivered by a Sylph." Aelish held up the one-line letter and Thagar gasped. Apparently, they both now believed in science as much as they believed in their own magical abilities.

"He is mine? He is *my* son?"

"Yes, my love. I suppose when you named him in Hentoria, it was written for the ages."

"Ohh, Aelish. You have given me a gift I could never repay."

"You already have, my love. You saved both of our lives. I love you now and forever."

And as if no time or events had passed of such monumental horror, Thagar and Aelish began making love as if it were the same night of Sartaine's Commitments Ceremony. She never thought she could feel this way again after everything that had happened to her, but it was all the same and as beautiful as ever. Their love had conquered the most evil kingdom and the most evil being who came out of it. They were alive, they had a son, a beautiful daughter, an incredible dog, and everything they had ever dreamed of.

They did not perform the Rapture, however. That was for another day.

28

A New Sanctuary

I T WAS NEARING the one-year anniversary of the Perfect Storm, August 25, 2025, the same date Hurricane Katrina hit in 2005. Every day a new heat record was broken, whether on land or in the oceans, and ice throughout the Earth was melting at an alarming rate. Thagar was growing concerned that all the Climate Refugee Intake Centers, within the U.S. and around the world, would not be able to handle the diaspora of displaced Humans on the horizon. While he and Drew had constructed additional climate refugee settlement sites, he knew the paradigm of relocating Humans from one place to another could only last for so long. Since the Perfect Storm, he'd been working on a long-term idea and was anxious to share his concept with Aelish.

Over the last two weeks, he'd seen how much she'd improved after discovering and disclosing to him that Elijah was their son and not Cardissius' offspring. Happiness began to permeate the household, once again, and with it came a calm.

He was hesitant to bring up the climate crisis on Earth, as he didn't want to cause Aelish any undue burdens. But they were leaving DAR and returning to Earth in a few days to attend Isabela and Drew's wedding. Prior to their departure, he felt the project he'd been working on might provide Aelish with some hope, especially since the overall global temperature was on the precipice of breaching the LECCS threshold. Even with higher vaccination rates, LECCS was still going to cause untold suffering. Additionally, it was the season when furious storms occurred. He couldn't imagine how Humans would be able to cope with another storm, like the Perfect Storm, in the middle of the LECCS crisis.

"You seem very far away, my love," remarked Aelish, walking into the kitchen. "Kiss your son and tell me what is on your mind." She leaned over so Thagar could kiss Elijah before putting him into his playpen.

Thagar began smiling at both her and Elijah, whom he kissed on the forehead. Elijah reached for Thagar's beard and began pulling on it. "He just loves to do this," said Thagar, extricating Elijah's fingers from his whiskers. Thagar stood up, took hold of his son, and began swooping him up and down, which made Elijah start laughing.

"I think he pulls on your beard so you'll play with him like that," said Aelish, chuckling.

"I think you're right," said Thagar, laying Elijah down in his playpen.

"He will be asleep shortly," said Aelish. "So, why don't you tell me what you were thinking about. Would you like me to make you an espresso?"

Thagar smiled at her. "Have I ever refused?" Aelish began laughing at him as she magically conjured a hot espresso for him. Thagar took a sip and said, "Delicious, as always. So, do you remember the day you presented the information on the Perfect Storm to the Head Council?"

"Of course. That was the day you told me about your vision to construct Climate Refugee Intake Centers and refugee settlement sites for those displaced by the storm."

"Do you remember me also telling you that I was working on an additional long-term concept even more complicated than the CRIC and the settlement sites?"

Aelish closed her eyes for a moment. "Yes! My goodness, that was nearly a year ago."

"A lot has happened since then," said Thagar. "Whilst you were in Yasteron, I realized I'd never told you about my other concept nor had I ever told you about my conservation work."

"Conservation work? Tell me, tell me!" Aelish smiled brightly at him.

How he'd missed their normal conversations. He took a deep breath and realized how grateful he was to see her green eyes shining in the morning sun. "Well, ever since we came to Earth in 2019 for Kaleigh's birth, I began reading about the Sixth Mass Extinction. Actually, my interest in saving species found in the magical world as well as the Human world began hundreds of years ago. That's why I took you to the Sanctuary in the S.E. Quadrant on our first date." Thagar smiled at her. "How long ago does that feel?"

"I'm really beginning to feel my first five hundred DARling years," said Aelish. "Things seem like they were a very long time ago. I loved that day, Thagar. It was otherworldly."

"Well, about two hundred years ago, the Sanctuary Learning and Educational Workers, or the SLEWs, began rescuing Earthly species they considered endangered. Finally, Humans realized the enormity of species being lost on Earth and created the Endangered Species Act of 1973 and its subsequent amendments.

The theory behind the law is similar to the Svalbard Global Seed Vault in Norway, established to protect the seeds and prevent the extinction of diverse agricultural crops, just like the Seed Vault of DAR, which you helped create."

Aelish nodded and said, "I remember the back-and-forth discussions with the Head Council as to whether DAR's rescue of endangered species constituted direct interference with Earthly affairs. It was determined DAR had not influenced Human free will, causing the species to become endangered in the first place, therefore, it was *not* considered direct interference. But despite the mammoth Human effort to halt extinctions, continued global deforestation has destroyed whole ecosystems within Earthly forests. The ongoing destruction of habitats is the leading cause of modern-day extinctions. The Head Council never thought Humans would let it get to this point, but they have. Thank heavens, DAR had the prescience to take decisive action, hundreds of years ago, to save species being lost to the Sixth Mass Extinction."

"Exactly," agreed Thagar. "Are you aware of the new Marine Sanctuary the SLEWs have created in the N.E. Quadrant to save endangered marine mammals?"

"I am! Your father and brothers told me all about it when we were searching for you after the bombings. I know it proved highly challenging to construct and several SLEWs lost their lives during its creation. Ultimately, the SLEWs only used DARlings who were able to breathe underwater to finish its construction. I'm so glad you reminded me of the Marine Sanctuary. I want to take Kaleigh there whilst we are living here. With the exception of myself, the entire family could have the full experience offered for those who can breathe underwater."

"Forgive me, my love, but I've already seen it," said Thagar, sheepishly.

"You went without me?" she asked.

He feebly nodded. "I also took Kaleigh. And we went with my entire extended family." He scrunched his eyes in anticipation of her response.

Aelish began chuckling. "Keeping secrets from me, I see." She deeply kissed him. "I'm glad you gave Kaleigh that experience whilst I was unwell. You're such a wonderful father. But take me and Elijah soon, okay?"

Thagar nodded and breathed a sigh of relief. "Well, I wanted to tell you two things today. Ever since we went to Earth in 2019, I've been keeping Targo, who is now the Master SLEW for all sanctuaries in DAR, apprised of all the animals, insects, marine mammals, etc., that have been placed on the endangered list, as well as those I felt should have been based on my research.

"In order to accommodate the numerous species verging on Earthly extinction, the SLEWs expanded their magical technology to encompass the necessary terrestrial ecosystems needed to foster the survival of the species brought to DAR, in order to prevent their extinction. This expansion of magical technology mandated the original Sanctuary in the S.E. Quadrant be greatly enlarged. And the SLEWs extensive new research and magical technology led me to the other project I'm envisioning, which I'd like to now share with you."

"I had no idea you were working with Targo at the Sanctuary," remarked Aelish.

"It became somewhat of a hobby for me," said Thagar. "You know how much I've always loved the Sanctuary and the salvation of so many magical and Earthly creatures."

"I am well aware," said Aelish. "Okay, so what's the other project you're envisioning?"

"When I took Kaleigh flying for the first time, to test out her breathing and the flying suit I created for her, I took her over

Mount Everest."

"Wow! I did not know that!" said Aelish. "Did she love it?"

"She did. Kaleigh told me that, one day, she wants to climb Mount Everest. It's such a breathtaking sight and always brings back wonderful memories for me of the mountain peak in the Sanctuary. And observing the Humans climbing toward the summit reminds me of the best Human trait—conquering the unconquerable."

Aelish nodded her head.

"After the Perfect Storm, I created the concept of the Climate Refugee Intake Centers as well as the refugee settlement sites. But recently, I've been thinking—what if I combined the concept of the CRICs and the settlement sites with the expanded magical technology of the SLEWs? Could DAR provide a sanctuary for Humans?"

"Okay, now you have my full attention, Director," said Aelish.

"In the very near future, Earth will become so volatile it will, most likely, not be able to sustain Human life or life for any of the species living alongside them. The SLEWs have been successful in creating new magical ecosystems for endangered mythical creatures, as well as endangered Earthly animals, insects, and marine mammals, by providing them with sanctuary here in DAR. So, I came up with a hypothesis—why can't we bring Humans, who are also severely endangered, to DAR?"

"I see. You want to combine the impending catastrophic Human displacement on Earth, with your original concept of the CRICs and refugee settlement sites and include the expanded magical technology of the SLEWS, in order to bring Humans from Earth to DAR, correct?"

"Correct," said Thagar. He remained quiet as Aelish analyzed his hypothesis.

"Thagar, there are nearly nine *billion* Humans on the Earth and there are approximately five *million* DARlings and other magical beings within the confines of DAR. What location in DAR has the capacity to accommodate that many Humans needing relocation?"

"Not to be morbid," said Thagar, "but once the Earth has finished its retribution for the lack of concern demonstrated for it by Humans, I imagine there will be far fewer Humans in the future than there are at present. They will die from a myriad of causes. Further, my concept is meant to be an intermediary solution, not a permanent one. But you're right, we'd need an enormous piece of land, even as an intermediary solution.

"In their present genetic state, Humans will soon be unable to live on what is quickly becoming an uninhabitable Earth; they will need a place of refuge. The gene editing of Humans could begin on Earth, but eventually, it will become too dire for it to conclude there. Therefore, DAR would need to construct a medical facility to accommodate the routine healthcare of Humans as well their genetic alteration.

"Whilst genetically modifying Humans may not be successful, let's assume that it is. Humans who have received Kaleigh's DNA key code could then be repatriated back to Earth. They'd be able to breathe its toxic atmosphere, be genetically immune to illness, and could begin restoring the Earth."

"Do you envision the Humans in a secure place in DAR?" asked Aelish. "Their inability to breathe our air would ensure they'd have to remain in the sanctuary DAR would establish. However, once they are genetically modified, they could breathe anywhere within the magical world and could become dangerous to their magical hosts."

"I completely understand what you're inferring," said Thagar. "But keep in mind, Humans will not be genetically modified to have magical capabilities. Magical beings would always have the upper hand. Having said that, you do raise a valid point. Left unchecked, Humans could potentially wreak havoc within the magical dimension, despite not possessing magical abilities, as they are both a peaceful and violent species."

Aelish sat at the kitchen counter thinking.

"Since you haven't yet burst out laughing," said Thagar, "should I take that as a positive sign you don't think the entire concept is ridiculous?"

Aelish narrowed her eyes and said, "Why am I getting the sense that I'm being told about this concept during the ninth inning?"

"What do you mean?" Thagar asked innocently, trying hard not to laugh.

"You've been working on this for some time, haven't you?" she accused. "I would go so far as to say, you've most likely had meetings and contact with senior policymakers within DAR and elsewhere in the magical world, to test out your new hypothesis. Am I correct?"

"Each time I think I might be able to outwit you, there you are!" Having been caught, Thagar started laughing. His intuitive mate had always been one step ahead of him. Even when he was ahead of her, once she became aware of a situation or project, she'd surpass him in a heartbeat.

He'd only had the momentary advantage because she'd been so mentally unwell. He knew she'd been somewhat aware he'd been working on a new project. Initially, he'd chosen not to share it with her to avoid adding stress to her recovery. But if he were being completely honest, he also liked taking the lead. Aelish's abilities in policy development were unrivaled. He'd only had the brief upper hand because she hadn't been fully informed about the project.

He continued laughing, as she was now sarcastically smiling

at him. Thagar stood up and passionately kissed her right on her sarcastic mouth. She instantly responded to his overture and did not object when he lifted her up and carried her into their bedchamber, taking advantage of Elijah's long nap.

Once they were in their bedchamber, he gently began undressing her, kissing each new spot of bare skin that he uncovered. He magically undressed himself while he was manually undressing Aelish. Seeing her react to him with pleasure, he was convinced that each time they made love, he erased one more bad memory from her captivity. It had become his own personal "Thagar therapy" and he was greatly enjoying it.

As he drove himself into her soft velvety flesh, she cried out and threw her head back in ecstasy. He lay atop her and remained inside of her, gently kissing her face and torso until she was ready for him again. He began thrusting himself harder and harder until they both experienced a release, heard by Elijah in his playpen, who promptly awoke wailing.

They both started laughing and lay side by side for a few minutes, catching their breath. Elijah calmed for a moment and Aelish began kissing him again. But Thagar stopped her from beginning anew as, right then, their son began pushing his vocal cords to the next level.

"I love our family," said Aelish. "You catch your breath, my love. I will take care of our DARlette. And after the males in my life have both recovered, we can resume talking about your new project. A project that is apparently *new* only to me." She chuckled and then deeply kissed him, prior to exiting the bedchamber.

He lay there listening to her soothe and comfort their son. Had he ever known such happiness? He didn't think so and was beyond grateful.

Elijah was in a wrap against Aelish, with his body facing outward. She was laughing with Drummond as he was preparing lunch for them. Drummond knew what she and Thagar had been up to, and he had a big smile across his face.

Thagar walked into the kitchen and sat at the counter. "I've worked up quite an appetite."

Drummond began snickering and set down a bowl of hot soup, two sandwiches, and a fresh salad in front of Thagar.

"This looks terrific, Drummond, thank you," said Thagar, who began eating with gusto.

Aelish turned to Thagar. "So, aside from missing the tour of the N.E. Quadrant's Marine Sanctuary, not being told about the Portal avoidance route for hundreds of years, as well as your conservation work with Targo, are there any other secrets you would like to share with me before we return to the subject of a Human Sanctuary?"

Thagar looked up from his food. He saw Aelish giving him another sarcastic smile, making him want to abandon his lunch and return to their bedchamber. He smiled and said, "I really like the sound of that—a Human Sanctuary. And no, I think that about covers everything you've been unaware of." He began chuckling and tickled Elijah's toes, which were right by his face. Elijah started giggling. "His laugh is such a beautiful sound, Aelish."

"You like it when Daddy tickles your toes, don't you, sweetheart?" asked Aelish. She began nuzzling his face and kissing the top of his head.

"Aren't you going to eat, my love?" asked Thagar.

"Yes, but first I'm going to give Elijah a little snack." She took the wrap off Elijah and placed him in his new high chair. "I am constantly surprised by how advanced DARlette development is from Humans. I imagine he'll be walking at five months." Thagar nodded at her.

"Here's the fresh applesauce I made this mornin' for little Elijah, Aelish," said Drummond, handing her a bowl with a baby spoon.

"Ohh, look what Drummond has made for you today," said Aelish to Elijah, who began smiling and laughing. He had his mouth open before she even put any applesauce on the spoon. "He's hungry all the time. I've never seen anything like it."

"DARlettes eat a lot in their first year," said Thagar. "You almost think there's something wrong, but that's why we can start him on solid foods so soon."

"Someone's been reading about infant DARlettes," said Aelish. Drummond winked at her and nodded. Thagar conjured the books he'd been reading from their bedchamber and they appeared on the kitchen counter. There was a stack of five books. "Wow, look at you!"

Thagar said, "It's incredible how much more quickly they mature from Human infants."

"It's like he's our first offspring," said Aelish, shaking her head. "My expertise from raising Kaleigh merely points out their differences to me. I feel like a first-time mother."

Elijah finished the applesauce and reached out his hands to Aelish for more. "My goodness, you are a hungry male. Drummond, would you mind giving me another bowl, please?"

Drummond placed another bowl of applesauce on the counter, but Thagar stuck his finger in it to taste it. Elijah cried out. "He doesn't like sharin' much, does he?" teased Drummond, who retrieved another bowl. "Here ya' go, little one. A fresh bowl, just for you." Drummond was chuckling as he handed Thagar a spoon for the bowl of applesauce he'd tasted with his finger. "We haven't seen much of Kaleigh. I miss her, and I miss cookin' her favorite meals."

"She loves boat-hopping from one of my family members to another," said Thagar. "I never knew how much she longed for a large extended family that included grandparents, aunts, uncles, and so many cousins. I know it's still a novelty, but I really miss her, too. Between boat-school and sleepovers on my father's boat, or one of my brother's, I fear our daughter is never coming home. She is very independent, which I suppose is a good thing. And her seventh birthday is only fifteen days away. I wonder how she'll feel when we return to Earth for Isabela's wedding. Do you think she will want to stay or hurry back, Aelish?"

"I truly don't know. I never thought she'd adapt so well to the magical world. I just worry she's not being challenged in school."

"Oh, don't worry, my love. They've brought in a Keeper from the Breanon to give her private tutoring lessons, during the time the DARlettes are learning magic. Keeper Granger's knowledge about Human and Earthly history is unrivaled. He also has Kaleigh's gift of languages. So, each lesson is taught in a completely different Earthly or magical language from the previous day."

Aelish suddenly began to tear up. Drummond motioned to Thagar for him to look at Aelish. "Why are you upset, Aelish?" asked Thagar. He got up and sat down on the stool next to her. He began rubbing her back while she continued to feed Elijah. "I thought you'd be pleased her education and emphasis on new languages was not lacking."

"No, it's really great, Thagar. Thank you for being the best mate and father. Sometimes, I feel like I've missed so many things whilst I was in Yasteron and during my recovery. You've been amazing at keeping everything running smoothly whilst I try to get well. I appreciate it so much." Aelish wiped away her tears with the back of her hands. Thagar noticed Elijah had also started quietly crying. Both he and Aelish observed him wipe away his own tears with the back of his tiny hands, just like Aelish. "Oh, my God! Did you see that, Thagar?"

"I certainly did!" exclaimed Thagar. "Inherited mannerisms—incredible! Elijah loves you so much he can't bear to see you cry without crying himself. He's so sensitive and loving."

Elijah stopped eating and stared at Aelish. "I'm all right, sweetheart," she said to him. He reached for her face. She put her face closer to him and he wiped away her tears with his little hands. "Oh, Elijah, now you're really going to make me cry." Aelish started laughing and crying at the same time. She stood up and unstrapped him from his high chair so she could embrace him. He reached for her breasts, indicating he wanted to nurse.

Aelish brought him over to the couch facing the ocean. She sat down and began nursing. Thagar sat next to them to make sure Aelish was all right. When Elijah was satiated, he fell asleep with his tiny mouth still against her breast. Thagar looked at Aelish with tears in his eyes. "You're such a good mother, Aelish. I love you so much." He inched closer to her on the couch so their heads were touching. "There were many times I thought I'd never see you again. And I, most definitely, never imagined a moment like this. We are so lucky, my love."

Aelish nodded. "I am so grateful for our family, Thagar. Thank you for saving me and Elijah from a destiny I believe would have killed us both."

"I love you from DAR to Earth, Aelish, now and forever."

The three of them fell asleep together in the bright afternoon sun, reflected off the ocean.

29

MINDELATA

WHILE IT WAS somewhat inappropriate to bring young ones to a professional meeting, Elijah was still nursing and Kaleigh was the only Human living in the magical world. Thagar felt her perspective might be useful and that she would also get a lot out of it. He considered it an educational field trip, while at the same time, satisfying his and Aelish's desire to spend more time with their daughter. So, this morning, the whole family was heading to the location the SLEWs had chosen for the Human Sanctuary.

Aelish had never been to this part of DAR and Thagar had only been here once before. It was the last remaining magical wilderness of DAR, and it bordered the magical dominion of Mindelata. Before working on this project, and even as Director of the POD, Thagar had never stepped foot inside of Mindelata. The dominion was not as secretive as Hentoria but most DARlings and other magical beings did not visit here, as many remained fearful of those who inhabited it.

Today's meeting was taking place inside of Mindelata, near the border of the magical wilderness. First, they were going to transport inside the magical wilderness and then walk until they entered Mindelata. Thagar was curious to see Aelish and Kaleigh's reaction to the Giant they were meeting with today. Of course, Aelish was aware of Mindelata, but the only DARlings who'd ever spent any significant time in this dominion were Master SLEW Targo and Head Council Member Cheswick, in her role as Special Envoy for DAR within the Alliance of Magical Dominions.

Mindelata was the home of Giants. Unbeknownst to many, Giants were actually part of the Faerie Realm. And while Faeries were usually considered tiny or small, Giants demonstrated that this was not always the case. Giants were also part of creation myths in both the magical and Human world.

Mindelata was considered the guardian of the magical dimension and everything which had been created there. Giants of the mountains, the forests, the rivers, and the oceans held the wisdom and power of the entire magical world. Their enormous footprints represented knowledge that still defied comprehension. Giants were consistent advocates for humility and championed the ideals that all magical species needed to live in harmony with one another, as well as in harmony with the remaining natural world around them.

Giants had one clear message: become greater than you are, stronger than you are, and more effective than you think you can be. The reason the magical wilderness had remained untouched by DARlings was because it bordered Mindelata. The land of Giants served as a constant reminder for DARlings to not only care for the magical natural world but to also care for the weak, the vulnerable, the timid, and the innocent. Giants often looked after that which was not properly valued, like the natural world.

The sheer size of the Giants demonstrated how the magical dimension's origins emerged from the areas of wilderness, located throughout the magical dimension, and that the wilderness should always be cared for and respected.

The magical wilderness of DAR was the same size as Canada, the country with the second largest land mass on Earth. The wilderness spanned the N.E. and N.W. Quadrants of DAR to the north, and the dominion of Mindelata sat to the north of the wilderness. The ocean of the N.E. Quadrant not only bordered DAR, it also bordered Mindelata and the wilderness to the east.

While donating the landmass of DAR's magical wilderness to create a Human Sanctuary was a great sacrifice, Master SLEW Targo felt it would serve as an excellent cautionary lesson for magical beings as well as for Humans: not caring for that which created you is a dangerous and reckless philosophy which can result in the loss of one's entire existence.

Giants have always played a role in creation myths for magical beings as well as for Human beings. The folklore of nearly every region on Earth incorporates Giants into their creation myths. While in Human folklore, Giants are often portrayed as violent or barbarous, they can be also be extremely gentle. They have the ability to amplify the fear expressed by those they encounter and they can, in turn, send this fear back. However, if respect and kindness are bestowed upon Giants, they are capable of returning these gifts many times over.

Master SLEW Targo believed that by situating the Human Sanctuary on the border of Mindelata, the magic of the Giants would permeate the sanctuary and relay a message to the Humans of what they had lost—their homeland, the Earth. And the magic of the Giants would also relay a message of what the Humans had been gifted—a place of refuge and sanctuary by the commonwealth of DAR. It was DAR's hope that by living in such close proximity to Giants, Humans might once again remember the importance of the Earth and ultimately wish to restore and rehabilitate their birthplace so it could once again be inhabited.

Reis was the representative of all the Giants who lived in Mindelata. He occasionally attended Alliance of Magical Dominion meetings but only rarely. If Reis was in attendance, it meant war or unrest was brewing in the magical dimension. Head Council Member Cheswick personally knew Reis. Over the last two months, she'd arranged and attended many meetings in Mindelata with Reis and Master SLEW Targo. And in the last few weeks, Cheswick and Targo decided to include Thagar in these meetings.

Thagar would never forget the moment when he first met Reis. The sheer size of the Giant made him feel as tiny as an ant. Reis towered over Thagar in every way, as he was over twenty-five feet tall and ten feet wide. Comparatively, Reis made the Hentorians appear short in stature. He was a gentle being and could speak for hours about the philosophy of caring for the natural world, within both the magical dimension as well as the Human world. He also had an excellent sense of humor and understood exactly why DAR had chosen to situate the Human Sanctuary on the border of Mindelata.

Reis explained to Targo, Cheswick, and Thagar that Humanity had completely forgotten their creation myths and legends. They'd allowed their natural world to decline to the point where it was on the verge of no longer being able to sustain Human life. All the lessons of Giants had been forgotten, mostly for the sake of greed and selfishness. And the Humans were about to pay an incredible, unprecedented price. He'd seen it happen in other worlds, now bare of life, with temperatures and atmospheres so inhospitable that life could never return. He expressed concern the Humans might be incapable of relearning the importance of their natural world. And he was horrified they'd let so many species that lived alongside them to simply perish.

Targo explained to Reis that she hoped DAR could provide a temporary sanctuary for Humanity. It was the hope of DAR that the magic of Mindelata would penetrate the Human Sanctuary and the Humans might, once again, remember their origin story and wish to rehabilitate the Earth into a new and different world, where this could never happen again. Reis expressed his doubts that Humans would be able to do so, but his optimism got the better of him, and he agreed to placing the Human Sanctuary on the border of Mindelata.

Thagar was very excited to surprise Aelish and Kaleigh today, by having them participate in a meeting with Targo, Cheswick, and Reis. It would also be the first time Aelish had seen Cheswick since her abduction and separation from her fellow peace delegates, during the Peace Accord negotiations back in January. And Reis was very excited to meet the Living Legend of DAR, born of the Earth. He'd heard the incredible stories of her bravery, courage, and endless devotion to Earth. He was also fascinated Thagar and Aelish had created a Human offspring within the magical world, as Kaleigh's conception occurred in DAR's Great Rotunda of Peace.

The family was seated in the living area near the kitchen, waiting for Drummond to finish packing up food for them to take on their journey. At present, other than Thagar, Drummond was the only being who knew where the family was headed. And he made it quite clear to Thagar that he was glad to be staying home. He was terrified to lay eyes on an actual Giant.

"I'm all done, sir," said Drummond.

"Wonderful! Thank you, Drummond. Okay, are we all ready to transport?" asked Thagar.

Aelish smiled at his enthusiasm. "Perhaps, Thagar, it might be wiser to tell us where we are headed today?"

"Yeah, Daddy, why can't we know where we're going?" asked Kaleigh.

"Because it is meant to be a surprise and a surprise means you don't know ahead of time," replied Thagar. "All right, then. Look, Elijah is smiling. Is the DARlette the only one up for an adventure today?"

"Should I climb onto your back now, Daddy?" asked Kaleigh, getting excited.

"Come," said Thagar. She jumped onto his back and Thagar magically affixed her there so she couldn't fall off in transit. "All right, Aelish, hold my hand and let's transport."

Aelish looked at Thagar. She reached up to kiss him and grasped his hand.

‡‡‡‡

They arrived inside the magical wilderness, close to the border of Mindelata. All they could see for miles were mountains, evergreens, deciduous trees, rolling green pastures, and fields filled with wildflowers under an exceptionally clear and bright blue sky.

"Wow!" exclaimed Kaleigh, still on Thagar's back. "There are no buildings at all!"

Aelish turned in a circle so Elijah could see everything from his carrier. "Why have I never come here before?" she asked. "It looks exactly how heaven is described in the Bible. It's absolutely beautiful and it's so quiet."

Thagar let everyone soak in the grandeur of the untouched

wilderness, before telling them, "We are going to hike for about a mile into the dominion of Mindelata."

Aelish exclaimed, "Mindelata!"

But before they could take one step, Thagar spotted Reis approaching them.

Without fear in her voice, Kaleigh yelled, "Daddy! There's a Giant coming toward us!"

"Oh, my God!" exclaimed Aelish. "Thagar, are we in danger?"

Reis was actually a mile away from them. But he was so enormous that he appeared closer. "No, my love, we are in no danger at all."

"Let's go see the Giant!" exclaimed Kaleigh. "He's waving to us." Still on Thagar's back, she began furiously waving to Reis, and Elijah began laughing. Aelish was the only one still responding with trepidation.

"All will be well, my love," said Thagar. "Come."

He took hold of Aelish's hand and they began walking toward Reis. After about twenty minutes, they saw a beautiful tent set up with stair-chairs and refreshments. "Look, Momma, they've set up a tent for us," said Kaleigh.

"I see, sweetheart. It reminds me of the Gala for DAR for some reason, Thagar," said Aelish, smiling. Thagar was pleased she no longer seemed afraid.

By the time they reached the tent, Aelish whispered to Thagar, "He's taller than a two-story building." They all looked up at him and he smiled broadly.

"Welcome to Mindelata, beautiful family!" bellowed Reis.

Thagar took Kaleigh off of his back and put her on the ground. She ran over to say hello to Reis. The Giant knelt down to greet her. He was now as tall as a slightly smaller building. She reached out her hand and said, "Hello, my name is Kaleigh Grace Carrigan."

"Hello, Kaleigh Grace Carrigan. My name is Reis." The Giant extended his hand, which was as large as a twin-size bed, and said, "Hop onto my hand, little one."

Thagar heard Aelish's sharp intake of breath, but he pulsed her hand twice to reassure her. Kaleigh climbed onto Reis' hand and said, "You are really big!"

Reis began laughing. The sound echoed throughout the magical wilderness and Mindelata and came back around as if in a canyon. "Are you the Human child of Aelish and Thagar?"

"I am. I also have a few magical traits, like I can breathe underwater and speak any new language I hear." Reis began speaking in one of the oldest languages of the magical world and Kaleigh responded in kind.

"Absolutely amazing!" exclaimed Reis. He lowered Kaleigh back onto the ground and approached Thagar and Aelish. Thagar could see Aelish was having the exact same reaction as he did to Reis' size and stature. The ground shook when he walked.

He nodded at Thagar and then bent down on one knee in front of Aelish, again shaking the ground. "It is my honor to meet such a brave and courageous female DARling, Director Aelish. Your reputation precedes you, and I have always wanted to meet you face to face. This is a dream come true for me. He bowed his head in respect. When he lifted his head back up, he looked into Elijah's eyes. Elijah smiled at Reis and began laughing. "Your son, like your daughter, has no fear of me. That's because they are intrinsically good and kind. Even at his young age, this is quite apparent. You should both be very proud of your beautiful family. Come, there are others who have already arrived."

As they began walking toward the tent, Aelish asked Thagar, "How does he know Elijah is our son? You've obviously met him before. Did *you* tell him? I just realized I haven't told anyone in DAR about his parentage and we really need to, in order to keep him safe."

"I never told him. Reis is magically intuitive and literally represents the creation myth of everything possible within the magical world. He is extremely kind, very funny, and very gracious. There is also someone here who is quite anxious to see you."

Before she could ask another question, Cheswick came out of the tent. Aelish gasped and they began running toward each other. They embraced with Elijah between them and they both began crying. "Oh, Aelish, how I've missed you," said Cheswick.

Thagar took Elijah and his carrier off Aelish so she could properly embrace Cheswick. They held onto each other for several minutes. "I thought I'd lost you forever," said Cheswick. "I'm so sorry for everything you've been through, my dear friend. You look absolutely stunning and none the worse for wear. I can't believe I'm staring into your beautiful green eyes again." The two females, who hadn't seen each other in seven months, couldn't seem to let go of each other as tears flowed down their faces.

They both sat on the ground and continued talking with one another while Thagar walked over to the tent. He introduced Kaleigh and Elijah to Master SLEW Targo, who had remained behind in the tent, not wanting to detract from the reunion of Cheswick and Aelish.

"It's wonderful to see you again, Thagar," said Targo. "Come, let's sit with our host. Let's allow the females some time for their reconciliation."

"It's good to see you too, Targo," said Thagar, smiling as he entered the tent.

Inside the tent, Thagar observed that Kaleigh had already learned how to climb the staircase attached to each chair, called a stair-chair. The attendees all needed to be seated higher than normal chair height so they could be eye level with Reis, who sat on the ground.

Thagar climbed up his stair-chair, with Elijah in his carrier, and sat down between Kaleigh and Targo. Reis sat opposite all the chairs. There were two stair-chairs left for Aelish and Cheswick. "Kaleigh," said Reis, "if you would like some refreshments, please help yourself." Kaleigh looked at Thagar, who nodded at her, and she bounded down the chair staircase over to the refreshment table.

Kaleigh turned to everyone and asked, "Can I bring anyone something to drink or eat?" Thagar was so proud of her courteous manner; he felt like his heart was going to burst.

Thagar and Targo thanked Kaleigh but declined. Reis said, "There's a specific lavender sweet cake on the table. Your mother adores them, and I will take one as well."

"How do you know my mother adores them?" asked Kaleigh.

"Giants know many things that others do not."

"Cool!" exclaimed Kaleigh.

Aelish and Cheswick finally came into the tent, red-eyed but smiling. They looked at the two empty stair-chairs and Aelish saw a plate of lavender sweet cakes on one of them. "Is this stair-chair for me? Those look like the lavender sweet cakes I used to bring Hamish, the Portal Gatekeeper, on my way to Earth."

"I am well aware, Director Aelish," said Reis. "I made sure they were here, specifically for you. I believe the recipe comes from a city on Earth called, Dublin, in a country called, Ireland, where you were born. You used to go with your father to a sweet shop in Dublin, and you magically stole this recipe, which has been with you your entire life. Am I correct?"

Aelish gasped, astonished. "How did you know that?" she asked.

Kaleigh replied, "Giants know many things that others do not, Momma."

Reis burst out laughing and made everyone else laugh as well. His echoing laughter could be heard not only in the tent but also for many miles away.

Targo came down from her stair-chair and greeted Aelish with a broad smile. "It has been too many centuries since we last laid eyes on each other at the Sanctuary in the S.E. Quadrant. What a legend you've become since the last time we met, Director Aelish. I am so honored to see you again and thrilled you're going to become part of this project, as there is no other DARling who matches your devotion to Humanity. She embraced Aelish and they both began crying.

"Females have such a gentle way about them. It is unique only to them," said Reis.

When everyone was finally seated with drinks and refreshments, the meeting began. "We've had several preliminary meetings, Director Aelish," said Reis, "but we were waiting on your input before we proceeded any further in bringing our concept of the Human Sanctuary to the Head Council of DAR."

"I am so honored and very flattered," said Aelish.

Reis nodded at her. "I apologize if the first question I'd like to ask you is a difficult one for you to answer. But I personally need to know what a DARling of your stature, born of the Earth, truly feels about creating a Human Sanctuary. Do you believe the Humans deserve such a gift?"

Aelish became pensive before answering. "When Thagar first told me about DAR creating a sanctuary for Humans, I did experience concern at the chaos Humans could potentially cause in the magical world. Whilst the magical world has been fraught with wars and tribulations, such as DAR's endless proxy wars with Yasteron, the Human world is far more complicated. Whilst here in the magical world there are often great disagreements, rivalries, and even persecution of particular magical beings, we still look upon ourselves as one species."

"Can you explain how that is different from Humanity on Earth?" asked Reis.

"Humans forget they are all one species," replied Aelish. "They rarely refer to themselves as Human beings, whereas here, we always refer to one another as magical beings. On Earth, Humans define themselves much differently.

"Skin color is the first barrier of shared commonality. Humans divide themselves by race, and from that point forward, unity collapses even further. Religion is another great divider. Humans often identify with a particular faith, which adds another impediment to shared commonality. The country of one's origin is perhaps the greatest obstacle toward Humans seeing themselves as one species. They identify with their country of origin and this particular divide comes with an allegiance to that area of land. It may have a language spoken only there and a flag, which is a distinctive piece of fabric, treated with divine admiration and respect. Countries also have defined borders, meant to keep others out.

"The Earth is a shared space, but there are many rules and laws which distract Humans from seeing one another as the same. Whilst gender has always been utilized to oppress or subjugate, as of late, there has been some progress on that front. The final barrier is wealth. Money affords specific Humans with a power they don't deserve and entitlements they haven't earned. For me, it is the quintessential and most irritating barrier to a shared commonality."

Reis asked Aelish, "So, how do you envision the Human Sanctuary? Would areas of the magical wilderness need to be cordoned off for those of a particular race, religion, country of origin, language, gender, or level of wealth?"

"No," said Aelish. "Replicating the barriers that exist amongst Humans on Earth, here in the sanctuary, would not provide the necessary lessons Humans need to learn, in order to overcome their implicit biases toward one another. And should the genetic modifications of Humans prove successful, in that they could ultimately return to Earth, I believe they would continue living in the same manner that caused it to disintegrate in the first place. They would have been given a gift of salvation but without progressive development, culminating in a totality of evolution as a species, nothing would change. Despite being genetically altered, to breathe Earth's toxic air and no longer succumb to illness or disease, the essence of Humanity—how they treat one another—would remain the same."

"It sounds as if you feel Humans need to be genetically altered, intrinsically," said Reis. "As if they need to be modified so they may evolve into a kinder and more respectful life form."

Aelish replied, "Whilst that might be exactly what is needed for Humanity to evolve, it raises many ethical questions about the use of science. I also doubt it would be feasible on a such a grand scale. There are nearly nine billion Humans on the Earth. Even if half were to die because of the disintegration of their world, it would still leave over four billion Humans. Altering them to be able to breathe or not succumb to illness is one thing. Altering the very essence of Humanity is quite another. I'm also not convinced the Human condition can change."

Reis asked her, "Do you feel we should abandon this project, entirely?"

Thagar observed Aelish looking at Targo whose face expressed great disappointment at the idea of abandoning the project. He knew Targo was a true believer in saving those facing extinction, even if they'd brought it upon themselves. Both he and Aelish highly respected her altruism. And then, he saw Aelish look over at Kaleigh.

"Up until very recently, Reis," began Aelish, "I worried constantly about my Human daughter's quality of life on Earth. If disease did not claim her life outright, what kind of future was she facing living upon the Earth? I have only just become aware that Kaleigh can breathe in the magical world and cannot succumb to Human illness. Further, it is her DNA that will provide the key code for genetically modifying Humans. It was also her biological matter that enabled a brilliant young scientist on Earth to create a vaccine to prevent the climate syndrome known as LECCS. My child has given more to save Humanity than I ever could.

"So, for all the families on Earth with children they fear will never grow up, I know we must establish a Human Sanctuary here in DAR. There are far too many innocents who will be deprived of a long life on Earth, and simply put, it's just not fair to the younger generations. DAR incorporated within its tenets and principles, protection of the Earth and Humanity, as this is where Earth born DARlings come from.

"I am an Earth born DARling born of Human parents. To this day, I miss them so much it makes my heart ache. And whilst I've clearly seen and personally experienced the failings of Humanity, I could never abandon all the Kaleighs who live there. But when structuring the sanctuary, it must be done with input from the greatest scholars and philosophers from both the Human and magical world. How do you teach a species to self-correct in order to survive?

"Built within the configuration of the dwellings, which will comprise the communities of the sanctuary, there must be unavoidable lessons that compel Humans to overcome their inability to see each other as one species. Through the involuntary lessons we create, Humans will have experiences which will further their evolution into a species who can accept and respect the difference of others, whilst at the same time, allowing those different from themselves to retain their dignity."

Kaleigh stood up and said, "Those who choose not to accept and respect the differences of others, doom us all to a life without dignity. Is that what you mean, Momma? You're talking about the words engraved directly above the doors of the Great Rotunda of Peace, right?"

All the DARlings began to tear up at the most eloquent phrase ever written to describe what the acronym of DAR—Dignity, Acceptance, and Respect—stood for. Aelish wiped tears away and said, "Yes, my sweet angel, that is exactly what I mean." Aelish smiled at Thagar, who smiled back. His face was beaming with pride as tears ran down his face.

"It appears DAR," said Reis, "has already taught your Human daughter a very important lesson of creation: treat all living things and the natural world which created them with endless respect and dignity. This is what Humans have forgotten and why they find themselves in such a precarious situation. The last Humans who still respect the Earth as one entity are the Indigenous Peoples and First Nations. The irony is they were also the First Peoples. They still hold fast to their creation myths, legends, and stories passed down through generations. They want their offspring to never take the Earth for granted and to understand how easily extinction can occur, when the natural world which created you is forgotten and polluted."

"Agreed," said Aelish. "I absolutely do feel the Human Sanctuary project should go forward. But as DARlings, it is our responsibility to design it in such a way as to further Human evolution. Humans need to finally understand that their fellow Human beings are all equal parts of Humanity, created by the Earth. And the barriers erected to divide them must disappear."

"In that case," said Reis, "I make a motion to move this project forward, so it can be brought before the Head Council of DAR. Do I hear a second?"

Cheswick raised her hand and said, "I second the motion."

"All right, motion approved," said Reis. "Targo, has there

been any progress in creating Human Portals throughout the Earth that would lead them directly into the Human Sanctuary?"

"Oh, my goodness," Aelish said quietly.

Targo smiled at Aelish and said, "Yes, Reis. The SLEWS have figured out a way to manipulate the magical technology of the Portal, so the new portals can be specifically adapted to accommodate the difficulties Humans have with transporting and breathing our air. Human Portals will be placed throughout the Earth so the climate refugees will not have to travel far to reach one. The portals will then lead Humans directly into the Human Sanctuary of DAR, as well as to another realm that has recently stepped forward and offered a sanctuary for the Humans."

"What?" exclaimed Aelish. She turned and looked at Cheswick, Targo, and then Thagar, who shrugged his shoulders and shook his head. "What other magical dominion has offered sanctuary for the Humans?"

Cheswick smiled at Aelish. "Two days ago, I was contacted by Special Envoy Ragdon from Yasteron." Aelish gasped. "Ragdon indicated that he'd just received permission from Queen Saia to begin discussions on donating their own magical wilderness, which borders a portion of the dominion of Hentoria, in order to create a sanctuary for the Humans escaping the climate crisis on Earth."

"Oh, my God!" exclaimed Aelish.

Cheswick continued, "The covert operatives of Yasteron wish to return to their homeland along with their Human mates and offspring, whom they call Yastermans. Further, they have volunteered to have their offspring and their Human mates be the first to be genetically modified on Earth, using the CRISPR technology, so the DNA key code that lives inside of Aelish and Thagar's daughter, Kaleigh, can be used to allow them to breathe in Yasteron. It has been determined by Yasteron experimenters that the Yastermans have inherited an immunity to Human illness, like most magical beings. Therefore, only their Human spouses would need to be genetically altered to prevent them from succumbing to any Human illness, like LECCS.

"Ryker, the covert operative's leader, stressed to Special Envoy Ragdon and Queen Saia that this will be the first reparation from Yasteron to Humanity for all the actions they've perpetuated, which contributed to the loss of Earth. Whilst Yasteron acknowledges that the DARling SLEWs have harnessed the ability to recreate different Earthly environments to accommodate the breathing restrictions for Humans within the magical world, the Yasteron covert operatives have offered up their Human mates and their offspring as the first to be experimented on, instead of Humans from the general population. This way, if anything goes wrong during the scientific process, Humans would benefit from any necessary corrections.

"Ryker added that whilst it may take centuries for Humans to be able to return to Earth, once it becomes unhabitable, Yasteron must offer this life-saving reparation to the Humans. They share the hope that Humans can be genetically modified successfully, so they may, one day, return to Earth, be able to breathe its contaminated atmosphere, not succumb to Human illness, and begin restoring its viability.

"And may I add one last thing: none of this would've been possible without the extraordinary sacrifices made by Director Aelish, Policy Director for Earth, who was kidnapped during the Peace Accord negotiations between DAR and Yasteron. She was held captive in Yasteron and forced to endure unimaginable circumstances for months. Thank you, my dear friend, for making this a reality." Cheswick blew Aelish a kiss.

Thagar sat there stunned, remembering what Amelia had said to him about the Yastermans in the drunken tavern in the lower-orders' section of Yasteron: '*Who knows? Maybe they will end up being a good thing for the Earth.*' He shook his head in disbelief that her words had already rung true.

And then, he looked over at his beautiful mate, who had tears streaming down her face. Everything Aelish had sacrificed and everything she'd put in motion during her captivity had brought DAR and Earth to this moment. Thagar could see the profound effect of Ryker's words on her. Ryker, the leader of the covert operatives, had received one of the four letters Aelish had given to Master Oba, in one last attempt to incite a revolution within Yasteron. Finally, with Queen Saia precariously in charge, the first act of contrition by Yasteron was on the horizon.

30

ISABELA'S WEDDING

A ELISH AND DRUMMOND were still packing and getting everything ready for the family's departure to Mexico City today. Isabela's wedding was taking place at the Hacienda de San Miguel, the new home Drew had bought for Isabela in memory of Abuela.

"So, whilst we're gone, Drummond, make sure Storm gets lots of exercise."

"I will, Aelish," said Drummond. "And I'll take him for walks on the beach, and we can also go into the woods so he can do a little huntin'. I will take good care of him. Don't worry."

Aelish's nerves were frayed. She was excited, nervous, and anxious all at the same time, and she kept dropping things while she was packing. Thagar walked into the cacophony and witnessed Aelish drop a platter, which crashed to the floor. "Oh, my God! What is wrong with me today?" she yelled.

While Drummond magically repaired the platter and put it away, Thagar came over to Aelish and tightly embraced her. "You need to take a breath, my love," he whispered into her ear. "All will be well."

His strong arms around her felt incredible and Aelish suddenly felt very tired. "Did you just put a calming spell on me?"

"Just a tiny one, to help you relax a little."

"Thank you," she said, still embraced in his arms. "The last time I saw Isabela was on January 8th. I can't believe her wedding is on August 8th—seven months to the day! I hope she will be happy to see me. However, I don't know if Marisol's idea of having me be in the bridal party is going to sit well with Isabela. I know she won't mind Kaleigh serving as a flower girl with Hector Rios' daughter, Elenita, but what if she doesn't want me in her wedding party?"

"Before I go wake Kaleigh, sit with me for a few minutes." He led her to the couches.

Aelish sat on the couch facing the blue of the ocean, which further calmed her. She took a deep breath and closed her eyes for a moment. Thagar sat opposite her with his back to the water.

"So, I spoke with Tozer yesterday," he said. "Did you know Isabela contacted him whilst we were in Hentoria?" Aelish's eyes opened wide. "Once she and her mother determined Yasteron did, in fact, burn our Bunker Hill home to the ground, Isabela knew Yasteron had decoded the Safeguard spell, which I'd placed on both our homes. So, Tozer crafted an elaborate new Safeguard II spell; he named it, I didn't. They've become such good friends. It made me so happy she felt like she could count on him to help her."

"I'm so proud of her," said Aelish. "Did Tozer come to Earth to apply the spell?"

"He did, and Marisol and Isabela made dinner for him."

"Oh, my God. He didn't try to seduce anyone whilst he was in their home, did he?"

"No, of course, not. He's incorrigible but was very respectful of Isabela's parents, especially in light of Marisol losing her mother to Yasteron."

"Thank goodness, he remembered his manners. So, our first stop on Earth will be to our burned house. Do you still agree Kaleigh should see it?"

"I do. She needs to know the house is, in part, why we have not returned to Earth."

"And are you still okay with all of us going to see Abuela's grave in Los Angeles?"

"Yes, I know how important it is to you, and it will give Kaleigh some closure, too. Oh! I almost forgot to tell you. Tozer informed me that Director Giles of Experimentation will be expanding the operations of Department 427. They are planning to create a new division for tracking the documentation of Humans who will placed inside DAR's Human Sanctuary.

Oh, wonderful! Tell me more," said Aelish.

"The Human Portals will be equipped with technology that can scan the identity of the climate refugees. Humans can use their passports, birth certificates, or other forms of identification, like their driver's license. Sometimes, there may not be time to retrieve documents stored in secure locations, like a safe deposit box. Inside the portal their photos will be taken along with an image of their ID, if they have one, and the names of those needing sanctuary.

"Tozer and his Satyrs will create a database to keep track of all those entering DAR. DAR, in turn, will share this technology with Yasteron so our two dominions can share data with one another to avoid any Humans getting misplaced. Just like the Climate Refugee Intake Centers, we will create intake centers within the landmass which will contain the Human Sanctuary. It will follow the same concept as the CRIC. Humans will be assessed, including their age, a complete medical evaluation, educational needs, languages spoken, and occupational skills. They'll stay within the intake centers until we've sorted out exactly where they should be placed within DAR's Human Sanctuary or if they should go to the sanctuary in Yasteron."

"I still can't believe Yasteron has agreed to create a Human Sanctuary and that our two dominions will be working in concert in the near future. It seems like a dream."

"It was a dream, Aelish. It was your dream," said Thagar, smiling at her. "Now, disease is one of the most concerning issues. We need to make sure the Komprathians, who are able to contract Human illness, are not exposed to any Human diseases, either directly or indirectly. Whilst I'm personally used to contamination issues like this from the CRIC, we have to be sure DARling Human Sanctuary workers are properly trained.

"I imagine Humans with medical expertise will work in the medical facilities we'll create for both general healthcare as well as for gene editing. Most importantly, Humans will need a purpose whilst they are here; a purpose for living will provide contentment. The sanctuary must also allow Humans to continue experiencing the arts, such as music, theater, opera, dance, literature, as well as the culinary arts. Boredom and idle hands will only lead to trouble."

"Agreed," said Aelish. "I will incorporate all of this into the report I'm working on with Cheswick for the Head Council and Melanthia's review. By the way, what's the name of the new division?"

"The Division of Human Documentation or the DHD. Tozer said the acronym reminded him of the DMV or the Division of Motor Vehicles—"

"Where one can literally lose their mind!" exclaimed Aelish. "I had to go there once to fix something with the registration of our SUV on Earth. It was positively maddening."

"Tozer felt it would make the Humans feel more at home," said Thagar, chuckling. "Okay, let's wake Kaleigh now. I want to make sure she still fits into the flight suit I created for her. I also made something for both Kaleigh and Elijah to wear over their eyes and ears to protect them from the noise of the thunder and the brightness from the lightning within the Portal." He saw the worried look on Aelish's face. "Don't worry, they will both be fine, Aelish."

"It's a shame we don't have time to use the Portal avoidance route," she said with a smirk on her face. "One day, I suppose you will show me how it works?"

Thagar stood up and came over and planted a big kiss on her mouth. "I most certainly will but do keep the route between us. No one was supposed to know about it, but I think that ship may have already sailed." He started laughing. "I assume we'll use Elijah's normal carrier? Oh, and I made sure both their retinal codes are in DAR's records for the Portal Gatekeepers."

"Yes, to the carrier and thank you so much for handling all of that," said Aelish. "Was it problematic for Kaleigh's eyes?"

"Not at all. She didn't feel a thing when they inserted the code."

"That could bode well. Perhaps a retinal code could be implanted into the eyes of Humans, whilst they are still inside the Human Portals, prior to entering the Human Sanctuary."

"Excellent suggestion. I will pass it along to Tozer. All right, let's get a move on!"

"Copy that, Director!" Aelish stood up and deeply kissed Thagar. "I love you so much."

‡‡‡‡

Everything went well through the Portal. The entire family landed in the woods, close to the park by their old house, where Aelish had encountered the Mystic when Kaleigh was a baby.

"How do you feel, Kaleigh?" asked Aelish.

"Can you first get me out of this suit?" asked Kaleigh. "It's so hot in here."

Aelish started chuckling at her daughter. While Thagar helped

Kaleigh out of the suit, Aelish removed Elijah's protective eye and ear coverings. He looked at her and smiled. "You were such a good male in the Portal, but I think maybe you need changing?" She felt around and determined he did, indeed, need changing. While Aelish attended to Elijah, Thagar put down a blanket on the ground. He magically shrunk Kaleigh's suit into his flypack. He then retrieved the breakfast Drummond had packed for everyone, which was also inside his flypack.

They all sat on the ground, including Elijah, who could now sit up on his own. Aelish and Thagar made sure the young ones were fed and hydrated before they began eating. "This reminds me of our first date at the Sanctuary in the S.E. Quadrant, Aelish. Do you remember?"

"I remember that I didn't know what a picnic was," said Aelish, chuckling.

Kaleigh started giggling. "How could you not know what a picnic was, Momma?"

"Well, I was born in 1546 and we didn't use that term on Earth yet. But Daddy loved picnics and in the Sanctuary was the first time I ever had one. It's wonderful to share Daddy's tradition of picnics with you and Elijah. Kaleigh, have you thought about what we discussed, regarding our former house? It's going to be shocking to see, so you need to prepare yourself."

"I know, Momma. I'm ready."

When they were all finished, they packed everything up, magically created a stroller for Elijah, and began walking through their old neighborhood. Aelish felt like she'd been gone for a century. As they came to the top of Bunker Hill Road, she gazed down toward the bottom of the cul-de-sac and saw the emptiness. All the beautiful trees which had graced the five acres behind the house were gone, as was the entire house. She'd chosen not to look at it from DAR through her Earth Viewer and decided to experience the moment with her family. Even Thagar had not taken a look through the Earth Viewer.

As they began walking toward the charred and burned-out lot, Aelish began crying. All the memories of buying the house with Isabela and Lady Antonia came flooding back. While she'd experienced so many conflicting emotions while living on Bunker Hill Road, including a longing for DAR, seeing the charred ground left her bereft.

"There isn't one piece of the house left," remarked Thagar. "At least they magically controlled the burn so the fire didn't spread to other houses." They stood on the street and stared at the property. Then, Kaleigh went running up to the very top of the hill. Thagar was so focused on Kaleigh that he didn't see Aelish's tears. Kaleigh now stood, where Aelish and Lady Antonia had first transported to view the house for the first time.

Kaleigh called to out to them, "It's so much bigger than I remember!"

Thagar turned to Aelish, "I think Kaleigh—" He saw Aelish's tears and embraced her.

Aelish said, "I can't believe Stannon did this to us, simply out of spite. I was gone from Yasteron. Wasn't that what he wanted all along? Why did he have to destroy the home where we made such beautiful memories?"

Thagar replied, "Because he was a rapacious, power-hungry being. He must have been furious Kaleigh survived the carbon monoxide event. I think he burned our house down more for that reason than in retribution for my rescuing you."

Aelish nodded. "What is she doing at the top of the hill?" she asked Thagar. "Kaleigh! Please, come down from there, now." But something had captured Kaleigh's attention.

Thagar climbed up the steep hill and waved to Aelish from the top. She saw them both digging at something in the ground, and then they both began climbing back down. Thagar was holding something in his hand.

"You don't have to look at this, Aelish, you really don't," said Thagar. In his hand was an envelope addressed to Lady Aelish. "It must have been placed up there after the fire started and was magically protected from the elements."

Aelish looked at the envelope and then at Kaleigh, who looked very worried for her mother. "I'm okay, Momma, but you look like you've been crying. Are you okay?" Aelish knelt down and embraced her daughter.

"If you're okay, I'm okay," said Aelish. She kissed Kaleigh on both cheeks. "Well, should I open it?"

"Open it and be done with it," said Thagar.

"Yes, Momma, open it," said Kaleigh.

Aelish sat down alongside Kaleigh on the sidewalk. Elijah was asleep in his stroller and Thagar stood at the ready. No other neighbors were around. She began reading the letter aloud:

My Dear Lady Aelish,

Never in my life have I been asked as a soldier to perform such a despicable act as burning down a family home. I hope you will forgive me. I found something in what I assume was your daughter's bedchamber. I knew it must have been very special to her, as I found it under the covers of her bed. I imagine she slept with it every night. When you are ready to receive it, use the Recover spell and it will appear. I'm so sorry I did not have time to save more keepsakes for your daughter.

With my deepest regret,

Captain Somerset

"Oh, my God!" exclaimed Aelish. "A Yasteron soldier with a conscience!"

"Do you know this soldier, my love?" asked Thagar.

"No, I have absolutely no idea who he is."

"Well, he obviously found Stannon's order detestable," said Thagar. "Use the Recover spell and let's see what Kaleigh is about to receive." Kaleigh began quietly clapping.

Aelish quietly recited the spell and a somewhat smoky-smelling bear appeared. Next to Big Bear, he was Kaleigh's favorite. She slept with him every night."

"Rex!" exclaimed Kaleigh. "Oh, my gosh, I never thought I'd see you again!" She put the bear next to her face and began crying. "I'm so happy we came back, Momma. We found Rex!"

Aelish used a spell to remove the odor of the fire from the bear. Although, she didn't think Kaleigh cared one bit about how it smelled.

Thagar said, "Drummond must not have been able to find it in time, because it was hidden under the covers. I'm going to send him a telly and let him know we found Rex." Aelish watched as Thagar put his hand against his temple. In a few moments, he began nodding at Aelish. "Drummond said he is so happy. He looked forever for Rex but couldn't find him. He was joyfully crying and said to send his love to everyone."

"I'm so happy!" exclaimed Kaleigh, who began walking down the street having an in-depth conversation with Rex.

"Well, that was a surprise," said Thagar.

"Truly," said Aelish, who began smiling. "I'm thinking of deeding the property to Isabela as a wedding gift from us. This way, they can build a new house and she can stay close to her parents as well her new CRISPR lab. I'm going to ask her if they could also build a small guest house on the hill, where the trees used to be. Then, we could stay in the guest house whenever we visit Earth. This would enable us to remain close to Isabela, Drew, Marisol, and Jorge, as well as the Climate Refugee Intake Center, when we want or need to come to Earth for an extended period of time. What do you think?"

"I think it's a beautiful wedding gift, Aelish," said Thagar. "So, we've decided, then? We will stay in DAR and Kaleigh will be educated there? Her educational model could be used as a template for how to structure education for the refugees within the Human Sanctuary."

"Yes, I think so, Thagar. And that's a great idea! Your extended family is providing Kaleigh with amazing stability in DAR. She's so happy spending time with your father and your stepmother, Scarlett, as well as your half-brothers and sisters who also have offspring, giving her even more cousins. And she adores Kane, Kaden, and Kaleb, as well as their mates, and all of their offspring. She has so much extended family in the N.E. Quadrant.

"And you and I will be working on creating the Human Sanctuary in the wilderness, so it just makes sense to primarily stay in the N.E. Quadrant. After all we've been through, I imagine the Head Council will allow us to also keep the Artist's House in the S.E. Quadrant. I couldn't bear to part with it because the house contains so many special memories, including where we performed the Rapture to create both Kaleigh and Elijah. And we can stay with Kaleigh in the Artist's House if she attends specific classes at the Institute or at the Breanon. We can then determine if those classes might be suitable to teach the Humans in the sanctuary. I think she can receive a good primary education in DAR. By the time she's old enough for college, if the Earth still has colleges and universities, she can come back and finish her education here."

"I like the idea of a guest house on this property," said Thagar. "It could easily fit a three-bedroom guest house on the top part of the hill. And we can plant new trees around it for privacy. I hope the township of Brookdale allows two dwellings on one property."

"If they don't," said Aelish, "somehow, I think Drew can make it happen. I really hope Isabela and Drew like the idea because then we could have the best of both worlds until the

Earth is uninhabitable. And I'd like Isabela's new baby and Elijah to be friends, as they will be less than a year apart in age. I've estimated Isabela's due date to be around March 12, 2027, and Elijah was born on April 16, 2026."

Thagar said, "Wow, incredible! And despite the fact that DARlettes mature so much faster, they really will be close in age. I'm sure they won't mind, Aelish. Deeding the land is a very generous gift, which will keep our families close together. And after all, what do you give a billionaire for a wedding gift? The property is perfect because it has sentimental value. And they could build a beautiful modern structure with the same magical materials created in DAR, used in all the climate refugee settlement sites here on Earth. No storm or evil magic spells could ever take it down. Somewhat the opposite of Yasteron burning our house down."

"I'm so glad you like my idea," said Aelish. She smiled at Thagar. "Okay, I think it's time we transport to Los Angeles to visit Abuela's grave now, my love. Here comes Kaleigh."

"Agreed." Thagar looked at Kaleigh, who had returned from her walk with Rex. "We are going back to the woods by the park so we can transport to Los Angeles to visit Abuela's grave. And you don't have to wear the flight suit. Hooray!" Kaleigh high-fived Thagar.

‡‡‡‡

They landed in a wooded area of the cemetery where there were no Humans, dead or alive. Everyone rested and Kaleigh drank lots of water along with her second meal of the day. Elijah woke up cranky and Aelish decided to nurse him to give him comfort.

When everyone was fed, had drunk fluids, rested, and Elijah was changed, they set off on foot for Abuela's grave. Marisol had sent Aelish a map of the cemetery, and Aelish had calculated the distance from the wooded area to where the gravesite was located.

"Now, remember to be respectful in the cemetery, Kaleigh," said Aelish. "Don't walk upon the graves and stay on the designated pathways."

Kaleigh shook her head at her mother. "Duh," she said, deeply exhaling.

While her response was less than what Aelish and Thagar would consider respectful, her sarcasm provided the precise level of humor for this somber occasion. Aelish looked at Thagar and they both began chuckling as they shook their heads at their daughter.

Kaleigh was the first to arrive at the headstone. "Here she is, Momma!" Aelish and Thagar purposefully stayed behind as they watched and used an auditory spell to hear what she was saying at the grave. They observed her touching the headstone as she continued speaking.

"I really miss you, Abuela," said Kaleigh. "I miss your stories, I miss speaking Spanish with you, but most of all, I miss how much you made me laugh and how naughty you were. You were so much fun to spend time with, and even though I have real grandparents now, I still miss you so much that my stomach hurts sometimes. But when I feel that way, I take out one of the books we used to read together in Spanish, and you come back to me.

"When Daddy took me flying, I felt so close to you. So, I know you are in heaven watching over us. And I know I will see you again after I get really old. But you might have to wait a little longer than usual, as I might live 500 years. We'll see. But I know you'll be there to welcome me, when it's my time to leave both DAR and Earth.

"The Earth is getting really sick, so Momma and Daddy are

trying to save everyone by bringing them to DAR. But I know you wouldn't have liked moving to DAR. So, you really aren't missing very much, but we sure do miss you. I hope you and Abuelo are having a good time together. I know how much you missed him. Please always remember me, Abuela. I will always love you, and I can't wait to see you again."

Aelish and Thagar watched as Kaleigh wiped tears away and sat down beside the grave. As they quietly approached Kaleigh, they were both in tears. Aelish asked, "Are you all right, sweetheart?" Aelish looked at the headstone and remembered all the fun she'd had with Abuela. She'd been a grandmother to her, and they'd shared so much, especially their faith.

"I'm okay, Momma. It's just very sad here because I wish she could speak to me, even one more time, ya' know? She was so funny, so nice, and such a good cook. I miss her food."

"Me, too," said Aelish. Aelish touched the headstone and said some internal prayers in Latin. She told Abuela how sorry she was that she'd lost her life because she knew them.

Thagar conjured a deck of cards and magically placed fifty-two cards all around her grave. "I miss our poker games and doing shots of tequila with you, when I'd let you win. Okay, I didn't always let you win, but I did most of the time." He started chuckling. As Elijah slept in his stroller, Aelish, Thagar, and Kaleigh sat together at Abuela's grave. They held each other's hands remembering Abuela, who'd meant something different to each one of them. Aelish could not believe Abuela had died because of Yasteron. It still seemed surreal she'd gotten caught in the crossfire of Stannon's plot to kill Kaleigh. Aelish said a prayer of thanks that her daughter had survived—that they'd all survived—and were on their way to Isabela's wedding. Aelish promised to pray for Abuela's soul to be at peace, every day.

"Whilst I wish we could take Abuela and Abuelo with us to

Mexico City to watch Isabela get married," said Thagar, "I think it's time for us to transport now."

They walked back to the woods by the cemetery and packed up all their things. Aelish turned to Thagar and said, "When we are less than a mile from the Hacienda de San Miguel, I'm supposed to text Drew with the code: Lavender." Thagar burst out laughing. "I can't believe Drew bought her a huge house in Mexico City. But what a great way to have close friends and family attend a destination wedding."

"It's also a great way to control security and the press," said Thagar. "Drew told me they were only allowing access to a few media outlets. And for the privilege of posting the photos or videos on their media platforms, they have to donate any profits to a climate-crisis organization."

"Oh, I love that idea," said Aelish. "In fact, it follows along the same lines of what I was thinking about regarding billionaires and the very wealthy receiving safe harbor in DAR. Since they won't need money in DAR, I think they should be required to donate one-half of their wealth toward the betterment and repair of the Earth."

"The price of admission to DAR?" asked Thagar, chuckling. "Well, we can certainly ask Drew how he feels about that whilst we are in Mexico. Very interesting concept, my love. Okay, are we ready?" Aelish and Kaleigh nodded. Elijah, who'd awakened, smiled. "Let's transport!"

‡‡‡‡

Never in her life had Isabela had such a beleaguered conversation about cheese. She was standing in the kitchen of the hacienda with her mother and Lucinda, Abuela's old friend whose son, José, owned the restaurant El Cardenal in Mexico City. She and Drew had hired mother and son to cater both the rehearsal dinner and the wedding. She stared at her mother and Lucinda, trying to understand why five choices of cheese had become such an issue, when the guests would be served hors d'oeuvres, later this evening, at the rehearsal dinner.

"We could have the servers rotate the cheese selections at each pass?" Isabela suggested.

"Or," said Aelish, standing at the threshold of the kitchen, "you could serve them all at the same time."

Isabela froze upon hearing Aelish's voice. She slowly turned around and saw the beautiful, smiling face of her Oraculi. "Oh, my God! Aelish! You're here!" Isabela went running over to Aelish and began hugging and kissing her. "Why didn't you tell me you were coming? Oh, my God, I'm so excited you're here!"

Marisol said to Lucinda in Spanish, "This is who we were waiting for while we kept the bride occupied with the discussion of how to serve the five cheeses." Lucinda started laughing as Marisol made her way over to Aelish.

"Hola, Aelish. My God, it's so good to see you." Marisol tightly hugged Aelish and yelled to the ether, "Did you all catch that on the cameras?"

They heard the static of an intercom and Drew's voice saying, "We did! And it was beautiful! We will be in the kitchen in five."

Isabela turned toward her mother and said, "The cheese thing was just a distraction?"

"Si, mija," said Marisol. "And it worked!" She high-fived Lucinda and began laughing.

Kaleigh came running into the kitchen. First, she embraced Isabela, and then she gave Marisol a big hug and a kiss. "I've missed you both so much!"

"You've gotten so big and are so beautiful, Kaleigh," said Isabela.

"Look, you're almost as tall as me," said Marisol. Kaleigh began laughing.

Thagar entered the kitchen with Drew. Elijah was in his carrier on Thagar, facing outward, so he could see everyone. He began laughing, which was like a magnet for all the females in the kitchen. Marisol got to Elijah first and tickled his toes and gave Thagar a big kiss on the cheek. "I've missed you so much, Thagar, and I'm so excited to meet your son."

"You are looking well, Marisol," said Thagar. "Are you feeling well?" Everyone knew Thagar was referring to her cancer and she smiled at him.

"All good for another six months!"

"Excellent," he said.

Jorge came into the kitchen and said, "Now that everyone is here, all the cameras and monitors have been turned back on." He shook hands with Thagar, gave a big hug and a kiss to Aelish, kissed little Elijah's hand, and then picked up Kaleigh, twirling her all around the kitchen. "Come, let's sit in the living room for a little while."

Isabela gave Drew a look, which she knew Aelish had caught, indicating Isabela's father was quite comfortable at the hacienda. With the exception of Lucinda, everyone followed Jorge into the living room and sat down. Isabela sat next to Aelish. She took Aelish's hand and kissed it. She whispered, "I didn't know if I'd ever see you again. You don't know how happy you've made me by coming to my wedding."

"I've missed you so much, Isabela. You will never know how much," said Aelish.

While Isabela quietly chatted with Aelish, Thagar asked, "So, when are the rest of the guests arriving?"

Drew replied, "Isabela's extended family and best friend Gaby are all upstairs, people from Devereux Enterprises are at a small hotel nearby, my father and his family will be here in an hour, Javier is out for a run, and Antonia and Amelia will be here tomorrow for the wedding."

"Oh, my God!" exclaimed Aelish. "I didn't know Antonia and Amelia were coming!"

Isabela said, "Antonia would've killed me if I'd gotten married without her present."

Just then, Javier came into the living room. "Hola, everyone!" As he made his way around the room, Isabela watched everyone greet Javier. Isabela was so proud of her brother. At twenty-six he was incredibly famous and highly respected in the world of sports. He'd always been handsome, but as he got older, he was only getting more handsome. And his physique matched his professional athlete status. She realized it'd been years since Aelish had last seen him. Watching Javier greet everyone, Isabela suddenly had an idea.

"Mom," said Isabela, "would it be all right with you if Aelish were my Matron of Honor? This way, you could sit with Dad after he walks me down the aisle and relax as the mother of the bride."

"I was praying you'd ask!" exclaimed Marisol. "Hector is Drew's Best Man, Aelish, so you and Hector will be on either side of Izzy and Drew. And Gaby and Javi will be attendants next to you and Hector. Elenita and Kaleigh will be flower girls. Would you like that Kaleigh?"

"Oh, my gosh, I would love that! Do I get to wear a white dress, like Izzy?"

"You do, and you will find it upstairs in the bedroom you'll be sharing with Elenita," replied Marisol. "You will be the first down the aisle, Kaleigh, with Elenita following, as you are the youngest. Then, will come Izzy and Jorge. Your mom, Drew, Hector, Gaby, and Javier will already be under the canopy, with the priest, where the vows will be exchanged."

"I get to be first down the aisle? That is so cool!" exclaimed Kaleigh.

Aelish turned to Isabela and quietly said, "I am so honored you want me to be your Matron of Honor, Isabela. Further, I can't believe you're getting married tomorrow. You're just a little older than most brides during the 1500s." Isabela burst out laughing. "Do I have a suitable dress here? If not, I could always conjure one."

"Wait, Mom!" exclaimed Isabela. "We don't have a dress for Aelish!"

"Of course, we do, mija. I bought one just in case. It's in the casita, waiting for Aelish."

"We do? The casita?" asked Isabela. "I thought that's where you and Dad were staying?"

"Oh no," replied Marisol. "We moved all our stuff out early this morning to one of the upstairs bedrooms while you were sleeping. The casita is perfect for Aelish, Thagar, and Elijah."

"You will also find a brand-new crib in there," said Drew, smiling.

"So," said Isabela, "everyone knew Aelish, Thagar, Kaleigh, and Elijah were coming except me, correct?" Everyone nodded. "Nice job! I'm impressed." She blew a kiss to Drew.

"Well," said Marisol. "Let's get you all settled in so you can have a little rest before tonight. A Mexican rehearsal dinner is just like a wedding reception, so get ready to party. Come upstairs with me, Kaleigh. I want to show you your dress while Izzy and Drew take your mom and dad to the casita. You can stay with them, of course, if you prefer."

"No, I want to stay with Elenita," said Kaleigh. "Is that okay with you, Momma? I just haven't seen her in so long."

"Of course, sweetheart. But listen to everything Marisol tells you, okay?"

Kaleigh rolled her eyes at Aelish and pulled on Marisol's arm to take her to her room.

As they all got up to go to the casita, Aelish turned to Isabela and said, "That's the second time today Kaleigh has sassed me. She's only going to be seven on August 18th, not thirteen."

"She's gotten so big and is so mature, Aelish," said Isabela. "Remember, her IQ is over 160. She's going to be a handful as she comes into adolescence. This is just a little taste."

"Look at you, Isabela! Ready to be a mom, already. Are you and Drew going to find out whether it's a boy or a girl beforehand, or are you going to wait?"

"We already know! These new ultrasounds can already determine the sex."

"Oh, my God, so soon! And?"

"What do *you* think it is?" asked Isabela.

Aelish tilted her head, looked upward, and then exclaimed, "A girl!"

"Bingo! You are correct!"

"Oh, my God, Isabela! I'm so excited. Have you and Drew chosen a name yet?"

"Juliette, after Drew's deceased mother and Maria, after Abuela."

"Ohh, that's so lovely," said Aelish. "Juliette Maria Torres Devereux."

"Drew says we'll probably end up calling her Jules, like his mom's nickname."

"Either way, it's a beautiful name, Isabela. I'm so happy for you."

‡‡‡‡

Aelish stood next to Gaby and across from Drew, Hector, and Javier under the canopy, covered in flowers. She watched Hector whisper something to Drew, who was exceptionally nervous.

Hector winked at Aelish. Watching Kaleigh come down the makeshift-white aisle on the grounds of the hacienda, was a moment she'd always remember. Kaleigh's white dress made her look like a princess, with its lace bodice and short sleeves, ballooning out at the waist into yards of tulle. A large satin bow on the back of the dress led to a four-foot train. On her head she wore a sparkling tiara. She sprinkled white rose petals from her basket onto the aisle as if she'd done it a thousand times before. When she reached the end of the aisle, she waited for Elenita, and then the two girls went to sit with Hector's wife, Marielena, as well as Thagar and Elijah.

Aelish and Gaby's dress mirrored the lace theme of the flower girls, except Isabela had chosen them to wear a light pink, form-fitting, short-sleeved gown. The short sleeves and entire bodice were made of pink lace, with a satin fabric belt at the waistline, and an A-line floor length bottom. Aelish wore her hair in an elaborate updo with flowers scattered throughout. Her bouquet, like Gaby's, was made of all white flowers. Around her neck, Aelish wore pearls, which had been her mother's.

When Isabela appeared at the beginning of the aisle with her father, Aelish fought back tears. Isabela's veil covered her face and her dress was a simple off-the-shoulder gown, with lace around the top of the bodice. It was form-fitting, made of a luxurious fabric, and the back of the dress had fabric-covered buttons from the top to the bottom of her ten-foot train. Her hair was straightened in a simple updo, underneath a stunning tulle wedding veil. Around her neck, she wore only the necklace of Saint Michael from Abuela and drop-pearl earrings, given to her today by her parents. She looked like a queen.

After looking at Isabela, Aelish turned to look at Drew, who had tears in his eyes. It was something she always did. After a brief look at the bride, she loved to watch the reaction of the groom. When they reached the canopy, Jorge lifted her veil, kissed his daughter, and Isabela handed Aelish her elaborate bouquet as she took hold of Drew's hand. Aelish looked out at the guests assembled and found Lady Antonia and Amelia, who were waving, crying, and smiling at Aelish. Lady Antonia had been right; Drew would marry once he found the right mate. And he had, in Isabela. Aelish still could not believe her bold decision to tell Drew about the magical world on his helicopter had led them all to this moment. It was one of the happiest days of her life. She blew a kiss to Thagar who was bouncing Elijah on his knee while Kaleigh remained standing, not wanting to miss a minute of anything.

The service was performed in Latin, in honor of Abuela, and was a traditional Catholic wedding service. Last night, Isabela told Aelish that while she was still an avowed atheist, being married by a Catholic priest was very important to Drew and her parents. So, she did not object. The Archbishop of Mexico City had to provide his authorization for the sacrament of marriage to be performed outside of an actual church. What sealed the deal was the fresco which sat in the hacienda from a 13th century church, making the hacienda a holy site.

When the priest pronounced them married, Drew and Isabela shared a passionate kiss. Aelish imagined, to them, everyone in attendance just disappeared. She could clearly see how in love they were with one another. She was so happy for Isabela. She'd finally gotten over all the heartache caused by Glen and had found someone who loved her for who she really was. Aelish let out a big sigh of relief. Isabela was whole again and ready to begin the next chapter of her life. And Isabela's happiness furthered Aelish's own journey of recovery and healing.

31

Amends & Adaptation

AELISH AND ISABELA were sitting together on the bench in front of Abuela's favorite tree, shaped like an elephant. All the wedding guests had departed, with the exception of Isabela's mother, father, and brother, as well as Aelish, Thagar, Kaleigh, and Elijah. Lady Antonia and Amelia had left on Sunday so that Lady Antonia could resume teaching at the Institute in DAR and Amelia could resume her classes. It was early morning and everyone else was still sleeping from the exhaustion of the weekend, with the exception of Isabela's household staff who were preparing breakfast.

The wedding weekend had gone off without a hitch, and all the guests had a fabulous time. Aelish still found it fascinating that the last time she'd seen Isabela was before Sartaine's Commitments Ceremony and the next time they saw each other was at Isabela's wedding; two weddings bookended their last encounter and their current reunion.

"So, how are you really doing, Aelish?" asked Isabela.

"I'm getting better, but I would definitely not say I'm back to normal. Knowing Thagar is Elijah's father has helped me more than anything, as well as his unconditional love. But I'm still haunted by sleepless nights. And when I do sleep, I usually have nightmares. Medicus Clove and I are working hard on my mental health treatment plan, and it is helping, but it's very hard work. I also hope to use how we are tackling my own mental health issues as a blueprint for the hundreds of captives once they are released by Yasteron."

"I'm so sorry for everything you've been through," said Isabela. "Do you really think Yasteron will honor the Peace Accord you sacrificed so much for?"

"I can only hope, Isabela. The civil war continues, but I believe in the end, Queen Saia and the revolutionaries will ultimately triumph. After it is over, we shall see if the queen will truly relinquish the monarchy."

"You're so strong, Aelish," said Isabela. "What you've been through is indescribable. But I know your sacrifices will be rewarded in the end."

Aelish looked at Isabela. "Perhaps and thank you. I'm so relieved you finally found some peace, Isabela, and the love of such an incredibly generous man."

Isabela looked deeply into Aelish's green eyes. "I'm so sorry for all the things I said to you before you left for Sartaine's Commitments Ceremony. I hope you have forgiven me."

Aelish smiled at her. "The first time I saw the magical glow on my abdomen, indicating I was pregnant with a magical being, was the morning of your twentieth birthday. I lay in my prison and thanked you for the best gift I could have ever received, in honor of your birthday. Once I got pregnant, Cardissius promised to leave me alone. And he did, until he forced me to marry him so Elijah could reign. Then, whilst pregnant, I had to perform the Endeavor, yet again, to consummate the marriage."

"Antonia told me in our letters that he forced you to marry him so the heir wouldn't be a bastard. But she never told me if he physically raped you as well as magically. Did he? Please, forgive me for asking. I suppose it doesn't really matter since you were raped, regardless."

"Oh no, it matters, Isabela. By the grace of God, Cardissius only magically raped me. He was never inside of me." Aelish looked at Isabela with tears in her eyes, which matched those in Isabela's eyes. "But it distorted my mind, you know? Thagar and I have yet to perform the Rapture. The first time with Cardissius, I was so confused. Why was the Endeavor so similar to the Rapture? At the time, I had no idea Yasterons had evolved from DARlings."

Isabela reached for Aelish's hand and held it tightly. "My God, Aelish. I'm so very sorry for everything you've endured. Did Thagar tell you he saved my life when I tried to kill myself in the psychiatric hospital? It was the darkest moment of my entire life."

"Yes, he told me. It had a tremendous impact on Thagar, and my heart broke in half at the pain you were in because of my decision to tell Drew everything."

"No, Aelish. That wasn't the reason." Aelish looked at Isabela. "I blamed myself and the hurtful way I spoke to you for your decision to go to Yasteron. I knew your life was in danger. Ultimately, I came to understand that regardless of the harsh things I said to you, prior to you leaving for DAR, you still would have gone to Yasteron. Drew explained that nothing was going to stop you from trying to secure peace between DAR and Yasteron. Was he right?"

Aelish nodded. "Yes, but after all Yasteron had done to you, I also knew I could never face you again if I didn't go. And I truly believed we were about to achieve something monumental, by finally bringing peace to the magical world. But it was all a ruse."

"Let's not speak of the past anymore. I don't want my questions to retraumatize you."

Aelish nodded her head. "Well then, before I tell you something I only recently learned about Yasteron, I'd like to give you your wedding gift whilst we are alone." Aelish conjured the deed to 5805 Bunker Hill Road and handed it to Isabela. "I want you and Drew to have this, so you can be close to your parents and close to your new CRISPR lab. You were the one who found me the house, so I've always felt like it was ours anyway."

Isabela looked at the deed and then at Aelish. "Oh, my God, Aelish. I can't accept this."

"Of course, you can," said Aelish, smiling. "But I do have one request."

"Anything," said Isabela.

"When you build an indestructible house on the property, using DAR's magical materials which no storm or evil magic spell can destroy, would you mind also building a guest house on the backside of the property at the top of the hill for me and Thagar? I don't want to feel far away from you ever again. I thought if our families lived close to one another, it would keep you and I close, forever. We are planning to live primarily in DAR, thanks to your incredible discovery of Kaleigh's DNA key code, but we will also need to be on Earth for extended periods of time. Would you be open to this idea, and do you think Drew would be okay with it?"

Isabela began to tear up. "I absolutely love this idea and so will Drew. I've been so sad because I knew once you learned Kaleigh could breathe in the magical world, you'd most likely go back and live in DAR. But now, we'll always be close to one another through the property. Have you realized that Juliette and

Elijah will be less than a year apart in age? Well, in Earth years anyway. I hope they can somewhat grow up together."

Aelish smiled. "I did realize that and was thinking the same thing before we left DAR. It's incredible!"

Isabela said, "I don't ever want us to be separated again because of hurt feelings and misunderstandings, Aelish. I love you too much for that to ever happen again."

"Me, too, Isabela. I'm so happy," said Aelish. They embraced one another as tears ran down their faces. They both wiped away their tears with the back of their hands and began laughing when they saw each other performing the same mannerism. "You won't believe it, but Elijah wipes his tears exactly the same way we do."

"No way! You're kidding me?"

"When Thagar and I first saw him do it, we couldn't believe it. It made me yearn for you. I couldn't wait for you to meet our son. Every day, I thank God that Thagar is Elijah's father."

"We've certainly come a long way since the first time you came into my bedroom when I was twelve years old. You changed my whole life, Aelish, and my mother is still alive! And please, don't blame yourselves for Abuela. She wouldn't want that. Thank you for everything."

"I miss her, Isabela," said Aelish. "Well, I have one other wedding gift for you."

"Absolutely not!" exclaimed Isabela. "The deed is already too much."

"Well, this gift is not something of a material nature." Isabela looked at Aelish confused. "Yasteron has managed to procreate with Humans."

"*What*?" asked Isabela. "But I thought that was impossible?"

"Whilst I was imprisoned in the kingdom, I was allowed the privilege of meeting their Master of Archives. His name is Oba. That's how I learned about the entire history of DAR and Yasteron.

To my dying day, I will never understand why Cardissius ever let me near him. Anyway, Oba told me how the covert operatives on Earth became aware of the fact that one of their youngest operatives, Glen, was undercover as the lover of a brilliant, young, Human scientist—you. They also became aware of the fact that he'd turned over all your research to the kingdom. After Glen gave your research to the experimenters in Yasteron, those who were politically aligned with the covert experimenters on Earth and wished to overthrow the reign of King Cardissius, eventually returned your research to the covert experimenters on Earth.

"So, Yasteron experimenters, both in Yasteron and on Earth, began studying the Human genome to see if they could discover a way to *stop* the extinction-looming event you were researching. They joined the SOS organization you initiated, working alongside Human scientists. Eventually, they discovered the bacterium you were searching for, which ultimately led to the discovery of LECCS—the experimenters were actually trying to *save* Humanity because they were in love with one specific Human."

"Oh, my God!" exclaimed Isabela.

"You see, whilst the experimenters were working on the bacterium, many of Yasteron's operatives throughout the Earth were in romantic relationships with Humans. They decided to marry them, without divulging that they were magical beings. There was great disappointment when they failed to produce offspring."

"Didn't the Yasteron operatives know they couldn't procreate with Humans?"

"The Kingdom of Yasteron was so insular, they were unaware of this fact. And then, something unexpected started to happen: female Humans and female operatives began to conceive, only to miscarry over and over. Unable to bear the suffering of their

Human spouses, the operatives came to a consensus—they decided it was time to divulge their secret."

"Did the mixed couples break up after that?" asked Isabela, completely intrigued.

"Not as many as you would think; love is a powerful force. So now, many of the operatives were exposed. But it was right around this time that Yasteron experimenters, on Earth and in Yasteron, made the astonishing discovery that a commensal strain of E. coli was going to morph into E. coli O157:H7 or LECCS. The Humans who'd married Yasteron operatives forgave them, as they'd unlocked the mysterious bacterium poised to extinct all of Humanity.

"Once you and other scientists, who Tozer vetted and confirmed were *not* covert Yasteron experimenters, began to work on the LECCS vaccine, the Yasteron experimenters, both on Earth and in Yasteron, turned their attention back toward finding a way to successfully procreate with Humans. From all their early research on the bacterium, the experimenters had become experts in the science of DNA, overall genetics, and the Human genome."

Isabela exclaimed, "That's why they're so good at genomics!"

"Exactly," said Aelish.

"Well, thank you for finally solving that mystery," said Isabela. "But wait, if so many of the operatives had Human spouses, why did Yasteron create a bioweapon of LECCS?"

"Master Oba explained to me that this was never their intent. Chief Minister Stannon, Cardissius' closest and most powerful advisor, discovered the experimenters in Yasteron were working on a Human bacterium. In reality, they were assisting the covert experimenters on Earth trying to *stop* the climate syndrome. But Stannon forced their hand. So, they lied and told him they were working on a bioweapon to kill Humans. Stannon never did discover that the *Earthly* covert experimenters had worked on the bacterium. If he had, things could've gone differently.

"However, lying about developing a bioweapon severely backfired on the experimenters in Yasteron. Once Stannon got a taste for bioweapons, he ordered them to take their bacterium research and turn LECCS into an *actual* bioweapon. In order to continue assisting the covert experimenters on Earth with their procreation research, the experimenters in Yasteron had to continue developing bioweapons to avert suspicion. The captive Komprathian drone rats were experimented on for the LECCS bioweapon, but Stannon wanted more. He ordered the experimenters in Yasteron to develop a specific bioweapon that worked only on DARlings. So, the experimenters were forced to experiment on the plethora of DARling soldiers, who still remain in captivity, to this day, until they developed the DARling Draft."

Isabela said, "Horrible! But how did they achieve success in procreating with Humans?"

"The first Yastermans were born in rogue labs on Earth, using the technology of in vitro fertilization along with a new technology that created an artificial womb. And obviously, a Yasterman is the name of the offspring between a Yasteron and a Human."

"Wait!" exclaimed Isabela. "I know science has made great strides for infants born prematurely to be placed inside of artificial wombs until they can complete their gestation. But to create a life through in vitro fertilization grown entirely in an artificial womb is decades away. How did they do it? Also, can Yastermans breathe in the magical world?"

"Oba told me that when they combined magic with science, procreation became possible. And no, the Yastermans cannot breathe in the magical world. But they've inherited an immunity to Human illness, like most magical beings. And this is the wedding gift I'd like to bestow."

Isabela looked at her utterly confused.

"Do you remember me mentioning Special Envoy Ragdon from Yasteron who served on the Alliance of Magical Dominions?" asked Aelish.

"Yes," replied Isabela. "He was the being who'd bring your conditions and stipulations of the Peace Accord to the attention of King Cardissius, right? I've always wondered if he was the one who betrayed you into being imprisoned."

"You truly are a genius, Isabela. He did, in fact, betray me. But he was forced to go along with Chief Minister Stannon and King Cardissius' plan to kidnap me during the Peace Accord mission. Otherwise, it would have been discovered that Ragdon was actually the conduit between the covert operatives on Earth and the revolutionaries in Yasteron who wished to overthrow King Cardissius. Shortly before I gave birth to Elijah, Master Oba delivered four letters for me which incited the civil war that Ragdon helped coordinate."

"Oh, my God, Drew was right!" exclaimed Isabela. "Drew told me once you were inside the kingdom, you'd have more power to effect change than through all the negotiations you'd attempted before. He knew you'd find a way to wreak havoc in Yasteron, and you did."

Aelish smiled humbly. It still did not feel like a victory.

"But wait," said Isabela. "What is the other wedding gift? The fact that you incited a revolution in Yasteron? Of course, that's an incredible gift—"

"No, Isabela. The gift is the Yasteron covert operatives, with the permission of Queen Saia, have offered up their offspring and their Human spouses to be the first to receive the DNA genetic modifications, using the CRISPR technology, to be done by *you*. And I imagine, you will find yourself working side-by-side with Yasteron covert experimenters who've been on Earth for some time. They are desperate for a successful outcome, which will afford their Human spouses and their offspring with the ability to breathe in the magical world so they can all return home."

Isabela stared at Aelish with her mouth open and an expression of disbelief on her face.

"And I suggest you perform this new science without asking permission from the United States government. First, be successful with the gene-editing procedure. Then, you will be in a much stronger position to ask for authorization to perform gene editing on the general population. Whilst I imagine the scientific community will continue objecting on ethical grounds, I also believe that once Humanity becomes desperate enough to survive the climate crisis, science and governments will ultimately acquiesce. In fact, I think Mexico is the perfect place to establish a rogue lab to begin your initial experiments on the Yastermans and their Human spouses." She looked at Isabela, who was speechless. "I can see your head is spinning from everything I've just told you. Especially, with regard to establishing a rogue lab. But sometimes it's better to ask for forgiveness than to ask for permission."

Isabela burst out laughing at her Oraculi. "You've become a revolutionary."

"Apparently," said Aelish, smiling.

After a scrumptious breakfast, everyone retreated into the living room to digest and relax. Aelish was thrilled by how happy Isabela was after everything she'd told her. Isabela was beaming and Aelish knew she was very excited to begin her new scientific research. LECCS was just on the horizon and it was going to be devastating for the Earth. But Aelish knew the gene-editing technology of CRISPR gave Isabela hope that Humanity still had a chance to survive. While under the elephant tree, Aelish had chosen not to tell her yet about the Human Sanctuary. She wanted to give her at least a couple of hours to process all that she'd relayed. However, she did plan on telling Isabela about the sanctuary, prior to leaving for DAR.

"So," said Javier, "not only have they installed a pitch clock in order to speed up the game, which I feel is totally ruining the game, but the overall rising global temperature is also allowing for more home runs. The warm air is less dense than the cool air, allowing for batted balls to fly much farther. It's fueling a home-run spree and we pitchers are getting all the blame."

"I never even considered that," said Thagar to Javier. "Absolutely fascinating."

"While baseball is my life," said Javier, "I can clearly see how the baseball executives are ruining the game, in their attempts to save it, by making it a faster game with a pitch clock. And at the same time, it's a home run free-for-all. The only sound that keeps me up at night is the crack of the bat. Unless, of course, I'm the one holding the bat." Everyone started laughing.

"I don't know how you stand the heat on the mound, Javi," said Isabela. "Aren't the players begging for more night games?"

"Oh, for sure. But you know, even though EMT's are taking fans from the ballpark to the ER because of heat stroke, the game must go on. I'm waiting for the day when a game is called on account of climate change."

"I actually can't believe that hasn't happened yet," said Aelish.

"Well, speaking of baseball," said Javier, "would you like to go outside and play a game of catch with me, Kaleigh? Did y'all by any chance bring a baseball glove or a mitt for her?"

Aelish sent a telly to Thagar and told him to magically conjure one inside the casita. Thagar said, "I did bring a glove for Kaleigh as we often play catch together."

Aelish sent Kaleigh a telly telling her to keep quiet and that her father was going to magically make a glove for her in the casita. Kaleigh nodded to her mother.

Thagar stood up and headed toward the casita. Aelish sent him another telly reminding him that the security cameras were active and to not be caught on camera using magic. Fifteen minutes later, he returned with a perfectly worn-in glove for Kaleigh.

"Here you go, sweetheart." Kaleigh put on the glove and punched it with her other hand.

"Thanks, Daddy," said Kaleigh. "I'm ready, Javi."

"Go easy on him, Kaleigh," said Jorge, chuckling.

"Very funny, Dad," said Javier. "Ok, kiddo, let's go throw some balls."

As they walked toward an open field on the grounds of the hacienda, Kaleigh said, "It's so cool you're an actual major league baseball player, Javi."

"It's a lot of fun," said Javi. "So, do you play baseball or softball in school?"

"Actually, we only play soccer. I don't really like it because I can't use my hands."

"Me, too," said Javier. "Although, I can play a pretty fierce game of soccer."

He handed Kaleigh a baseball and began walking about twenty feet away from her. "Okay, do you want to throw underhand or overhand? Underhand is easier."

"I want to throw the way real baseball pitchers do," said Kaleigh.

"Are you sure? Because underhand is easier than overhand."

"I'm sure."

"Okay," said Javier. "I'm ready. Throw the first pitch."

Kaleigh threw the baseball, overhand, which landed with a

smack into Javier's glove. "Wow! That was really fast," he said. "Maybe I should back up a little farther." Javier walked another ten feet, making them thirty feet apart. They were about half the actual distance between a pitcher and home plate in a professional stadium, which was sixty feet, six inches. He threw the ball back to her; she caught it with absolutely no problem. "Okay, throw me another pitch."

Kaleigh threw the ball again—same thing. The speed of her throw was astonishing for a seven-year-old, and it landed precisely in his glove.

"Wow, Kaleigh!" exclaimed Javier. "You've got some arm on you. I didn't expect that."

"Thanks," said Kaleigh. "One day, maybe I can play for the Red Sox in DAR."

"In DAR? What's DAR?" asked Javier.

"You know," said Kaleigh. "The magical commonwealth where my parents are from."

"There's no such thing as a magical world, Kaleigh," said Javier. "Quit playing with me. And the only Red Sox are in Boston."

"Don't tease me, Javi. You know my parents are from DAR."

Javier stared at her. "Hey, Kaleigh, I'm going to go inside for a second to get some water. I'll be right back. You can still practice by throwing the ball above you and catching it."

Javier walked into the living area where Elijah was asleep in a playpen and Aelish, Thagar, Drew, Isabela, Marisol, and Jorge were all talking and laughing.

"Excuse me, everyone," said Javier. "Sorry for the interruption, but can anyone here tell me where DAR is?"

Everyone froze and stopped talking. No one said a word.

"Why isn't anyone answering me?" he asked. "What the hell is going on?"

Suddenly, Kaleigh appeared in the doorway of the living room and went running over to Aelish. She whispered into her ear, "Momma, I think I told Javi something I wasn't supposed to tell him. But I assumed he knew because he's Izzy's brother." She began crying.

Jorge came over and went to embrace his son, but Javier evaded the hug. Marisol stood up and came over to Javier. Aelish knew his anger was only masking his feelings of betrayal. "Mijo," said Marisol, "I know you feel like your family hasn't been truthful with you. You're confused and you feel like we've hidden something from you, and you'd be right—we did. But it wasn't because we didn't trust you. It was because we were trying to spare you from the burden of knowing about the magical dimension."

"There is no magical dimension! Are you all insane?" Kaleigh began crying harder.

Jorge said, "Javi, your mother and I only recently learned about the magical dimension this past January. Izzy was the one DAR recruited to help save the Earth and Humanity from the climate crisis."

Aelish could see Javier was furious. He began pacing the room. "Izzy, why didn't you tell me?" he asked. "I thought we always promised to never keep secrets from one another."

Isabela began gently crying and walked over to Javier. "I'm so sorry, Javi. Aelish swore me to secrecy because if the governments on Earth knew about the magical dimension, it would undoubtedly put the magical world in danger. DAR is a commonwealth in the magical world, and they've secretly been working to help Earth and Humanity survive the climate crisis."

"Well, they aren't doing a very good job now, are they?" accused Javier.

Kaleigh was still buried in Aelish's bosom and continued crying. Aelish whispered something to Kaleigh and then stood up. She walked over to Isabela and embraced her. "Here we go again, Isabela. I'm so sorry." Aelish began softly crying. Through her tears, Aelish observed that the tears from the females in the room were having a profound effect on Javier, as even his mother had begun crying. She knew he'd never want to upset his mother, especially after all Marisol had been through. He finally sat down on one of the chairs and put his head in his hands.

After a few moments he looked up and asked, "Why didn't anyone tell me about this?"

Marisol knelt before Javier and said, "Izzy agreed to work with Aelish and DAR because Aelish was able to put No Pain spells on me, which helped me endure and survive the experimental cancer trials. While magic cannot cure disease, Javi, Izzy agreed to work with DAR for my sake. I knew nothing about any of this until this past January, when Aelish told me everything after Izzy became so mentally unwell and had to go to the psychiatric hospital."

"That's why you survived the trials, when nearly all the other participants died?"

"Yes, mijo," said Marisol. "Without the No Pain spells, I know with certainty, I would not be alive today. Aelish and the commonwealth of DAR saved my life. But it's Izzy and Aelish who've paid the greatest price for trying to save Humanity from extinction by the LECCS syndrome, caused by the climate crisis, which continues to deteriorate conditions on Earth.

"However, no one has forgotten the sacrifices you made, by delaying college and your baseball scholarship at UCLA, so you could take me to my treatments and help Abuela care for me throughout the entire ordeal. When it came time for you to leave for school, only Izzy knew about DAR. Your father and I knew nothing. We haven't even known for a year."

Isabela said, "Glen was actually a covert operative from the

Kingdom of Yasteron. He was a very talented baseball player who stole all of my research and gave it to the kingdom, that then turned LECCS into a bioweapon. He lied to both of us, Javi. Aelish and Thagar only discovered who he was because of a new spell invented by Antonia's husband. Thagar was severely injured while interrogating Glen in an underwater bunker in DAR, which Yasteron blew up."

"There isn't anyone in this room, including you," said Thagar, "who hasn't lost something or someone because of Yasteron. They infiltrated Earth a long time ago to exacerbate the climate crisis, sow war and overall chaos, pushing Humans to destroy themselves. Aelish was born on Earth of Human parents, as was Antonia and her late husband, Roger. The Earth born DARlings have the greatest magical capabilities within the magical world."

Looking at Thagar, Javier asked, "But how has Yasteron affected me?"

Everyone cast their eyes downward, but it was Kaleigh who shocked everyone. She came over to Javier and stood in front of him. "This past January, Yasteron tried to kill me."

Aelish gasped. "Oh, my God, Kaleigh! You know this? Daddy and I never told you!"

Kaleigh replied, "After Drummond came to Hentoria, you got really sick, Momma. One day, I was sitting by your bedside and you were talking in your sleep about how Yasteron soldiers tried to kill me in the carbon monoxide poisoning event. I knew you didn't want me to know about it, so I never told you what I heard you say." Aelish put her hand over her mouth.

"Momma has been trying to make peace with Yasteron for a very long time, but they are very difficult," said Kaleigh. "They tried to kill me in order to hurt Momma, but it was Abuela who ended up dying. At the time, no one knew I had magical traits, not even my own parents. Izzy discovered it after she got out of the psychiatric hospital. I can breathe toxic air, like carbon monoxide, as well as the thinner air of the magical dimension, which is very high up. I'm so sorry you lost Abuela, Javi. And I'm so sorry about how I told you about DAR. I made a mistake. I thought you knew because you're Izzy's brother. I miss Abuela so much."

Suddenly, Javier began crying. "That's why Abuela died? Oh, my God."

For the next two hours, they all explained everything to Javier, who was still in shock but was no longer angry. He began to understand why they'd let him live in peaceful ignorance.

"Well," said Aelish, as the mood in the room shifted, "I suppose this is as good a time as any to tell you all about the Human Sanctuary."

"The *Human* Sanctuary?" asked Isabela. "I know there's a sanctuary for extinct species."

Aelish said, "DAR has taken the same technology used to save mythical and extinct species on Earth and expanded it. They can now magically engineer the atmosphere and terrestrial ecosystems needed to sustain Human life, within the magical world. DAR is donating the last of their magical wilderness in order to create a Human Sanctuary. It is approximately the size of Canada."

Isabela said, "That's incredible, Aelish. Humans get a Plan B!"

Aelish said, "Thagar and I will be working on this new project together, which is primarily why we need to stay in DAR. The Human Sanctuary will be to the north of DAR's N.W. and N.E. Quadrants, spanning the distance of both, from the west to the east."

"And the N.E. Quadrant is where all of my extended family lives!" exclaimed Kaleigh. "I have grandparents now, and aunts and uncles, and tons of cousins."

Marisol smiled at Kaleigh and came over to give her a big hug and a kiss. She looked at Thagar and said, "The whole concept of the Human Sanctuary reminds me of the CRIC and the new settlement sites built for climate refugees. It sounds so similar, with the exception that people will be relocated from Earth to the magical dimension. Am I correct in my thinking?"

"You are, Marisol," said Thagar, smiling. "And we were hoping you'd take on the role of Human Sanctuary Director." Marisol put her hand over her heart and smiled at Thagar.

Aelish also smiled at Thagar and sent him a telly: *Nice one, my love! Really beautiful!*

Thagar winked at Aelish. She said, "Ultimately, the Earth will become uninhabitable."

Marisol nodded, saying, "It used to be a distant reality, but it's coming faster and faster."

"It's incredibly generous of DAR," said Drew, "to try and accommodate so many Humans. But the landmass size of the Human Sanctuary and nearly nine billion Humans is not adding up to me. How could the entire population of Earth fit inside of Canada?"

"Not to be grim," said Aelish, "but by the time the Earth becomes uninhabitable, there will no longer be nearly nine billion Humans on the Earth. Those who chose not be vaccinated before the overall global temperature flips the switch on LECCS will die. And even if we include those who rush to obtain the vaccine, within the seventy-two-hour window of effectiveness, many will have waited too long and die. This will be Earth's first major Human die-off. Then, as the global temperature climbs, cascading climate events will occur, killing more and more Humans. And as the Earth heats to unimaginable temperatures, new pandemics will emerge, which the Human fever will no longer be able to kill, as pathogens will have adapted to the extreme heat of the planet. We won't know the exact number of Humans who'll have survived until it's time to evacuate the Earth. But it certainly won't be close to nearly nine billion."

"I understand now," said Drew. "We are a very sad species. But what about the CRISPR technology Isabela plans to use to genetically modify Humans?"

Aelish replied, "Isabela can begin that science here on Earth, but there will never be enough time to finish all the modifications before the Earth becomes uninhabitable. DAR will construct a facility for her to continue her scientific work so that, one day, Humans can return and make Earth viable once again."

"Wow!" exclaimed Javier. He stood up from his chair and poured himself a whiskey. "This is really complicated! No wonder you had a nervous breakdown, Izzy. Eight years?"

"Some of it has been horrible, Javi, but some of it has also been wonderful." Isabela smiled at Aelish. "Please, forgive me for not telling you sooner. I almost did the day you came to see me in the psychiatric hospital before we all left for Abuela's funeral."

"But you didn't want to burden me further, correct?" Javier asked. Isabela nodded. "Well, I guess my baseball days are coming to an end."

"No, Javier, not at all," said Aelish. Javier looked at her puzzled. "Now that you are part of our inner circle, I was hoping you could help us plan the proper sporting facilities we'll need within the Human Sanctuary. Sports have always been one of the greatest barrier-breakers between Humans. We'll need sporting arenas where Humans can continue competing in a variety of sports whilst they're in DAR. After all, you were Thagar's inspiration for bringing baseball to DAR. And now, there's a multitude of teams there that mirror Earthly teams—"

"Like the Boston Red Sox in the S.E. Quadrant!" exclaimed Kaleigh. "But unlike on Earth, girls are allowed to play. Also, until I was playing catch with you earlier, I had no idea I had a good arm. I'm so excited! I never thought of myself as a baseball player."

Thagar looked at Javier and asked, "She has a good arm?"

Javier replied, "I've never seen anything like it for someone her age. Wait! If she never played baseball before, how did you have a broken-in glove with you that fit her perfectly?"

Thagar wryly smiled at Javier. "Oh, my God," said Javier. "You went to the casita and magically made one, right?" Thagar nodded at him. "Well, I know there are security cameras all over this hacienda, but I think after the day I've had, I'm definitely owed a magic show."

Everyone burst out laughing.

"Your head must be spinning, Javi," said Drew. "I know mine was when I met Aelish on my helicopter, who appeared *mid-flight* after I'd been shot at the WHO. And then, she and Isabela just vanished off the helicopter when it was time for them to leave." He shook his head remembering. "But DARlings are very good beings, Javi."

"Not like those from . . . what was the name of the kingdom?" Javier asked.

"Yasteron," said everyone together.

Thagar said, "My beautiful mate suffered horribly during her captivity as a prisoner of Yasteron. She was kidnapped during a peace mission and was held for over four months. But in that time, she managed to set in motion a civil war which may finally allow the citizens of Yasteron to develop into a more egalitarian dominion. In the near future, we hope they will dispense with their monarchy and finally live in peace alongside us."

"And one final bit of news, Isabela," said Aelish. "Yasteron has offered up the last of their magical wilderness for a *second* Human Sanctuary. I still can't believe it. Thagar and I only learned about this a few days ago. So, along with what I told you earlier this morning, Yasteron has also offered to create a Human Sanctuary, in furtherance of the reparations they feel they owe Humans because of all their heinous actions."

"Oh, my God!" exclaimed Isabela, shaking her head.

"So," said Aelish, "at some point, in the not-too-distant future, all of us will be living in DAR. I bet you never imagined that was going to happen!" Aelish started laughing, as did everyone else, including Javier, who'd finally come around.

"Let's celebrate!" exclaimed Jorge, who popped open a bottle of expensive champagne.

Aelish caught another look between Isabela and Drew about how comfortable her father was in the hacienda. She imagined they were saving that champagne for when the baby was born. Aelish internally told Abuela: *I know you are here with us, and everyone is doing great.*

32

SUMMATION

THE OVERALL GLOBAL temperature flipped the switch on the Lancaster E. Coli Climate Syndrome a week before Christmas, 2026. But the temperature didn't stay at 1.4°C for long. By New Year's Day, it was at 1.5°C and climbing. Even with a worldwide vaccination rate of seventy-five percent, billions of people died. Some of those who'd hedged their bet and took the vaccine within the seventy-two-hour window of the onset of the 1.4°C temperature did survive, but they represented only two percent of the worldwide population.

LECCS had killed 2.07 billion people or twenty-three percent of the worldwide population of nine billion people. Only two percent were saved by the seventy-two-hour window, but it still represented 180 million souls. LECCS had killed more people than all of the bubonic plague outbreaks combined, estimated at 200 million people, over the course of more than 1,000 years. LECCS had killed billions in a matter of one week—seven days. All of Isabela's dire predictions had materialized. While science may have regained its reputation, it came at a horrific cost of Human life.

LECCS mercilessly killed the elderly and young children who were severely immunocompromised, despite being vaccinated, due to their comorbidities. Isabela and her team of scientists had hoped this wouldn't happen, but the climate syndrome was horrific.

The Earth was in complete chaos, as the loss of life occurred predominantly in the industrialized nations, causing the global economy to come to a complete standstill. The supply chain wasn't interrupted, it was completely broken. LECCS had a drastic effect on the Earth and caused immediate social and economic devastation. Over the last few months, the lack of food production and delivery had already started a famine in parts of the world that relied upon the agrarian systems of the larger nations.

Aviation was only operational for emergency food and medical supply drops and shipping was the same. Ports were closed, airports were closed, and telecommunications were severely interrupted for over a month, with no internet and no cell service. It was like the Human world went from 2027 to 1027 in a matter of seven days. People died so quickly, they didn't even have time to get home. Many died right where they stood, causing railway accidents, car accidents, and airplane crashes. While most pilots were mandated to be vaccinated in order to be cleared to fly, there were still over five airplane crashes within a thirty-six-hour period.

Isabela was devastated by the deaths that rocked society and brought Human civilization to a virtual standstill for the last three months. But today, Isabela brought a new life into the world as March 12, 2027, was Juliette Maria Torres Devereux's birthday. And because Isabela had taken the vaccine, Juliette was inoculated for the first two months of her life, having inherited her gut microbiome from Isabela. But once Juliette was two months old, she'd have to receive a smaller dose of the vaccine to ensure her survival in the new world of LECCS.

Many new mothers were afraid to give the vaccine to their babies, despite having taken it while pregnant. The clinical trials showed it was safe and effective for both pregnant women and two-month-olds. Yet there was still resistance to do so. Many infants died by three months of age, adding even more numbers to the Human death toll of this deadly climate syndrome, which was now a permanent part of Human life.

Marisol sent a Sylph with the birth announcement, which included photos of Isabela and Juliette minutes after she was born. Juliette had porcelain skin and light brown hair, like her father, and Marisol joked in her letter to Aelish and Thagar that Isabela had given birth to a "gringa" baby as "blanca" as snow. The new Abuela was beside herself with joy, especially since Isabela had no complications during her delivery and Juliette was a healthy eight-pound, eight-ounce baby. There were also photos of Drew holding his daughter as well as Jorge and Javier. It was the happiest day Aelish had experienced since LECCS had devastated the Earth.

Aelish left the photos on the dining room table for Melanthia to see during their luncheon. They'd planned to meet on this day at the cove house about two weeks ago, despite it being Isabela's due date. Aelish just presumed first babies always came late, but this one didn't.

Drummond had prepared a beautiful spread for the Council Chair and had subsequently retired to bed with Storm by his side. Ever since the family had gone to Earth to attend Isabela's wedding, Storm had gotten very attached to Drummond. Aelish had a sense the dog was keeping a watchful eye over him; they'd become inseparable.

Thagar promised he would be home in time to see Melanthia before she departed for the S.E. Quadrant. He'd taken Kaleigh to boat-school and had also taken Elijah with him to Mindelata for a meeting with Reis and Targo. He needed to bring them up-to-date, regarding the conditions on Earth since the arrival of LECCS.

Aelish sat in the living area of the cove house dressed in a lovely pink shift dress, with a boatneck, capped sleeves, and a belt made of the same fabric as the dress. She also wore low-heeled, strappy sandals. Her hair was uncharacteristically loose and she wore makeup as well as simple gold hoop earrings. She hadn't seen Melanthia since Sartaine's Commitments Ceremony, over a year ago, and she wanted to look her best.

As she waited for Melanthia to arrive, she was feeling anxious. When Melanthia had requested they meet, Aelish had never pushed her for the reason why. However, knowing the Council Chair as well as she did, Aelish assumed the reason for their meeting was important. Melanthia had waited a respectable amount of time for Aelish to recover from her abduction and imprisonment. The Council Chair was aware she was under the care of Medicus Clove for mental health issues. But Melanthia never pushed Thagar or Cheswick for private details of Aelish's condition other than by inquiring in generalities to get a sense that she was improving.

Suddenly, Aelish heard three gentle knocks on the front door. She stood up and opened the door to the smiling face of an aged Melanthia. Aelish compared her appearance to when she'd visited Thagar in the N.W. Quadrant after the bombings in 2022—the last five years looked more like five hundred upon Melanthia's face. She had dark circles under her eyes and her face was filled with pronounced lines and crevices.

Aelish embraced the Council Chair and said, "Thank you so much for coming to see me today, and thank you for this beautiful home, which has helped me to heal." She could feel Melanthia nodding. After a few moments, they disengaged from their embrace.

"The setting of this house is magnificent. The ocean truly holds restorative powers."

"It absolutely does," agreed Aelish. "Please, come inside. The views are magnificent from inside the house as well."

Melanthia put her sweater down on one of the kitchen stools and began walking around the house, looking out at the ocean from each vantage point in the main living areas. She saw the table spread and exclaimed, "Oh my! This is too much, Aelish. Where is Drummond?"

"He begged your forgiveness for not staying up until you arrived. He's finally starting to feel his age and tires more easily now."

"I understand that all too well," said Melanthia. "Why don't we eat first, and then we can have ourselves a chat over by the couches facing the ocean?"

Aelish prepared a bountiful plate for Melanthia and then made one for herself. They dined together and spoke of nothing serious or important and gossiped about the most mundane things. They laughed and had some spirits, which helped them further relax with one another. And Melanthia greatly enjoyed the photos of Isabela's new baby; it cheered her. After they were satiated, they retired to the couches in the living area off the kitchen. Aelish allowed Melanthia to sit on the one facing the water and she sat across from her with her back to the ocean.

Melanthia deeply exhaled and said, "Life is the greatest currency in DAR. And DAR's devotion to peace is the greatest weapon we will ever have, Aelish. But it comes at a high price for those who truly embrace its tenets and philosophies, like you and I do. Sometimes, peace must be fought for. But most times, it simply requires the greatest ingenuity, patience, and endurance not to break faith with the beliefs of peace. It is the hardest thing to do."

Aelish said, "And sometimes, for peace there must be war. But no war is ever truly finished unless it is permanently replaced by peace."

"Very true, Aelish."

"During my captivity, I learned two astonishing things, Melanthia. First, DARlings from the N.W. Quadrant formed Yasteron millions of years ago and second, Yasteron is what DAR would have become had the females who assumed the leadership of DAR from the males, not insisted that all citizens take and live by an Oath of Peace every single day."

Melanthia asked, "Where did you learn that DARlings formed Yasteron?"

"From the Master of Archives for Yasteron. His name is Oba and he has the only remaining piece of physical evidence left in the magical world, stating this is the case. Whilst it became too dangerous for him to release the document from the spells which protect it, for me to see it firsthand in my prison, I know it to be true."

Melanthia said, "Many times, as young DARlettes, we heard of this myth. But we were told by our greatest scholars and Keepers in the Breanon that it was not true. Unbelievable."

"Oba said something I will never forget: 'If words are not written down and read from one generation to another, ignorance spreads like a wildfire and burns knowledge into ashes. The written word is more powerful than any weapon or evil magic spell ever created because it is the truth, and the truth is divine. When actual history can be turned into a lie or conspiracy, the truth is lost forever. And whoever is in power at the time, can claim ownership over what was once the truth. Falsifying the truth is allowed by those being ruled, as those being ruled *choose* to remain ignorant. To be literate, to be able to read, especially about history, is dangerous to those in power. Always beware the ignorant, Lady Aelish.' You would really like, Master Oba."

"Absolutely profound, Aelish," said Melanthia, with tears in her eyes. "I would like to meet Master Oba one day."

"I believe you will," said Aelish, smiling.

Melanthia said, "Whilst DAR must always be prepared to sacrifice any of our citizens for the greater good of the commonwealth, when DAR's Living Legend became that citizen, it was unbearable for me. I was shackled to the principles that DAR's devotion to peace must supersede the rescue of any one specific DARling. It became an untenable reality for me, Aelish. I completely understood the Earth born DARlings' desire to directly war with Yasteron on your behalf. But it is the responsibility of the Council Chair to uphold the principles of peace, even when the commonwealth is threatened. However, your abduction and imprisonment has forever changed me. Something died inside of me, Aelish, and I simply cannot reclaim it."

Aelish could feel Melanthia's unbridled torment in every word. She knew when Melanthia cast her tie-breaking vote *not* to war directly with Yasteron, after Kaleigh addressed the Head Council, that was the moment Melanthia felt something die inside of her.

Melanthia continued, "We had peace in the magical world for nearly 400 years and it allowed a commonwealth like DAR, devoted to peace, to become complacent about war. Our tenets backfired on us, as we were no longer on guard about evil forces at work, sowing discord leading to the inevitable outbreak of war.

"Personally, I will always feel as though I failed you, Aelish. The tenets of the Doctrine of DAR have broken me. I cannot reconcile my decision to not have directly bombed Yasteron in retaliation for their actions against DAR in the N.W. Quadrant. I also cannot reconcile my decision to not have burned Yasteron to the ground for what they did to you. I am ashamed, yet I know if

I had to do it all over again, as Council Chair, I would do nothing different. And that is my endless torment.

"But the one thing I refused to do was stand in the way of Thagar developing a covert mission to rescue you, regardless of my knowing that if he succeeded, the result could be war between DAR and Yasteron or a magical worldwide war. Yet I still feel as though I didn't do enough for you.

"Despite being imprisoned, repeatedly raped, and forced to bear what you thought at the time was Cardissius' offspring, you never took one life. You've become an even greater Living Legend than you were before. Once again, you saved another kingdom from tyranny. You also gave Earth a fighting chance to survive, whilst at the same time, ushering in the possibility of perpetual peace for the magical world. How you convinced Queen Saia to turn Yasteron into a matriarchal dominion defies comprehension. Yes, you incited civil war. But as you know from the statute I found in the Breanon, all those centuries ago after you freed Komprathia in a similar vein, you did not violate any of DAR's tenets and principles. I am in awe of you."

Aelish smiled tentatively at the Council Chair. But just like when she first met her, at the age of twelve in Brólaigh Castle, she sensed Melanthia was leading up to something life-altering.

"After what needs to be concluded with Yasteron is finished," said Melanthia, "which I will tell you about shortly, I am resigning as Council Chair. I am tired and feel defeated. The weight of my decisions has profoundly affected my desire to continue living. I'm sorry for my complicity in allowing the continuation of your suffering in Yasteron, which I know despite you being freed, continues to this day. I'm sorry for depriving Thagar of his mate, and I'm sorry for depriving Kaleigh of her mother. And finally, I'm sorry for depriving Isabela of her Oraculi whilst she was hospitalized for mental illness.

"By threatening Yasteron with Roger's spell, I negotiated a tentative peace agreement through our mutually assured destructive capabilities. Yet all the while, DAR continued to supply Komprathia with weapons to enable them to continue directly warring with Yasteron. It became a tapestry of mangled tenets and principles. To me, the policy of mutually assured destruction will always be a despicable method of maintaining peace; it is no peace at all.

"And despite considering myself a Keeper at heart, it was you who uncovered a piece of DAR's hidden history. Your discovery of the archive, revealing that DARlings from the N.W. Quadrant founded Yasteron millions of years ago, is a world-altering revelation. DAR has never known a being like you. And whilst it will never make up for what you've endured during your captivity, I can assure you of this: there will be monuments, sculptures, and literature written about your accomplishments and achievements for millennia yet to come. I hope you can find it within your heart to forgive me, Aelish."

Aelish stood up and came over to embrace Melanthia on the couch. They were both crying. Aelish said, "There is nothing to forgive, my dear friend. You are the greatest Council Chair that DAR has ever known, precisely because of how you are suffering. You hold fast to DAR's beliefs and are the being I measure my own behavior by. You set the bar, Melanthia."

Melanthia wiped away her tears with a proper handkerchief from her pocket, something Aelish never seemed to have when she needed one. Aelish stood up and sat back down on the couch across from Melanthia and said, "The singular event of the deaths of my parents from plague set me on a course for the rest of my life, Melanthia. It was the catalyst that set off one action after another. Once Thagar told me King Gidius was using his drone rats as weapons against Humanity by spreading the plague, I risked everything, including my own life. I was focused on one thing and one thing only—stop the rats and, hopefully, stop the plague.

"I risked banishment from DAR for life, by conducting a covert mission into Komprathia. I worked toward starting a civil war in that kingdom, in order to overthrow Gidius. I cultivated my asset, Cagélét, and pledged DAR's military support, when I had no authority to do so. The grief from the deaths of my parents propelled my actions.

"Once DAR was successful in destroying Gidius' reign, ending the relationship between Komprathia and Yasteron forever, I incurred the wrath and psychopathic love of Cardissius for nearly four hundred years. He stealthily exacted his twisted love and revenge on me for what I'd done in Komprathia, by inserting covert operatives throughout the Earth to foment the climate crisis. He wanted to destroy Humanity to ensure that no more DARlings could be born of Human parents. He succeeded; there hasn't been a birth of an Earth born DARling for over a century.

"After Glen was captured as a Yasteron covert operative sent to kill me, Thagar, and Isabela, King Cardissius bombed the N.W. Quadrant killing many innocent DARlings. They were ordinary DARling citizens, not soldiers. Thagar was nearly killed and has never been the same since. Yasteron unleashed their newest weapon of mass destruction, killing their own operative, Glen, as well as Thagar's entire team in the underwater bunker.

"Isabela was nearly killed in her own lab, her research on LECCS was stolen and turned into a bioweapon, and she was a target of assassination in Geneva at the WHO. She went there to tell the world about the LECCS syndrome, poised to extinct Humanity. She was under my care and has been put in harm's way so many times, it is a disgrace for any Oraculi.

"Cardissius exacerbated the climate crisis, causing LECCS, killing billions. And Cardissius bombed the N.W. Quadrant, killing innocent DARlings—all because of the choices I made nearly four hundred years ago. LECCS has brought a chaos to the Earth that no living Human has ever experienced. Despite the discovery of the syndrome and a vaccine to prevent it, nothing could have prepared Humanity for the aftermath of billions of Humans dying within a span of one week. The Earth is on its knees.

"But to vanquish an enemy like Yasteron was always going to scar the vanquisher. Imprisoned in a room for months on end, deprived of all my magical capabilities was a form of torture that defies description. Yet I was determined to use my imprisonment to instigate desperately needed changes within Yasteron. Because I was inside the kingdom, I learned things I could have never learned otherwise: Yasterons were originally DARlings and there was tremendous unrest brewing. The unrest was not only amongst the lower-orders who'd been enslaved since Yasteron's inception, but there was also dissension amongst the covert operatives on Earth and even amongst the nobles who had tired of Cardissius' endless machinations.

"Through a hand-written letter, I tried to empower Queen Saia to channel her innate female DARling magical capabilities. Whilst I turned a queen into a murderer, by hanging all the ministers who ran Yasteron, she now rules the kingdom. She's pledged to make it a matriarchal commonwealth, but who knows if she will actually remain peaceful?

"I endured being magically raped night after night, by a monster who professed his undying love for me and who wanted to create a lineage of preeminent magical beings with an Earth born DARling. He turned my mind against Thagar, left me bereft of all my magic, and if I tried to hurt the offspring we created, or myself, Cardissius would kill Thagar and Kaleigh. I was trapped. Acquiring the Magical Sunlight Heart Deprivation Syndrome, poised to kill me shortly after I delivered the heir, was a relief. My impending death brought a freedom I could not bring about myself, without killing Thagar and Kaleigh.

"But in the end, if Cardissius hadn't held the lives of Thagar and Kaleigh over my head, I would have inadvertently killed Thagar's son, Elijah, as well as myself. When I think about how circumstances and obstacles came together to prevent me from doing something I was so desperate to do, I can only attribute those circumstances and obstacles to divine intervention.

"I set out on this journey nearly 400 hundred years ago, Melanthia. I blame you for nothing. I made all of my own choices and decisions with a clear conscience. And DAR owes me nothing, but I owe DAR and Earth my life. I pray they will both survive long after I've left this life. There is nothing to forgive you for. You've been a second mother to me, and I will always love you. You need to stop tormenting yourself because you held fast to your principles. Kaleigh told me everything she said to the Head Council before they voted on whether to directly war with Yasteron. Everything Kaleigh said was true—do not engage in war in my name, as that's not what I would have wanted, no matter how much I was suffering. No, Melanthia, war is never the answer—you taught me this. You did the right thing by voting no, and further, by dissuading me from using Roger's spell. Since Yasterons are DARlings, I could have killed all of DAR."

Melanthia gasped.

"So, I hope you will reconsider your resignation as Council Chair," said Aelish. "I cannot imagine any other female who could handle what you have these last five years. Thagar said something to me the other day that I will never forget: 'DAR is a great dominion because the females are in charge. Males are not as strong as females. They fall apart when they lose or get injured, and they retaliate in order to drown their sorrows and humiliations. Males are incapable of turning off their desire for revenge. They start wars, lose their way, and become frantic when they can't find a way out, making everything worse. They do not possess the ability to juggle war, peace, and the necessary advancements needed for progress. Males should never be in charge. They need females to lead them.'

"Once I realized Yasterons were actually DARlings, when I wrote my letter to Queen Saia, I wrote it as if I were speaking to a family member. Saia was like my sister, or like Cheswick, or like you; she was really a DARling. She would ultimately understand what I was proposing for her kingdom and come to realize what she and every other female in Yasteron had been denied under the reign of the males. The male reign was abhorrent and it was time for her to lead. She just needed a push."

Melanthia shook her head in disbelief at Aelish's litany of accomplishments. "Well, Aelish, Queen Saia contacted me a week ago. She expressed her desire to meet with DAR's Head Council as soon as possible to discuss how to go about changing Yasteron from a male primogeniture monarchy to a matriarchal commonwealth. The civil war is over and she wants to be rid of the lower-orders' caste system, immediately. She wants to form an equitable and egalitarian dominion. Saia wants Yasteron to be a commonwealth devoted to art, science, music, medicine, but most importantly, to peace. And she will honor all the conditions of the Peace Accord. I will never know how you managed to have the strength to instigate these unfathomable changes in Yasteron. Especially, living under such heinous conditions and with the knowledge that you were dying. You truly are a Living Legend, Aelish, and I am so honored to know you."

Aelish's mouth was agape. "The civil war is over? Will Queen Saia free the prisoners?"

"Yes, Aelish. We are in the process of planning a ceremony

together for their release on the shores of the N.W. Quadrant. The DARling soldiers will be returning to DAR and the imprisoned drone rats will be returning to Komprathia. She is planning to honor all the conditions and stipulations of the Peace Accord in the weeks to come. She wrote me quite an intimate hand-written letter about her love for Cardissius as well as her love for all the citizens."

"Oh, my God. Is it really almost over?" asked Aelish.

Melanthia pulled out a letter. "I've brought the letter with me so I could read it to you.

Aelish sat up straight and took a deep breath. Melanthia read:

Dear Council Chair Melanthia,

I was a stupid female who gave her heart to a bad king, a cruel king. And then, I discovered he actually preferred another and had for centuries. It's a bitter feeling to be so betrayed. He was the blood in my veins and every beat of my heart. And now, he's torn that same heart out of my chest, smashed it upon the ground, and flattened it with his boot. I'm trying to find a meaning to the unending loneliness which has become my life; it still eludes me. I am miserable and I imagine Director Aelish suffers still. The only one who was happy for a time, until he was ultimately betrayed, was Cardissius. It has always been this way. He always got whatever he desired; his father spoiled him thus.

The king humiliated the queen in front of the entire kingdom. Why did he do this to me? I thought I was the only one he ever desired, the only one he ever truly loved. I feel like I was born blind. He charmed his way into my heart, and I went willingly. And despite it all, I can't stop loving him. How disgraceful is that? If he were still alive and asked me to forgive him for all of it, I know I would. It's revolting how I love him still, how I need him still, and how I feel him still, despite him being in a grave.

I read Director Aelish's letter to me, possibly, one hundred times. And it helped me to realize only I could free myself from the chains of love that bound me to Cardissius. When I arrested and imprisoned Chief Minister Stannon, after learning he'd murdered the love of my life, I took the first step in freeing myself. And when I learned of all the king's ministers who were complicit in allowing Stannon to rule my kingdom, I hung them all. Special Envoy Ragdon, Master Oba, the leader of the lower-orders, Kam, and the leader of the covert operatives, Ryker, have helped me to free not only my kingdom but also myself.

Thank you for being so generous in supplying the revolutionaries with an endless supply of weaponry and warcraft through Commander Orión of Komprathia. Without his assistance and yours, we would have been at an impossible disadvantage.

Please, tell Director Aelish we are planning to release all the prisoners to the custody of DAR and Komprathia next week, by ship, on the shoreline of DAR's N.W. Quadrant. Over the next months, we will destroy all stockpiles of bioweapons created to kill Humans and DARlings. The same goes for our newest bomb. We will be sending DAR the research that went into creating not only our heinous, destructive bomb but also all of the bioweapons. We look forward to receiving Roger's spell, as an act of good faith, although I completely understand if you are reluctant to give it yet to Yasteron. We are still an unstable dominion, and if you'd prefer to wait some time before doing so, that is acceptable to me. I look forward to seeing you on the shoreline next week in DAR, where we will sign the Peace Accord. It has been a long time coming.

Sincerely yours,

Her Royal Majesty Queen Saia

Melanthia looked at Aelish and said, "The original letter will, of course, go into the Breanon along with all of our other historical documents. But this is a copy, which you may keep. I felt it was the least I could do for you."

Aelish sat lost in her own thoughts for a few moments. All the years spent working on the Peace Accord, all the arguments with Thagar about trying to make peace with Yasteron, and all the suffering she'd endured during her captivity were at the forefront of her mind. Was it worth it? She imagined once she witnessed the prisoners being released, as well as the actual signing of the Peace Accord, it would finally feel like a victory. She wondered if, one day, she and Queen Saia could be cordial with one another. Having her forgiveness was still important to Aelish, despite not having done anything to intentionally hurt the queen.

"You made all of this happen, Aelish. Be so proud of yourself, I know I am. Ah! Before I forget, DAR issued a proclamation to Yasteron and the Alliance of Magical Dominions, stating Thagar is Elijah's father and not King Cardissius. We hope this will always keep him safe."

"Oh, thank God," said Aelish, who burst into tears. "I've never been able to relax whenever we take him anywhere. I'm constantly worried that he remains a weapon of revolution or a weapon of restitution to Yasteron's Crown. Thank you, Melanthia."

Just then, Thagar returned home with Kaleigh and Elijah. "Oh, wonderful!" exclaimed Thagar. "I was so afraid I'd missed you! The meeting in Mindelata went longer than expected."

Kaleigh went running over to Melanthia and jumped onto the couch and gave her a big hug and a kiss. Thagar came into the room with Elijah in his arms. It was the first time Melanthia had ever laid eyes upon him. Thagar put him down and Elijah went running over to meet Melanthia. He climbed onto her lap, reached up and touched her olive-green cheek, and stroked it. He smiled broadly at the Council Chair. "Hello, Council Chair," he said. Melanthia practically melted from his sweetness.

"Ohh, you're quite the charmer, aren't you Elijah?" she asked.

Elijah responded by kissing her cheek. "He's absolutely beautiful. You must be so proud to be a big sister, Kaleigh."

"I am, Council Chair," said Kaleigh. "And I'm so glad he's almost a year old because now we can finally play together."

Aelish took a deep breath and smiled at Melanthia. She felt the inkling of inner peace.

✝✝✝✝

Aelish stood on the shoreline of the sea between DAR and Yasteron with Thagar, Kaleigh, and Elijah, who was in Thagar's arms. The Head Council, the peace delegation, and other dignitaries from DAR stood alongside them, waiting for the ship of prisoners to arrive from Yasteron.

When the ship appeared, Aelish realized it was the same royal ship that had taken her to Yasteron along with the peace delegation. It didn't feel so long ago.

Medical personnel lined the shore. They set up the same type of field hospital used after the bombing of the N.W. Quadrant. She saw Medicus Clove, who waved to her from a distance as well as Captain Lena, who saluted her. Lady Antonia, Quentin, and Amelia also waved to her.

But the one being Aelish had been most eager to see again was Lieutenant Commander Stavros. He now stood right next to her. It was important to Aelish that he knew she did not blame him for her abduction. He seemed reluctant to accept this. As the ship came into view, she felt him momentarily touch her hand. She squeezed his hand back in acknowledgment of this long-awaited accomplishment.

Aelish gave Queen Saia a lot of credit for not cleaning up the prisoners before they boarded the royal ship. The queen wanted their suffering to be in plain view of everyone in attendance.

After they received a medical evaluation at the field hospital, if they were mentally well enough, they would be reunited with family members. But Aelish knew many had lost family members during their captivity and no longer had anyone to go home to.

The drone rats were taken off the ship in cages. Under the direction of Commander Orión, the cages were loaded onto an airship headed directly for Komprathia. He saluted Aelish when he saw her and Aelish blew him a kiss. Thagar caught the interaction between them. "Am I to lose you to Commander Orión? His king cobra hood was especially flared when he saw you."

"Not today, but keep it in mind," teased Aelish, coyly. Thagar chuckled at her.

As the prisoners began to disembark, some unable to walk on their own, Aelish calculated that some had been imprisoned since 1300 and others since the Proelium in 1360. The DARling soldiers had been in captivity between 667 and 727 years. Aelish began to tear up. The rags they wore were filthy and nearly all exhibited signs of severe frailty.

As they began making their way to the medical personnel awaiting them, the crowd erupted in cheers for their DARling soldiers and the applause had quite an effect on them. Some began to walk taller and others even smiled and waved at the crowd assembled to greet them. Hope was a powerful thing and they were finally home.

The last to disembark were Queen Saia, Special Envoy Ragdon, the Queen's guard, and two other males she had never seen before. As Aelish studied the faces of the unknown males, she saw the similarity between one and her lower-order-in-waiting, Katrina. She instantly knew he was Katrina's brother, Kam, leader of the lower-order revolutionaries. He had survived the civil war. And the other male had to be Ryker, leader of the covert operatives on Earth.

As the delegation from Yasteron greeted all the dignitaries from DAR, when they stood in front of Aelish, they all curtsied, including Queen Saia. The crowd gasped at this incredible sight. But when Aelish returned the curtsy, the crowd began whistling and applauding, realizing it was the Living Legend to whom the Yasteron dignitaries were showing reverence. The queen reached for Elijah's cheek and stroked it gently. "He's beautiful," she said to Aelish and Thagar.

Aelish smiled at the queen and Thagar bowed out of respect, saying, "Thank you, Your Highness." When the delegation had walked away, Thagar turned to Aelish and said, "Don't ever forget that moment, my love. The Queen of Yasteron just curtsied to you and thinks our son is beautiful." Aelish nodded and started chuckling at him, releasing some of the nervousness inside of her. She kissed Elijah on top of his head. The Yasteron delegation made their way to the area set up on the beach for the momentous signing of the Peace Accord, as did the dignitaries from DAR.

The peace delegation from DAR was permitted to stand behind the Head Council and witness the signing of the Peace Accord up close. As the signing between DAR and Yasteron began, Aelish realized she was standing in the exact same spot where she'd waited for days, during the search for Thagar. After nearly five years, peace had come to the same place as the wreckage that preceded it.

When the signing concluded, a tent was set up for a dinner in honor of the Yasteron delegation, the Head Council, and the peace delegates from DAR. While Aelish stayed behind to dine with the dignitaries, Thagar transported home with Kaleigh and Elijah.

When the dinner was over, Queen Saia came over to Aelish and said, "I hope our two dominions will enjoy a lasting peace in perpetuity, Director Aelish. Thank you for your letter."

Aelish stood up, curtsied to the queen, and said, "Thank you, Your Highness. That is my hope as well. One other thing." The queen looked at her quizzically. "When we first met back in January of 2026, you complimented my gown. Do you remember?"

"Ah, yes, I actually do," remarked the queen, smiling.

Aelish said, "In your state room, aboard the ship, you will find a gown I promised you a long time ago from the designer of my own gown, which you so admired when we first met. The designer's name is Naz. I hope it is to your liking and that you will accept it as a gift of friendship not only between our two dominions but also between you and I."

"How incredibly kind of you to remember such a thing. And to situate it as a surprise for me to enjoy on the voyage home. Thank you, Director Aelish. It is most appreciated."

"You are most welcome, Your Highness," said Aelish. They curtsied to one another.

As Aelish watched the queen walk away, Melanthia came up behind her. "There hasn't been this much curtsying in the commonwealth for centuries. I feel like we need to do some cleansing spells." Melanthia began laughing, which made Aelish laugh as well.

"So, it's done," said Aelish. "I can't believe it, Melanthia."

"There is one more surprise today, Aelish," said Melanthia.

Melanthia handed Aelish the coordinates of a mountaintop in the S.E. Quadrant. "We would greatly appreciate it if you could join us all there. We are transporting now. Thagar, Kaleigh, and Elijah will meet you there.

"What is going on?" asked Aelish.

Lady Antonia snuck up behind her. "Are you ready to go?" she asked. "Let's transport holding hands, Aelish."

Aelish began laughing and grasped Lady Antonia's hand.

Right before they transported, she heard Melanthia say, "It's time everyone! Let's transport to the mountaintop!"

‡‡‡‡

Aelish and Lady Antonia landed on a mountaintop in the S.E. Quadrant. It was across from the Great Rotunda of Peace and had no other structures upon it other than the most magnificent monument Aelish had ever seen. Thagar, Kaleigh, and Elijah came up behind her as did Melanthia and the entire Head Council. Melanthia said, "This monument has been created in your honor, Aelish, for your devotion to peace and for your devotion to DAR."

Aelish looked more closely at the monument and realized it was her own image she was staring at. An enormous sculpture of Aelish stood at the crest of the mountaintop. It must have been fifty feet high. In her left hand, she clutched the Peace Accord document against her chest, and her right arm was raised with a lantern of light in her hand, which hung over the crest of the mountaintop. Behind her were all the DARling soldier prisoners, dressed in filthy rags, along with the drone rat captives scurrying upon the ground next to the soldiers. Scattered throughout the monument were benches so citizens could sit in contemplation of how Aelish had forged a peaceful coexistence between DAR and Yasteron. Since it was now nightfall, the entire monument was lit with light. It could be seen anywhere from within the S.E. Quadrant.

"The Head Council commissioned it in your honor, Aelish," said Melanthia. "Remai, the most famous sculptor in DAR, led a team of burgeoning young sculptors to create it. Its beauty rivals the majesty of the Great Rotunda of Peace. It will be illuminated every night, just as the Great Rotunda is, and you will be able to see it from your home in Bencarlta. We are all so very proud of you." Melanthia embraced Aelish as she continued staring at the monument.

"What's the name of the monument, Council Chair?" asked Kaleigh.

"The Aelish Monument of Peaceful Contemplation," replied Melanthia.

Thagar came over to Aelish and kissed her cheek. "No one deserves this more than you."

"Absolutely," said Lady Antonia.

It brought Aelish an internal quietude to see the sacrifices she'd made for peace immortalized in this incredible monument. With tears in her eyes, she said, "I am so honored. Thank you all so very much."

‡‡‡‡

Years later, when the last of the remaining Humans were safely ensconced in the Human sanctuaries, Aelish picked up her Earth Viewer. She gazed at the uninhabitable Earth, still reflecting DAR and Earth's shared sun into the magical world, which was finally at peace.

Author's Note

Thank you so kindly for reading *DAR & Earth: Evolution*. Writing the *DAR & Earth* tetralogy has brought me great joy, however, the scientific research that went into these books has also brought me great sorrow. And ten years out, the goals of the 2015 Paris Agreement, which nations promised to abide by, feels like a broken pledge.

In book one, *DAR & Earth: Oraculi*, I was fortunate to have been able to include the report from the United Nations Intergovernmental Panel on Climate Change, entitled: *Global Warming of 1.5°C*, released on October 8, 2018. The report stressed the importance of not allowing the overall global temperature to exceed 1.5°C. Unfortunately, the overall global temperature not only hit 1.5°C during most of 2023, it reached 1.6°C in 2024, making it the first calendar year to exceed this important threshold. While scientists state the temperature must remain at 1.5°C or above for a sustained period of ten or even twenty years before the threshold can be considered truly breached, I think we can all agree, we are heading in the wrong direction.

Based on my research, I was convinced the overall global temperature was going to exceed 1.5°C before I finished the last book—and it did! In *DAR & Earth: Evolution*, the temperature hits 1.5°C on January 1, 2027. Despite writing approximately two years into the future, I was off by four years! Always concerned this might be the case, I built in some scientific cover for the accuracy of the research in the series. In the books, DAR has been scrubbing greenhouse gases out of fantasy Earth's atmosphere for years, buying humans more time. Whew! And further, unlike on fantasy Earth, real Earth does *not* get a Plan B, like it does in the last book. There is no place to relocate to after the Earth becomes uninhabitable.

I often wonder, if global leaders could gaze into the future world of their children and grandchildren, would this vision stop them from being this ineffective in halting the progression of the climate crisis? I doubt it. I experienced political intractability during my career in politics. I'd often say to elected officials—if you wanted to do, you'd do it—but you don't want to. When there's no will, there's really no way.

For me, this is the most frustrating aspect of the climate crisis. We've developed so many new technologies to halt its progression. Yet there is hesitancy to implement grand changes. Why? I believe it's because these new technologies don't turn enough of a profit to be appealing to those in positions of power. Those in power are not ordinarily known for their benevolence. They want a high yield on solutions to solve the climate crisis and unless human life can turn a profit, it's a worthless currency. But that's always been the human condition and why we find ourselves in our current predicament.

At some point, everything will change. I believe the younger generations to come will be responsible for changing the moral construct of humanity, as they will have suffered the most from its immoral obsession with money and power. I wish them so much good luck. After all, I wrote the *DAR & Earth* series for them, as I've always believed this.